D0886620

Brighten to Incandescence

17 Stories
by Michael Bishop

GOLDEN GRYPHON PRESS • 2003

Introduction copyright © 2003 by Lucius Shepard

Edited by Marty Halpern

LIBRARY OF CONGRESS CATALOGUING–IN–PUBLICATION DATA
Bishop, Michael.
    Brighten to incandescence : 17 stories / by Michael Bishop ; with an introduction by Lucius Shepard.
        p.   cm.
    ISBN 1-930846-16-9 (alk. paper)
    I. Title.
PS3552.I772   B74   2003
813'.54—dc21   2002151200

* * *

Contents

For Michael Hutchins,
conscientious bibliographer, web-site magician, friend.
As Mr. Porter wrote,
"You're the top, you're the Colosseum."

Acknowledgments

Writers often derive a particular sort of inspiration writing for a particular editor or set of editors, and here I would like to note my debt to the editors who first ushered sixteen of these stories into print. My hat is off to Gardner Dozois, Scott Edelman, Edward L. Ferman, Charles L. Grant, David Hartwell, Edward E. Kramer, Byron Preiss and Robert Silverberg, David Pringle, William Schafer and Bill Sheehan, Roy Torgeson, Eric Vinicoff, Jacob Weisman, and the editorial team of Jennifer Hershey, Tom Dupree, and Janna Silverstein. And let me not forget Marty Halpern, here at Golden Gryphon Press, for recurrent heroic feats during the compilation and revision of these seventeen pieces and also the production of the volume showcasing them. Blessings upon you all, *mis amigos*.

*   *   *

Introduction

WHEN CALLED UPON TO INTRODUCE A WRITER AS
widely known to the general readership as Michael Bishop,
I'm tempted to put aside the traditional notion of introductions and
turn to the music business for a model, to the MCs of early rock
concerts, hirsute young guys with no shame and freshly damaged
brains who would stand before a shabby closed curtain at, say, the
old Eastown Theater in Detroit, trying to appear cooler than the
glassy-eyed stoners clamoring for music. These quasi-luminaries
would invariably tell everyone to chill, the band was having set-up
problems (code for the drummer's passed out or some such), and
when this admonition merely agitated the crowd further, they
resorted to inept jokes, crude sexual allusions, and acts of self-
debasement in order to pacify the beast. I had a particular fondness
for this one kid, a lanky drug-inspired fellow with freckles and a
prominent Adam's apple, his dyed-red hair butchered into a
mohawk, who—should all else fail—would fall on his back and
hump his way back and forth across the stage. Though a literary
approximation of this freakish yet (at the time) mildly entertaining
performance might be appropriate to the moment in that it would
serve less as an introduction than a delaying action, something to
fill a few minutes before giving way to the featured attraction, I'm
not sure such a display would suit the character of what is to follow.

But then thinking about Bishop in terms of a classic r&r band, a group whose music has survived shifts in fashion, changing hairstyles, et al., and still rocks as hard as ever, is not in the least inappropriate. Bishop's lucid narration, his spiritually complex characters, and carefully employed moral sensibility have altogether fashioned a style that has managed to ring out clean and true above thirty years or thereabouts of science fiction's ever changing Next Big Things, from bell-bottom prose to sampled tropes and acid house hallucinations. Indeed, it would be apt to view this collection of seventeen uncollected stories as an album of outtakes and singles that did not make it onto previous albums, not because they were of lesser quality, but because they did not quite suit the tone of those collections, and now, gathered together, can be seen to have themselves a unity that derives from a constancy of obsession. From "A Tapestry of Little Murders" (1971) to a group of stories that saw print in the new millennium, we are able to bear witness to the continual revitalizing of Bishop's great themes and familiar passions (spirituality, family, paleontology, rock and roll, et al.). All in all, it's rather like coming across the bootleg of a lost concert by Hendrix or the Clash.

Truth, like good whiskey, like a great song, burns along the nerves, and whenever I've read Mike Bishop's work, I've gotten that burn. When I started thinking about trying my hand at science fiction and fantasy, it was the writers who gave me that burn—Le Guin, Disch, Wolfe, Ballard, Aldiss, to name a few others—who nourished what was then only a vague urge and caused it to grow into a firm intent. I took something from each of them—not elements of their styles, but a comprehension of what was possible to impart through fiction, of how truth (and by truth, I mean not what George Washington never strayed from, but a natural measure of the world distilled into words) could be injected into a story, how it could *become* the story. Attempting to say exactly what I derived from each of these authors would be a difficult chore, because the quality of this sort of honesty in fiction is ineffable, much easier to detect than to define. However, I feel more commonality of purpose with Mike than with the other writers named, and I believe that the apperception I had of his novels and stories, what gave me the burn, was the sense of a man with a clear moral focus who declined to make facile judgments about a clearly amoral world and, instead, allowed that world to speak through him. This is not to suggest that Mike is without bias or agenda in his writing, but rather to say that his biases and agendas always seem the servants of his experience and not its masters. And that strikes me as a remarkable and enviable quality, more remarkable and enviable even than Mike's considerable gifts with language.

The thing that makes writing—art of any sort, for that matter—suspect as to its worth is that jerks can become proficient at it. Indeed, it might be said that being a jerk is something of an asset for a writer, affording him or her a flexible moral platform from which to declaim. But long before I met Mike, I was quite certain that he was no jerk. I actually thought I would be able to pick him out of a crowd by his expression and demeanor, despite never having even seen a photo (I failed in this, but was more or less right in my pre-judgments concerning his general aspect). Though I had only exchanged a couple of phone calls with him, I knew him from his stories . . . and he *is* there in his stories with less deception and camouflage than any other writer of my acquaintance, visible as a good-humored, honest man who earns a living by telling exotic and mesmerizing lies, doing so with such heart and skill that we believe him utterly. I read somewhere that on the Hindu Wheel of Life incarnation as a poet precedes incarnation as a thief. If this is the case, then speaking as one of the jerks, it seems that Mike may be slumming from a much higher plane, for he brings uncommon honor and integrity to our profession.

The stories in *Brighten to Incandescence* would be astonishing if we were only to consider their range. Here we have the comic metaphysics of "Simply Indispensable" cohabiting with the sinister allusiveness of "Thirteen Lies About Hummingbirds"; the Laffertyesque "Of Crystalline Labyrinths and the New Creation" cheek to cheek with the moving Vietnam piece, "The Tigers of Hysteria Feed Only on Themselves"; a powerful horror story, "Help Me, Rondo," concerning the cult film actor, Rondo Hatton, sharing the covers with the quiet humanism of "With a Little Help from Her Friends," a story that features an appearance by the Beatles (having always hated the Beatles—galled by their music, which my parents thought was "nice" and I considered overly sentimental—let me say that it takes an extremely persuasive author to get me to stick with a story involving them); the Cretaceous adventure story "Herding with the Hadrosaurs" in intimate propinquity with the marvelous 9/11 story, "Last Night Out." My personal favorite of this collection, "Sequel on Skorpiós," a stunning poetic recasting of the life of Christ, has the impact of a compressed novel, bringing to mind the effect—though not the dry academic tone—of Jorge Luis

Borges's fictions. It makes one wish that one could go on reading it, that the author had expanded upon his materials; but because he does not, it forces the reader to do his own expansion, and this is the finest gift any story can bestow—to fire the imagination, to create a fiction within the soul of the reader that is so real and important, it lives with him for the rest of his days.

This has happened to me with Mike's stories more than once. For instance, I recall wandering around in Guatemala in 1982, stopping at a seedy hotel in Flores, a little regional capital set on an island in the middle of a jungle lake, and finding under the bedside table a coverless rain-damaged fragment of a Terry Carr anthology that contained the Nebula-winning story "The Quickening," which illuminates the unsettling transformation of a culture. I was headed back to the States, having just left behind the brutality and turmoil in El Salvador, a country then being gutted by civil war, and partly because of my troubled mental condition, partly because of the shifting nature of rain forest culture, partly because of the strangely dissolute appearance of Flores itself, with its children's playground half under water, swings and seesaws sticking up from the lake, and crumbling buildings whose support posts were lashed to telephone poles and whose porches were held aloft by crutches of wood and stone, but mostly because of the artfulness of the writing, I began to see Guatemala in terms that the story had imprinted upon me; to perceive that everything around me was at the point of potential transformation; to understand that our culture, all cultures, were fluid, malleable, amoeba-like in the resilience of their form, yet frail at the center—that the apparent iron of the world was supported by an illusion.

As every writer knows, finding a way out of a story, a means of exiting gracefully, is among the thorniest problems facing anyone engaged in the art, and I am discovering that this same problem is true of introductions. I had in mind to return to the conceit with which I began the piece, the rock and roll concert, and to conjure the image of a crowd (of readers, this time) stamping their feet and throwing lit cigarettes at the MC, demanding that this stammering preamble be done, calling for the curtains to open and the Michael Bishop Band to make its overdue appearance. But now that I'm here, I feel compelled to take the metaphor in another direction. Unlike the dinosaur bands of the '60s who refuse to fade away, continuing to play on in retro-slanted clubs and VH1 specials, proving by their performances that the height of their creativity has long since passed and that they are merely cashing in, Mike Bishop continues to grow as an artist. I've been privileged to read several recent stories that have not yet seen print. They mark an astonishing evolution in his work, and I look forward to seeing them put between covers and celebrated for their beautifully etched particularity and their loving yet unflinching rendering of the American experience. Until that day, we have *Brighten to Incandescence*, a collection that not only offers seventeen wildly entertaining stories, but displays for us the paths its author has traveled and provides us with a strong intimation of the world he soon intends to show us, a world that—albeit familiar in its essential things—will seem newly immediate, freshly defined, and entirely Michael Bishop's own.

Lucius Shepard
May 2002

Brighten to Incandescence:
17 Stories

* * *

Thirteen Lies About Hummingbirds

ER NAME WAS MEMORY YANG. AT KYSER, GODWIN & Kale, she had just come aboard as a junior marketing researcher. The first thing I noticed about her—once past the nifty frisson of her name—was the way her Amerasian features resisted pigeonholing. From certain angles, she radiated the pale gauntness of a film-noir beauty; from others, the innocent sultriness of a geisha.

I was smitten once again. Absolutely snowed.

One night about a month after she joined our firm, I stayed late, working on the secondary accounts that were my burden at Kyser. When Memory left, I followed her to the fourteenth-floor elevators, and we rode down together in a glass-faced capsule.

It was spring. Streetlights illuminated the eerie white plumes of the dogwoods in a pocket park across from our building. From my briefcase, I pulled three tissue-wrapped, long-stemmed red roses. One would have been too ostentatiously modest, a dozen too vulgarly smug.

"Pretty," said Memory Yang. "And they smell nice."

"They're for you."

Memory lowered her head in a parody of maidenly embarrassment. She was embarrassed not because she had attracted my attention and my unexpected gift. She was embarrassed *for me*.

3

"Corny?" I asked. "*Too* corny?"

Head still down, she looked aside.

"Memory?" No answer. "*Miss Yang?*"

"Mr. Jurusik—"

"Peter. Pete."

"Mr. Jurusik, I hope what I tell you won't endanger my job."

That made me angry. "I'm not your boss, Memory."

"Mr. Jurusik, the problem is this: You're one of our hottest hot-shots in copy-and-layout, right?"

"So they say."

"And your idea of a brilliantly rad come-on is . . . roses?"

"*Three* roses."

She raised her eyes to me. I saw then that Memory was no kid. She was a woman at least as old as I: a woman of some experience, a late career-starter. Any advantage imparted by my position at KG&K or my man-about-town sophistication evaporated like windshield fog under a roaring defroster.

"I thought it was the thought that counts," I said.

We were down. Foyer ferns, a vast slab of water-smooth marble flooring, and a uniformed security guard slid into view.

"The thought *does* count," Memory said. Side by side, we walked out to the hedge-protected parking lot.

"What's the trouble, then? Do you doubt the sincerity of my thought?" I clamped my briefcase against my side and brandished the rejected flowers.

"Not the sincerity—the quality."

"The quality? Then what would do it for you? The keys to my Audi? An airline ticket to Acapulco?"

Memory stopped walking. She took my lapel between a thumb and forefinger. "I'm not talking money." She tweezered my lapel in a vaguely intimidating way. "Not necessarily, at least. I'm talking . . . imagination."

"Imagination?"

Under the greenish-yellow arc lamps, Memory peered into my eyes without really seeing me. To reestablish contact, I had to twist free of her gently pinching fingers.

"Roses are better than a gold-plated zodiac charm," she finally said. "But not much. For the charm, you'd've at least had to find out my birthday."

"How about giving me some suggestions?"

For a moment, I thought she was going to climb into her car—a Volkswagen beetle, recently repainted—and drive off, leaving me to

simmer in my chagrin. But she didn't. Brow corrugated, she turned back to me, defiantly lobbing examples:
"A baseball signed by Hank Aaron. A full-color poster of the National Palace Museum in Taipei. A novel by García Márquez."
"Great. Go on."
"A shark's tooth. A ginkgo leaf. A geode."
(The self-conscious list of a Granola-eating nature lover.) "Fine. Anything else?"
"A hummingbird." And then she *did* climb into her bug and putt-putt regally away.

A hummingbird? Had Memory given me her real wish list or just a suggestive schema? It would be easy to get Hank Aaron's John Hancock on a National League baseball; a friend of mine labored in public relations for the Braves. Travel posters weren't hard to find. And every bookstore in town had *Love in the Time of Cholera* stacked up so high that it looked as if García Márquez had put a move on Stephen King's floor space.

The hard part of making use of Memory's examples, I saw, would come in *determining beforehand* what would suit her. How could I have known that she liked baseball, Taiwanese art, Latin American novelists? Or, finally, hummingbirds?

So I played detective. I found out that Memory's birthday was less than a week away; that her ex-hubby was doing time for a drug conviction in Macon's Central Correctional Institute; that, as a result of wounds sustained during a holdup at his health spa two years ago, her father, an immigrant from Taiwan, was now disabled; that, late in Carter's presidency, her mother had suffered a fatal stroke; that her only brother, Tom, lived in Connecticut; and that her favorite poet was Wallace Stevens.

I did *not* go out and buy her a first edition of *Harmonium*. Not only would that have been nearly impossible, it would have been —in Memory's eyes—show-offy and obvious.

Instead, I had the jeweler wife of a copywriter friend make a three-inch-long (i.e., life-sized) hummingbird out of semiprecious gemstones, gold wire, and lacquered cellophane. I lowered it into Memory's cubicle on a thread. A hand-lettered card accompanied my gift.

The card said, "*Happy Birthday, Memory. There are at least thirteen lies I can tell you about ruby-throats. This is the first one: 'I am a hummingbird.' The remaining lies will follow in turn.*"

I signed it—almost sincerely—"*Love, Peter.*"

*   *   *

Memory, true to her name, remembered our less than auspicious meeting. She caught the nod to Stevens's "Thirteen Ways of Looking at a Blackbird." She agreed to go out with me.

We began carefully. No pushing. Movies, not art films. Ball games, not museums. Del Taco's, not Nikolai's Roof. And when our inevitable shoptalk began to give way to heart-to-hearts, I cooled down and backed off.

Five *good* days, full of subsurface sexual tension. It was the first time in my life I enjoyed seeing Dale Murphy fan in four out of five at-bats. Or Sly Stallone do anything at all.

On our sixth day, I decided to tell her Falsehood Number Two. After work, Memory and I drove to an old-fashioned tearoom in Madison, Georgia, three counties away. We ordered spinach salad, scalloped potatoes, and lemon chicken. Later, our white-jacketed waiter came out and set a desert plate in front of Memory.

"Your fortune cookie, ma'am."

Memory eyed it suspiciously. Then she cracked the cookie open, removed the fortune slip, perused it.

As I already knew, it said: *"The blood spot on the gorget of the male is an outward sign of its passion."*

My tie was crimson silk. I waggled it at Memory—a lascivious Oliver Hardy impersonation.

"Two down." Memory smiled, then added: "Female ruby-throats don't have red gorgets, Peter."

"According to Mr. Audubon, no, they don't."

Memory read the tiny scroll again. "So does this"—holding the fortune aloft—"imply that the females lack passion?"

I took the scroll from her and used a ballpoint to write on its unprinted side. "Here. A corollary to Lie Number Two." I passed the slip back to Memory.

She read its message: *"The female suppresses her blood spot from an inborn sense of propriety."*

Another smile. "You wish," she said, and I didn't know whether she meant that females actually did lack passion or that my attempt to unsuppress hers was a transparent botch.

Hopefully, I returned her smile.

Memory didn't lack passion. Even though the following day was a workday, she agreed to an interlude. At a bed-and-breakfast in a remodeled antebellum house, we spent most of that night playing out the feverish impulses of our blood.

In the morning, we made separate long-distance calls to KG&K to tell our bosses that we were sick and wouldn't be in.

"This is something I don't do," she said.

Jaybird-naked next to her, I had to laugh.

"Lie about being sick," she said sharply. "We can't do this again, Peter."

My stomach lurched as if I *did* have a virus. "Memory—!"

"During the week, I mean. It's unprofessional."

We argued, but Memory was adamant. Although I felt sure that later, under the lash of desire, she would change her mind, she never did. In fact, Memory went back to work that very afternoon, claiming that her attack of flu had been a feeble one. I, however, stayed out the entire day, angry and resentful. She had sabotaged the perfect pleasure jaunt.

The next weekend, I took Memory to my friend Jeremy Taggart's hunting and fishing cabin in the mountains of Pickens County. This was no rustic, ramshackle hideaway, but a well-appointed bachelor's lair featuring a music-and-video center, a wet bar, and a series of erotic lithographs at those spots on the walls where most Good Old Boys would have hung deer heads, shotguns, or pur-loined electric beer signs.

Memory thought the lithographs vulgar. Fortunately, the cabin had something that she liked: the hummingbird feeder hanging from a shingled eave of Jeremy's toolshed. A picture window in the loft bedroom permitted us to lounge limb in limb on Saturday after-noon watching the fleet, metallic hummers (most, white-throated females) pop into sight at the feeder's phony scarlet blossoms, hover there siphoning the sugar water that Memory boiled for them, and flit off into . . . maybe another dimension. They were feisty birds. One territorial female, feinting and attacking, repeatedly chased away all the others seeking to drink from the feeder.

"The little bitch," Memory said.

Then that green-jacketed harridan vanished too, and for a long moment the air was birdless—spookily so. I used this interlude to tell her my third premeditated lie:

"*'Hummingbirds do not fly; they matter-transmit.'*"

Memory considered this. Then she kissed me on the temple and pointed at a spot between the bed and the picture window.

"You're right," she said. "There's one . . . *now!*"

I blinked. So emphatic was Memory's suggestion, I thought a male ruby-throat had materialized in our bed loft. The sound of its whirring wings, the ebony syringe of its beak, and the pulsing fire of its gorget burned into my retinas as if a flashbulb had exploded. Then the mirage was gone, and all I could hear, as I clutched Memory's warm, supple body, was laughter. The laughter of a sorceress.

"Another," she demanded.

We wrestled. Memory kept laughing and, through this laughter, daring me to manufacture a fourth fantastic lie.

" 'Sex for hummingbirds is an exquisite agony,' " I finally said, spitting out my epigram. " 'To imagine it, stick your finger into the blur of an electric beater.' "

She liked that. "Very good, Peter. Nine to go."

Yet more laughter, followed by a spontaneous binge of inventive sex — none of it, its exquisiteness aside, the least agonizing.

The next present I gave Memory was a circular aquarium containing a dozen flamboyantly colored tropical fish, several muck-eating snails, and an underwater forest of seaweed and sinuous ferns. I installed the aquarium in her apartment on a Friday afternoon while Memory was still at the office. When she arrived home, she found the glowing tank, the beautiful angel wings and clownfish, and, in a near-invisible Lucite cube suspended at the aquarium's heart, one iridescent hummingbird.

"Peter!" she said, approaching the radiant tank.

The hummingbird wasn't real. It was the same one I'd lowered to her desk as spectacular proof of my interest. Distorted by the fish-peopled water, though, it looked real. I kissed her on the forehead and slipped out the door, allowing her to find and read for herself the lie on the accompanying card:

"Eventually, a hummingbird in a tank of oxygenated sugar water will sip its way to freedom."

A major Atlanta soft-drink firm employing Kyser, Godwin & Kale decided to create, name, and test-market an energy-boosting drink in direct competition with Gatorade. Logan Metasavage gave this account to me and told me to have my entire campaign worked out in brilliant detail yesterday. I got to it.

I named this drink — some sort of citrus-flavored, sugar-laden, cherry-colored, additive-doped swill — NRG-Assist, and I designed a bottle resembling a hummingbird feeder, a label on which a pair of cartoon ruby-throats are prominent, and a series of animated TV ads featuring the energetic hummers as product spokescreatures.

The makers of NRG-Assist were delighted; they gave us a handsome bonus for executing the campaign so quickly. Thus did I vindicate—that week, at least—my reputation as a company hotshot.

On Sunday, Memory and I attended a free symphonic concert on the grass in Chastain Park. Between sets, a light plane buzzed the crowd, trailing an advertising banner. This banner bore the burden of my sixth falsehood, a public falsehood for which the company and I were generously reimbursed:

"Hummingbirds prefer NRG-Assist."

As an additional reward, KG&K gave me a twelve-day vacation in Palm Springs, Florida. Memory couldn't go, but I stayed in touch with her via postcard and Southern Bell.

In the seventh week of our itemhood, Memory had a pregnancy scare. It was only a scare, but it fell between us like a sword; and the lie I handed her on a postcard purchased during my getaway to Florida—a card showing a red-gilled lizard on a palm tree—did nothing to ease her mind, even though I'd meant it lightly:

"The first hummingbirds were the get of an oversexed chameleon and a bewildered dragonfly."

What eased her mind was the arrival, nearly two weeks late, of her period. That tardy event calmed some of my midnight anxieties too. Some. Not all.

Two nights after Memory told me that everything was copacetic, I had a psychedelic nightmare. A plague of hummingbirds swept up from South America and hurtled into Atlanta in a whirring cloud of invisible wings and chittering, batlike squeaks—a cloud so dense, begemmed, and mobile that the sun was eclipsed; traffic disappeared behind a series of shifting emerald scrims; and humming-bird guano began to fall like wet caulking on sidewalks, gutter guards, window ledges, awnings, rooftops.

This vile bombardment went on and on. If you stuck your head outdoors, the backwind from a myriad ever-beating wings would knock you down. Rays of sunlight struggling to penetrate the metallic cloud sparked blinding flashes off it. Those Atlantans who weren't cowering in parked cars, or in the revolving doors of department stores, or in streetside bus shelters, lay on the pavement with their hands over their heads, like actors in old Civil Defense films about the Soviet nuclear threat.

I woke up sweating. Is a plague of hummingbirds what I would have sired on my Oriental dragonfly if Memory had really been pregnant? Out of my lover's womb, a noisy litter of ruby-throats? A tape recorder lay on the end table next to my bed. I kept it there in case midnight inspiration seized me during my efforts to devise a full-bore ad campaign for one of our clients. I picked it up, found its built-in microphone, and spoke my lie:

"*One plague in Egypt was of hummingbirds: Pharaoh's people died with emerald plumage in their mouths.*"

An evening later, when I played this back for Memory, she said, "There aren't any hummingbirds in the Old World, Peter. And there never have been."

"Don't be so literal-minded," I said.

Memory wanted me to meet her daddy. I needed to see that she had strong ties here in Atlanta. So, in her VW beetle, we drove to her father's clapboard house in Decatur.

Mr. Yang, wearing a pair of smoky sunglasses, sat in a lawn chair illegally watering his drought-stricken grass. The hose lay in a narrow trench next to the driveway, eeled up into some weedy vegetation at his sneakered feet, and, thereby hidden, spilled its liquid bounty into all the nether reaches of the yard, which the hose had flooded to a condition of squishy marsh.

"Howdy," the old man said, tilting his head like a dog.

He had on a Day-Glo orange jumpsuit and a paint-freckled Braves cap. At seventy-plus, he looked only about five years older than I did. Memory had told me that the bullet wounds responsible for his retirement included a blasted-away calf muscle, a shattered elbow, a mangled hand. But only when he stood to greet us did I notice his injuries.

"Daddy, there's a water shortage. You could be fined."

"Only if they catch me." Limping, he herded us up the walk to his air-conditioned house.

In the tiny living room, Mr. Yang felt his way into a low-slung easy chair. Next to this chair lay the corpse of an aged, silvery, lion-maned chow, the handiwork of a taxidermist.

"That's Chiang Kai-shek," Memory explained. "Daddy's last and longest-surviving seeing-eye dog."

She said that her father had been a masseur in Taipei, Taiwan (blind persons have a monopoly on the massage profession in that island nation), and that he had founded a thriving, wholly upright massage parlor in Atlanta soon after coming to Georgia in the early 1950s. As Memory spoke, her father absentmindedly scratched the dead animal's muzzle.

A shiver helixed my spine: I wasn't much comforted to hear that Mr. Yang had had Chiang Kai-shek stuffed because the faithful chow had given its life for him in the same brutal robbery attempt that had forced his retirement.

While Memory was in the kitchen, Mr. Yang informed me that his daughter loved me. Moreover, I was the first man for whom she had felt such tenderness since her divorce.

"Memory tells me you lie to her, Peter."

I was too stunned to reply.

"Lies about hummingbirds," he specified, smiling. "As a way of wooing her."

"I guess that's so," I said, only a little relieved.

"It can be hard, coming up with clever lies." Mr. Yang tilted his blind head. "Would you like to borrow one?"

"I guess so."

"Okay. Here you go, then. It's a direct steal from Stevens, but it's a 'lie' you must keep in mind if Memory is really in love with you."

I waited, my hands clammy and my irritation building.

Mr. Yang stared through his silver lenses at me: " 'A *man and a woman are one. A man and a woman and a hummingbird are one.*' "

A coldness unrelated to the air conditioning bludgeoned me, for this "lie," echoing some lines in Stevens's blackbird poem, embodied a subtle threat. Mr. Yang wished me to understand that my intentions toward Memory had better be honorable.

"Lie Number Nine, Peter," Mr. Yang said. "Feel free to tell it to Memory when you leave here this evening."

"I will," I said. "That's exactly what I'll tell her. Thanks, Mr. Yang. Thanks a lot."

"I don't think her ex-husband—the womanizing no-account doing time in Macon—ever saw the truth in that lie."

"He didn't?"

"No, he didn't. He was a runaround. When the feds arrested him on a drug charge, I told Memory to speak the truth about his activities. She did, too. In court."

"Good. Good for her. Really great."

"You're tense, young man. I can tell from your voice. Let me give you a massage."

This offer frightened me. The simple thought of the old man's touch set goose bumps sprouting. "But your hand . . ."

"With one hand, I'm better than most sighted people who have a healthy pair. If I didn't tire so fast, I'd still be working."

For some reason, I submitted. In a back bedroom, I lay naked on an aluminum table. The old man kneaded the flesh at my nape, my shoulder blades, the small of my back, and my upper buttocks as if he wanted to sculpt them into completely other shapes—hummocks of loamy soil, maybe, or the body parts of a bipedal alien being. My muscles stayed as taut as clock springs.

"Try to loosen up," the old man said.

"I can't." My face lay on a stiff folded towel.

"Maybe it's because you've been mixing Memory and desire." He chuckled, not kindly. "Do you suppose?"

"Mmmmf." I had no memory. I had no desire.

"I can feel it in my fingers. There's something cruel in you, Peter. Something bleak and unforthcoming."

He told me my birthdate. He gave me the names of the last four women I had romanced "seriously." He alluded to my parents' divorce and told me where my father was buried. He informed me that I had never been a baseball fan and that I had no more interest in poetry than I had in hummingbirds. Never fear, though—he wouldn't tell. Memory was a big girl and could find out these unremarkable secrets for herself—probably by a method akin to the tactile one that he was presently employing. Indeed, she might know my secrets already.

I wanted to flee, but the old man's single good hand held me to the table. Neither his massaging technique nor his menacing patter seemed likely to freshen or relax me.

Twenty minutes into this delicate sadism, he said, "Do you know why I named my daughter Memory?"

"No, sir."

"Memory is a form of knowledge." Mr. Yang leaned the heel of his hand onto my spine. "What one remembers, one knows. Memory—Mnemosyne, the Greeks called her—was the feminine source of all human creativity. I hoped our daughter would please her mother and me just as happy memories do. Also, I trusted that memory—our daughter's, I mean—would serve her as a shield and an ever-present solace. Do you see?"

"I don't know. Yes, sir. I think so."

"What one remembers—really remembers—one stores. I named Memory years before the personal computer; but, in terms of memory storage, Memory's my computer. My memory is lousy, Peter. Some days, I scarcely know my own name. But if I want to hear about my late wife, Memory calls up her recollections and gives them to me in forms well suited to my sightlessness—stories, songs, poems. Do you follow, young man?"

"Yes, sir." But I didn't. I just didn't want to give Mr. Yang an excuse to shatter a vertebra.

"*I* may forget, Peter, but *Memory* won't. And when she tells me what she knows, I always remind her . . . not to forget it."

Eventually, he released me. Eventually, the three of us—the old man slumped in his chair with a plastic plate on his lap and the silver-furred Chiang Kai-shek beside him—ate what Memory had so painstakingly prepared for us.

I don't recall what that was, nor do I wish to.

Later, standing in the lobby of the Fox Theater on Peachtree, I told Memory her father's lie: "'*A man and a woman are one. A man and a woman and a hummingbird are one.*'"

"Nice," Memory said. "But I hope it isn't a lie."

"It's not *my* lie, Memory."

"I tell Daddy everything, Peter."

"You tell him everything," I said numbly. Suddenly, I had an unsettling suspicion.

"In that robbery your dad got shot up in . . ."

"What about it?"

"Were the holdup men caught?"

"Chiang Kai-shek tore one of them up. That gave Daddy time to shoot the other. In fact, he crippled the second creep even worse than those cowardly bastards did for him."

"Not bad for an old geezer shooting blind," I admitted, without enthusiasm.

"No," Memory agreed. "It wasn't."

On Friday afternoon, eager for solitude, I went up to Jeremy's cabin by myself. I filled the hummingbird feeder and watched until dusk as a pair of females flew aerial dogfights around each other—a battle for exclusive sipping rights.

When no birds appeared the next morning, however, I hurried to check out the feeder. Small red ants paraded up the wall of the shed, under the eave, along the feeder's drop line, and down the sticky glass bottle to the four plastic blossoms dispensing sugar water. Although a few ants had drowned in the clear syrup inside the cylinder, most hadn't—they swarmed like coolies all over the bottle. No wonder my hummingbirds hadn't returned.

I found a garden hose, leveled a cleansing spray on the feeder and the ants crawling over the shed, and tried to find a better spot for the feeder. Where? No place seemed absolutely safe from ant attack—so, finally, I dumped the bottle's gluey contents on an ant hill next to the shed and lugged myself back inside.

Later, lying on Jeremy's king-sized bed and staring at nothing, a fresh lie came marching into my mind—like a train of ants, each insect carrying one syllable of the conceit that I could not evict from my consciousness:

"Anteaters sometimes impersonate hummingbirds in order to gorge on the ants that have overrun their feeders."

Ha ha, I thought bitterly. Very amusing.

At which moment I had a disturbing picture of Memory playfully straddling me, her glossy hair hanging down around my temples, her nipples moving over me like the pink felt nubs of Magic Markers. What was her eidolon doing? Tracing on my chest, I realized, the very words that she was whispering to me inside the hallucinatory veil of her perfumed tresses:

"Often, Peter, some of these imposters—anteaters pretending to be hummingbirds – have trouble staying aloft."

Memory's smart-ass corollary to Falsehood Number Ten. For, even after her naked phantom had vanished, there was no doubt in my mind that she was calling me—subtly, very subtly—an imposter.

By dint of real effort, I sidestepped her for a whole week. I took lunch an hour earlier or later than she did, I stayed well out of her territories in the KG&K building, I stopped telephoning her in the evenings, and I let my answering machine reply to every call to my apartment, even when I was there to interrupt my own recorded spiel. To Memory's credit, or maybe as a sample of her shrewdness, she called me only once that week, and her voice among my messages sounded neither desperate nor sad:

"My father enjoyed talking with you last week, Peter. Let me hear from you in the next day or two, and he'll stand us to dinner at one of his favorite restaurants. Love ya. 'Bye."

I ignored the call, which came on a Tuesday evening. In fact, I made it until Thursday afternoon without Memory's spotting me on the fourteenth floor or chasing me down in the parking lot. As it was, she cornered me right after an unscheduled marketing meeting called by her boss, Vivian DuPriest, to which Logan Metasavage, my boss, had sent me as his proxy.

Throughout this meeting, at which I learned that my animated NRG-Assist hummingbird ads would debut that evening on Ted Turner's Channel 17, Memory behaved to everyone, including me, as if nothing were wrong. When she buttonholed me outside the meeting room afterwards, she displayed a possessiveness—fingering my tie, patting my pocket handkerchief—that nonplussed me.

"You *must* be busy, Peter. Well, Vi's kept me on the go, too, and it won't hurt Daddy to wait a while to see you again."

"Ah." (That old Jurusik wit in action.)

"Which reminds me. It's time for a hummingbird lie, Peter."

Criminy. The woman was insatiable.

"Don't get uptight. I know you've been busy. I have too, but I decided it was time for *me* to do one."

"Pardon me?"

"This one's my treat. You should like it. It makes reference to advertising. Ready?"

I just gaped at her.

Memory laughed and kissed me on the forehead. "'*Hummingbirds regard the imperceptible eyeflashes of subliminal TV ads as heavy reading.*'"

I heard the words, but they didn't register at the level of my conscious understanding. Memory smiled and repeated them.

"Number Eleven," she said. "The last two are yours, but if you want me to take over or just to drop the whole game, fine. We'll find a less phony way to make our relationship meaningful. You're too bright a guy for this crap, Peter."

That night, I drove straight to my apartment, locked myself in, and heated a low-calory gourmet dinner in the microwave. Peter, I told myself, switching on the TV, take a few minutes to review your situation.

Just then, one of my NRG-Assist spots came on. Two animated hummingbirds flew a *pas de deux* around a cartoonish bottle of the stuff, chittering lies like "*For instant energy replenishment*" and "*Fly with the fleetest when you NRG-Assist.*"

But I noticed something weird about the ad—an annoying blur at the bottom of the screen, twin streaks of spectral characters that came and went so fast it was impossible to tell if they were real. During the crummy sit-com afterward, I shoved my tray aside and went looking for my Polaroid. Finally, camera in hand, I returned to my chair for the next commercial break.

A repeat of my NRG-Assist spot was squeezed between an upbeat Toyota ad and a dull brokerage-firm come-on. During this rerun, I took four hasty pictures of the screen. One of my shots, developed, clearly disclosed the illegal eyeflash message that I had suspected to be there.

It said, in computer-printer letters that convinced me paranoia was a legitimate, survival-oriented response: "A *hummingbird's min-*

iscule heart can beat up to thirteen weeks after the bird itself has died. How long do you think yours will beat?"

That was Lie Number Twelve. Truly heavy reading.

How had that ominous message appeared in my ad? Well, at least one version of the spot must have gone to our client's offices from KG&K that way. I had a hunch that Memory was the marketing rep who had fed the doctored clip to our client—who, in turn, had passed it on to the TV people for broadcasting. Her doctoring was clumsy and obvious, but when it was discovered, as it eventually would be, *I* was the ad exec who'd catch the flak.

That night, I packed. On Friday, I went to work as if nothing were wrong. I continued to avoid Memory, whom I once saw staring into copywriting-and-layout from the edge of her research-and-marketing warren. Later, pleading a queasy stomach (the truth, the honest-to-Jesus truth), I left three hours early.

But I didn't go home. I drove to the bank, withdrew every last cent in my savings account, and got on I–20 West out of Atlanta, to Birmingham and whatever unknown spots farther west the evil designs of Memory Yang might ultimately force me to flee.

I cruised for hours. I didn't stop cruising until the air had an unfamiliar, high-altitude sting.

For the past ten or twelve days, I have been writing this on motel stationery in a variety of motels across the Rockies and the Pacific Northwest: Econolodge, Day's Inn, Motel 6, Scottish Inn, you-name-it.

I jump every time I see a Volkswagen, and yesterday morning my heart nearly burst when I entered a mom-and-pop grocery in Klamath Falls, where I'd been holed up for two days, and saw a hummingbird broach on the floral-print blouse of the proprietress.

"Where did you get that?" I demanded.

"Pretty lady handed it to me yesterday right after you'd bought something from us. Said, if I didn't mind, to let you have it the next time you came in."

She shouted something after me as I fled, but with no time to waste I beat it back to the motel to gather up my belongings and hit the road again. I drove south, into California, and continued treading asphalt long after night had fallen.

Two nights ago, in a ramshackle boardinghouse in Bakersfield, California, I dreamed that a wrinkled, gnomish old man sat astride my hams pulling my spinal cord, knob by Tinker Toy knob, through a hole he had punctured at the base of my neck. He reeled it out (even flat on my belly, I could see the moist, cartilaginous column emerging from between my shoulder blades) like a man drawing a knotted rope out of a well.

On each knob—on each knot—shone a tiny photo-booth portrait of a young woman I had pursued, screwed, and alienated. The gnome on my back felt the blood-smeared face on each picture with a crooked thumb, grunted his pitying recognition, and continued extracting my spine. At last, finished, he climbed down from the bed and stumped out onto the boardinghouse's second-story landing using my flaccid backbone as a not very serviceable walking stick.

Later, a series of noises wakened me. It was a dog's furious barking.

Face down on my room's lumpy daybed, I could not move. It took an hour—at least—to scrunch myself into a wormlike parody of uprightness and to shuffle to the door. The moon was still up, and standing on the sidewalk across the street from the boardinghouse was a silvery, lion-maned dog. Even as it barked, it snapped and slavered at me.

I slammed the door, grabbed my gear, and hustled down the rear steps to the eucalyptus-guarded yard sheltering my Audi.

I have just returned to my roach-infested second-floor room in a motel on the outskirts of Socorro, New Mexico. I was out less than forty minutes, long enough to buy some Kentucky Fried Chicken and a new set of fingernail clippers. The first thing I saw when I came back in—a shock worse than those afforded by either Memory's hummingbird pin or her father's resurrected seeing-eye chow—was a small hardcover book lying open on my bed.

A tiny creature rested in the crease between the book's yellow pages, a creature that I could not identify until I went across the room and lifted it squeamishly by a tail feather. I don't know whether this bird is male or female, for the blood spot on its gorget consists of real blood—as if whoever brought it to me first sliced its throat with a razor blade. Some of its blood stains the elegant poetry of the volume, a first edition of *Harmonium*.

My phone line has been cut. When I peeked through the curtains a few minutes ago, two shadowy figures stood on the landing across the courtyard from my room. And the silhouette of a lion-maned dog wavered in the gloom beneath their lodgings, a canine statue no more substantial than moonlight.

The dead telephone rings. I answer it with a nervous "Hello."

"Hello," says the party calling me, a young woman. I already know who she is, of course. "This is your imagination speaking," she goes on, but it is so obviously Memory that I must clench my teeth to keep from calling her on her lie. "And you have a good one, Peter, better than I would have ever guessed. Forgive me for doubting you."

"What do you want?"

"That first lie you told me: *'I am a hummingbird.'* Don't you remember it, Peter?"

I grip the dead phone, resolutely saying nothing.

"It wasn't a lie. That makes it the truth. Which, given the game we were playing, makes it a lie again. See?"

"I'm finished," I blurt. "I'm finished playing."

"Close your eyes, Peter."

I try to resist this command, but I can't. Memory's powers of coercion, even through the cut line, are preternatural.

"You're not finished until the last lie is spoken, Peter. But even though you started the game—and even though you've long since broken your promise to play it through to the end—I'll let you off the hook. *I'll* be Official Finisher, okay?"

I start to open my eyes.

"Don't!" Memory shouts at me through the handset. Both she and her blind daddy can see what they shouldn't be able to access. How do they do that? Imagination or memory?

I keep my eyes closed.

"Here," Memory says. "Our thirteenth lie. *'A dead hummingbird symbolizes unspeakable grief.'* "

Does she mean me? Is her lie, like Mr. Yang's, a barbarous physical threat? No, I don't think so.

But my eyes open anyway, and when I look at the bed, I see that the first edition of *Harmonium* is really a Socorro phone book and that the butchered hummingbird in the crease between its pages has turned into the jade-green hand comb that I ordinarily carry in my pocket with my car keys.

Doesn't Memory understand—didn't she ever know?—that hummingbirds don't pair-bond? That's the truth, perhaps the first truth I ever learned about myself.

Suddenly, there is a low hum in my ear—a busy signal, abrupt and raucous – and I am all alone in a shabby little room somewhere not too far from either the White Sands nuclear testing grounds or the treacherous Jornada del Muerto.

How did I get here? I can't help wondering. And why do people always lie to one another?

The Unexpected Visit of a Reanimated Englishwoman

T HE FOOTFALLS ON THE STAIRS HAD WEIGHT. I COULD hear not only their impress on the lacquered heartpine but also the successive creaking of each riser and the begrudging pops of the handrail balusters. I stopped taking notes and listened harder.

I half expected — I *always* half expect — my father to climb as he often did in life to my second-story office and to bark, "Let's go for a sandwich, Michael." If he had come today (March 11, 1996: the 178th anniversary of the publication of *Frankenstein; Or, The Modern Prometheus*), he would barge in wearing a ratty parka, a woolen watchcap, and grimy, checkered trousers, his feet shod in army-surplus boots, for a deep cold held sway. The saucer magnolia in my front yard had lost its pink blossoms to a weekend frost; those still clinging to it fluttered like tiny flags of beige nylon.

In the dark upstairs hall, the temperature had not risen above forty-five degrees Fahrenheit. To my right, a propane-burning space heater labored to keep my teeth from chattering; they clacked anyway, for whoever had materialized on the stairs continued to climb them, producing more groanings in the wood and a mounting jitteriness in me. Still, the intruder's tread did not suggest the coming of a large person, certainly not a marauding golem. A child, I figured, or a woman. Jeri would not return from her counseling job in Hogansville for another four hours, though, and because I

19

had heard no one twist the bell-key on our front door, *materialized* seems the aptest word for my guest's advent on the bottom landing.

The phantom on our steps shoved through the stuck door at their top, just outside my office. I don't keep a pistol in my desk — but would a burglar or a potential assassin have bothered to knock? I coasted back in my chair and croaked more than called, "Come in!"

She entered, without flamboyance. Tentatively, in fact; courteously. If she had expected either elegance or order, my office — two cramped squares, with floor-to-ceiling bookcases on four of the six walls — disappointed her. She hesitated before a stack of books on the floor. The door gaped behind her; cold air swept past her shawled body like a williwaw from the final chapter of her teenage masterwork.

"Shut the door," I said. "We'll freeze if you don't."

At her own careful speed, she obeyed. Her gaze took in the prints on my walls and the weird windowed machine on my rolltop. The garish spines on the paperbacks in my bookcases also seized her notice.

Only a few of these titles and authors could have meant anything to her: *The Aeneid* of Vergil, *The Republic* of Plato, the plays of Shakespeare, and a smattering of early titles by Charles Dickens. Robert Louis Stevenson, whose *The Strange Case of Dr. Jekyll and Mr. Hyde* has horrific affinities with *Frankenstein,* had only just passed his first birthday when she died. George Eliot (Mary Ann Evans Cross) did not publish her first book until seven years after my visitor's death. Joseph Conrad, H. G. Wells, G. K. Chesterton, and Virginia Woolf first saw daylight six, fifteen, twenty-three, and thirty-one years, respectively, after her 1851 demise — compatriots all, but all of course forever strangers to her.

And what could she possibly make of writers named Aldiss, Ballard, Bradbury, Clarke, Delany, Disch, Le Guin, Silverberg, and so on? Trembling a little, she let her gaze linger on the Dan Simmons titles *Hyperion* and *The Fall of Hyperion,* but the clutter on my floor kept her from going to them and unshelving one or both.

I nodded at the paperbacks. "They make great insulation. Please sit in my chair."

"No, thank you. I fear my arrival inconveniences you."

Of course it did. My office has only one chair, and no other decent place to sit except the three-step stool that my father-in-law built to provide access to my topmost shelves. The inconvenience meant nothing, though. I knew my guest for the daughter of protofeminist Mary Wollstonecraft, author of *A Vindication of the*

Rights of Woman (1792), and William Godwin, author of *An Enquiry Concerning Political Justice* (1793). In 1714, a month shy of her seventeenth birthday, she had eloped with the married writer Percy Shelley. Later, she had written many books herself, including *Frankenstein* (1818) and *The Last Man* (1826), as well as the five supernatural tales about which, owing to an unexpected writing assignment, I was now obsessively ruminating.

Inconvenience? No, call her arrival an *opportunity.* She arranged herself and her skirts on my stool and clasped her gloved hands in her lap. Her presence heartened as well as spooked me. I wanted to tell her about automobiles, airplanes, movies, television. To chauffeur her to the Little White House in Warm Springs. To treat her to a Popsicle. To show her the plastic lemon in our refrigerator. (Would she think it witty or just grotesque?) To play her snippets of my Miles Davis, Abbey Lincoln, and Chris Botti CDs. (So much, good and bad, has happened since Mozart.)

We began to talk. She recognized me as a fellow writer, but implied no knowledge of my work and offered no assessment of my gift. (I regarded her forbearance as a kindness, for I quailed before her opinion and had no idea how she could have reached one.) Like the heroes of her essay/tales "Valerius: The Reanimated Roman" and "Roger Dodsworth: The Reanimated Englishman," she had won through to some sort of second-chance resuscitation. I wondered what had awakened her, revivified her, and sent her climbing the stairs to my office in a country far from either England or her beloved Italy.

"I had an inclination this way whilst you set down your odd sequel to my Prometheus," she said. "And came when you decided to write a commentary about my supernatural tales."

"Yes, but *why* did you come?"

"To help. Whatever else?"

"Do you think a lot of money figures in an assignment like this?" I said.

She smiled. "It never does, does it?"

"What do you want? Accuracy? A positive spin?"

"'Spin'?"

"You've got a sympathetic mouthpiece here. I *want* to give today's readers your take on these stories."

"Accuracy, certainly," she said. "Insofar as any fallible mortal has the capacity to ensure it. I would also desire that you neither overpraise these pieces nor claim too much for them as exemplars of . . . *science fiction?*" She cast a skeptical glance at the multicolored paperbacks converging in the corner behind her.

"Brian Aldiss—" I began.

"Yes, I know of *him*," she said. "I would have visited him ere calling upon you, but that the prolificity and the reputed excellence of his work have to some extent cowed me." Here she shrugged enigmatically within her shawl.

"Well, I see neither of those things kept you from coming to Pine Mountain. Anyway, Aldiss says that *Frankenstein* sired the literary genre known today as science fiction."

"Yes. But of *The Last Man* he wrote that my prose had 'run a little to fat'; that 'one often wishes for more conversation and fewer descriptions, and altogether less rhetoric' in it."

Had that comment, even more than Aldiss's formidable output and reputation, derailed her plans to visit him? Swallowing the question, I noted that three of her five supernatural tales— "Dodsworth," "Valerius," and "The Mortal Immortal"—clearly represented short-fiction forays into the category that she had inadvertently or intuitively invented as a teenager.

She smiled again. "We must forgive adolescents their excesses." Perched before me as a fifty-three-year-old woman who had died in the winter of 1851, restored to health and animated by her own singular *élan vital*, she looked strangely at home on my stool. Her center-parted hair had more silver than chestnut in it, and the lines around her mouth and nose heightened the dry, satiny quality of her skin. "Before I intruded, what *had* you intended to write in your remarks?" she said.

"That I thought I knew why the reanimation of the dead had such centrality in your work."

"Pray, enlighten me as to your thesis."

I really didn't want to do that—*in her presence*. I wanted to hide it in a pseudo-Freudian essay and hope that no one but pseudo-Freudians ever stumbled upon it. To say it aloud struck me as tantamount to bludgeoning her over the head with, well, a baseball bat. At last I said, "Subconscious wish-fulfillment fantasies."

"Louder, man. The seething of that queer device," nodding at my space heater, "obliterates your utterance."

Obliterates. Utterance. (Aldiss had her pegged.) But I repeated my suspicion, louder, and my face grew hot.

"Do you hypothecate I never saw this bent in myself? Fie. Who among us wouldn't resurrect a departed loved one?"

I hesitated.

"You don't wish to pursue the matter?"

"I guess. It definitely inclines us to more conversation and fewer descriptions."

"As for the rhetoric, let us each stand watch." She lifted her hands in a quick minstrelish gesture.

"Possibly you lost more than your fair share of loved ones to death," I said.

"Not possibly. Unquestionably."

"Your mother, Mary Wollstonecraft, died as a consequence of delivering you. Your first baby by Percy Shelley, a daughter, died only eleven days after her birth. Your next two children, William and Clara, died young in Italy, the girl at only a year and two days, the boy at three and a half. In 1819, you gave birth to the only child to survive both you and your husband, Percy Florence, who came on November 12—by a mild coincidence my birthday in a distant future year. Another child miscarried in the summer of 1822, shortly after your stepsister Claire's child Allegra by Lord Byron died, and not long before Shelley and a friend drowned off Leghorn when a squall capsized the boat *Ariel*. Which isn't to mention the suicide of Shelley's first wife, Harriet Westbrook, that allowed you to marry, or the laudanum overdose of your half sister Fanny Imlay, which the Godwins gave to the world as a somehow natural demise. Or the fact that in Missolonghi, two years after Shelley's death, Lord Byron, your friend and Claire's former lover, contracted a fever and—"

"Please. Your recitation fatigues me. I inly rehearse it more often than you may surmise, but I much prefer to dwell on the beautiful and the good."

"Like what?"

"At age five I beheld the Frenchman Andre-Jacques Garnerin accomplish the first parachute jump in England. My father took me outside to see it, for M. Garnerin dropped himself from a balloon over the fields behind the St. Pancras church, in whose graveyard—" She stopped.

"—your mother lies buried," I said. "A biographer says that you and Shelley first made love behind her tombstone in that graveyard."

"That, too," she whispered, not looking at me. "At sixteen I found that experience as galvanic as, at five, I had found the Frenchman's spectacular descent."

"This biographer also says that Godwin taught you to read by tracing the letters on the tombstone's inscription."

Head up, she rebuked me: "The beautiful and the good! Sir Walter Scott praised *Frankenstein* in *Blackwood's*. Later, he said that he preferred it to any of his own novels. How I took cheer from that unsought encomium."

"What else heartens you?" I said.

"The success, then and now, of that novel."

"Elias Canetti has said, 'Whoever can embue mankind with a myth has accomplished more than the most daring inventor.' He cites you as one having that 'rare distinction.'"

"I know him not, but I earnestly thank him."

"Even so, Mrs. Shelley, I think I know where both that myth and your obsession with the idea of reanimation come from. I'd planned to say so in my introduction—without however disputing your genius in dramatizing it."

She ignored me. "I also take great pride in having edited and annotated my husband's poetry. I preserved and elucidated it, I vindicated his character. It required too many years for the world to laud my contributions there."

"Mrs. Shelley—"

"We dared, both he and I. My novella *Mathilda*, which I composed even as Shelley brought his verse tragedy *The Cenci* to completion, had no publication during my lifetime for the very reason that his play had no staging during his. They both deal forthrightly with incest, and our age had no stomach for such a theme. My novella entered print—in your country, I must tell you—only after I had endured bodily extinction one hundred and eight years. That Shelley and I continually hurled aesthetic defiance, however, even yet gratifies me."

"Yes," I said. "You pushed the envelope."

"Oh, no. More often we posted it overland to the Channel."

"Mrs. Shelley—"

"Yes, yes. Say what you so obviously wish to say."

I shuffled through my notecards to a *Journal* passage dated March 19, a month after her first child's death: "'Dream that my little baby came to life again—that it had only been cold and that we rubbed it by the fire and it lived—I awake and find no baby—I think about the little thing all day . . .'"

My visitor merely looked at me.

"Reanimation," I said. "A *year* before you, Shelley, Byron, and Polidori held your little ghost-story contest in the Villa Diodati. I think it signifies."

"Every life signifies, and a lost life sends out as many ripples as the sun has rays, even if one does not always stand at a place to break and disarrange them."

If she meant this epigram to cut, I sidestepped its point.

"I feel—" I began.

She again lifted her hands. "I thank you for the impulse behind, but reject, your pity. Only children who die young get through life without some dreadful loss, and generally such children represent that most dreadful loss to those who love them. Life chastises as well as exalts. Anyone of even idiot ken knows that. Raise me not to sainthood on the commonplace foundation of my sufferings. Given so easy a criterion, even you might merit a quarter arc of halo."

This hit, even if rhetoric-freighted, stung. "Pardon me if I find biography a key to your reanimation hang-up."

She actually laughed. "Consider my pardon bestowed. But also that my Prometheus and these five stories constitute only a fraction of my life's work."

"An *important* fraction."

"I would hope every fraction in some measure important, as you must regard each constituent arc of your incomplete halo a promise of future wholeness."

"This halo crap has a vicious circularity, Mrs. Shelley."

"My, my. No need for such unimaginative vulgarisms, sir."

"Could we get back to your stories?"

She lifted her eyebrows and her hands.

"Roger Dodsworth comes back to life," I said. "You shift him from Cromwell's time to your own. You speculate briefly on all the 'learned disquisitions' that some future humanity would produce to account for the huge gap between the birth and death dates on Dodsworth's tombstone. How do *you* account for them? Did he *thaw* into life?"

"Doesn't the story say so?"

"What about Valerius in 'Valerius: The Reanimated Roman'? In his case, the story *doesn't* say."

"Then why not assume that he thawed into life too?"

"In Italy?"

"Italy also has snow. Romans did not always sit in the sun watching African beasts maul unrecanting Christians in the ensanguined arena of the Colosseum. Indeed, Valerius during his original incarnation never encountered a Christian, nor had any presentiment of the Emperors."

"He dislikes the priest whom he meets in your own time and despairs of the fact that Rome now bears the title 'the Capital of Christianity.' "

"That troubles you?"

"Oh, no. It rings true."

"I concur, but tell me why you think so."

"It rings true to Valerius's character, but also to yours. As a girl—a young woman, actually—you twice went to live in Dundee, Scotland, with the family of a wealthy sailcloth maker, Mr. Baxter. You formed a lasting friendship with his daughter, Isabel, four years your senior. In your story, Isabell Harley, although you give her first name an extra 'l,' forms a fast friendship with poor anachronistic Valerius, who calls her 'the only hope and comfort of my life.'"

"The name Isabel, whatever its orthography, has always appealed to me. Why shouldn't I christen a suitable character with a favorite name?"

"No reason at all. But the Baxters belonged to a strict Calvinist sect called the Glassites. During your second stay in Dundee, from June 1813 to March 1814, attention to the Glassite's strictures destroyed any lingering respect that you may have had for Christianity."

"Their *practice* of it," my visitor corrected me.

"When the Glassites excommunicated Isabel for marrying her older sister's widower, calling the union incest, your disgust grew. Some of this attitude colors Valerius's negative view of Christianity, even if that opinion has real credibility in the frame of his fictional predicament."

"Thank you, I suppose. How you do enjoy speculating."

"Anyway, your treatment of Valerius points me to a passage in 'Dodsworth' where you argue that if philosophical novels had an audience nowadays, someone could write a good one 'on the development of the same mind in various stations, in different periods of the world's history.' Because you wrote 'Valerius' in 1819, seven years before 'Dodsworth,' I see you explaining in the later tale your aim in both."

"Bravo." She clapped—a brief velvety thumping.

"Did you know that twentieth-century science fiction *has* exploited the idea of translating figures from the past into other time periods and turning them 'naked of knowledge into this world'?"

"Truly?"

"Occasionally. We call such tales alternate or alternative histories. You may have pioneered them."

"But not very deeply into the wilderness. You flatter me. You also discover in these quotations the reason—the foremost reason—for my visit to you today."

I leveled a cynical squint at her.

"You have a dilemma?" she said.

"You didn't exactly arrive here 'naked of knowledge.' "

"Ah. A lady—even if she practices rebellion against the grosser conventions—never arrives anywhere totally naked, and even in death I have kept my eyes and ears open."

I chuckled. "And as Emily Sunstein says in her biography, you always had an abiding faith in the imperishability of 'the spirits of all aspiring and great individuals.' "

"An abiding faith," she said, "that often flickered."

"In 'The Mortal Immortal: A Tale' you present the reader a character, Winzy by name, who—"

"Yes. It troubled me to find after the story's publication in 1833 that some readers saw Winzy as a Dickensian name, like Pickwick or Gabriel Grub, when, in fact, as many scholars have since noted, it comes from the Scottish *winze*, or 'curse,' for my Winzy must bear his life and growing estrangement forever."

I scratched a note. "Still, it doesn't strike me that Winzy, who frets over the appearance of one gray hair, bears a curse as terrible as do Swift's *struldbrugs*, who not only live forever but suffer continuous enfeeblement."

My visitor shrugged. "If decay proceeds continuously, then the mind will at length cease to comprehend its predicament. Indeed, the author of these grotesqueries"—*the pot calling the kettle black?* I wondered—"himself confessed that the least miserable among them had dwindled into dotage and lost their memories. Swift neglected to foresee that all his *struldbrugs* would one day reach a state of irreversible fatuity. My Winzy, however, must live in daunting knowledge of his immortality and separateness. Forever."

I conceded the point. "I had started to say that Winzy attains to immortality by drinking an *elixir vitae*, a potion scientifically, or at least alchemically, decanted. In fact, that detail has led some to label your story science fiction."

"Good for them."

"The American writer Gary Jennings once even published a tale in *Fantasy and Science Fiction* using some of your story's prose and naming you—'Mary Wollstonecraft Shelley'—as his collaborator in its byline."

"Really? Then integrity persists. Here and there."

"Do you see the alchemist Cornelius Agrippa's potion as the end result of a technological or a magical procedure?"

"I have no authoritative opinion."

"Why not? You wrote the story."

"The potion forwards the plot but has no value as an index of its theme. Winzy carries the theme, Winzy's character."

"As character focuses the tales of Dodsworth and Valerius?"

"Yes, but Valerius exercises more influence over his tale's mood and direction than does the icy Dodsworth over his."

"One more point about 'The Mortal Immortal' before we move on to 'Transformation' and 'The Dream.' "

"Move quickly," she said. "My time here has contracted—*com-pressed*—to a vibrating point, and this point desires to abstract me from my place among the living for . . . who can say?" Finger by finger, she removed a glove and laid the back of her pale hand to her paler brow.

"Do you feel ill? Can I get you a Coke?"

"*Coke?* You employ *coal residues* as a medicament?"

"Coca-Cola. A soft drink." In desperation, I added, "Would you prefer a *hot* beverage? Some tea?"

"No, no. I recover, sir. Proceed." She lowered her hand and essayed a grim wan smile.

"The passage in 'The Mortal Immortal' where Winzy begins to notice his, well, out-of-placeness among the villagers affected me strongly. They aged. He didn't. Eventually, they came to regard him with 'horror and detestation.' "

"Yes. True."

"In my followup to *Frankenstein*, the creature has a like experience in the Eskimo village Oongpek." I took a paperback copy of the novel from a niche in my rolltop. "Listen: '*That I appeared immune to these natural depredations, continuing youthful in my hideousness, did not go unremarked. Many Oongpekmut, especially those of generations subsequent to mine, regarded my persistence among them as uncanny. . . . I watched in dismay as they . . . withdrew from me their trust and affections.*' " I looked up for my visitor's reaction.

She smiled ambiguously, not unlike Emma Thompson in *Sense and Sensibility*. "Masterfully derivative. But I do ken the similarity of the experiences of my Winzy and your pasquinadal version of my confiscated creature."

"Mrs. Shelley, I treat your creature with respect. I—"

She waved a hand. "Did I venture here today to talk about *your* book? Please. Eternity loses patience."

I calmed myself, breathing as deliberately as a Buddhist monk —Thich Nhat Hanh, perhaps.

My visitor waited me out. "Better?"

"Yes." I cleared my throat. "The two fantasies among your super-natural tales—how do you feel about them?"

"I prefer 'Transformation' to 'The Dream.' 'The Dream' I had to rewrite—partially—to accommodate the details of Miss Louisa Sharpe's illustration for *The Keepsake*. By moving an indoor scene outdoors for this painting's sake, I sacrificed a portion of my vision and a degree of the story's integrity and excellence." She sighed. "The things one will do for money."

"'The Dream' has some fine atmospherics anyway," I said. "The dark boat gliding, the soundless oars, Constance stretched out on St. Catherine's couch on the ledge above the Loir. Any fan of Poe would get off on it."

"Thank you. If 'get off on it' implies approval."

"You outface Poe, though, by arranging a character-driven happy ending, in which Constance's dream allows her to see—my favorite line in the story—that 'to make the living happy' doesn't mean 'to injure the dead.' "

"Something I, too, had to learn. And I cannot think of 'The Dream' without thinking of dear John Keats's lovely 'The Eve of St. Agnes.' "

I had led her, circuitously, to the last undiscussed story of the supernatural five, "Transformation."

"It puts me in mind of Poe, too," I said. "Specifically of 'Hop-Frog'—the dwarf business—and 'William Wilson' with its use of the theme of the double."

"Poe died not quite two years before me. He could hardly rival Shelley as a poet, but he had an independent sensibility that reminded me in some ways of Shelley's." She closed her eyes. "'*From childhood's hour I have not been / As others were—I have not seen / As others saw—I could not bring / My passions from a common spring.*' Poe's words, not Shelley's, but they would serve well as a caption under a portrait of my husband."

"Or under your own portrait."

She shook her head. "Do you know the story of how a friend of Shelley's mother told her to send her boy to a school where they would teach him to think for himself?"

"No," I said.

"Well. Mrs. Shelley's eyebrows shot up and she exclaimed, 'Teach him to think for himself? Oh, my God, rather teach him to think like other people.' "

We both laughed, I louder than my visitor.

"True, my character Guido in 'Transformation' has much of

Shelley in him, both before and after the metamorphosis which gives the story its point."

"At the end, Guido's priest tells him that the dwarf who so nastily impersonated him might have embodied a good rather than an evil spirit. Did you intend a moral?"

"Most people despise change, particularly in themselves. But without continual, even continuous, intellectual and moral transformation, one dies by pieces and joins the dead whilst yet upright. I seek transformation even in my death, else I would not have visited you here."

She shifted, placed both feet on the floor, and stood. I stood, too. The air in my office felt thin and unsustaining.

"You have to go?"

"Yes. At once. Thank you for tolerating my intrusion."

I tried to wave off her thanks and extend my own, but she stopped me. She declined my invitations to stay over with us, even to escort her down the stairs. Instead, she commanded me to remain in my office while she descended alone.

"But why?"

"I can easily see myself out."

"I mean, why deny me the pleasure of accompanying you?"

"You would hardly relish accompanying me to the immaterial demesne from which Volition and Time distilled me into your presence here."

"I don't understand."

She started to reply, but restrained herself. I seldom kiss a woman's hand, even as a joke, but I seized my visitor's and touched my lips to its back. It had a brittle texture, but no taste or temperature. If I overstepped propriety, she allowed the violation, then gently withdrew her hand and exited my study. The door shut behind her, and I heard her carefully descending footfalls.

I slunk from my office to the stairs and leaned against the wall to see my visitor's foreshortened body on our bottommost landing. She kept going down, but like a soldier marching in place, making no spatial progress—until the cold, or maybe Time and Volition, spun a helical sheath that she must have felt tightening nooselike around her. This sheath abstracted her, giving me a view out the landing window of two weathered rocking chairs and a black metal porch railing.

My father died believing that he would sleep, insensible, until the putative End of Time roused him and all his faithful coreligionists. My visitor would probably tell him that heavy sleepers do not reanimate. Perhaps she already has.

Story Sources

[From this list, Sunstein's biography and Robinson's notes in *Mary Shelley: Collected Tales and Stories* proved most helpful.]

Aldiss, Brian. "Introduction." *The Last Man* by Mary Shelley. London: Hogarth Press, 1984.

Bishop, Michael. *Brittle Innings.* New York: Bantam, 1994.

Crowley, John. "The Reason for the Visit." *Antiquities: Seven Stories.* Seattle: Incunabula Press, 1994.

Noyes, Russell, ed. *English Romantic Poetry and Prose.* New York: Oxford University Press, 1956.

Poe, Edgar Allan. "Alone." *Great Tales and Poems of Edgar Allan Poe.* New York: Washington Square Press, 1960.

Robinson, Charles E., ed. *Mary Shelley: Collected Tales and Stories.* Baltimore: John Hopkins University Press, 1976. (Softshell reprint, 1990).

Shelley, Mary. *Frankenstein; Or, The Modern Prometheus.* Afterword by Harold Bloom. New York, Toronto: New American Library (Signet Classic), 1965.

"Shelley, Percy Bysshe." *The New Encyclopedia Britannica.* Macropedia, Vol. 16. (*Encyclopedia Britannica,* 1979).

Stevenson, Robert Louis. *The Great Short Stories of Robert Louis Stevenson.* New York: Pocket Library (Pocket Books), 1954

Sunstein, Emily W. *Mary Shelley: Romance and Reality.* Boston: Little, Brown, and Co., 1989.

Swift, Jonathan. *Gulliver's Travels.* Foreword by Marcus Cunliffe. New York: New American Library (Signet Classic), 1960.

*   *   *

Chihuahua Flats

IN A DUSTY PANEL TRUCK WITH A SLACK TRANSMIS-
sion and no spare, Dougan bumped into the cactus-lapped
verges of Chihuahua Flats. He came nudged by a fitful Texas
sirocco, desperate to expand his territory. Behind him, in the cargo
bay, a dozen or more economy-size bags of N.R.G. Chunx in slick
double-lined red paper, the dogfood itself dry as potsherds and
frangible as old biscuits.

Even over the engine's banging and backfires, Dougan, his good
ear cocked, could hear a deranging insect rustle in two or three of
the bags. Well. So what? How much could the blamed roach borers
eat?

About a block from the kennel, he began to brake. He rode the
rubberless pedal or else he fiercely pumped it. The truck squealed
in the gust-driven desert blow, jounced in a perpetual sand scour;
when it shuddered to a rolling ebb, Dougan wrestled it into the
crazed adobe driveway of the kennel to which he had pointed it
these past howevermany hours. Dead on the ground, Dougan's
truck neither sighed nor swayed.

A sign in the yard—a huge red-cedar shake on oily chains, its
letters heat-gouged out and dyed in char—said MILLICENT T.
CHALVERUS / CHIHUAHUA FLATS KENNELS / BOARDING * GROOM-
ING * BREEDING * SALES. It bucked and twisted, its chains glinting,
its face sun-shellacked.

32

The sprawling house had a whitewashed mission look. Behind it, cockeyed on the rattlesnake-peopled steppe, blazed a three-story concrete run with a roof of terra-cotta macaroni halves.

Dougan pushed the door buzzer and got back through the wall a lizardly metallic hiss. The sweat-plastered hair on his nape struggled to stand, giving him an almost pleasant chill—so he buzzed again, and then again, leaning with his decent ear hard to the doorframe.

Come around! You got to come around! said a speaker unit next to him, a grill like an Aztec medallion.

Miss?

Come around! This so piercingly that Dougan nigh on to stumbled off the porch. He recovered, though, and circled on a hurried limp to the fenced-in compound out back.

I'm Millie Chalverus, said the woman at the gate. Who are you? Whaddaya want? N why should I care?

She had green eyes bracketed by hard-to-see laugh lines, skin like coffee-colored suede, and, shoehorned into a pair of ebony-and-gold-embroidered pedal pushers, a haunch like a ripening matador's. A velvety black haltertop crossed her upper torso. Her toenails peered up at Dougan from her scuffed huaraches like lacquered violets. Ankles, midriff, shoulders, arms: continents of glistening suede.

Talk to me, lover. I got stuff to do.

Dougan said, Vernester Dougan, Kennel Supplier.

Zatso?

Yes, Miss. Outta Lubbock. Specializin in high-protein, super-vitaminized bugproof feed. Not to mention assordid n sundry groomin, trainin, n recreational products.

How you do talk. What you got beyond a downpat spiel?

Miss? Dougan's eyes bounced. A bowel south of his navel went slack and took on a windy cargo of doubt. So much skin. Such lakegreen eyes. A mouth you could press a kiss on thout ever quite reachin her teeth.

By the way, Dougan. It's mam, not miss. I got a little too much age on me to truckle to miss.

Sorry, Dougan said.

Yeah. Well. Don't sweat it.

Beneath him, a quick yip and a helium-high growl. A dog no bigger than a heifer's stool had reared up against the chainlink gate. It had raised its paltry brindle hackles, and the fudge pools of its eyes stuck out like a mantis's. Dougan could have snapped off those eyes and sent the dog on a looping fieldgoal arc by slamming his boot against the gate. Except for Millie Chalverus, he would have surrendered to the idea and launched the mutt.

Instead he said, Nice dog.

He don't like you, Dougan. Thet's a fac.

He don't know me. I only jes got here.

Conchos has a built-in sense bout folks. You don't tickle his fancy cep mebbe crosswise n backards.

Conchos, huh? Hey, Conchos, howya doin? Dougan knelt in front of the dog. He moved a forefinger toward Conchos with a thought to rubbing his nose through the mesh, but Conchos leapt against the gate, snarling and pogo-sticking. Dougan fell over sideways.

Chalverus chortled. Dougan brushed himself off.

Guess if Conchos don't like me, *you* don't either, he said. Guess I got as much chanst to sell you on my bidnus as I do to drop me a baby nex Friday.

Don't give up so quick.

Mam?

Conchos cain't judge character worth a sue. Why, he'd bite Mother Teresa on the tush n lay a sloppy wet one on a liar like Ollie North.

Dougan blinked in the magnesium glare of the sun. To the northwest, a hawk floated between Chalverus's stockade and the salmon and mint ridges of a distant rampart. Below Dougan's left eye, a tic began to cycle.

If Conchos don't like you, you must be okay.

No shit? Dougan turned crimson. His last word rang in the air like a bell. No *lie*. I meant, no lie.

No lie, Chalverus said. Whynt you show me what you got?

Dougan recovered. Currying combs? Choke chains? Bugproof feed? Jes name it n I'll go gitter.

Whynt we try some food? Conchos aint gonna come round to you, honey, for no choke chain or metal brush.

Food it is. Good choice. *Great* choice. N.R.G. Chunx're flat-out worth their weight in Taos silver.

Dougan broke into a pebble-skittering trot. Thank God Conchos didn't like him. Stupid pile of crap. Why'd anybody own a Chihuahua? Why'd a gorgeous gal like Millie Chalverus *breed* the bat-eared midgets?

In the oven of his cargo bay, Dougan wrestled with the dogfood bags. He scrutinized them all for punctures, tears, and bore holes, then selected out a bag as glossily seamless as the Messiah's robe. This one he toted in a Groucho Marx crouch back to the kennel.

As soon as the Chalverus woman let him in, Conchos seized his trouser cuff, snarling through clenched teeth and flapping like a pennant on his instep until they reached a feeding area under a wide green plastic awning. All along the three-tiered run next to it, a chorus of unseen caged Chihuahuas whimpered and yipped.

Chalverus cried, Let go, Conchos. *Let go!*

Conchos released Dougan's cuff, reared like Trigger, and scuttled holus-bolus away, fussing without relent. Grateful, Dougan lowered the dogfood bag and bent over it like a soldier over a gut-shot buddy.

Thanks, he said. Much bliged. It jes gits hotter. As if to prove this remark, clammy drooping semicircles had bloomed under his workshirt's arms, big cancerous splotches. He split the bag with his pocketknife and doled out onto the concrete a handful—a prodigal double handful—of N.R.G. Chunx, brickred pellets craggy as owlcasts and burly as paperweights. Conchos pricked his ears, tilted his head, scented the spill, skipped from foot to foot like a balsawood puppet. Several Chihuahuas on the tiers, also smelling the food, began to yammer and bay, a doggy munchkin chorale.

Awright, Dougan told Conchos. Come git yore picnic.

Conchos looked at Dougan, then at Chalverus, then at the mound of N.R.G. Chunx. Go on, Chalverus said. I don't mind. Have yoreself a go. So Conchos tiptoed over and tried to mouth a chunk, but not one in the pile was less than half the size of his head. Conchos could not even crack a piece with a forepaw on it to hold it down. Stymied, he danced a bemused do-si-do, looking up again at Chalverus.

You must feed these boulders to St. Bernards, she said. Or starvin African pachyderms.

We give you a lot for yore money.

Well. It's useless to me if Conchos n his sort cain't eat it. N it shore as shivers looks like they cain't.

Wait, said Dougan. Jes you wait. Outside the run, he saw a steppingstone long and wide as a breadloaf. Gimme a minit, okay? He wedged himself through the kennel gate while holding it ajar with an outstretched leg, prised up the stone, and eased back through the gate with it before him at groin height, an honest-to-Jesus threat to herniate him. See, he said. See, now. He dropped the stone on the N.R.G. Chunx, picked it up, dropped it again. He put one boot sole on the stone and ground it from side to side. There. See. He nudged the stone aside, disclosing a pile of rubbly fragments and a scatter of brickred powder.

Conchos pitter-pattered up and fell to. He chewed what he could, cracking the kibbles in his jaw teeth, and licked what he couldn't. He did a little jig as he ate.

The put-up-or-shut-up test, Dougan said. The taste test. I think this stuff's done passed it. Don't you?

Looks thet way, Chalverus said. But am I myself gonna have to pulverize ever bag I decide to buy?

Nome. No way. Place you a long-term order n I promise you plenty of prepulverized N.R.G. Chunx whenever you ast.

Deal, Chalverus said.

She and Dougan shook hands. Her palm and fingers, Dougan noted, had a breezy dry silkiness. Even her calluses had a well-cared-for feel, as if she refused to allow the desert any tyrannical say-so over the expression of her womanhood. What a find, thought Dougan.

On Christmas Eve, four months later, Dougan married Millie Chalverus in a Catholic ceremony in the den of her house on the outskirts of Chihuahua Flats. About seven years back, she had lost her previous husband, Joseph Worrill, to an oilfield fire between Midland and Odessa, Texas. Starting up Chihuahua Flats Kennels had rescued her from the blues and maybe even poverty, for the biggest part of Mr. Worrill's insurance money had gone to cover a slagheap of outstanding debts. Dougan cared nothing for the petty facts of Chalverus's past life, particularly her marriage and any earlier romances—except insofar as her past, sprouting up as memory or as unfinished business, derailed her happiness or blighted his and her itemhood. Even today, the rolling gravel in her laugh and her skin's swarthy flush made Dougan swoon standing up.

I do, Chalverus had said, keeping her own name, as she had kept it with Mr. Worrill (for business purposes and to feed her soul). Anyway, at that *I do,* Dougan had begun to live—to live in sweet truth—for the first time since his release from Dooly Correctional Institution in Unadilla, Georgia, where he'd spent five years on a DUI unlawful-death conviction. (Driving blotto on cheap corn liquor in Macon, he had fender-glanced with his pickup an old woman walking home. Except for a vicious bump to his right ear, he had killed her without half noticing.) Even operating his own shoestring kennel-supply business in Lubbock had failed to drain from Dougan a melancholy unease, and this subtly toxic ache had poisoned him on every long-distance haul through the panhandle or across the hot alkaline flats of the Jornada del Muerto. But one *I do* had changed that, nullifying the poison.

Dougan abandoned Lubbock. He threw over his kennel-supply business. Chihuahua Flats Kennels had work enough for two, and Millie Chalverus, now his beloved wife, had no objection to his coming aboard and shouldering a man-sized moiety of the labor. He toted bags of Chihuahua chow, hosed down the runs, patched gaps in the chainlink, replaced fallen roof tiles, and haggled at the doorstoop with jewelry-freighted high-pressure salesguys besotted with their own stale hormones and decades of worn-out macho propaganda. And so, in many ways, the union of Vernester Dougan and Millie Chalverus seemed to Dougan the recipient of a sure-nough heavenly blessing.

Conchos, though, never came around. He despised Dougan. He yapped whenever Dougan entered the house. He tried to guard the master bedroom against Dougan's certain arrival. Failing that, Conchos fell back to protect the bed itself, an immense two-layer wheel under a spread of the same embroidered fabric from which Chalverus had made the pedal pushers in which Dougan had first beheld her delectable croup.

Yip yip yip, went Conchos, yap yap yap, meanwhile snarling his outrage and prancing in strategic if hopeless retreat. Dougan wore heavy suede gloves to deal with Conchos and always picked him up and moved him aside whenever such run-ins took place. It annoyed him, Conchos's implacable hatred along with all the silly ass threats, but Dougan never—not once since the day of his first N.R.G. Chunx delivery—felt the least urge to strangle Conchos, dropkick him into orbit, or render him unpeelable roadkill. Dougan had resolved not to hurt Conchos because Chalverus loved Conchos and what Chalverus loved Dougan respected unconditionally.

I love you, Chalverus told Dougan on their wedding night, but—

But what, babe?

But my soul—my deepest privatest heart—is tucked away in thet little dog. I jes cain't help it.

You don't have to, Dougan said. I respec whatsoever you love n'll try to love it myself n hope thet one day Conchos'll take to me too.

Although Dougan heard the nobleness of this pronouncement, he found that in town for his weekly haircut he had a hard time being faithful to it. Pete Mosquero, his barber, liked to rag him about Conchos:

You don look to me like a Chihuahua esorta guy.

No?

No. I jess refuse to blieve you *like* em.

I don't, Dougan said, but—

You see, I magine you an Espringer espaniel esorta guy or mebbe a golden retriever.

Thanks, but—

As I esee em, Chihuahuas are estupid popeyed prisses, n you got too much class to be messin widdem.

They've got their points.

Yeah. On the ends of their ears. Mosquero laughed at his own joke, sclipping his scissors to punctuate it.

Back out at the kennels, Conchos's despisal of Dougan went unallayed. The dog chewed holes in his jockey shorts, shat in his Sunday oxfords, peed on the mahogany valet that Chalverus had given him as a wedding gift, and either strewed about the house or punctured irreparably every foil-wrapped condom in a box of three dozen that Dougan had bought at Best Buy Drugs. Conchos scrabbled at the bedroom door every time Dougan and Chalverus grew amorous. When they declined to admit him and made love to spite him, Conchos stood in the hall baying like a plangently deflating balloon. If they did admit him, Conchos straddled Dougan's back and aimed penetrating nips at his nape and shoulder blades. This misbehavior had earned Conchos the sharpest scolding he'd ever got in Dougan's hearing and a quick exile to the utility room.

Couldn't we jes kennel him when we git frisky? Dougan said.

Why?

I lose concentration.

I don't. Mmm. Mmm mmm *mmm*.

S different for a man.

Yeah? Howso?

But Dougan could think of no explanation that did not imply that he might surrender total focus on her even in the throes of climactical passion. So Conchos remained indoors, if not in their bedroom, even when Cupid attacked.

Outside the boudoir, Conchos played other games. He sat on the couch between Chalverus and Dougan. He guarded his daily allotment of N.R.G. Chunkletz—Chihuahua-sized pieces that the company had begun producing for smaller breeds—as if fearful that Dougan might hijack it and eat it himself. Conchos never carried any of his rubber squeak toys or his leash to Dougan, and on early-morning winter walks through the cacti he refused to take a dump until Dougan's lips had visibly blued and his bladder had grown as taut as a volleyball. Often, once Dougan had unzipped and made steam, Conchos would give in and unload, eyeballing him from a crayfishing squat that only a smart aleck could have choreographed.

Little dog, Dougan would say, you make me sad.

But not sad enough to go back to the bottle. And, setting aside the hatred of one muleheaded Chihuahua, he viewed his new life with Chalverus as charmed.

I have a new idea for our bidnus, Vernester.

Yeah. Like what?

Races.

Whaddaya mean, *races?* Dougan stood baffled, transfixed by the applegreen fire in Chalverus's eyes.

Chihuahua races. Daily doubles. Trifectas. The whole ever-lovin pari-mutuel schmeer.

Ha ha.

S no joke, honey. It's legal for greyhounds, idnit? Why not for my little Toltec babies?

I don't know why not, Dougan said.

So they built it. Or, nigh on to singlehandedly, Dougan did, a track not much bigger around than the public swimming pool in Tucamcari, with two sets of seven-tiered bleachers on the eastern side so that paying spectators would not have to peer like nuclear-test observers into a blazing sun when the evening races started and the first nine to twelve Chihuahuas broke like windup toys from the miniature gates.

From the beginning, business at Chihuahua Flats Raceland boomed, even if the dogs themselves failed in heat after heat to have a like impact on the sound barrier. Breeders from across the country fell upon Dougan and Chalverus's little town to strut their dogs and place flashy wagers. By mid-April, sometimes as many as two hundred people occupied the stands; and on that redletter night in early May when the one-thousand-and-first Chihuahua hit the track for its maiden handicap, the raceland noted the event with a barrel drawing, a cowboy band from Portales, and a videocassette giveaway.

Dougan announced. As the bell rang to start each heat, he intoned over the public-address system, *"There . . . goes . . . Ricky!"* and the mechanical rat that paced the Chihuahuas on a mobile pole lurched out to a herky-jerky lead, heading around the track via a concatenation of twitches and fits. Maybe a dozen times since the raceland's opening, the lead Chihuahua had caught, or caught up to, Ricky, but owing to the rat's size—it stood almost as high at the withers as the pursuing dogs, else even patrons with binoculars would have had a hard go seeing it—no dog had yet halted Ricky or dragged Ricky off its jerkily advancing lever. Dougan thought it unlikely that even a *pack* of Chihuahuas, cooperating as stranger dogs almost never did, could pull down Ricky and turn a decent money heat into a yelping group feed.

Dougan enjoyed calling the races, updating the odds, and introducing such celebs as the owner of the biggest local car dealership, the latest homecoming queen, and the weatherman at the NBC affiliate in El Paso. But Conchos, the winner of four tiptop stakes races and a first or second runnerup in several others, liked Dougan no better. Floodlamps burned through half their nights, and Chalverus often seemed distracted by success, drunk on the picayune details of public relations, concessions stocking, and the twelve thousand applicable state and federal tax laws. Such crap made Dougan long for the desert serenity of Chihuahua Flats before the boom. Sometimes, then, he took a beer; sometimes, even, a hit of the hard stuff.

Chalverus throve. An interviewer from a TV newsmagazine asked her questions against the backdrop of the sawdust track and its electronic toteboard, the hubbub of spectators, touts, bettors, and boozy hangers-on counterpointing the audio:

What led you to open a Chihuahua track, Ms. Chalverus?

The Chihuahuas. What else?

Why not cocker spaniels or miniature poodles?

I knew when my first hubby died thet whatever I did had to have a really cheerful grounding in my own selfhood. It also had to like start with the Chalverus sound. Thet was my first true ch-ch-ch-challenge.

Challenge?

To myself. To my womanly Chalverus spirit. At first, you see, I figgered chinchillas. A chinchilla ranch. For the furs n the cheap cheeky glamour.

Okay. What killed that idea?

Havin to kill the chinchillas. Also, you cain't cuddle em. They have a odor n they bite. You have to kill em to git any use from em. The pelts don't come off thout you brain the varmints then flat-out strip off their skins.

So you turned to Chihuahuas?

Didn't want to cherry-pick. Or charm rattlesnakes. Or try out for cheerleader. N chow dogs're too danged mean.

Tell us, Ms. Chalverus, who's your little friend?

Oh. Him? Thisere's Conchos. Say hello to all the folks, Conchos.

Dougan, standing back, watched his wife take Conchos's paw and wave it at the nation.

Cute dog, said the interviewer.

Thanks. My soul lives in this little dickens. Him n me're jes like this. She crossed her fingers. So to speak.

How does your new husband and business partner feel about the colossal upheaval in your lives, Ms. Chalverus?

Dougan? Dougan honestly loves me. Whatsoever I love, even a persnickety n possessive little booger like Conchos, well, he tries hard to love, himself.

So he's *happy* with a thousand-and-one Chihuahuas aswarm in your backyard?

Shore. Who wouldn't be? We're doin what we love n gittin royally flush in the doin.

But Dougan wasn't happy, and he didn't love Chihuahua Flats Raceland, and Conchos's spitefulness gnawed like a true *rata* (rat) at his bruised and tender *alma* (soul). This condition was so painful, and yet so inward, that it billyclubbed him when Chalverus, less than a week after her interview, received a medical diagnosis of inoperable pancreatic cancer. Before he could chew up and swallow this news, she had to start a series of radiation and chemical treatments in Las Cruces. Her hair let go. Her skin turned sallow and squamous. Her eyes played daily host to floating graygreen clouds.

By the end of summer, Chalverus was so sick that it hardly mattered, except to her, in which venue, public or private, she forsook the struggle and died. So Dougan brought her home. PR guys, gamblers, and uninformed Chihuahua breeders still stopped by occasionally, but all racing activity had long since ceased, and Dougan knew in his bones that Chalverus had contracted her terminal disease as an apology to him and a huge unrepayable gift. He said as much, in rougher words, as Chalverus lay abed amidst the air-conditioner drone and the brittle night hush of the desert.

Nonsense, she said. Thet's all pure nonsense.

It ain't, babe. It purely ain't.

Lissen, you. I had to've had this damn ol cancer *before* we even begun our raceland. *Had* to've. If I hadn't, I wouldn't be this far along to—

She stopped, not for her benefit but his. They both knew dying was the missing fill-in-the-blank word, and even unspoken it dropped between them like a wall.

You think I got sick apurpose?

Dougan sat with his long hands holding the insides of his knees and his long eyes downcast in craven abashment. Even so, he managed a mortified nod.

Sick apurpose? To give us cause to undo the nightly to-do round here? S thet what you think? Tell me.

Yessum, I do.

I got me a cancer to make you happy?

Yessum. You're like selfless thet way.

Awright then. Let me ast you. You happy?

Course not. How could I be? You think I'd trade off my precious wife dead jes for some lousy quiet?

Chalverus rolled her face toward Dougan on her pillow and smiled. No, she said. I never thought thet off the top of my brain or deep down in its kinks, neither one. Which shorely orter tell you somepin, lover.

Dougan began to cry. He kept looking down, though, and his tears plunked the backs of his dangling hands like beads of hot candlewax.

On the bed beside Chalverus, Conchos fought to his feet, peeled back his whiskery lip, and growled at Dougan in pitiable quivering disdain. Chalverus took Conchos's snout between her thumb and forefinger, tugged on his papier-mâché skull, and in spite of her weakness easily rolled him over.

Hush thet disrespecful noise. You silly cur you.

Dougan swept a forearm across his eyes and looked over at Chalverus with a question or maybe just a thanks.

Take care of Conchos when I go, she said. Do what you want with them others, but save Conchos to home. Promise?

Babe, you know me. You *know* me.

Thet's right. I do. I shorely do. N the Lord'll repay.

A week later, eased through at least a stint of her going by old Eddie Arnold songs and a morphine drip, Millie Chalverus forsook the struggle and died.

Conchos, sitting on her sheeted midriff, lifted a long bittersweet howl.

Dougan sold most of the Chihuahuas in the kennel's runs and shut down its top two floors. He remained in Chihuahua Flats. He remained in his late wife's house. He fed and watered Conchos, who went on eyeing him askance, hitching growly rides on his trouser cuffs, eating his socks, and awakening him from dreams of Chalverus with vampire nips at his earlobes, fingers, and groin. But Dougan forbore, in obedience to the deathbed charge, Take care of Conchos.

One evening a month after the funeral, Chalverus appeared to Dougan in the kennel yard as he played hose water over the concrete in slate-thin tides. In haltertop, pedal pushers, and a wavery cape, she hovered three feet off the ground between a storage shed and the multilevel runs. Her image had so little substance, so little hue, that it looked to have faded from a hard medium like china onto a flimsy one like rice paper or old silk. It rippled as it hung, melting and remanifesting in the twilight like a Jornada del Muerto mirage.

Dougan, she said. Dougan.

This voice—no question that it was hers—sounded distant and tinny, like Franklin Delano Roosevelt on the radio. The voice startled him, though, even more than had the apparition. It startled him so much that he unwittingly put his thumb over the hose's nozzle and sprayed the floating eidolon of his wife with a piercing burst. Chalverus billowed backward, dissolving on the fusillade, and then came together again, wavering, much dimmer than before.

Babe, I'm sorry, he cried. Real real sorry.

I cain't stay, she said. I ain't got the strenth. But I'm with you always anyways n won't ever wholly depart.

Like Jesus? he said.

Lissen, honey, I love you. Even if, as thisere proclaimin shade, I've got to fade off to Lethe. So to speak.

You only jes got here. You cain't go.

Don't beg me, now. I'm leavin you with a comforter.

It's too danged hot for a comforter. Dougan flung the hose aside and trotted wet-faced toward the melting spectral figment that was, or had been, Millie Chalverus.

Adios! she called in her fading cathedral-radio voice. To God, my darlin!

When Dougan went inside that night, Conchos stood guarding the circular bed. The dog growled, feinting forward and back. Dougan opened the top drawer in his chest-of-drawers, found his gloves, pulled them on.

Hush, you popeyed rat, he said. Then he picked Conchos up, carried him in outstretched hands to the bedroom door, set him down gently in the hall, and, ashamed for even considering such an act, slammed the door on him with a bang that shook windows and toppled bric-a-brac. He slept soundly, though, a dreamless slumber of scouring purity.

In the morning, Conchos greeted Dougan with a wriggly butt, a toothy Chihuahua grin, and an ecstatic four-footed jig. When Dougan walked to the kitchen, Conchos followed at heel, yipping in excitement and homage rather than in provocation or spleen. Outdoors, Conchos took care of business in two minutes flat and returned to the utility room for breakfast. When Dougan poured N.R.G. Chunkletz into his bowl, Conchos licked Dougan's hands; when Dougan pivoted to leave, Conchos reared up and begged for a noggin rub.

What in heavenly rip's got into you?

Mmm, Conchos whined. Mmm mmm *mmm.*

And Dougan knew. Chalverus had sent him a comforter. He let Conchos finish eating, then scooped him up, perched him in the crook of his arm, and took a reminiscent stroll through every room in the house and across every sandy stretch of his and Chalverus's arid acreage, however Gila-monster-haunted or boobytrapped with cacti. As they went, Dougan murmured sweet nothings to the dog, and Conchos rode like a raj in a howdah, lordly as all get-out. From that day forward, in fact, Conchos went everywhere with Dougan.

Even to the barbershop.

Esorry bout your loss, Mosquero said, trimming Dougan's hair as Conchos sat upright one swivel chair away.

Thanks, Dougan said. But the dead can do things the livin cain't.

Mosquero had no reply to this epigram. He clipped and snipped. Eventually he said, I never esaw you as a Chihuahua esorta guy.

You didn't, huh?

Course not. They're aw like that one. Mosquero waved at Conchos with his comb. Ugly little rats. Deesgustin popeyed prisses. You musta had to take him to the vet or esomepin, eh?

Mmm, said Dougan.

That one he's an especial laugh, eh? No more hair than a piglet. Legs like crippled finger bones. A face like one of them pickle-jar abortions. I mean, it's—

Dougan knocked Mosquero's hand away and jumped from the chair. No more insults! he cried. Not another nasty word! Or I'll danged shore deck yore ass!

Easy, Mosquero said, conducting a calm-down symphony with his open hands.

Easy? We're sick of yore insults!

I'm jess talkin, hombre. It's jess my esame ol haircuttin esorta way of time passin.

Well, don't do it like thet no more!

Okay. *Okay.* You got my esolemn word.

Dougan and Mosquero held a long wary look. Conchos perched attentively in his swivel chair, a lopsided grin on his snout. Dougan sat again, and Mosquero resumed cutting his hair with a sharp *sclip!* of the scissors.

A little later, taking care to say it behind Dougan's bad ear, Mosquero whispered, But he's *estill* ugly.

* * *

With a Little Help from Her Friends

TWO YEARS AGO, CARLOS KNEW, THE WOMAN'S LIPS had been sewn together by the rightist vigilantes who had over-run and occupied her medical compound on the Pacific coast of the tiny Central American country of Guacamayo. The govern-ment had regarded her humanitarian efforts among the Indians as a subtle but insidious brand of Marxism. Therefore, while sewing her lips together, the agents of the Guacamayan status quo had de-clined to use antiseptics or anesthesia.

Today, on the pine-shaded lawn of the Amnesty International Torture Victim Rehabilitation Center in Warm Springs, Georgia (one of seven such sanitariums worldwide), Eleanor Riggins-Galvez sat in her wheelchair fielding the video correspondent's questions. Her voice was clear, but the aftermath of the vigilantes' barbarism revealed itself in the persistent twitching of her mouth and the involuntary fluttering of one dry eyelid. Nevertheless, her red-rimmed eyes still held a disturbing sparkle.

"They didn't want me cheering up the other hostages with talk and songs," she was saying. "That's why they did it."

"You sang?" Carlos Villar asked, surprised by this revelation. "What songs did you sing?"

"That's enough questions about her ordeal," said Dr. Karen Petitt, chief neurologist at the center. She was pushing the woman's wheelchair down the walk, and she indicated her disapproval of the

46

correspondent's line of questioning by tilting its lightweight, blue-enamel frame away from Carlos.

"Why did you tell him that?" the wheelchair's passenger asked, glancing over her shoulder with one farcically screwed-up eye.

"I think you know why," the neurologist said.

"To keep from reminding me of the horrors I've been through," the torture victim said in a mocking singsong.

"I suppose that's an acceptable paraphrase of center policy."

"Karen, I'm reminded of those horrors every time I look into a mirror. Let Carlos put all the questions he wants."

"Do you want me to leave you alone with him?"

The correspondent's heart leapt. He worked for Video Verdadero, a satellite news service and broadcasting firm headquartered in Bogota, and it had taken him seven months to wangle this exclusive interview with *La Gran Dama de Misericordia*. He had succeeded, Carlos had no doubt, only because a maternal uncle living in Mexico City had funded so many of the *señora's* quasi-saintly activities on the Guacamayan coast. By talking to him now, she was doing little more than acknowledging her debt to another man, and so far this afternoon she had told him nothing that had not come out already, shortly after the spectacular liberation of Casa Piadosa. If Dr. Petitt left, maybe she would open up.

"Why not?" Eleanor Riggins-Galvez replied. "He can walk me down to the fish hatchery. If he asks me anything *too* painful, I'll feed him to that ugly spotted gar in the main pool."

And so, hands plunged deep in the pockets of her lab coat, Dr. Petitt sauntered resignedly back to the treatment center. A brown thrasher scurried out of her way, and the October sunlight sifting down on Warm Springs gave every item on the lawn—gazebo, bird-bath, wrought-iron benches—a pastel fuzziness altogether alien to Bogota. Only the nineteenth-century French Impressionists, Carlos felt, could truly do this light justice, but they were a school not much in favor here at the near beginning of the third troubled millennium since Christ's birth.

October 9, 2013.

Carlos began to ease the wheelchair down the long walk to the National Fish Hatchery. His passenger gripped her armrests as if she did not quite trust him. But, of course, torture victims always found it difficult to trust.

"What songs did you sing to cheer your coworkers and patients at Casa Piadosa after the government takeover?"

"First of all, Carlos, I didn't *sing* the songs."

"I don't understand."

"You would if you heard me sing. I have a voice like a stuck pig. I played the harmonica instead."

"Very good, *señora*. But what songs?"

"That's a second thing. Do you really believe Video Verdadero's audience is going to give a good damn about my repertoire?"

"Human interest. It's for the program *El Tiempo Turbulento*. When it comes to news of heroes, the vidsat audience is insatiable, and we've done to death every bit of trivia about the members of the United Nations antiterrorist force that rescued you and the others. Besides, who's to say what's trivial and what's of enormous consequence? I, for instance, would greatly like to know what you played. What was it that provoked those animals to take needle and thread to your lips?"

"Needle and fishing line. Top-grade Filimar fishing line. That's why I've got the mouth of an Amazonian shrunken head."

Carlos remained silent. Carefully, he negotiated a turn and pushed his charge onto the apron of the main display at the hatchery. Here, hundreds of unfamiliar fish, including many diamond-backed carp as long as his forearm, dozed under lily pads or finned from one shady spot to another.

A party of shirt-sleeved Japanese tourists, who had probably just visited the Little White House of Franklin D. Roosevelt, milled about the display pond and the blond-brick aquarium next to it. Most of them evinced the same world-weary aloofness and torpor exhibited by the fish in the pale green water. Carlos did not feel comfortable around them and so kept his silence. The *señora* smiled and nodded at the Japanese, however, and seemed saddened when they boarded an orange gyrobus in the parking lot and departed the hatchery.

"What songs?" Carlos asked again.

"Mostly, I'm afraid, it was Beatles stuff."

"Beetles?"

"Not bugs, Carlos. That group of English-born musicians who disbanded more than forty years ago. The most controversial member was shot by a deranged fan outside his New York apartment building about ten years later."

"John Lennon?" said Carlos tentatively.

"You *do* remember, then?"

"Hardly, *señora*." The correspondent laughed. "I was born five or six months after this Lennon *hombre* fell dead on the pavement. I've read some things, heard a few tapes, seen some video. It's not really my interest, though. I like Ravel and Debussy."

"Good for you. Anyway, it was Beatles songs I found myself playing in the compound while El Presidente's thugs were holding us prisoner. 'Love Me Do,' 'I Feel Fine,' 'Eight Days a Week,' 'Yellow Submarine,' 'Here Comes the Sun.' Oh, a whole passel of such songs."

"Because they were cheerful?"

"Yes. And because they came back to me unbidden across all the years. I hadn't even *thought* about most of them since college days. Too many other things to worry about. During the government's illegal siege of Casa Piadosa, though, they all came back — like doves alighting in the waiting branches of my memory."

" 'Like doves alighting,' " Carlos echoed her. "You should have been a poet."

She laughed self-deprecatingly. "You're applauding doggerel, young man. Nevertheless, a facility with words is what I have in place of a singing voice. It's my God-given compensation."

"You have many compensations. You heal the sick —"

"Not anymore."

"Let me finish. You have deep feelings for the poor and the dispossessed. You have friends in high places all over the world. Your name is a benediction to almost everyone who hears it spoken. You play the harmonica —"

"And I'm dying, Carlos."

"On the contrary, *señora*, you're making a remarkable recovery from a brutal ordeal."

"I'm getting well enough to die. El Presidente's stooges latch-hooked my lips together. Then, for the next eight days, they fed me on a tainted IV solution that introduced a slow-acting virus into my system. No antidote exists. El Presidente's despicable regime may have toppled because of his own recklessness and that unprecedented United Nations strike, but this is his revenge on me, Carlos. I call it *La Fiebre Furtiva*."

The correspondent squinted at her. "The Secret Fever."

"It's not contagious. No one at the Torture Rehabilitation Center has contracted it. Karen — Dr. Petitt — tells me that *La Fiebre Furtiva* is a figment of my imagination. A tenacious paranoid delusion growing out of my abhorrence of our captors' tactics."

"Did they rape you?"

"Don't be naïve. That goes without saying. And broke my legs four or five times each for good measure."

Carlos glanced at a huge mottled carp gliding through the waters of the pond. How removed it seemed from the conflicts and atrocities of the upper world.

"May I return tomorrow with my video equipment, *señora?* Dr. Petitt told me on the telephone that if I brought it today, she would not allow me to see you at all. So all I brought was this recorder." With a manicured fingernail he tapped the miniature device on his belt.

"Tomorrow, Carlos, bring your camera. I'll intercede with Karen. After all, what's a vidsat interview without pictures?"

"Radio," Carlos said, and they both laughed.

The chimes of a local Protestant church began to reverberate through the pine-scented dusk. In obedience to their tolling, the young Colombian escorted Eleanor Riggins-Galvez back to the treatment center.

That night she could not get the correspondent's visit off her mind. No, that wasn't entirely accurate. Neither the images of Carlos Villar himself nor the vividness of his foray into her life had made her insomniac. Rather, it was that offhand bit of business about the Beatles. *That* had her helplessly casting back, combing through the detritus of her days to find the beginnings of her half-forgotten infatuation with those four Liverpudlian rock 'n' rollers. Her infatuation had long since turned into something else, of course — a dogged subconscious refusal to admit to herself that she had ever enjoyed their music or a rare burst of nostalgia spotlighting the teenage Eleanor Riggins in the dim but tolerant amusement of her latter-day self. The Beatles. Lord have mercy, the Beatles.

In Guacamayo (it was true), the music of her young girlhood had come spilling out of her harmonica in spite of her adult self. Further, this music — these melodies — had almost certainly played a key role in stiffening her resolve in a situation of otherwise untenable terror. At first even El Presidente's thugs had been charmed by her performances of the Lennon-McCartney material. But, finally realizing its part in boosting morale about the compound, they had retaliated by confiscating her harmonicas (she had five or six stashed among her belongings), and then by closing her mouth in as cruelly dramatic a fashion as they could devise without killing her.

Ah, but why Beatles music? Why not Christmas carols, Negro spirituals, Appalachian folk songs?

At Casa Piadosa she had never really considered the matter. She had merely let the music flow through her as if she and the harmonicas voicing it were a single unthinking instrument for its peremptory expression. She was not so much playing the Beatles

tunes as being played by them. That this music inevitably heartened the other hostages and even a majority of their swaggering
guards—payrolled rapists, torturers, and assassins—was a happy
accident. At first, anyway. At first.

Now Eleanor sat in her wheelchair trying to recall a bygone
era. . . .

JFK, Khrushchev, John Glenn, Lee Harvey Oswald, and the
British invasion of the American popular-music charts.

At first . . . well, at first the Beatles had not interested her. When
they appeared on a long-running CBS variety hour early in 1964,
she was a socially backward, intellectually precocious thirteen-year-
old whose most passionate longing was to become a medical mis-
sionary in Africa or Latin America. She watched *The Ed Sullivan
Show* that Sunday night only because her older brother, Marshall,
had to see the mop-topped quartet make their American television
debut, and because even her folks could scarcely contain their
curiosity about this unlikely show-business phenomenon.

During the program Eleanor made up her mind that these four
British boys were silly looking and their songs energetic but primitive pieces of nonsense. Although the elder Rigginses exchanged
disbelieving glances and acidulous remarks about the musicians'
haircuts and singing voices, they remained almost as attentive as
Marshall and Eleanor to the band's performances. Afterward, more
amused by her parents' behavior than by the Beatles', Eleanor went
to her room to do her homework. What was all the fuss about?

Two years later she was still relatively untouched by the fevers of
Beatlemania. Of course, she could not turn on the radio without
hearing one of the group's songs or go into a store without encoun-
tering some sort of makeshift shrine to their ubiquitous appeal (tee-
shirt displays, magazine covers, Beatle wigs, outsized posters).
However, her own private goals (divinity school, Johns Hopkins
Medical College, a tour in the Peace Corps) kept her from idolatry.
She knew her own mind, and the uncompromising rigor of her
goals isolated her so that she could pursue them.

Then, one Saturday morning, Susan Carmack—Eleanor's only
close friend in the tenth grade—stopped by her house with a copy
of the new *Revolver* album. In Eleanor's bedroom, Susan put the
vinyl disk on the turntable of a tacky portable stereo and insisted
that she listen to a ditty called "Eleanor Rigby." This proved to be a
driving but melancholy song with a haunting lyric.

"It could be about you," Susan said, "if your name was Rigby
instead of Riggins."

"Thank goodness for that syllable's difference, then."

"Why?"

"Because it's a depressing song, Susan. Eleanor Rigby dies alone in her flat, and nobody comes to her funeral—that's why."

"Still," said Susan Carmack.

"Still what?"

"I'd be ecstatic if John and Paul wrote a song called 'Susan Carmody' or 'Susan Carlisle' or something. I wouldn't even mind if the girl in the song got knocked up and had an abortion and finally went to live in a Mexican whorehouse."

"I'll bet you wouldn't."

Laughing and arguing, they listened to "Eleanor Rigby" two or three more times, then to the other songs on the album. Along with a whimsical photomontage, the record's cardboard sleeve featured Beardsleyesque pen-and-ink portraits of the four elfin fellows. Eleanor found herself staring at these portraits with genuine respect. Elfin or not, the Beatles had added the startling dimension of social consciousness to their work. Good for them. Thus inspired, in fact, she put down the jacket and hurried into her brother's bedroom to borrow the harmonica he kept hidden in one of his dresser drawers. With it, back in her own room, she played impromptu off-key accompaniments to "Taxman," "Yellow Submarine," and several others. Susan, giggling, egged her on.

And so, like a sinner fussed over and prayed for by tenacious fundamentalists, Eleanor finally surrendered to the spirit animating her peers. At the advanced age of fifteen, she, too, was a victim of Beatlemania. . . .

Dr. Petitt, silhouetted against the dull fluorescents of the corridor, stood in her doorway.

"Mrs. Galvez, don't you want me to help you into bed?"

"Please."

"And just what are you doing up at this hour?"

"Remembering the first time I was tortured, Karen."

Maneuvering Eleanor's wheelchair closer to the narrow bed, Dr. Petitt said nothing. Her silence was not hard to interpret. She was undoubtedly wondering why her patient had chosen these lonely moments before bedtime to call up such unpleasant memories. Further, she was probably cursing herself for permitting Carlos Villar to come to the center to plague Eleanor with questions about the siege at Casa Piadosa.

"Karen, the first time I was relentlessly tortured was when I was fifteen. It had nothing to do with Guacamayo."

"Good." The neurologist pulled the bed linen over her patient's body and then began to plump her pillow. "Do you want to tell me about it?"

"Why do you suppose I brought it up?"

"Go ahead. I'll sit in your wheelchair while you talk."

"Oh, I'm going to sing a little, too—even if I do sound like a stuck pig. You see, off and on during my last three years of high school in Richmond, the boys in my classes would taunt me with a parody of the Beatles' 'Eleanor Rigby.' It went like this:

> 'Eleanor Riggins
> Scrapes at the lice
> In her hair with her fingers and comb,
> She's all alone.
>
> 'Stoops by the teacher,
> Browning her nose
> In the crease of that fat lady's ass.
> O what a gas.
>
> 'Such a homely harpy,
> She's not the smoochin' kind.
> Such a homely harpy,
> We love her for her mind.'"

Eleanor's wavering, birdlike falsetto ceased. Turning her head, she saw that Dr. Petitt, as if in spite of herself, was smiling. She smiled, too, just to let Dr. Petitt know that she had intended to provoke her amusement. Of course, the boys' cutesy "torture" had not been funny at the time—not to her, anyway. It had, of course, played well to their sycophants and to new arrivals who had never heard it before. Eleanor had survived—she had even managed to preserve a little of her dignity—by steadfastly ignoring these performances. But you could hardly hope to emerge unscathed from that kind of protracted belittlement, and she had not. Finally, in fact, even Susan Carmack had deserted her, and those last three years of high school had been a friendless hell.

"I don't have a ready treatment for that one," Dr. Petitt admitted.

"Time," said Eleanor Riggins-Galvez, relishing the bromide. "Time heals all wounds."

Carlos, who was staying at the Peachtree Plaza Hotel in Atlanta, returned the following day with his video equipment, a CD player, and a CD of the Beatles' *Abbey Road* album that he had purchased at an all-night music bar not far from the hotel. The CD had cost forty American dollars, and having listened to it back in his hotel room, Carlos felt grimly certain that the dealer had burned it from somebody else's imperfect copy of the original recording. Well, it would have to do. He meant it as a memento of his regard for Mrs. Galvez, not as something she would want to play over and over again.

Walking from the Warm Springs heliport to the Torture Victim Rehabilitation Center, Carlos passed many of the hospital's patients on the lawn. He had seen them yesterday, of course, but his involvement with Dr. Petitt and Mrs. Galvez had prevented him from paying much heed. Today their faces jumped out at him, masks in which only the eyes truly lived. Their bodies, whether propped in aluminum walkers, jammed in wheelchairs, or hobbling along with the aid of rubber-tipped canes, seemed to be encumbrances that the eyes in the masklike faces either despised or resented. And why not? Their bodies had betrayed them. The enemies of their deepest moral and political beliefs had tried to use their bodies to make them renounce or recant those beliefs. Even the strong-willed survivors who had withstood the agony inflicted upon them had not yet escaped the memories of their degradation. Most of these patients never would, not even the ones who walked upright and bore no outward signs of their ordeal. As a result, their own bodies were strangers to them, mangled suits of armor imprisoning their souls.

Time, apparently, did not heal all wounds—unless, of course, you regarded death as an acceptable panacea.

Inside the hospital, Carlos filmed Mrs. Galvez taking her afternoon meal with a man who had recently lost both hands to a cadre of Argentine guerillas on the pampas. Beaming, this man fed *La Gran Dama* spoonful after spoonful of Brunswick stew with the living prostheses bioengineered for him by a Swiss company often engaged by the seven rehabilitation centers of Amnesty International. After this meal, Carlos recorded Eleanor trading good-humored insults with an orderly, wheeling herself down her gloomy first-floor corridor, and playing a game of video chess with a patient undergoing therapy at a facility in Toronto.

Back in her own room, Carlos played the *Abbey Road* CD for her. A young Peruvian torture victim wandered in and leaned against the doorjamb to listen. He wore only a pair of faded gray gym shorts and a suede vest on which he had pinned dozens of sloganeering buttons: *"Gente Arriba, Junta Abajo," "Don't Sell the*

Moon to General Motors," and so on. Carlos also noticed that purple welts ran up and down the insides of the empty-eyed victim's arms. Eleanor introduced him as Ramon Covarrubias, but the man only nodded. He took his leave as soon as the CD had finished playing. The *señora* was little more communicative; she thanked Carlos for his thoughtfulness.

"I have something else for you," he said.

"Indeed?"

Carlos produced a harmonica from his pocket and urged her to play along with "Here Comes the Sun," a song by Beatle George Harrison that she had often performed during the siege at Casa Piadosa. The old woman demurred, insisting that the damage done to her mouth and lips by El Presidente's henchmen had robbed her of the necessary strength and skill. She laid the instrument on an end table and stared out the window with a faraway frown so devoid of condemnation that Carlos, condemning himself, felt caddishly opportunistic. How could he make amends?

"At this stage in your life, Mrs. Galvez, what would make you most happy?"

"Ah. You ask because I'm dying."

"I ask because you're recovering," Carlos said, parroting Dr. Petitt's own cheerful prognosis. "You have a future in store—twenty more years at the least. It's not your dying wish I want to know."

She looked through him. "What would make me most happy?"

"Yes, *señora*."

"Do you want a hypothetical response, something grandiose and far-fetched like World Peace or An End to Poverty? Or would you prefer something within the pale of possibility, something that would really increase my small stores of happiness?"

"The latter, of course." But Carlos found these finicky qualifications baffling and wondered if he had answered correctly.

"Are you going to try to grant my wish if I reveal it?"

"Well, Video Verdadero might. If it's grantable."

"Queen for a Day," said Eleanor Riggins-Galvez abstractedly. "World Peace, Carlos. An End to Poverty. Those are the things that would make me most happy. I wish Video Verdadero great success in bringing them about."

Caressing his video gun, Carlos sat down on the window seat near the old woman's wheelchair. She had withdrawn into herself, and he wanted to reestablish contact. "In Atlanta last night, I did some checking on the Internet. Three of the members of this group —the Beatles, yes?—are still alive. One lives in England, one divides his time between Scotland and the West Coast of the United States, and one has a domed villa in the Sea of Rains on Luna. The low gravity eases a peculiar medical condition that has been troubling him for the past few years."

Mrs. Galvez laughed, a birdlike titter. Then, less than enchantingly, she sang three or four lines of "Fly Me to the Moon."

"What would you say if these former members of the Beatles got back together to commemorate your recovery?" Carlos said.

"They must be in their seventies. They're older than I am."

"Would it make you happy—such a stellar reunion?"

"Not if it discomfited *them*. Let the rich old farts live out the remainder of their days in peace. Me, too, for that matter."

"Video Verdadero may be able to arrange it."

"Why bother? There've been partial reunions before, Carlos, and John Lennon's dead. Besides, nobody cares anymore."

"It wouldn't gladden your heart to see these three men singing together again?"

"I don't know. Maybe. If it didn't convulse me with laughter."

"Ah," said Carlos. He played the *Abbey Road* CD again. This time Ramon Covarrubias, still in his gym shorts, returned to the room with a party of more conventionally clad torture victims from the same wing. Eleven well-mannered auditors, ranging in age from a pale young woman in her early twenties to a balding Oriental-looking gentleman not much younger than Mrs. Galvez, crowded in. This last patient, Carlos was surprised to note, had tears in his eyes.

With his hostess's permission, then, the correspondent used his video gun to record the entire surreal scene. It gave him almost exactly what he wanted for a segment of *El Tiempo Turbulento* to be devoted to the Saint of Casa Piadosa.

This segment ran on the Video Verdadero network on the last Thursday in October. The staff and patients at the Warm Springs Torture Victim Rehabilitation Center convened in the cafetorium and entertainment hall to watch it on the enormous wall screen there. The onlookers wore earplugs that provided simultaneous translation of the Spanish commentary for any who required it. Much laughter and applause greeted *La Gran Dama*'s sallies at either the previous Guacamayan government's or her earnest young interviewer's expense. In fact, the laughter and applause frequently overrode the segment's embarrassingly upbeat narration. A good thing, too. The subject of the piece was beginning to choke on Carlos's unadulterated praise.

At the conclusion of the program, when the hall had pretty much emptied, Karen Petitt came to Eleanor and handed her a printout of a standby front page for the following morning's *Atlanta Journal-Constitution*. The lead story was labeled "special to the *Journal-Constitution*," and its author was Carlos Villar. Dr. Petitt conjectured that the wire services would pick up the story and distribute it to the print and electronic media worldwide. This likelihood appalled Eleanor. In a fashion that made even fulsome praise seem a blessing, the story's headline sabotaged her dignity:

Saint of Guacamayo's Dying Wish: That Liverpudlian Rock and Rollers Reunite for Warm Springs Torture-Rehab Concert

"Oh, no," said Eleanor.

"Oh, yes," said Dr. Petitt. "It's a lot of garbage about Beatlemania and *La Fiebre Furtiva*."

"Oh, no, Karen."

"He had the good sense—the decency—to leave both those topics out of the video broadcast, but he's playing them up now in the hope of staging an even bigger coup for Video Verdadero."

"A show in my honor here at the center?"

"Exactly. He refrained from using *El Tiempo Turbulento* to make such an appeal only to preserve his employer's credibility—to save face—if the appeal fails. His own credibility, too, so far as that goes. He's really an unscrupulous schemer, Mrs. Galvez."

Eleanor laughed. "Handsome, though. And sincerely solicitous in person. I've got a kind of radar for such things."

"Do you really want him to show up here again with two or three doddering ex-Beatles in tow?"

"I'd be happier," said Eleanor after pondering for a moment, "if he showed up with Adolfo, my Adolfo, instead—but I certainly wouldn't turn away Messieurs McCartney, Harrison, and Starr. I just regret not having mentioned the chance to see Adolfo again when young Villar asked me what would make me *most* happy. At the time, though, that seemed as far-fetched a wish as World Peace, and certainly a more selfish one."

Adolfo Galvez, an Argentine by birth but today the director of a classical theater group in Maracaibo, was Eleanor's estranged husband. They had been separated for twelve years, a schism dating back to the third year of her mission in Guacamayo. And if any person (the long-suffering Dr. Petitt aside) had received dramatic proof of Eleanor's unworthiness for canonization, it was Adolfo

Galvez. To further her work, she had married this taciturn wealthy man as a matter of convenience, believing that Adolfo fully understood and acquiesced in the nature of their partnership. He was to sponsor her activity in the field; she was to boost his reputation in theatrical circles by reflecting on his surname the glamour of her high-profile humanitarianism.

Instead, Adolfo had come to live with her at Casa Piadosa, a declaration of commitment that he abandoned only when it became clear to him that his wife was never going to retire from the compassion business into orthodox domesticity. In the meantime, though, she had let him know how unsuited he was to such simple menial tasks as taking a temperature, dressing a superficial wound, or comforting a frightened child. More often than not, he had been in the way—a clumsy well-intentioned man whose demonstrated aptitude for management she had chosen to ignore. After all, Casa Piadosa was *hers*. More saintly than she, Adolfo had hung on for two years before confessing his unhappiness and retreating to the bright lights of Buenos Aires, Caracas, and finally Maracaibo. Then, in order to increase his contributions to Venezuelan artistic causes, over a five-year period he had gradually phased out his financial support of the Guacamayan mission.

"Adolfo came to see you soon after you got here," Dr. Petitt reminded Eleanor. "You ran him off."

"I regret that, too. I didn't like the way I looked. And I didn't want to face anyone I'd treated as badly as I had Adolfo."

"But you're ready for the Beatles?"

"If our friend Carlos can arrange it, bring them on. I've never done anything to hurt *those* chaps." And to hell with my "dignity," she thought. Maybe I'm finally old enough to dispense with it.

Two days later, in Bogota, Carlos was startled to receive a televideo communication from the chief neurologist at the Warm Springs center. The woman did not like him, and as soon as her face materialized on the console screen in his office, he braced himself for a torrent of invective and recrimination. After all, he had trespassed on her grudging hospitality by releasing to the American press word of Mrs. Galvez's fatal illness—an illness, moreover, in which neither Dr. Petitt nor he truly believed. Also, there was Carlos's altogether outrageous call for a reunion of superannuated rock 'n' rollers at the treatment center itself.

"My superiors at Amnesty International, London, have given their okay," the woman said, obviously trying very hard to be pleasant. "You may arrange the concert, and if the event actually occurs, you have our permission to provide video coverage. Other details you'll have to work out with the principals themselves. They may not wish to grant your organization exclusive rights to their performance."

Dumbfounded, Carlos gaped at the neurologist's image. At last he said, "*Muchísimas gracias,* Dr. Petitt. How have I won your cooperation?"

"Wars and rumors of wars abound, Mr. Villar. Political hit teams kill three or four people every day. Territorial disputes make enemies of former allies. Terrorist activity has increased every decade since the 1960s, and, after electronic surveillance, torture has become the most widely used instrument of oppression in the world. The Asian nuclear 'demonstrations' of the past five years have claimed more victims than anyone but bleeding-heart alarmists ever supposed possible, and recent numbing real estate negotiations between multinationals have put even the moon at risk. In comparison, your own petty opportunism pales."

"Thank you," said Carlos.

"What I'm trying to say is that against such a climate of perpetual crisis, my superiors think your self-serving scheme may be good for morale everywhere—especially here at the center. Do you understand me?"

"Yes, Doctor. But what of Mrs. Galvez?"

"I have some things to tell you about her, too. Please keep my confidences in mind while you're planning this event."

"Of course, Doctor. Of course."

Karen Petitt talked for ten more minutes. Although his vidcom unit was automatically recording their conversation, Carlos took notes in longhand. This activity, by focusing his attention, always steadied his nerves. Then, when the neurologist had signed off, he set to work pulling strings, calling in IOUs, renewing potentially useful contacts, and, in general, pretending to be an entrepreneur of staggering clout and competence. Over the next several days he was astonished to learn how many people were willing—even eager —to believe in his masquerade.

At the Torture Victim Rehabilitation Center, reporters from dozens of American and European print publications, video magazines, and web outlets tried to call on Eleanor, but Dr. Petitt and the uniformed security personnel held them at bay. One afternoon, in fact, while taking the sun on one side of the hexagonal walkway surrounding the gazebo, Eleanor heard a man with a battery-powered handmike call, "Mrs. Galvez, Mrs. Galvez, are you really dying? Do you have any last words for the millions of people who admire you?" But this reporter beyond the fence palings fled before a leash-tugging German shepherd, and she never replied.

Then the weather turned cold, Eleanor could no longer sit on the lawn, and the world press corps, for all it impinged on the day-to-day routine of her life, went into something resembling hibernation.

Carlos Villar was a remote memory. Eleanor was certainly not thinking of him when she set about putting her affairs in order so that when *La Fiebre Furtiva* claimed her, no one at the hospital would have any doubt about what to do with either her body or her belongings. Cremate the former. Sell the latter and divide the money between the World Health Organization and Amnesty International. She had absolutely nothing else to divest.

In the second week of November, then, she was thinking that perhaps she should make Ramon Covarrubias a gift of the harmonica that Carlos had given her, when an orderly knocked on her door. The orderly had brought with him a stranger, a portly septuagenarian with sad eyes, a heavy mouth, pendulous dewlaps, and a crown of white hair cut in the Roundhead style of Lord Cromwell's seventeenth-century followers. This man walked with a noticeable limp, almost dragging himself across the room to shake her hand.

"Richard Starkey, mum. Pleased to meetcha."

"Starkey?"

He showed her the ornate ruby ring on his little finger. "Me nom de nativity, I'm afraid. It's an incognitoism I've taken to using here on Mother Earth. As if it mattered much anymore."

"You're the one from the Sea of Rains," Eleanor said. "The drummer."

"Only I'm not selling anything, mum. Meself, p'raps. I've come to see yer because me agent said I should." With obvious pain, he eased himself down on the window seat next to her wheelchair. "If I may. It's been an age since I banged the skiffle cans. Or acted, for that matter."

"You live on Luna for your health, don't you?"

"Right," the mournful little man said. "It's more exciting than Flagstaff and closer to heaven."

Eleanor cast about for a response. "How do you like Georgia this time of year?"

"Arfly warm, ain't it? Actually, though, it's not the heat, mum, it's the gravity. The bare-O-metric pressure, too. I'll adjust well enough inna nother coupla weeks. Me doctors say I'm a Methuselah-in-the-making."

"I'm so glad," said Eleanor, meaning it.

Their conversation, to this point little more than an exchange of awkward pleasantries, ran up against a brick wall. So this was one of the surviving former Beatles. Just to look at, he could have been a greengrocer (a prosperous one) or a vice president of a late twentieth-century dotcom. Nice enough, of course, but what did the two of them really have to say to each other? Her zeal for the Chaplinesque figure he had cut in his youth had always taken a back seat to her late-blooming enthusiasm for the Lennon-McCartney team; even the aesthetic-looking George Harrison, the group's single-minded proponent of sitar and tabla, had initially seemed a more likely candidate for idolization. And then, of course, she had set aside such childish concerns by tackling the demanding disciplines of theology and medicine. The Beatles had disbanded about the time she was coming into her own. Now, she and this wrinkled simulacrum of one-quarter of a former legend were struggling to exchange their credentials as human beings. And only narrowly succeeding.

"You said your agent told you to come?"

"Right. To see if you'd really like us to put on a show here. Most of the video loot we'll shove along to the rehab centers, keeping a moiety for ourselves to cover expenses and feed the hangers-on. Whaddaya say, mum? Would you like us to do yer a Christmas gig?"

"Of course, Mr. Starkey."

"Call me Ringo. Or Ishmael, if you'd rather." He pointed his nose at the harmonica in her hands. "You play that, doncher?"

"Once upon a time. No more."

"John was our harmonica player. Remember 'Love Me Do'? We did fifteen cuts o' that one before George Martin was satisfied with the instrumental track. John's mouth went running back 'n' forth on the grill. Fookin' hard work, that. If you'll pardon the expression."

"I'll second it if you like."

Mr. Starkey laughed, brushed off the thighs of his trousers, and stood. "Well, I'm off to Californication Land, then. When I come back, we'll do for you and yer friends here just like the Beatles of yore. That's a promise."

"Your harmonica player's dead," Eleanor heard herself say. The words leapt out before she could stop them.

"And the rest of us've gone plump—well, maybe not George—
and grizzly-gray. You'll just have to fill in, Mrs. Galvez. That's all
there is to it." He saluted her and limped out of the room.

November passed on. Seasonal decorations—flocked trees,
Santa Claus cutouts, even elaborate Yuletide mobiles revolving in
the corridors—popped up around the center as if by magic.
Eleanor drew Ramon Covarrubias's name for the annual gift-
exchange, but she could not bring herself to give up the harmonica.
What Ramon really needed, she told herself, was a brand-new pair
of cotton Winterskins.

In a conference room in Southern California, where hanging
green plants and the amplified white noise of the surf did little to
soothe his nerves, Carlos Villar listened to the "principals" debate
the merits of a private performance for recovering torture victims,
foremost among them Eleanor Riggins-Galvez. Repeatedly, Carlos
assured the three men—only two of whom were in the room,
Harrison auditing the proceedings via a television hookup in London—that a videocast of their concert would go out to the world at
large only after they had edited the tapes.

"This is exactly what John didn't want to happen," said McCartney, big-eyed and pudgy in a fuzzy beige sweater. "Didn't he swear
we'd be four rusty old men playing out somebody else's fancy? It'd
be even worse now, wouldn't you say?"

"That's why we get to edit the bugger," said Starkey. Carlos had
worked long and hard to persuade him to make the three-day crossing, first to sound out Mrs. Galvez and then to attend this meeting
as his most powerful ally.

"We're pretty bleeding likely to stink," McCartney said. "Is
Video Verdadero going to be happy with a two-minute program?"

"The old lady wants us," said Starkey. "She's a saint, and she's
dying."

"Do you want to give her tarnished goods, then? The notion's
crackers. John would—"

"Are you really invoking John again?"

"John would undoubtedly puke is all I was going to say."

"Seems to me," said Harrison's image from the vidcom unit at
table's end, "John's past worrying about it."

"*Gracias*," murmured Carlos under his breath.

Of the three surviving members of the group, only Harrison remained svelte, almost hungry-looking. His close-cropped white hair
accentuated his leanness.

"It doesn't matter anymore," said Starkey. "To three quarters o' the folks alive today we're about as timely as the bloomin' caveman."

McCartney turned on his heel. "I dunno about *that*."

"Speak for yourself," said Harrison from the vidcom unit. "Timely is as timely does."

"I always speak for meself, I do, and I say we're old enough to make fools of ourselves. We've earned the fookin' privilege, 'ticularly if we befool ourselves in a good cause. This one qualifies."

"Three Lads Who Rooked the World," said Harrison from the screen.

Even McCartney laughed, and Carlos hurried to interject, "This reunion will be much more legitimate—honest, I mean—than that silly Agatha Christie thing you did a year or so ago. You all had cameos, but not a single scene together."

"Why don't you take a short hike?" Starkey said. "I *liked* that silly Agatha Christie thing, and you're queering me pitch."

Flustered, Carlos let himself into the carpeted antechamber, where three attorneys, a pair of high-powered personal agents, and an executive of Video Verdadero's American affiliate stood gossiping together. They shot looks of anxious inquiry at Carlos, who shrugged, walked across the room, and sat down in a lounger equipped with headphones and a video hood. Twenty minutes later he felt a hand on his ankle.

"It's set, mate," said Starkey. "Don't hold yer breath till it comes off, but I do believe it's set."

Eleanor had a front-row seat in the cafetorium and entertainment hall. Dr. Petitt occupied the chair to her left, and the remaining patients and staff—a number that had swelled by thirty or more, owing to the influx of the various local officials claiming affiliation with the center—filled nearly every inch of space behind the two women. Where no people sat or stood, up sprouted remote-controlled video equipment or a battery of triangulating theatrical lasers. Nestled about the hall were dozens of miniature speakers to provide the occasional orchestral accompaniment that the group could not generate itself. Montage projectors recreated the myth of Swinging London and the legend of the Fab Four on a scrim of translucent indigo hanging down behind the band. These images slowed for love songs, ricocheted back into action for the hard stuff.

How small the guys seem, Eleanor thought. And how old.

In their white tuxedoes the four of them resembled well-dressed refugees from a Busby Berkeley musical. At present, suitably enough, McCartney's husky voice was doing a respectable job on the lyric of "Yesterday." Somewhat apart from the others and more ethereal in his imaginary old age than his living comrades, Lennon fingered his guitar strings.

Something bumped Eleanor's right elbow, and Carlos Villar eased himself into the only vacant chair remaining in the hall. "Pardon me, Mrs. Galvez," he whispered. "I had some last-minute business to attend to."

"The Lennon's remarkable," Eleanor whispered back. "Just the way I'd envision him looking after all these years."

"Stereoholography. We had to get his sons' permission, of course. It took some doing." He squinted at the scrim. "Has he sung lead yet?"

"On 'Strawberry Fields Forever,' yes. Utterly convincing."

In fact, the eidolon's appearance stunned her. Never in her life had she undergone such a racking but joyful experience. Many others felt the same. This feeling—this thankful and expectant gaiety—had more to do with the aura of long-deferred rapprochement emanating from the performers than with the songs they had chosen. The songs heightened the general breathless gaiety, of course, but they had not created it, and they did not sustain it. Something else was at work. Eleanor found at the heart of this unlikely get-together a gospel akin to the one she had taken into the field with her splints, bandages, and pills.

A short while ago, these aging men, and one utterly convincing apparition, had sung "All You Need Is Love." And, setting aside the demonstrable impracticality of this precept, a roomful of men and women who had suffered insidious mental and physical abuse had listened to "All You Need Is Love"—on its face, bouncy idealistic cant—as if the song's repetitive lyric embodied a real solution to the world's ills. Absurd. Crazy. Tomorrow, of course, they would know better again, but tonight they had willingly suspended their adult disbelief in the foolish notion of universal amity.

Absurd. Crazy.

McCartney finished his solo on "Yesterday," and a pair of overlapping lasers lifted the wizened face of Ringo Starr into front-and-center relief. He did some flashy business with his sticks, and the cymbals on his drum kit rang with a noise like hail hitting tin.

"We've got a request for a song we just can't do anymore," he said. "It's called 'When I'm Sixty-Four.' We've got beyond such childishness, I'm afraid. We could change it to 'When I'm Eighty-

Four,' but it would be hard to credit such an arbitrary substitution, it being based so baldly on the fleetin' feet of time."

"Time's got bald feet?" said the stereohologram image of Lennon, looking up from the fingerboard of his guitar. Laughter. Until now, the Lennon analogue had merely played and sung. It was startling to hear it engage in dialogue with the living group members.

"Yes. Well," said Starr. "I won't play footsie with you on that one, John me lad." He struck the cymbals an emphatic blow. "Besides, I didn't speak up to announce another song, but to say we've got a special guest on the premises, and it's me duty—me pleasure, I should say—to intromit 'im."

"Introduce," said Harrison, looking pained.

"I looked up the word, George. It's *intromit*, 'to cause or permit to enter—'"

"Ha!" barked the Lennon analogue.

"Or 'to introduce or admit.' It's got a coupla meanings bagged up in one package. I'm only saying what I mean."

"Who is it, then?" asked Harrison.

Oh, no, thought Eleanor. They're not going to take public notice of me, are they? Everyone knows I'm here. What a waste of time. Then she recalled that Starr had said "him" instead of "her," and her heart began to beat very fast.

"Patience, podner," said Starr. "Patience, patients." He played a roll. "Here from Maracaibo, Venezuela, direct from *El Teatro Clásico Nacional*, is Adolfo Domingo Galvez. Get out here, Alfie. Ain't this what it's all about—rejoining for a time what fate and various lawsuits have put asunder."

Half-aghast, half-exhilarated, Eleanor watched her estranged husband emerge from one wing of the tiny stage and stroll past the four applauding musicians to the footlights. He looked sleek, gray, and uncertain; a mustache of sweat beaded his upper lip.

This is just like *Queen for a Day*, Eleanor thought. Or any one of a dozen others of those corny video concoctions of her distant girlhood, programs that delighted in wringing pathos, warmth, and high ratings from artfully engineered, otherwise inconceivable reunions.

Queen for a Day.

Adolfo held the harmonica that Carlos had brought into her room back in October. "*Vengas, querida,*" he said when the applause had died. "You must perform with these gentlemen."

"No," said Eleanor. "I can't."

"Of course you can," Carlos Villar assured her, and before she could protest again, he had gripped the handles of her wheelchair and pushed it onto the mechanical lift at one end of the stage. This platform carried her upward, and Adolfo, after kissing her forehead, pulled her clear of the lift and positioned her chair so that she was facing the expectant crowd. Then he placed the harmonica in her hand and touched his lips to her brow again.

"This one's 'Love Me Do,'" McCartney said. "John's got the vocal, but Mrs. Galvez has the mouth-organ riff. *One, two . . .*"

The group began to play. The houselights dimmed again. The Lennon analogue began to sing. The hospital staff and the recovering torture victims clapped their hands in time. Eleanor, trembling, raised the harmonica.

"Take it!" McCartney cried, but she shook her head. She couldn't. The band backed up, deforming the song to compensate for her reluctance. The stereoholographic image of Lennon drifted across the stage and superimposed itself on her person by sitting down with her in the wheelchair. The eidolon of the dead musician buttressed her, strengthening her resolve by inhabiting her body. Eleanor felt reinvigorated, galvanized. And with the aid of the Lennon analogue she played the crucial harmonica riff.

During and after her playing, the hall shook with cries of "Bravo, Mrs. Galvez!" and "Thattagirl!" Her head reeled. The Lennon analogue separated from her, and Adolfo reappeared to help her back to her place between Dr. Petitt and Carlos Villar.

The neurologist, however, gave up her seat to Adolfo, and before Eleanor could reorient herself to her swift transposition back into the audience, the group onstage was singing something new. Something old, rather. What the devil! Old or new, the rhythms of the piece summoned memories—Susan Carmack, *Revolver*, the bittersweet torment of her high school years. Only the words were different:

> *"Eleanor Riggins*
> *Plucks at our hearts*
> *With a courage so icy it's hot.*
> *We've not forgot.*

> *"Brought us together,*
> *Singing our songs*
> *For the last swingin' times of our lives.*
> *Magic survives.*

"Such a gritty lady,
Her work is never done.
Such a pretty lady,
She lifts us to the sun."

There was more, including a communal singing of Lennon's "Happy Xmas (War Is Over)," but Eleanor could not take it all in. She held Adolfo's hand. At concert's end, she smiled and nodded at the patients, staff members, and outside well-wishers who filed by her chair. She even spoke to the individual Beatles—once, that is, the hall had emptied of everyone but Adolfo, Dr. Petitt, Carlos Villar, and the musicians themselves. What they said to her she scarcely heeded. What she said to them had little importance beyond its bemused communication of her gratitude.

In one otherwise inconsequential eddy of time, at a place far from the centers of world power, something good had happened. Tomorrow the bombs might fall, or aliens invade, or the planet spin off its orbit into a collision course with the sun. No matter. Something good had happened.

Queen for a Day, thought Eleanor as her husband propelled her down the dark corridor to her room. Queen for a Day.

Rewarded by Video Verdadero with an extended leave of absence, Carlos Villar flew from Bogota to the capital city of Guacamayo. From there he took a bus to the medical compound where Mrs. Galvez had worked for so many years. It seemed to him, walking the grounds of Casa Piadosa, that he had come to a place combining the lingering horror of Auschwitz, Buchenwald, and Dachau with the sanctity of a religious shrine. Driven by a spontaneous impulse, he fell to his knees and kissed the ambiguous earth. Then he stood, wiped the dirt from his hands, and returned to Ciudad Guacamayo for dinner with the president of a Central American firm in competition with Video Verdadero. After dinner, back in his hotel, he learned that early that morning Eleanor Riggins-Galvez had died.

*   *   *

"We're All in This Alone"
with Paul Di Filippo

*B*AM! THE MORNING NEWSPAPER HIT THE SCREEN. Harry Lingenfelter sloshed coffee onto the mess littering his tabletop: two weeks' worth of prior editions of *The Atlanta Harbinger*, all creased open to the same damned page; stacks of unpaid bills and scary envelopes from his wife's lawyers; dishes crusted with the remnants of sour microwave bachelor meals. Lingenfelter gulped a calming breath and raked the stubble on his jaw with well-bitten fingernails.

Blast old Ernie! Couldn't he—for once—plop the paper gently on the grass? Every morning, Ernie Salter nailed the screen door. And every morning since the acrimonious departure of his wife Nan, Lingenfelter *jumped.* Nan's decamping to her sister's house in Montana, almost a continent away, had not surprised him, but it rankled yet. His gut never stopped roiling. In fact, nowadays even the trill of a house finch could unnerve him.

But what most rankled, even shamed, Lingenfelter was his intolerably foolish preoccupation with a feature in the *Harbinger* called "The Squawk Box." How much longer could he indulge his crazy, self-generated obsession with a few column inches in a two-bit newspaper? "The Squawk Box" ruled his waking life. Sometimes it invaded his dreams. Work on his latest Ethan Dedicos mystery novel had almost stalled, even as his deadline neared, and one look at the kitchen—hell, at any room in the house—disclosed the humiliating magnitude of his bedevilment.

"The Squawk Box" ran daily in the *Harbinger*. It resembled similar columns in newspapers across the nation. A friend in Illinois had forwarded Lingenfelter copies of a feature called "The Fret Net," and at airport newsstands he had run across others titled "The Gripe Vine" and "The Complaint Department." An outlet for pithy bons mots and rants, these columns consisted of anonymous submissions from the paper's own readers. The *Harbinger's* readers generally squawked via telephone or e-mail. An unnamed staff member, self-dubbed the "Squawk Jock," winnowed these quips and printed the wittiest. Although the Squawk Jock never inter-jected private opinion, Lingenfelter had concluded from the evidence of the columns that he had right-of-center leanings and no taste for controversy. You rarely encountered a squawk about abortion, gun control, ethnicity, the death penalty, or religion.

The clumsy phrasings, the naiveté, and the *smugness* of the resulting mix usually irked Lingenfelter, but he could not stop read-ing it. Like the trend of "reality television," the window that "The Squawk Box" opened onto the citizenry's collective soul afforded a glimpse of a purgatory where sinners freely uttered their uncen-sored thoughts, however self-serving or -damning.

Lingenfelter had begun reading the column in earnest only after Nan's departure. To that point, he had only scanned its entries or, on Sunday mornings, jumped to the highlighted "Squawk of the Week." But just two days of involuntary solitude had forced him into new patterns of time wasting, and five days of reading the feature from top to bottom had addicted him.

Most squawks clearly originated with their submitters. Unhap-pily, some readers plagiarized their submissions, rephrasing ancient jokes, ripping off cartoon captions or the punch lines of magazine anecdotes. Often, the Squawk Jock printed the cloned lines along with the authentic ones, without distinction. (Undoubtedly, the pressure to fill space explained the Jock's lack of discrimination.) Still, by and large, the kudos and complaints making up each column exhibited the vivid eccentricities of those who had com-posed them.

- *Ever notice how the faces of drivers in an Atlanta traffic jam look just like the mugs of "clients" at the cheapest mortuary in town?*

- *Our new President has problems above the neck rather than below the waist.*

- A *fool and his money are soon dot-com investors.*

- *I'm so broke that if it cost a quarter to go around the world, I couldn't get from the Fox Theater to the High Museum.*

- *The latest census shows a lot fewer married couples. Folks have finally figured out that they can fight without a license.*

This last squawk had made Lingenfelter wince.

But his fascination with these outpourings of the community mind had soon morphed into something unexpected and embarrassing, namely, a desire to *join* the voluble herd. He wanted to compose a squawk so succinct and biting that the Squawk Jock not only featured it in one of the paper's daily columns but also showcased it on Sunday morning as "Squawk of the Week."

Having set this goal, Lingenfelter felt sure of success. After all, he had some small cachet as a writer. Three modestly selling mysteries starring his gutsy private dick Ethan Dedicos (with a fourth in progress—*slowly* in progress, true, but certain to appear to good reviews eventually) all testified to his skill and success. Or so he and his agent almost daily reassured each other.

From this position of superiority, Lingenfelter had written and e-mailed off a half dozen brilliant squawks, then sat back to await the appearance—the next day—of three or four of them. After all, who could more intelligently tap the Zeitgeist? Who could more eloquently encapsulate the furor and the folly of these portentous days at the beginning of a new millennium?

But neither the next day's *Harbinger* nor any of that week's succeeding issues had featured his work!

Doggedly, Lingenfelter repeated the process—with identical results. Subsequent barrages of squawks—all of which he polished to a high gloss using time that he should have spent advancing Ethan Dedicos in his investigations—likewise met with rejection. Clearly, the Squawk Jock found no merit in his work. Given the crap that did make the column, the Squawk Jock may have even *hated* Lingenfelter's fastidiously crafted quips.

As of today, with neither money nor publicity as likely trophies, he had wasted three *weeks* in this pursuit. What foolishness! No, what quixotic *idiocy*! But he could not stop. He had to make that jerk—that bitch—that Grub Street hack, male or female—acknowledge the beauty and power of his vision, and feature one of his killer witticisms in "The Squawk Box"!

*   *   *

Opening today's paper, Lingenfelter could already feel his pulse throbbing. What bloated japes and mindless yawps had crowded out the twelve gems that he had zapped to the *Harbinger's* virtual mailbox yesterday? Hope flickered in him, but dimly. Either to forestall disappointment or to fuel himself for another round of squawking, he scrutinized the front page, then studied the traffic reports, obituaries, and crime accounts in the Metro section.

A small headline on an interior Metro page caught his eye: *Airline Employee at Hartsfield / Victim of Gruesome Murder.* The details of this slaying would have given even the hard-boiled Ethan Dedicos pause. A check-in clerk for Southwest Airlines had been found in an elevator in the North Terminal with the top of his skull cut away and his brain primitively extracted. As bloody embellishment, the killer had chopped off the ill-fated clerk's right hand.

Lingenfelter mumbled, "Jesus," as he peeled back the pages of the Diversions section to "The Squawk Box." Then he stopped and stared at the ceiling. The bizarre particulars of the airport murder plucked at his memory. He set today's paper aside and rummaged about for last Sunday's. In it, he found the "Squawk of the Week," which struck him as insupportably petulant: *"Asking the brainless counter help at Hartsfield International for a hand is a waste of time. A prison inmate might as well ask a guard for a massage."* An eel of discomfiting coldness wriggled down Lingenfelter's spine. His nape hair bristled.

Grisly coincidence? Surely. Anyway, this squawk had no more wit or grace than a dozen others that had appeared last week. The Squawk Jock had spotlighted it only to plug a recent investigative series in the *Harbinger* on the breakdown of services at the airport and attendant customer frustration. Lingenfelter sighed heavily. Some of his own experiences at Hartsfield had nearly moved *him* to murder, although not to a murder as complex or gory as this one.

He laid the old Sunday paper aside and returned to today's edition. Fumblingly, he checked out "The Squawk Box," confirming his suspicion that its editor had stiffed him again. As always, it consisted of the banal, tongue-tied, and pilfered submissions of dolts and plagiarists. Two thirds of these troglodytes, Lingenfelter smirked, had to be the Squawk Jock's creditors. Or inbred cousins.

Thirty minutes later, he refilled his coffee cup and slunk into his study. At his computer, he ignored the guilt-provoking icons symbolizing his stalled novel and clicked instead on his Internet connection. The Squawk Jock's ignorance and pettiness had to have a natural limit. A fresh baker's dozen of his canniest topical epigrams would sound that limit and result in his first published squawk. One of his efforts might even earn enthronement as "Squawk of the Week"! Gamely, Lingenfelter curled his fingers above his keyboard.

- *Confession is good for the soul, not to mention the prosecution.*

- *Marriage institutionalizes love, sex, parenting, and, sometimes, one or both partners.*

- *My 4-year-old niece has a toy pool table. She shoots peas into its pockets with a plastic straw. The kid really knows her peas and cues.*

- *Caller ID is a fine innovation. Now we need another, Callee ID, for those of us who forget whom we're calling.*

- *Pity my estranged wife, a designer-clothes exclusivist. She was confined to our home last winter by a swollen dresser drawer.*

- *If my mood depended on the regular publication of my squawks, I'd need a truckload of Zoloft just to elevate my feet.*

Lingenfelter savored these recent submissions, as if they belonged in *Bartlett's Quotations*. But Sunday had come again, and the Squawk Jock had nixed them all. Despite both the day and the early hour, Lingenfelter knocked back a jolt of Wild Turkey, neat. Granted, he had stolen that barb about Nan's fussy taste in clothes from Hoosier humorist Kin Hubbard (1868–1930), but the others had all originated with him alone. How could anybody bypass them in favor of crap like—well, like the crap the Squawk Jock preferred?

The "Squawk of the Week," for example, struck Lingenfelter as a whimper of no distinction at all: *"The fat of our great land has rendered us into a nation of grasping fatties."* It barely warranted a place in the column, much less in a box at the feature's top. Lingenfelter poured another shot and tossed it down. Let the dork responsible for that *fatuous* line relish his brief moment of glory. Alcoholism and altruism alike delude, Lingenfelter thought. A moment later, he twigged to the fact that his words had . . . yes, squawk potential:

Alcoholism and altruism alike delude.

He wobbled off to catapult this saying through the ether and to compose another batch of epigrams for his nemesis. When his phone rang in the midst of this activity, Lingenfelter ignored it on the grounds that his agent—thank God for Caller ID—would scold him rather than root him on.

During the following week, Lingenfelter took to meeting his deliveryman, Ernie Salter, at curbside at 6:25 A.M. and seizing the *Harbinger* right out of his hand. Monday morning witnessed the first of these addled rendezvous.

A heavyset African-American with muttonchop whiskers and a foul cigarillo, Salter hunched forward in his spavined pickup truck and cocked a scarred eyebrow at Lingenfelter. The two had already talked about Lingenfelter's "Squawk Box" hang-up, and Salter obviously thought him tetched. Dashboard glow shadowed his bulldog jowls and the chest of his faded Olympics tee shirt.

"No luck last week, eh?"

"Maybe this morning." Lingenfelter paged immediately to "The Squawk Box." Several blocks away—the two men lived in Mountboro, eighty miles southwest of Atlanta—a rooster crowed. As the sky to the east pinked up prettily, Lingenfelter tilted his paper into its sheen. His brow furrowed. Then he refolded the section and thwacked it against the pickup, hard.

"A moron chooses these things! A spiteful, *dyslexic* moron!"

Ernie asked, "How much does the *Harbinger* pay for a squawk, Harry?"

"Not a copper cent. You know that."

"Yeah, I know that. Do you get your name in the paper?"

"Every squawk is printed anonymously. You know that, too."

"No wonder you're losing Zs trying to crash this market," Ernie said. "The big bucks. The fame."

"Damn it, Ernie. I can get sarcasm from my agent. Or from Nan, long-distance."

Ernie's cigarillo waltzed over to his other lip corner. "Get back to your Ethan Dedicos stories, Harry. I really dig that guy."

"You and fourteen other people."

"I got to go. Stop squawking. Start writing again." Ernie let out the clutch, and his clattery old pickup began to roll.

Lingenfelter trotted along behind it. "I'll see print yet!" he cried. "I'll make that jerk sit up and take notice!"

"Don't write so damned highfalutin!" Ernie shouted back. "The Squawk Jock *hates* highfalutin!" Apparently, Ernie's patience had just run out. Lingenfelter jogged to a bemused standstill.

But he showed up hopefully at curbside every morning, anyway —to no purpose but the further exasperation of Ernie Salter, who on Friday exited his truck, hooked elbows with Lingenfelter, and walked him back inside. "They aint nothing in here from you, Harry. Nothing." He shoved Lingenfelter into a kitchen chair and poured him a cup of his own godawful molasses-like coffee. "I'd lay odds. Check it out."

Lingenfelter checked. Ernie was right. Another strikeout. No, a whole *clutch* of mortifying whiffs!

With a tenderness that reduced Lingenfelter to tears, Ernie gripped his shoulders and squeezed. The massage lasted not quite a minute. Then Ernie said, "Let the damned bug in your ball cap go, Harry," and slowly clomped out.

Lingenfelter picked up the *Harbinger.* On the front page of the Metro section, this: *Bank President Found Mutilated / In Abandoned Car Dealership.* The headline alone yanked him erect. The story itself shoved a flaming rod down his spine. His hands shook, and the newspaper's pages rattled as if burning.

A night watchman had found the bank president's decapitated head sitting on the hood of his new Ford Exorbitant in the roofless courtyard of a car dealership that had just gone bankrupt. The dealer had sold economical imports from Eastern Europe. The watchman found the overweight victim's body hanging in the boarded-up showroom like the carcass of a butchered hog. The air conditioning, which should not have worked at all, blasted away at its highest setting. Meanwhile, an iron kettle next to the SUV boiled merrily over a fire of scrap wood, rendering the man's internal organs into soap scum and tallow. A pair of severed hands gripped the Exorbitant's steering wheel, like claws. The whole ghastly scene suggested that the culprit had fled only moments before the arrival of the watchman.

Lingenfelter picked up last Sunday's paper again. Shaking like a man with delirium tremens, he tore from it the "Squawk of the Week." He then cut out the story about the bank bigwig's murder/ mutilation, stapled the squawk to its corner, and stuffed both items into an envelope, which he addressed to the Atlanta police department. By now, some law-enforcement official *must* have noticed the connection between the *Harbinger's* featured squawk and the particulars of the killings at both the airport and the car dealership. How many earlier featured squawks had provided a sick human specimen the impetus for murder? How many prize squawks of the future would prod that same wacko to slay again?

Don't mail this in, Lingenfelter told himself. Phone it in. You can't waste time—oh, the irony of *that* self-admonition—going through the U.S. Postal Service. You need to speak to somebody *now!* Although he didn't really want to get involved—a cliché with a shame-engendering edge—he steeled himself to call. Even as he touched the numbers on his keypad, though, he wondered if the police would suspect *him*. Tipsters sometimes turned out to be perps, and even if the police congratulated him on his civic-mindedness, they would file his name and number for future reference.

A polite female functionary took his call, promised to pass along his tip, and admitted that several other people had already telephoned with the same concern. In fact, the policewoman said, detectives had noted not only the squawk-as-murder-incitement angle but also the head-and-hands obsession of the killer or killers responsible for these latest mutilation slayings.

"Latest?" Lingenfelter said. "Others have occurred?"

"Thanks for doing your duty as a citizen," the woman replied. "We'll call if we have any further questions." *Click.*

Lingenfelter set the envelope with its provocative clippings aside and reexamined the squawks in today's paper. His heart, whose pounding had eased a bit, began to hammer again at his ribcage. One item annoyed him intensely: *"Now that 'The Squawk Box' has printed me, I have an agent ready to sell movie rights to my life to the highest bidder."* What an egomaniac! What a self-deluding boob!

Oddly, Lingenfelter's own agent, Morris Vosbury, chose that moment to call him again. He let the phone ring. Just as his answering machine prepared to kick in—provoking Morris's departure, for he refused to talk to a machine—Lingenfelter relented and picked up.

"Finally," Morris said. "How goes the latest Ethan Dedicos? You gonna make your April fifteenth deadline?"

"Tax day?" Lingenfelter moaned. "That's less than a month off."

"Yeah, well, we chose it as a mnemonic aid, Harry. Remember how you forgot your own birthday as a deadline for the last Dedicos?"

"That book drained me spiritually," Lingenfelter said. "I had to go deep—deep into myself—for *Blessed Are the Debonair.*"

Morris's long pause suggested that he was biting his tongue. Eventually he said, "So how goes *Seven Terriers from Bedlam?*"

"Not bad until you broke my concentration." After a few closing pleasantries, Lingenfelter hung up. A pox on Morris, anyway. How, after such an intrusion, could he hope to concentrate on his fiction

writing? Better to soothe his nerves with a little Wild Turkey and a
new strategy for cracking "The Squawk Box."

- *Some self-obsessed fame seekers think that enlightenment occurs at the pop of a flashbulb.*

- *Cell phones have as much business in the front seat of moving motor vehicles as uncapped whiskey bottles.*

- *Ever notice how the mayor's mustache makes him look like Adolf Hitler in an elongating funhouse mirror.*

- *My condolences to the person who spent two weeks in Los Angeles for brain surgery. Even without surgery, L.A. can appallingly alter the brain.*

- *In the long annals of crime, Fulton County's counterfeiter of Beanie Babies hardly qualifies as an Al Capone clone.*

- *Yesterday I got a mailing from an "intellectual" magazine begging me to subscribe: "Think for yourself. Just send in our card." I thought for myself. I ash-canned the card.*

One more, Lingenfelter thought, just one more, and I'll get
back to my novel. He tapped out: *"Journalism is to literature as a
stomach flutter is to all-out panic."* What did that mean, exactly?
He had no clear idea. He did know that he had killed yet another
afternoon, and when none of these submissions appeared in the
paper that week, he knew, too, that his career was down spiraling
like a missile-struck F–111.

How did other writers maintain their focus when day-to-day
living threw so many distractions at them? He checked the Activities page in the *Harbinger*. Conferences and book signings were
rampant in Atlanta this weekend, with visits from such eminences
as John Updike and A. S. Byatt, such mystery-writing stalwarts as
Sue Grafton and Joe R. Lansdale, and such up-and-comers as Ace
Atkins and Atlanta's own Chick Morrow. Lingenfelter had met
Chick last year at a Georgia Author of the Year program. Although
he had liked Chick, he had also felt a twinge of impending competition. This Saturday the younger writer had a signing, albeit a
modest one, at the Science Fiction & Mystery Bookshop on Highland Avenue.

Chick bore down and wrote. He deserved his success. Lingenfelter could not imagine him sweating manuscript staples to place a
silly one- or two-liner in an amateur forum like "The Squawk Box."

This thought sobered Lingenfelter, literally. He set aside his bourbon bottle and applied himself all morning to *Seven Terriers from Bedlam,* his first long stint of work on the novel in over six weeks. At noon, he felt like a hero—or, at least, a competent human being.

On Sunday, he paged to the squawks out of habit rather than compulsion. The "Squawk of the Week" leapt out like a mocking jack-in-the-box, but he thought it amusing—and incisive—and wished that *he* had written it, for it gibed with his own experience:

"Having met several authors at book signings, I can report that most writers are smarter on paper than in person."

Amen.

Hold on, Lingenfelter warned himself. If the "Squawk of the Week" provides our anonymous serial killer fantasy fodder for his next murder, why couldn't he settle on *you* as his next victim? Ridiculous. For one thing, the previous murders both took place in or around Atlanta, not out in the country. For another, even in the South, writers abound. If you know where to look, writers wriggle like maggots.

Lingenfelter observed the Sabbath. He walked to Ernie Salter's and played him several games of two-handed poker. And the next week he wrote—on his novel, *not* on a battery of desperate doomed-to-rejection squawks. Life seemed almost tolerable again. One night, in fact, he called Nan in Montana—hey, not a bad title for a Western—and apologized for his crazy work schedule and net surfing, which together had pitched their relationship into the crapper.

On Thursday morning, though, he opened the *Harbinger* to find this headline on the front page: *"Rising Atlanta Mystery Star Chick Morrow / Himself the Subject of a Mystery: / Body Found Strangled in Ponce de Leon Apartment."* An inset head read, *"Police suspect that killer / uses popular* Harbinger *column / to target victims."* Jesus, Lingenfelter thought.

Apparently, the murderer had surprised Chick Morrow at his desk and choked the life out of him. Then the fun began. The intruder affixed a dunce cap to Chick's head, rolled out a sheet of butcher paper, and laid Chick on the paper. Then he sketched a red outline around Chick's body with a grease pencil, just as the police draw a chalk outline around a murder victim for investigative purposes. This time the killer had not mutilated or dismembered his victim. But when the police moved Chick's body, they found the paper inside his outline teeming with mathematical formulae, some so abstruse that only Steven Hawking could have deciphered them.

According to the newspaper, one detective said, "Think last Sunday's 'Squawk of the Week.' You know, '*Smarter on paper than in person.*' Get it? Pretty highbrow. Pretty sick."

I'd say, Lingenfelter murmured.

Bam! Bam! The screen on the kitchen door banged open and shut.

Lingenfelter jumped up from his computer table. Had the killer come for him, too? He kept no handgun in his house, and this morning he regretted that scruple. In a panic he looked about for a heavy object—doorstop, paperweight, or dictionary—to use for self-defense.

Ernie Salter manifested in the doorway. "Hey, Harry, how you doin?"

"Not so good." Lingenfelter patted his heart. "A friend of mine up in Atlanta was strangled dead yesterday."

"That's why I come over. That damned 'Squawk Box' thing. You hear how the paper aint gonna run a 'Squawk of the Week' no more?"

"I just read it—last paragraph in the story."

"Oh man," Ernie said. "Sorry bout your friend. Weird how it's got this screwy squawk tie-in. Weird n spooky."

"Take me to Atlanta. I've got to see about Chick, help the family, something. I'll pay if you drive me." Nan had taken their car when she skedaddled for Montana, but Lingenfelter had not missed it until now. He got around Mountboro just fine on foot or bicycle.

"You got it, bro. When you want to leave?"

An hour later, Ernie drove Lingenfelter up I–85 toward Atlanta. Traffic streamed about them, and by chance they fell in behind a slow-moving Parmenter's chicken truck. White fluff from its stacked cages blew back at them in a diffuse blizzard, along with a sickening stench.

Ernie said, "Now those birds got something *real* to squawk about."

"You mean Chick Morrow's murder doesn't qualify?"

"I mean I'm glad you gettin over your squawk hang-up. Even as I'm sorry bout poor Chick."

"I'm just jumpy, Ernie. Chick's murder has really hit me. The other killings made me feel weird, but this one wrings my heart. There's more to all this than a robotic 'Son of Sam' character taking random instructions from a newspaper. 'The Squawk Box' strikes me as—well, flat-out *evil.* Look at the hold the damn thing had on me. It's like all my aborted squawks fed something bad, a monster living off ill-will."

Ernie chewed his unlit cigar. "You trying to say the *Squawk Jock*'s the killer?"

"No. Well, maybe. Damn, I don't know! The cops probably grilled the Jock, once they saw the link between the column and the murders, but he's still running free. I don't know *what* to think."

"Best not to think at all then." Ernie dialed in some gospel music and hummed along with it.

Traffic in the metro region had worsened nearly every month for the past decade. Today it crawled. Unable to pass the smelly chicken truck, they suffered with rolled-up windows and no air conditioning in the moderate late-March heat.

Chick Morrow's well-maintained apartment building rested between an electrical supply store and a laundry-processing plant—hardly the most elite neighborhood. But Lingenfelter knew just how little beginning writers usually earned, and he admired Chick for doing as well as he had. The place had a low redbrick wall in front of it and majestic oaks rearing in back. Lingenfelter stepped onto the sidewalk.

"Coming with?"

"I aint no Hardy Boy. Got a sister on the South Side who wants to see me."

"Okay. I need to visit some other places here, anyway. But I can get to em on the bus. See you later."

Ernie scribbled on a matchbook. "Here's my sister's number. Call me when you're ready to head on home." His pickup grumbled off down the street.

Lingenfelter climbed the condo steps. The name *Chick Morrow* on an embossed strip identified the apartment. He mashed the button.

A woman's dispirited voice issued from the speaker grille: "*Yes? Who is it?*"

"I'm a friend of Chick's. Harry Lingenfelter. I just—well, I just wanted to talk to someone about Chick."

"*Come on up.*"

The door to Chick's apartment opened on the blotchy face of a red-haired young woman, who introduced herself as Lorna Riley. She surprised Lingenfelter by observing that Chick had often talked about him.

"Don't worry about defacing the 'crime scene,'" she said, waving him in. "Once the police had finished, they put me in touch with a company that specializes in cleaning up murder scenes. Can you imagine making your living that way? *I* never did, before all this. Now, such a service seems a gruesome inevitability."

Inside the modest apartment, Lingenfelter had no idea how to proceed, or what he hoped to learn, or how he could help. He asked impulsive questions. Did Chick have any enemies that Lorna knew about? No. Was Chick despondent? No, Lorna rejoined. His first novel was about to receive a favorable review in this Sunday's *Harbinger*, and his agent had already fielded a half dozen inquiries from Hollywood. He had everything to live for.

Lingenfelter disengaged from his role as inquisitor. He had to go. He extended his hand to Lorna, who flabbergasted him by falling into his arms, her whole body slack with despair. She wept quietly as Lingenfelter patted her back. Eventually, she regained her composure, apologized for the lapse, and told him that the funeral would take place on Sunday in a church near Emory University.

"Will you come?"

"Of course." He gave her both his phone number and that of Ernie's sister, then tripped down the stairs and strolled to the nearest bus stop.

Like many freelancers, Lingenfelter often took quick assignments for the ready cash. Among these jobs, he most enjoyed writing book reviews for the *Harbinger*. His editor was Heather Farris, a woman from Rhode Island with a degree in comparative lit from Brown University. He had never met her in person, but on the telephone she had a scrappy personality and a sharp-tongued sense of humor. Surely, she could introduce him to the Squawk Jock. Once he detailed his own minor complicity in feeding the beast loose in Atlanta, she *had* to help him, journalistic ethics be damned.

Suppose Heather did introduce him to the Jock—what then? Did he confront the man as an accomplice to the murders? Ask him if he knew the identities of any likely serial killers? Badger him about his failure to print any of Lingenfelter's own squawks? And if he learned something that pointed to the killer, did he call the police? Or did he put on the persona of his own Ethan Dedicos just as Bruce Wayne put on the regalia of Batman? What role *should* he play?

A block from the newspaper building, Lingenfelter got off the bus and walked to its towering facade. At the security desk in the lobby, he explained that he had come to see Heather Farris, the

Book Page editor. The guard spoke briefly into a headset mike and nodded him to a bank of elevators with copper-colored doors. Riding an elevator up, Lingenfelter felt like a surreal avatar of himself.

Heather greeted him warmly. She had a mole on her left jaw on which he fixated. At some moments the olive-complexioned editor glowed like a movie star, at others she went as sallow as a jaundice sufferer—shifts that discomfited Lingenfelter as he tried to explain why he had come and what he wanted. Her mole had him hypnotized. His mission had him stuttering.

Finally, Heather broke in: "Our so-called Squawk Jock doesn't meet folks face to face. He wants to avoid bribery, intimidation, even outright threats on his life. Some people will try almost anything to get a squawk of theirs in print."

"I believe it," Lingenfelter said. "But Chick's strangulation—this whole series of murders—should alter things radically."

"It has. We've dropped the 'Squawk of the Week.' And the police already know the Jock's identity. *Your* need to know, however, seems low-level, if not nonexistent."

Lingenfelter said that he had deduced the link between the "Squawk of the Week" and the murders early on, that Chick Morrow was a friend, and that he had a powerful sense that "The Squawk Box" channeled a current of amorphous evil in the city. The Squawk Jock's weekly selection of a champion squawk focused this evil and put it into deadly real-world play. He, Lingenfelter, understood the mind of the typical squawker as well as, if not better than, anyone. Moreover, for the entire city's sake, Heather had an *obligation* to tell him the Squawk Jock's identity.

"My God, Harry, you really *do* believe you're Ethan Dedicos. What can you do that the police can't?"

"*Something*—something more than they've managed. Tell me, Heather."

"He'd kill me." Heather locked her fingers and extended both hands in a tension-reducing stretch. "Oh, not literally of course."

"I'll say a friend on the police force tipped me. He'll never suspect you."

Review copies of books—bound galleys, photocopied typescripts, finished hardcovers—teetered on Heather's desk in misarranged stacks. She drummed her fingers on the dust jacket of an illustrated art book titled *Topographical Abstracts of the Human Body*. She squinted at Lingenfelter. She exhaled and said:

"Sylvester Jowell."

"The *Harbinger*'s art critic?" This revelation was so unexpected that Lingenfelter thought it bogus, an obvious dodge. "You're kidding."

"Go see him. Check the far end of this floor." Heather gestured, accidentally toppling a stack of books. "The next time you visit, don't ask me to play stool pigeon."

Lingenfelter nodded goodbye and wandered among the reporters' workstations toward Sylvester Jowell's office, fearful that as soon as he had stepped out of earshot, Heather would telephone the police to confess what she had just done.

Sylvester Jowell! Lingenfelter marveled. The man wrote hoity-toity reviews of art gallery openings, single-artist retrospectives, etc. He had two Harvard degrees, a Pulitzer Prize for art criticism, and a citywide reputation as an erudite snob. Had he really agreed to take on the proletarian task of editing "The Squawk Box"? Did his duties as art critic give him so much leisure—and so little leftover discrimination—that he gladly compiled that daily burlesque of good taste? Maybe his well-known fondness for outsider art had a literary counterpart. Atlanta's squawks probably charmed him in the same way as did the childlike visual artifacts of Grandma Moses and Howard Finster.

Jowell's cubicle stood empty. A reporter dressed in satiny gray, including even his tie, intercepted Lingenfelter. The illustrious Mr. Jowell, this reporter said, had taken himself for the umpteenth time to the High Museum for yet another encounter with a special exhibition of the horrific paintings of the late British artist Francis Bacon. If Lingenfelter hurried over there, he could find Mr. Jowell in the galleries devoted to this prestigious show.

As Lingenfelter turned to go, the reporter asked, "Do you like Bacon?"

"Usually only on a BLT."

The High Museum suggested a modernistic castle-keep made of big bone-white Lego blocks. The long-running Francis Bacon exhibit had not attracted families or young children—a parental outcry had put an end to one scheduled middle-school field trip—and its most devout fans had already seen it many times. So Lingenfelter had no trouble getting in—for ten dollars—or striding up the access ramp to the maze of rooms filled with Bacon's unsettling images.

Lingenfelter declined a headset providing commentary on each of the paintings. He peered about in foreign-feeling awe. The hardwood floors seemed to rise under him like concrete slabs on hidden hydraulic lifts, and the pictures, many under glass, assaulted him with bloody reds and opalescent grays. Moving slowly, he gaped at Bacon's huge renderings of screaming popes, butchered cow carcasses, feral dogs, and distorted three-part crucifixions. The show bemused and sickened Lingenfelter, who sidled into a small room with only a water cooler and a wicker bench for furnishings. He sat on the bench, his head hanging forward.

"Too much for you, eh?"

Lingenfelter raised his head. Sylvester Jowell—recognizable from the photo that accompanied his art columns—stared at Lingenfelter without pity or even much interest. He modeled a burgundy jersey with its sleeves pushed up and thrust his hands deep in the pockets of pleated gray trousers.

"I've never seen such ugly work on canvas before."

"Didn't you read my eloquent warnings in the *Harbinger?* I've written about this show like no other."

Lingenfelter's nape hair bristled. "I know who you are," he said. "In addition to the *Harbinger's* art critic, I mean."

"Then you have the advantage of me."

"You're the Squawk Jock."

Sylvester Jowell winced. "I loathe that sobriquet. I loathe the feature's *title*, for that matter. I lobbied for 'Cavils and Kvetches,' you know."

"I had no idea. A friend said the Squawk Jock hated highfalutin stuff, but 'Cavils and Kvetches' sounds pretentious as hell."

Jowell crossed his arms. "Perhaps I *do* know who you are."

Lingenfelter repressed an urge to scream. "Who?"

"The psychopath using my 'Squawk's of the Week' as templates for outrageously nasty murders."

This accusation stunned Lingenfelter. He wanted to shout it down—to jump up, wrap his fingers around Jowell's neck, and squeeze until, flushing scarlet and wheezing, Jowell recanted the insult. Of course, those very actions would fulfill Jowell's every vile expectation of him. As Lingenfelter shook with rage and self-disgust, Jowell took two or three steps back, his body limned against the folds of the pearl-hued drapes cloaking the opposite wall. He glimmered before these drapes like an object in a cheap special-effects shot of a matter-transmission field.

"Don't abandon me here," Lingenfelter said. "You know I'm not the killer."

"How do I know that?"

"Because you're either doing the killings yourself or artfully directing them."

"Ah." Jowell smiled. "Rest assured that I have no intention of abandoning you here, Mr. Lingenfelter."

His image—as shiny as a tinfoil cutout—steadied before the headache-inducing dazzle of the curtain.

At that moment, three figures—like three-dimensional projections of the images in some of Francis Bacon's paintings—walked through the chamber in single file. The first was an airline clerk wearing a bloody cap and a bloody bandage over the stub at the end of his right arm. The second was a portly man in a chalk-striped Italian business suit carrying his own swollen, shocked-looking head in his handless arms. These grotesque persons passed through the chamber without speaking. The third figure—a fit-looking priest in a black cassock and a jaunty black biretta—halted directly in front of Sylvester Jowell. He turned to look at Lingenfelter, who prepared to avert his gaze.

"Excuse me," the interloper said in an odd nasal voice. "Do you know in which room I can find *Study after Velazquez, Number One?*"

Lingenfelter experienced profound relief that the shade of Chick Morrow, bearing the signs of his strangulation, had not posed this question. "No, sir, I'm afraid I don't," he said belatedly.

The priest consulted a photocopied list. "Then how about a painting called *Blood on the Floor?*"

"I'm wandering lost in this place, Father. But, to my eye, every painting here seems to celebrate lostness."

"Do you think so?" the priest said. Then he recited, "'*If all art is but an imitation of nature, then this Francis Bacon character must have really liked imitating its nastiest processes.*'"

"That sounds like a squawk," Lingenfelter said.

"Sadly, an unpublished one." The priest either smiled or scowled. "Forgive my intrusion." When he walked from the chamber into the next room, the air in his cassock's wake actually crackled.

Sylvester Jowell touched a finger to his face, which shone like a life mask lit from behind by a candle. Overlapping taped commentaries buzzed in the headsets of people in other rooms, a faint out-of-sync chorus.

"What did you want of me?" Jowell asked Lingenfelter.

"A telephone number. An e-mail address. A name. The identity of the 'Squawk of the Week' killer."

"What if I admitted my sole culpability?"

"I'd turn you in to the police as a prime suspect. I'd also fight to haul you into the stationhouse to sign such a confession."

"'*Prime*'?" Jowell said. "Provocative word." He shimmered in his slacks and jersey. His skin glimmered. The folds of the gray curtain behind him foregrounded themselves so that they resembled the bars of a cage. Jowell grabbed them with his pale hands. Then he let go and peeled back the front of his knit shirt to reveal the fatty wings of his own ribcage. Without wholly dissolving, his face melted. His mouth opened, but no sound issued from it. The curtain at his back flickered like an electric field, its folds continuing to mimic the solidity of prison bars. Jowell's body and face phased in and out of reality, wavering between freedom and encagement.

Elsewhere, the sounds of shuffling feet and talking headsets told Lingenfelter that he had *not* suffered a psychotic break. Upon entering the show, he had seen a framed black-and-white photograph of Francis Bacon, middle-aged and shirtless. Triumphant in his own frank animality, Bacon held aloft in each hand a naked flank of meat. The distorted image of Jowell with his chest split open qualified as a living take on that still photographic image.

Lingenfelter leapt to his feet.

Jowell vanished like early-morning fog. The isolated little room congealed around Lingenfelter like aspic. The drapes on the wall had folds again rather than bars, but the chamber held him fast. It held him until a member of museum security and two Atlanta policemen hurried in, handcuffed him, and escorted him out of the exhibit under the astonished gazes of a dozen visitors. Lingenfelter wondered where all these people had come from.

- *Stone walls do not a prison make, nor iron bars a cage, but tell that to somebody who can't interpenetrate them like Superman.*

- *Tomorrow my wife will receive word that I am taking the spring short course in license-plate design.*

- *If the measure of a good resort is the quality of the people you meet, this one deserves a minus five stars.*

Obsessively, Lingenfelter mentally framed squawks of a confessional sort. (It looked as if he had been framed himself.) Doing so helped pass the time. He had used his one telephone call to ring up Ernie's sister's house. Then he had asked Ernie to contact his lawyer, his wife, his agent, and Heather Farris at the *Harbinger*.

Maybe she had some pull with local law enforcement. She could certainly testify to his good character, his reliability as a book reviewer, and his essential innocence, even if he did write down-and-dirty mystery thrillers.

In the presence of his daunted attorney, Cleveland Bream, the police had grilled Lingenfelter about the squawk murders. Nan did not call. Later, the police summoned him from a fusty basement cell for a visit with Ernie Salter in their favorite interrogation room. All through this low-key talk, Lingenfelter knew that detectives were watching through a two-way mirror, eavesdropping on every word. Ernie promised to do all he could to help and then drove home. Heather Farris neither telephoned nor visited. Back downstairs, Lingenfelter wrote his private squawks.

Eventually, a guard approached to inform him that he had another visitor. "Don't get up," the guard said. "This one's coming to you—an honest-to-God Catholic priest. So don't do anything antisocial or violent, okay?"

"A priest?"

The guard read from a manifest: "Diego Fahey, S. J."

"I'm not Catholic," Lingenfelter protested. But the guard simply ignored him and left. Minutes later, the same spectral priest who had spoken to him in the High Museum loomed over him like a vulturine confessor.

Lingenfelter's hands went clammy, as if encased in latex gloves. His stomach cramped repeatedly. Did anyone ever bother to search a priest? This one's cassock sleeves could have concealed a National Guard arsenal—or, at least, a carving knife or two, an automatic pistol, and a fold-up machete.

"Pleased to see you again," Father Fahey said. "Sorry it's under these dreary circumstances."

"What's the S. J. stand for?"

"Society of Jesus." Father Fahey's pupils glittered like bits of obsidian. "Why? What did you *think* they stood for?"

"I couldn't have said. Do you happen to know Sylvester Jowell?"

"No, I don't. Interesting name, though."

"Interesting initials, too."

"I suppose so. Did his initials lead you to assume a connection between him and us Jesuits?" Without asking, Father Fahey sat beside Lingenfelter on his narrow cot and gripped his knee. "Because we don't know him. We've never known him. His opinions distress us. His motives defy our comprehension." The grip on Lingenfelter's knee grew more insistent, as painful as the flexion of a raptor's talons. Father Fahey's pupils—his dark-brown irises, for that matter—abruptly clouded, as if someone had pressed disks of smoked glass over them "Shhh," he said. "Don't cry out. Love is the Devil, but silence gets all manner of wickedness done."

From one cassock sleeve Father Fahey pulled a wooden ruler with a thin copper edge and some sort of writing implement. From the other he extracted a switchblade that Lingenfelter dimly associated with the Cross. . . .

Heather Farris perched at Lingenfelter's bedside in Henry Grady Memorial Hospital. For twenty minutes she had apologized for ratting him out to the police after identifying Sylvester Jowell to him as the Squawk Jock. She apologized for failing to heed Ernie Salter's notification of his arrest. She apologized for the peculiar wounds that the priest had inflicted upon him in a fugue of profound enthrallment after cajoling his way into Lingenfelter's cell. As Heather spoke, the mole on her jaw occupied almost all his attention.

Apparently, Father Fahey had placed the wooden ruler across Lingenfelter's windpipe until Lingenfelter blacked out. Then he had measured the cell's dimensions in feet and inches. He wrote the length, height, and breadth of the cage on its rear wall in bright pearl-gray numerals. Then he placed Lingenfelter on the floor, cut away his shirt, and used the switchblade to gouge four star-shaped badges of flesh out of his torso. He was bent over Lingenfelter carving a fifth star into his chest, right above the heart, when the police broke in and seized him. If the cuts had gone much deeper, Lingenfelter would not have awakened.

Heather said, "You don't know how glad I was to see your eyes open, Harry."

Lingenfelter nodded. He wondered how Diego Fahey, S. J., had read his mind. He wondered if capturing and subduing the priest, whom Heather said had no memory of assaulting him, would put an end to the squawk murders. He feared the opposite. If the *real* agency behind the slayings could inspire new killers with epigrammatic thoughts out of the mental ether, the bizarre assaults would go on. Fahey struck Lingenfelter as a mere cat's-paw whom Sylvester Jowell had felled by channeling and focusing the destructive essence of innumerable malign squawks, brilliant and banal.

The ruler across Lingenfelter's throat had rendered him temporarily mute. He knew this without even trying to talk. Heather detected his agitation and handed him a notepad and a pen. He worked to position them properly and then scratched out on the pad's top sheet: **What's happened to Jowell?**

"He's disappeared," Heather said. "I think he knew that Diego Fahey, S. J., had outlived his usefulness. What serial killer in his cunning right mind attempts a murder in a locked jail cell?"

No one knew where Jowell had gone, but Heather had an idea. The Francis Bacon exhibit at the High closed tomorrow and moved across country to a museum—Heather could not remember its name—in the San Francisco Bay Area. This fact struck her as suggestive. Lingenfelter pondered it for about thirty seconds and then scrawled a message on his notepad: **Need to rest.**

Although his doctors had advised him not to, on Sunday Lingenfelter attended Chick Morrow's funeral. He sat with Lorna Riley in a pew reserved for close friends of the deceased, but he could not stop thinking of a melancholy Lily Tomlin observation: *"We're all in this alone."* So far as Lingenfelter knew, no one had ever ripped off this clever remark and submitted it to "The Squawk Box."

The young priest officiating at the service did his earnest best to contradict both this unspoken sentiment and the artist Francis Bacon's love affair with portraits of caged and screaming popes. He exuded humility and calm. Some of his serenity passed into Lingenfelter. After all, Chick Morrow had considered Lingenfelter a friend, Lorna Riley had invited him to come, and not one mourner looked at him as if his presence in any way profaned these rites.

An alien thought—a squawklike saying—struggled to rise into Lingenfelter's consciousness. He could tell by its alien edge that it had originated elsewhere—in the troubled, alcoholic depths of Francis Bacon's own personality, in fact. At length he had this terrible epigram firm and entire in his head: *"I always think of friendship as where two people can really tear each other to pieces."* Lingenfelter's mouth opened in awe and horror.

Lorna Riley nudged him and whispered, "What's wrong, Harry?"

Lingenfelter tried to tell her, but all that he heard escaping his lips was a hideous, inarticulate squawk.

* * *

Sequel on Skorpiós

i

YESHUA HAS DIED, AN OLD MAN WITH TANGLED NOSE hairs and rotten teeth. I place two of Caesar's denarri on his eyes, to blind his death-stare. Soon, in this Ionian island's fierce heat, his body will release the first odors of its corruption.

Many people believe that Yeshua died forty years ago on a cross on Skull Mount outside Jerusalem. Many others believe that two days later he rose from his tomb, not as a ghost but as a death-changed cutting of God's selfsame vine. In truth, Yeshua did not die on that cross, and so had no call to come alive again. Our plot entailed bribing two Roman soldiers and so much risk to so many others that even now I marvel that we accomplished it.

In our hovel on Skorpiós, the dead Yeshua hardly resembles the young rabbi whom the soldiers scourged that day, pressing a mock crown onto his head and scarring his back with flails. The crown's thorns and those flails dripped with an opiate I had boiled out of a wilderness lichen. This substance helped Yeshua endure the pain of crucifixion and lapse by the gradual slowing of his heart into a limpness akin to death.

One bribed soldier argued against breaking Yeshua's legs. "He's gone," he said. "Why waste more effort on him?" When another legionary crowed, "For the fun of it," our soldier, to stymie a worse

89

assault, stabbed Yeshua under the ribs with his spear, delivering another dose of opiate. This sustained his deathlike slumber until Sunday morning.

But on Friday evening, Joseph of Arimathea came with an ox cart and several women to Skull Mount, to take Yeshua from the cross. I also came, in woman's garb, and wrestled him into the cart. Later, I carried him into the garden tomb. After I laid him out there, Mary, Mary of Magdala, and Joanna massaged his body with spices and bound him in clean linen strips.

Tonight Yeshua's aged corpse has none of his younger self's poignant beauty. (What foolishness, attempting to reform the corrupt Judean religion by shamming a death and a return!) In its fleeing slumber, his crucified body had appeared ready to soar out of itself on viewless wings. How did so lovely a man dwindle into this grizzled wreck?

In this wise:

On that long-ago Sunday, Joseph and I crept into the tomb through a hidden tunnel. When Yeshua awoke, we unwrapped his body, robed him, and led him back out to a juniper grove several hundred paces away. From there, Yeshua fled, at length reaching Nazareth in Galilee. Meanwhile, some soldiers moved the tomb's stone (for a rumor had spread, that someone would steal the body) and found nothing inside but Yeshua's discarded wrappings.

Later, on a Galilean mountain where the rabbi had given his most famous sermon, we feigned a resurrection event. Even more people believed. When the Romans came to investigate, Yeshua and I hiked to Tyre and boarded a Greek merchant ship, yielding the preaching of his gospel to an army of beloved dupes.

ii

Cephas, the brothers Boanerges, the man once named Saul, and many others carried our false good tidings (believing them implicitly) to the Gentiles, to every major city on the jagged northern shore of the Middle Sea. Soon, colonies of Christ followers pocked the coastlands, suffering the scorn of pagan neighbors but infecting many others with belief. Yeshua, whom some of these evangels would have recognized even in disguise, avoided his old comrades.

We settled in a small village on Skorpiós. I made and sold rare medicines. Yeshua carpentered or fished. He nearly undid us, though, by urging baptism on amazed pagans and casting his cryptic parables before them like pearls.

And then a fishing accident left Yeshua unable to move any

body part but his eyes. If God had chosen Yeshua (as Yeshua had always said, even during our Passover ruse), why had this paralyzing injury befallen him? I could not believe that God would so cruelly humble his anointed son, but my affection for Yeshua led me to serve him as physician and slave. I fed and cleaned him, turned him to keep him from growing pallet sores. Beyond assisting in his lie, though, what had I done to render myself this imposter's keeper?

Observing me at work, an islander asked me why I did not abandon Yeshua and return to Palestine. I recalled Yeshua's admonitions to visit the sick, to go to the prisoner, and I stayed. The plealess dignity of his gaze also spoke to me. Heal yourself, I silently begged him. Meanwhile, my ministry to him stretched into years. Often I prayed that he would die. His eyes, though, kept me from denying him food, or the solacing rubdown, or the occasional clumsy story.

Travelers to our village sometimes told me of the spread throughout Asia Minor, Greece, and Italy of a queer Judean sect trumpeting a savior who had died but who now lived again as an emblem of eternal hope. I said nothing in contradiction, even though the savior himself, eating and eliminating, mocked this hope every time I rubbed ointment on his sores or added fresh ticking to his pallet. My faith in the man had died long ago, even before the accident at sea.

iii

This morning, in his seventy-third or -fourth year, long after most other chronic invalids have passed on, Yeshua in fact died. I have leisure to write. The dead do not rise. Even worse, God does not preside.

Yeshua's corpse, its aroma unbearably high, sits propped against the parapet in mute witness to God's silence. I should bury the man, but the act has no urgency for me, even in this heat. Does it matter that our lives have no follow-on, that we sleep rather than soar? Tonight, as Yeshua's corruption rises, mere oblivion seems a gift.

iv

God forgive me, I burned him on the beach. I made an oven of stones and torched his tenantless body. The smoke climbed both sweet and foul into the evening sky. His skull failed to burn. More disturbing to me, so did his heart.

If only in the here and now we have hope in Yeshua, we who

loved him constitute the most pitiable people on earth—as I, a slave in bondage to a lie partly of my own devising, have known for years. And now

coda

Yeshua has appeared to me. Without even opening a door, he stood before the table in my hovel cupping his unburnt heart in his hands. He laid the heart on my table. He looked like an old man, but an old man in perfect health with a strange bronze nimbus about him. He said to me, after years of invalid muteness, "Congratulations, Lebbeus," and vanished as startlingly as he had come.

I do not know what this means. But Yeshua's heart still rests on my table, and I did not visit the beach to fetch it here. (Nor have I gone mad, like those from whom Yeshua once evicted demons.) Meanwhile, his heart smells sweet, less like braised flesh than new roses, and what I begin to know is that I must open my own to its fragrance.

* * *

Murder on Lupozny Station

with Gerald W. Page

ALIVE, THE MAN HAD UNDOUBTEDLY INTIMIDATED his subordinates—a heavy-browed colossus of a stationmaster, with a muscular upper torso and hands like iron pincers. Now he lay face-down on the floor of his private quarters aboard Lupozny Station, light-years from the "civilized" worlds of the Ecumos Confederacy. The blood that had spilled across the floor from the wound near his heart put me in mind of cooling lava, for the emotional vulcanism that had powered Frederick Lupozny's life seemed far from extinguished. In falling and lurching forward, his second-in-command had discovered, the stationmaster had bent the haft of the knife that his unknown assailant had plunged into him. His right hand, meanwhile, was still outstretched toward an object that lay only centimeters from his fingertips: a small, old-fashioned telescope.

Two hours ago, summoned from the aft astrogational room, Chaish Qu'chosh and I had set eyes on Lupozny Station for the first time. We had seen it from the positive-space conning module of the light-skater E.C.S. *Baidarka*, of which my tall alien dyadmate and I were then new crew members. This ship, under our guidance, had just emerged from the medium of faster-than-light travel that veteran skaters refer to as Black Ice; and there on our forward screens, glowing against the inky backdrop of normal space like so many incandescent coals and flinders, were the central cylinder, and the closely orbiting storage canisters of Lupozny Station.

Those canisters, Captain Ishmaela Sang told us, housed the nickel, iron, molybdenum, and various other ores dug by Lupozny's miners from the errant asteroids constituting the entire solar retinue of Anless 32, a small and lukewarm star. It was this ore that the *Baidarka* had come to pick up and to haul back to the Twin Ruby system and the factory world of Greater Bethlehem. But, by a coincidence which Captain Sang deplored, we had arrived at the station an hour or so after an unfortunate incident that would probably delay our enterprise.

"Someone over there has murdered the stationmaster," Captain Sang said, swiveling distractedly in her conning chair. "The facility's second-in-command, a man named Sinclair Toombs, wants an impartial party from the *Baidarka* to evaluate the matter. He thinks he's found the murderer, but until he has the support of a disinterested outsider or two, he's not going to rest easy. Ecumos is likely to view everyone over there as a suspect, and Toombs is anxious for the heat to be off. He wants you to begin."

"Us?" I said, looking warily to Chaish Qu'chosh.

"Why not, Mr. Detchemendy?" Captain Sang replied, ceasing to swivel. "Have you no faith in your powers? Chaish and you are an astrogational dyad, the *Baidarka*'s skategrace."

"But this was our first actual—"

"No matter," Captain Sang interrupted me. "Your judgments, once shared and reconciled, give you an advantage over mere human and chode mortals. Or should." She smiled slyly. "Go over to Lupozny Station and help poor Toombs."

Chaish and I exchanged a glance. A dance of phosphenes— "stars," say human beings who see them after receiving a blow to the head—told me that Chaish Qu'chosh had triggered them in my brain and retinas by means of an electromagnetic emission similar to those used by electric eels as a sense system. I nodded at Chaish, bowed to Captain Sang, and led my towering dyadmate out of the conning module to the *Baidarka*'s spaceboat bay.

Murder? Chaish signaled me. **One of your kind has killed —taken the life of—another member of your species?**

Preoccupied, I didn't reply.

But let me explain: The chode purposely trigger phosphene patterns in one another's optical fields. These quasi-visual phenomena, in fact, constitute their "language," and their people have distinguished among forty-eight different naturally occurring or electromagnetically provocable categories of phosphenes (more than three times the number originally detected by human researchers)· quivering plaids, translucent snowflake characters, pinwheels, complicated moiré effects. For all of these the chode have either assigned specific meanings or deduced certain absolute innate meanings. In human circles, in fact, some say that their people are busily working out the secret code of the cosmos itself. Maybe. Maybe not. During our dyadship, Chaish never made any claim to Ultimate Knowledge, and it may have been my imagination leading me to suspect that she was remorselessly on its trail.

During the three Earth-standard years in which Chaish Qu'chosh and Raymond Detchemendy trained to be dyadmates, her human partner learned the complex symbology of the phosphenes she transmitted; she, in turn, learned the phonetic patterns of three different human languages. Her task was the more difficult. Chode from widely separated regions of their home world —which human beings call Voshlai, in the Suhail system—are instantly able to communicate, unless physiologically or emotionally powerless to trigger phosphenes in others, an extremely rare disability. The meanings of phosphene patterns are universal on Voshlai, and even the blind among the chode are able to see and interpret them—for their "language," although often stimulated from without, originates from within. Human beings, I should add, can see phosphenes by closing their eyes and vigorously but carefully rubbing their eyeballs.

"Chaish Qu'chosh," by the way, is an arbitrary phonetic transliteration of the phosphene pattern by which my dyadmate invariably referred to herself. Assigning different sound values to the characters comprising her name, we could just as easily call her "Pob Ra'pib" or "Blej Lu'blaij."

In a matter of minutes our spaceboat closed the distance between the *Baidarka* and Lupozny Station, which orbits Anless 32 almost at the outer edge of that star's feeble gravitational influence. The system's ore-bearing asteroids inscribe their crazy ellipses much closer in, darting like mercurial fish.

As Captain Sang had said, Chaish and I were a skategrace. We had just brought an interstellar vessel across Black Ice for the first time in our joint career, only to find that Frederick Lupozny's murder had upstaged our performance. No chance to celebrate our accomplishment. Of course, had we failed, the *Baidarka* would have been frozen forever in The Ice.

A dyad skategrace is the soul of a faster-than-light vessel. Early on, when ships were first tentatively easing themselves out of positive space into the translight regions, their crews fell into a state of unconsciousness akin to death. Only ships whose contingents had a particularly quick-thinking captain, or crew members less immediately susceptible to the siren song of The Ice, were able to return. Therefore, interstellar travel took place at sublight speeds and "skating" remained an untested theoretical possibility—except, of course, by a few stalwart or addlepated captains who risked everything for a breakthrough.

Sheer serendipity came to the rescue. Aboard the freighter E.C.S. *Osprey*, nearly ninety years ago, were a human astrogator and a chode auxiliary pilot who had grown up together on Voshlai. They had been raised in the consciousness-sharing tenets of a sect called, by Ecumos demographers, Essencialism, a sect lightly regarded even by many of the chode, if regarded at all. No matter. On their fourth or fifth cruise, in a linkage as much philosophical as physiological, the human astrogator and the chode pilot survived the *Osprey*'s accidental side-slip into the wastes of Black Ice. Wholly awake, they exercised their complimentary talents not only to lift their ship free of danger but to skate across the gelid subtemporal blackness to their home world, Voshlai. In only two hours of feverish activity, they had guided the *Osprey* a distance of three light-years.

This unlikely pair, then, was the first dyad, and Ecumos took their serendipitous triumph to heart. Within a year training programs had been instituted on five different Confederacy worlds, including Voshlai itself, Earth, and Greater Bethlehem; within a decade the sublight mercantile and military vessels of the Confederacy had all become, with very little design or technological alteration, "light-skaters."

Chaish and I were one astrogational dyad out of five thousand, give or take a hundred or so. Nevertheless, considering a total E.C. population of better than one trillion, we were sufficiently uncommon that I viewed my partner and me as a splendid *rara avis*. I tremendously resented the fact that Frederick Lupozny had got himself murdered just in time to ruin our maiden run across The Ice. I was forty-four at the time, old for the human half of a skategrace; and because Chaish was approaching the chode equivalency of middle years, I was hungry for all the glory that our past lives had deferred.

Our spaceboat entered the hangar in the bay perpendicular to the cylinder of Lupozny Station, and we waited for the air pressure to equalize with that of the station itself. Although both Chaish and I were wearing suits, neither of us cared to exit into near vacuum. Fortunately, we didn't have to.

"Have you touched the body since you found it?" I asked Sinclair Toombs, a lean, gray-eyed man of about my own age.

"Of course—to examine the wound. The knife is from Lupozny's desk. So is the telescope. Our stationmaster enjoyed surrounding himself with mementos from his career."

"The telescope?" I asked, nodding at it. "Does it function?"

"It's strictly for amateur stargazers," Toombs said, trying, without success, to look neither at Lupozny's corpse nor at Chaish Qu'chosh—who roamed the perimeters of the room like a prepossessing wraith of silver and gun-metal blue. "The captain whose skater first surveyed this system gave every crew member and passenger one of those 'scopes to remember their adventure by. Lupozny was aboard, and he brought that gadget with him when he and his partners began their operation here."

"How long ago was that?"

"About eleven years, standard reckoning."

I walked to Lupozny's feet and stared across his body and beyond. The discomfort of his living second-in-command was increasing, visibly. It seemed that the mining operation around Anless 32 was an exclusively human operation; contact with the chode was rare, and Toombs was reacting to my dyadmate's presence as if I had invited an impossible variety of dinosaur into his hermetic castle. Maybe, in a sense, I had. Sometimes I felt that, despite the occupational intimacy of our dyadship, I knew absolutely nothing about Chaish.

Toombs, however, was in sullen terror of her. His gray eyes shifted after her as she moved from Lupozny's bunk to the door of his tiny water closet to a rack of prefabricated shelving.

"What's over there?" I asked, pointing in the direction that Lupozny had fallen. All I could see beyond his outstretched right hand was a small, relatively dark corridor mouth.

"The lifeboat bays for this part of the station," Toombs answered, glad to have his attention directed away from the corpse and Chaish.

I looked back at the door by which we had entered Lupozny's quarters; there were no other entrances or exits. The station's control center, its hub, lay farther along the passage by which Toombs had directed us to the victim's room. After meeting us outside the spaceboat hangar (the station's principal airlock and primary means of access for off-board visitors), he had led us down here without even offering to introduce us to the people in the control center. At first I suspected that he feared the reaction of his associates to Chaish. Although that worry may have contributed to Toombs's brusqueness, I now began to realize that he desperately wanted his own deductions confirmed and the case taken out of his hands.

"Is Lupozny's room serviced by maintenance crawlways?" I asked.

"I know who killed him," Toombs replied testily. "You're needlessly complicating things if you think—"

I cut him off by repeating my question.

"No, it's not, Mr. Detchemendy. There aren't any maintenance crawlways on Lupozny Station. It was constructed so that we could make most of our minor, day-to-day repairs from our living and working areas. We suit up and go outside to take care of many of our problems."

"Which brings me to the lifeboats. Have you checked them since Lupozny was killed?"

"As soon after we found him as we had the chance," Toombs said wearily. "Our lifeboats—our remora craft—are all fully pressurized. No one could have entered or exited the station through a lifeboat without leaving it evacuated. If someone *had* managed to open the exterior hatch of a remora, all of its air would have blown out into the void. That just didn't happen."

Suddenly I was seeing Toombs through an ice storm of phosphenes: Chaish had encoded a question for me to put to him.

"Would your on-duty crew in the control center have seen anyone using the corridor connecting this room and the hub?"

"No question about it, Mr. Detchemendy."

"And undetected access through the only airlock at this end of the station—which would have permitted the murderer to sneak across the main passage into Lupozny's cabin—is an impossibility because the depressurization alarm would have alerted the crew. Is that another reasonable assumption, Mr. Toombs?"

"Ordinarily."

I didn't register the grudging note in this response because Chaish had seeded my field of vision with another secret blizzard: **There seems no way at all that anyone could have killed Lupozny and escaped detection,** she was declaring. In the way her message oscillated in and out of focus, I read both her bewilderment and her distaste for our enterprise.

I spoke aloud for Toombs's as well as her benefit: "We've got something of a locked-room murder on our hands. Except that our 'room' is a station in space."

"Damn it, Detchemendy, I've already told you that I know who killed Lupozny. The murderer's in custody, in fact. Don't complicate this for the sake of an imaginary challenge of your own asinine invention!" The outburst seemed to restore a measure of Toombs's confidence. "Let's talk in a vacant office, near here. I'm tired of wading back and forth through Lupozny's blood."

Although nettled by his tone, I agreed. At the door, however, I realized that Chaish had made no move to follow us. Looking back, I saw that she was squatting beside the corpse, her intricately scaled torso bent at an angle that must have struck Toombs as either hysterical or predatory.

"Hey!" he shouted.

Chaish looked up at him, and he fell back—involuntarily—from her stare. Fascinated by the man's ill-concealed horror, I tried to see my dyadmate as he saw her, as if for the first time.

Her eyes, which resembled large ball bearings, floated in a containing matter the color and consistency of mercury; they were slitted vertically by milky, diamond-shaped pupils like a poisonous snake's. On her head and upper body she appeared to be wearing iridescent mail, whose platelets flashed blue and silver. Closer scrutiny revealed that this mail was her skin: She was as naked as a newt. Her abdomen, buttocks, and upper thighs, meanwhile, were not scaled at all, but girded in a blue-gray integument like the scar tissue that forms on the backs of dark-coated animals whose fur has been stripped away by fire or boiling water. Her lower limbs were again clad in natural mail, terminating in a pair of calloused, blue-gray feet.

I let my eyes sweep back to Chaish's head. It was shaped more like an extinct hominid's than a reptile's . . . but for the bulge at the base of her brain stem. This hard but movable lump housed an evolutionary-directed extrusion of gray matter from the cerebral lobes above it. In front this bulge was mimicked by a loose, shimmering throat sac whose principal function among the chode seems to be as a sexual signal. And on both sides of Chaish's head, where a human being would have ears, were those horizontal strips of bright violet flesh that anatomists call "respiration ribbons."

No wonder Chaish had disrupted the already well-battered control of poor Sinclair Toombs.

"Get away from the body," he said, his voice quavering.

Chaish ignored him. She gripped Lupozny firmly by the shoulders and pulled him over to his back, revealing the bent haft of the knife. With her left hand (only four digits, but immense ones) she pulled the knife out. Then, letting the blade dangle between her two middle fingers, she rose and approached the door. Toombs pushed past me into the station's central corridor.

If they have a scanning electron microscope in their assay room, Chaish told me, **they could check the haft for fingerprints.**

I relayed this suggestion to Toombs, who urged Chaish to go to the control center and to give the weapon to Synnöva Helmuth, the station's assayer and metallurgist. Toombs shouted a series of instructions at the control center, telling Helmuth precisely what she must do with the knife. Helmuth came forward a few steps from the consoles up that way, and Chaish strolled nonchalantly toward her, bearing the bloody, outsized bodkin.

"Neat," I told Toombs. "You get Chaish briefly out of the way and likewise ensure a thorough examination of the knife."

"He makes me nervous," Toombs confessed.

"She," I corrected him.

"*Chode* make me nervous. Irrational, maybe—but there it is. I've done nothing to be ashamed of, but that one—just the way she moved around Lupozny's room was an accusation."

I finally said what I had been thinking ever since Chaish had first looked down on the stationmaster's corpse: "They don't kill their own kind, Mr. Toombs. That ancient rumor is true: The chode don't take one another's lives."

Toombs gave me an incredulous moue. "Never?"

"Never," I echoed him. "Not for vengeance, or profit, or meanness, or mercy. Self-defense is never even an issue among them."

"Let's go in here," Toombs said, gesturing me into a nearby room and bemusedly shaking his head.

The room into which Sinclair Toombs directed me was small, clean, and bleak. It contained a metal desk and three metal chairs, all bolted down against the unlikely prospect of a failure of the station's artificial-gravity generators.

"One of Lupozny's partners maintained an office here," Toombs said, sitting down behind the desk. "Back in the days when Lupozny had partners, that is. No one's used it in years."

I eased myself into one of the metal chairs. "How many unused rooms are there in this part of the station?"

"This is the only one. If you're trying to imply that someone might have hidden in here after killing Lupozny and then slipped out again, you're prospecting barren rock."

"Why?"

"We've accounted for the whereabouts of everyone aboard the station during the time that the murder had to occur. Besides, the people at the control center never saw anyone in this corridor."

"Who's your murderer, then?"

Toombs cocked his head to one side. "You may not believe this, but Lupozny himself told me."

"Lupozny?"

Toombs's lean face revolved toward me; his eyes, glittering, intercepted mine. "Let's just say that even toppling face-forward to his death, he was mean enough—just sufficiently cagey-mean, Mr. Detchemendy—to want to pin his murder on the appropriate party. That's how and why he managed to leave us a clue."

"The telescope?"

The new stationmaster nodded.

"Just who does that point to, Mr. Toombs?"

"Listen: Here was the situation just before the *Baidarka* emerged from Black Ice. All but four of us were in the control center. We're working with minimal staffing because Lupozny could never stomach the expense of an adequate payroll. As for our mining crews, they're either out among The Rocks or manning the far-side fetch station."

"Which four weren't in the control center?"

"Not counting Lupozny, who'd given us instructions not to disturb him until the *Baidarka* arrived, only Misha Block, Corcoran Skolits, and me."

"Alibis?"

Toombs raised his right eyebrow. "I was in my office on the other side of the control center, sweating over the cargo-release forms you'll be taking with you when you leave."

"What about Misha Block and—?" The other name had escaped me.

"Skolits. He's a journeyman asteroid miner, long in the company's employ. He came into the spaceboat hangar several hours ago with a partial load. His was the other craft you saw in there when you and your dyadmate arrived aboard the station."

"He didn't report immediately to the control center?"

"No. Just off the hangar, through a small accessway, is a recuperation facility for incoming miners. It's not unusual for them to shed their suits, shower, and settle in for a well-deserved rest.

Skolits had been out prowling about nineteen hours. In any case, once aboard, we always knew where he was; he couldn't have been anywhere else."

"All right. That leaves this person Block."

"Misha's the station's astronomer and remora-craft controller." Toombs lofted this statement into the air like a target balloon.

"You think the telescope was Lupozny's way of fingering the station's astronomer — is that it?"

"That's the obvious interpretation, but there's more. You see —"

"Wait a minute. Before you slip the noose around Misha Block's neck, how did you discover that Lupozny was dead? You seem to enjoy springing the gallows trap even before you've produced a body."

Toombs stood up. "Listen, Detchemendy, you've *seen* the goddamn body!"

"Tell me how you found it."

Up and down at the pit of his stomach Toombs shook one of his gourdlike fists. "When the *Baidarka* broke through The Ice," he began angrily, "Hans Verschuur, our communications officer, tried to notify Lupozny of your arrival. Lupozny didn't answer. So Verschuur got in touch with me; and I tried to summon the stationmaster. Still no response." Toombs's oscillating fist continued to accent his story. "I went to the control center and found Skolits talking with Synnöva Helmuth about an ore sample he'd brought in."

"Skolits? I thought he was in the recuperation facility by the lifeboat hangar."

"He *had* been." Willfully asserting control, Toombs halted his shaking fist. "He had been. But he'd come in from the lounge to check in formally and present a sample of his partial load. I asked him and Helmuth to go with me down the central corridor to Lupozny's quarters. The stationmaster's door was locked . . . from the inside. I had to ask Loraine Block, our computer officer, to countermand the lock from her console in the hub. When Skolits, Helmuth, and I finally entered the room, we found Lupozny just as you've seen him."

"Loraine Block? This is your astronomer's wife, I take it. Misha and she have an old-fashioned marriage contract?" I was surprised. You found very few couples, either het or isoclinic, who did. Toombs sat down again. He turned toward the wall, giving me his hard, lupine face in profile. "Yes, an old-fashioned marriage contract," he said tonelessly. "That's important. Misha and Loraine aren't giddy adolescents; in fact, they're both in their thirties. But. . . ."

"But what?"

"But they're genuinely, passionately in love with each other. In my experience that's a rare thing. And that's why Misha killed Frederick Lupozny."

"Because Misha loved his wife?"

"Because, Mr. Detchemendy, about a month ago—" Toombs turned toward me again, almost accusatively "—Lupozny escorted Loraine Block to his cabin, supposedly so that she could make a series of minor repairs to an auxiliary personnel computer. Once there, however, he took her."

"Took her?"

"Carnally. Against her will. But it happened behind closed doors, Loraine's word against Lupozny's, and the tension aboard this station has been close to unbearable ever since. Because Misha believed his wife—I do, too, for that matter—he made sure that the story of her violation reached everyone from his own point of view. Of late we've been especially jittery because three or four days ago Misha and Lupozny almost came to blows in the observatory."

I said nothing.

"Even in the best of times," Toombs went on, unbidden, "Lupozny had a way of keeping everybody pushed right to the edge. He was demanding, arbitrary, egotistical, insecure, physically intimidating. On the other hand, he could go weeks—or several days, anyway—exuding a low-key sweetness that scared the living shit out of us. The hell of it is, Mr. Detchemendy, any one of us aboard this station could have killed that man. Misha Block just happened to be the one to do it. The rape of Loraine, and Misha's preoccupation with it even after Lupozny had apparently bought them both off with apologies and bonuses, finally pushed him over the edge."

I was growing more and more uncomfortable. For three years, back on Middlesaint in the Menkent system, my contacts with other human beings had been rare and meager in content. So cloistered had been our skategrace training, in fact, that Chaish and I had often gone three or four months without seeing anyone but our dyad mentor and a few other uncommunicative chode-and-human pairs in collateral skategrace programs. Now, it seemed, Sinclair Toombs was mercilessly reacquainting me with the unique and persistent follies of my kind.

"How does your station's crew abide it here?" I asked.

"Most of us are on one-year contracts. That gives us the sensation that our sufferings are finite. Besides, once you get *on* the payroll, the money isn't bad. Since there's nothing much to spend it for out here, it steadily accumulates for us on our home worlds."

"Do people ever choose to renew their contracts?"

"I'm on my second year. Not many of the station personnel work beyond their initial contracts, though. Miners are more likely to opt for contract extensions, primarily because they don't have to put up with the abusive, demoralizing guff that Lupozny plied."

"How long have the Blocks been working here?"

"Seven months."

I tacked about: "Does Lupozny's death elevate you to his position in the company?"

"It elevates me to acting stationmaster," Toombs replied angrily, his right hand again tightening into a fist. "I'm an employee, Mr. Detchemendy, not a business partner or a shareholder. An *employee!*"

A veil of phosphene characters fell between Toombs and me, and I realized that Chaish had returned from the control center with Synnöva Helmuth.

The knife haft reveals a number of Lupozny's own smeared fingerprints.

As my dyadmate and the station's assay officer entered the tiny room, I stood up. Toombs also stood, gamely struggling to demonstrate that Chaish's presence did not disturb him. He was folded as many ways as a paper finger puppet.

"Nothing else?" I asked, after nodding curtly at Helmuth.

Perhaps the wear pattern of a glove. The assay officer probably has very little experience making such determinations.

I turned and told Toombs what Chaish had just said. He looked to Helmuth for confirmation, and she, somewhat bewilderedly, supplied it. They may have believed that Chaish had spoken with me telepathically, mind to mind, when the truth was in many ways stranger and more complex. Recovering, Toombs commenced a round of introductions, for Helmuth still did not know Chaish's name and recognized me only as the chode's anonymous human associate from the *Baidarka*. She was a trim, silver-blonde woman with a generous nose and chaffinch-quick eyes.

"Glove markings on the knife haft?" Toombs asked her, motioning her to one of the bolted-down chairs. "Are you sure?"

"I've got to get back," she said, declining the invitation to sit. "No, I'm not sure—but the oily micropattern on the haft suggests that some kind of flexible material effaced some of Mr. Lupozny's old fingerprints and badly smeared several others. It *might* be the synthetic fabric of a spacesuit's glove that did that, but it's hard to be positive."

"As far as I'm concerned," Toombs said, looking at me, "that's corroborating evidence. It points directly to Misha Block." Synnöva Helmuth nodded deferentially at Chaish and me and disappeared with a sprightly step into the corridor. My dyadmate, meanwhile, stationed herself to the right of Toombs's desk like a piece of painted statuary. Her mail shone almost blindingly in the cold, flat light.

"If Block's your murderer," I asked, "how did he get into and out of Lupozny's room undetected?"

"He had help," Toombs replied, glancing warily at Chaish. "Misha claims he was in the observatory developing some photographs, the sort we use to find and spectrographically evaluate asteroids. Really, though, he was putting on a vacuum suit and preparing to murder Frederick Lupozny. He let himself into the auxiliary airlock near the observatory, went out through it onto the station's hull, and walked forward to the auxiliary airlock just beyond Lupozny's room. From there it was a quick dash across a small section of corridor into the stationmaster's cabin. Block took his revenge on Lupozny and returned to the observatory the same way he had come." Toombs vibrated his right fist for emphasis. "Helmuth's electron-microscope scan of the knife haft supports this chain of reasoning. The murderer was wearing gloves, you see—the gloves from a spacesuit."

What about the airlock alarms? Chaish asked. **Would not they have sounded?**

I put these questions to Toombs.

"Ordinarily, yes. But Misha and Loraine Block were acting in concert. When Misha first climbed onto the hull, Loraine intercepted the alarm trigger at her console in the hub, through which almost every function of the station can be monitored—even locking and unlocking the doors of our people's private cabins. That's a capability upon which Lupozny had insisted when this station was built, not even exempting his own quarters. In any event, because Misha left both the observatory airlock and the airlock near Lupozny's room depressurized after exiting them, Loraine—again from the master console—activated the appropriate pumps to restore airlock pressurization. Those actions effectively covered her husband's tracks."

"Not if you managed to see through them," I countered, annoyed by Toombs's smug omniscience. "Where are Misha and Loraine Block now?"

"Under house arrest in their quarters, Misha for premeditated murder and Loraine for aiding and abetting him. If you come to agree with me, I hope you'll take the Blocks aboard the *Baidarka* for conveyance to the proper Ecumos authorities. I just want to be rid of the matter, Mr. Detchemendy."

Would a murderer take himself into the territory of an intended victim without carrying a weapon? Chaish asked.

Rephrasing the query, I conveyed it to Toombs.

For a brief moment he looked taken aback. Then he said, "Everyone knew that Lupozny kept that knife on his desk. Misha has no discretion, no real self-control—but he's very smart. Killing a man with his own weapon obviates the necessity of securing one of your own and then trying to dispose of it."

"You have it all figured out, don't you?"

Toombs turned away, showing me his haggard profile. "I'm sick of this business. I want it to be over."

"Let me talk to Loraine Block," I said.

The interview with Misha Block's "partner in crime" (if you accepted the new stationmaster's interpretation of events) took place in a room well away from the murder site; it gave off the main corridor beyond the hub of the station, not too far from the observatory.

In fact, it was Toombs's own office, a cubicle appointed with lime-green vinyl flooring, models of interstellar ships, baroque specimens of ore on wooden stands, and a gallery of hologramic portraits, apparently of members of Toombs's family. The cargo-release forms on which he had been working several hours ago were still on his desk.

As for Lupozny, the dead man, a crew consisting of Chaish, Hans Verschuur, and me had helped Toombs remove the corpse to a cold coffin, in which we would transfer him to the *Baidarka*. Although death had pretty obviously resulted from the stabbing, our shipboard physicians would perform an autopsy to see if there were any incongruous foreign substances in his blood. We also intended to send over the contents of Lupozny's medicine cabinet for analysis. Considering the locked-room peculiarities attending his death, it wasn't altogether impossible that Lupozny had committed suicide and for eccentrically spiteful reasons of his own *disguised it as a murder.* Toombs dismissed this over-clever hypothesis out of hand, nor did I really seriously credit it—but Captain Sang had wanted her investigating dyad to put a skeptical T-square to every angle, and so the body, along with a box of harmless-looking medications and toilet articles, awaited shipment to the *Baidarka* in the bleak little room adjacent to the murder site.

Where the body had lain, bright green-yellow chalk marks outlined the man's attitude in death. Another vivid chalk loop showed where the telescope had fallen.

Now Chaish and I were awaiting Loraine Block in a cluttered room almost at the other end of the station.

Soon Synnöva Helmuth escorted Loraine Block in to us, dropping her off in the same affectionate, distracted way a parent deposits a child at school. Helmuth, at least, did not regard Chaish and me as threats. That was comforting, for Toombs had been peevishly reluctant to let us interview Loraine Block in his absence. Finally I had asked him point-blank if he feared the outcome of such an interview, and he had angrily acceded to our demand, knowing that he had no other choice.

Loraine Block seemed, at first glance, a beautiful child-woman. Small in stature, she wore her dark hair long, clasped at the nape in a butterfly barrette. Both Chaish and I towered over her, a fact to which she was wholly indifferent. More remarkable, she was unperturbed by the presence of a chode.

I pointed this petite computer officer to the swivel chair behind Toombs's desk, and when she sat, she ceased to convey the vulnerable daintiness of a child. I made brief introductions.

"I can answer your first question without your even having to ask it," she said. "Shall I do that?"

"Go ahead," I urged her.

"No, I definitely didn't intercept the airlock pressurization alarms at my computer console." She paused. "What's my prescience quota?"

"Did your husband kill Lupozny?"

Mildly piqued that I hadn't accepted her gambit, she again turned her attention to Chaish, who, partially concealed by a microfiche cabinet, radiated satiny glints of silver and blue, her eyes like melting mirrors.

"You're a lovely representative of your people," Loraine Block told her. "Misha and I once had a brief stopover on your world— Voshlai, that is; not a colony—when we were employed by the Ecumos freighter *Newfoundland* eight years ago." She looked back at me. "No, Misha didn't kill our stationmaster. My husband was in the observatory when the murder apparently occurred. He *might* have killed Lupozny, given half a chance—but that chance never presented itself, and after he got into a stupid scuffle with Lupozny a few days ago, I warned him that he was jeopardizing everything we've worked for out here."

"Which is what?"

"The chance to visit as many different inhabited solar systems as we can. That's always been our life's goal together."

I stared intently at the demoralizing lime-green floor. "Lupozny raped you?"

"Yes."

"Did you hate him?"

"Despised him. But I had despised him *before* he raped me, Mr. Detchemendy. After it happened, I. . . ." Her voice trailed off.

"You told Misha."

She ignored this. "He used his size to overpower me. It was as if he were manipulating a doll. I think he would have derived as much joy from his own clenched fist. It certainly wasn't an erotic impulse that prompted his assault."

"What, then? A desire to humiliate?" I looked up.

"Partially," she replied. "A more compelling motive, though, was his need to reaffirm his authority over everyone aboard this station. I think his real target was Sinclair Toombs."

"Raping you was a slap at Sinclair Toombs?" Behind Loraine Block, the new stationmaster's family smiled down on Chaish and me from the hologramic gallery on the wall: a woman, two children, and a set of gracefully aging parents or in-laws.

"I think it was. Mr. Toombs—with admirable discretion—has invited me to bed with him on three or four different occasions. Unlike Lupozny, he was—maybe he still is—truly taken with me. Or maybe he just envied my relationship with Misha and hoped to share in it in some silly, even harmless way—by making love to me. In any case, Lupozny picked up on his longing. And Toombs irritated Lupozny with his efficiency, his ability to stay on top of matters that had slipped Lupozny's own notice. Because Lupozny's sexual wiring was basically isoclinic—same-to-same, you understand—I think he raped me as a complicated sort of rebuke to Toombs. Any humiliation to me was incidental."

"If Lupozny picked up on Toombs's longing, what about Misha? Did he?"

"Never."

"Why not?"

"He's absorbed in either me or his astronomy, not much else. And Toombs, as I said, was always discreet."

"How did Toombs behave when you refused him?"

"How is anybody supposed to behave when unequivocally rejected? I don't think he *liked* it. He usually just smiled. He certainly didn't shout or throw things."

"Do you think he's trying to frame you and Misha?"

"It's a definite possibility, isn't it?" Loraine Block smiled.

Why? Chaish suddenly asked.

I turned to her. "Toombs may be attempting to punish Loraine for refusing him."

Why does he also seek to punish Misha?

"Out of envy," I hazarded. "None of this is certain, Chaish. We're exploring the possibilities."

Even though I anticipated another brief flurry of phosphenes, Chaish simply stared at me.

"I know how you two communicate," Loraine Block suddenly said. "Crystals of inner light. Your companion generates them out of your own brain and optical equipment. Misha and I tried to acquaint ourselves with the phenomenon when we were on Voshlai. We attended a mechanical simulation—projections on a wall—in a visitor's temple outside a northern lake city. But I've never seen the real thing."

"You'd like to?"

"Very much—if it's possible."

Chaish, understanding, glided forward and squatted purposefully before Loraine Block. The transmission of phosphene images requires that the chode have a mental fix on the retinas of any potential communicant, as well as some small handle on her frame of mind. Chaish was attempting to secure these things, probing to locate Loraine's foveae in order to transmit an electromagnetic signal into their sensitive depressions and so from there to the young woman's brain. The rebounding of this signal along the foveal tracks would, in turn, create the "crystals of inner light" which Loraine wanted to see. Later, more familiar with her subject, Chaish would be able to beam this encoded signal straight to the visual cortex.

A moment later Loraine Block had seen her gentle explosion of phosphenes. She blinked and put the heels of her hands to her eyes. Chaish returned to her corner.

"Lovely." The computer officer lowered her hands. "Just lovely."

I watched the beatific expression on Loraine Block's face dissolve into one of bewilderment. She turned to me.

"But it's all abstract patterns and floating lacework. Are you really able to interpret it?"

"Sure—but there's three years of sweat, hypnopedia, and mental anguish in that accomplishment."

Lifting her chin, she looked to Chaish. "Please tell Mr. Detchemendy what you've just told me. Please. So that he can translate it for me."

After Chaish had regaled me with the same message, I relayed it —in English—to Loraine: " 'I wish for you and Misha all anticipated fulfillment of your life's plan, that and a great deal more.' "

Then I said, "Tell me who was in the control room with you when you were supposedly intercepting airlock alarms for your husband."

"Hans Verschuur," she responded readily enough. "And Daphne Kaunas, the life-systems officer. Synnöva was there, too, of course. And Corcoran Skolits, the pilot of a mining boat, was talking with Synnöva about something he'd found during his work shift among The Rocks. They're pretty good friends, those two."

"Was Skolits there the entire time?"

"I don't know what you mean by 'entire time'—he came into the control center about twenty minutes before the *Baidarka* arrived. All hell broke loose when Hans was unable to rouse Lupozny."

"From which direction did Skolits enter the control center?"

"The only way he could—from the access corridor to the spaceboat hangar, the same way you and Chaish did."

"There was no way he could slip down to Lupozny's quarters without being seen by the personnel in the hub?"

"Everyone saw you, didn't they?"

"Just long enough to nod or wave. Toombs hustled us down there before we could even say hello."

"But you were seen?"

"Yes," I admitted. "Everyone gawked."

Loraine Block absentmindedly examined one of Sinclair Toombs's light-skater models, then blinked and said, "I don't know who killed Frederick Lupozny. It's hard for me to see how any of us could have done it. What I do know is this: I intercepted no airlock alarms, and Misha didn't kill the bastard. That's my story."

"Tell me about Corcoran Skolits."

"I don't know anything about Corcoran Skolits." Loraine Block shrugged dismissively. "Only that he's in and out of the station at odd intervals and that he's an old hand out here."

"Anything else?" I waited, expecting nothing.

"Oh, yes," Loraine Block said with a small surge of enthusiasm. "Oddly enough, Skolits is something of a pocket expert on the chode. It's his pet avocation. I once overheard him tell Synnöva that as a boy he had hoped to be the human half of a skategrace."

Chaish, noncommittal, sent me no excited or disbelieving snowfalls. Her calm was almost admonitory.

When Toombs returned to his office, I told him that I wanted to talk with Corcoran Skolits. This request plainly annoyed him. He heaved himself into his swivel chair and banged his right hand down on its padded arm.

"Talk to Misha Block instead."

"I've just talked to his wife. She said she intercepted no alarms and that your frustrated longings have disposed you to be vindictive."

Toombs continued to exercise a precarious control over his emotions. "The longings I freely acknowledge. The vindictiveness I don't. Everything points to the Blocks. Even if Loraine is ordinarily the most forthright of women, she would lie for Misha. She'd do virtually anything for him."

"Including refusing the advances of a man who wasn't her husband?"

"Talk to Misha Block, damn it! If you're such a magician at distinguishing between our illusions and our squalid realities, he'll topple to your magic touch in a goddamn nanosecond!"

"I'd rather talk to Corcoran Skolits."

"Why?" Toombs blurted, profoundly exasperated.

It would be better not to tell him, Chaish cautioned me.

Heeding this advice, I met Toombs's question with one of my own: "Isn't it true that even if Loraine Block intercepted the airlock alarms, the actual functioning of the airlocks would have registered in the memory circuits of the computer?"

"It would have, certainly—but Loraine, in turn, is smart enough to know that and to have erased the memories."

"But a good computer officer could either locate the alarm memory or tell if anyone had recently cleared the circuitry where those memories are stored?"

"Loraine Block," said Toombs wearily, "is a good computer officer, but she's under house arrest, and she's not likely to incriminate herself and her husband by untooling her own cover-ups for us."

"Then we'll send to the *Baidarka* for Françoise Loizos, our own computer officer," I told him, growing angry. "Would you have Verschuur, your communications man, ask Captain Sang to get her over here? She might as well send over our cargo master, too, so that he can supervise the loading of the ore." I turned away.

"Where are you going?" Toombs demanded.

"To visit Skolits. I assume he's back in the miners' recuperation facility near the main airlock." I waved a hand at the new stationmaster. "Don't bother to get up. Chaish and I can find it."

"Listen—" Toombs said, rising.

I turned back, my anger escaping me in a kind of hiss. "Listen, yourself. Whether from laziness or duplicity you're sitting on a pet hypothesis. So tell me something, Toombs: Did you ever have anyone check out the pressure suits in the airlock near the observatory?"

"No," he confessed, nonplused.

"Then why the hell don't you do that?"

Chaish and I exited the cluttered office. Side by side, we stalked down the dove-gray and chlorine-green corridor of Lupozny Station, a skategrace caught out in a realm of ice at least as dark as the one through which we had piloted the *Baidarka*.

Corcoran Skolits turned out to be a man of fifty or so, as leathery-skinned as a baked Newhome pear. When Chaish and I entered the miners' recuperation facility, he was sprawled shirtless across an air-divan, engrossed in an ancient vid program. Men in long-billed caps and striped pantaloons were standing half-crouched on a kelly-green field. Occasionally they lunged after a ball struck into the field by another such man wielding a bottle-shaped club.

Without looking up at us Skolits said, "They told me I couldn't leave until you'd talked to me."

"Who did?"

"Toombs, I guess. Synnöva was the one who relayed word."

Skolits neither looked at us nor invited us to sit down; he continued to watch the arcane goings-on of his vid program.

"They have a hideous crop of vids in this place," he finally said. "Lupozny bought them wholesale from a supplier working out of the Pollux backwater. 'Baseball,' this one says on the filing slip. It's really pretty amusing if you let yourself get into the play."

A group of people on benches behind a retaining wall suddenly began spilling onto the field where the men in pantaloons and caps were standing. One player bludgeoned an amok-running interloper to the grass with an elongated and pincerlike piece of leather.

"This part doesn't seem to have anything to do with scoring points," Skolits declared. "I turned down the accompanying sound because the blather of the overvoice was truly incomprehensible."

I interposed myself between the air-divan and the screen. Skolits gave me a pained look, then glanced sidelong at Chaish—whose presence he had not detected until now. Pulling himself up, he turned almost respectfully toward the chode, his baked-brown face perceptibly fading a tone. I turned off the vid program. Now a solitary fluorescent lit the miners' recuperation room, and Skolits struggled to his feet. He was wearing slippers and a pair of netherjohns with a nylon draw cord.

"You're a skategrace," he said, surprised but not dumfounded. "What are my chances of riding back to Greater Bethlehem with you aboard the *Baidarka?*"

"When does your contract with Lupozny's company expire?"

"In about two and a half standard months."

"Then you're probably stuck here at least until then. Were you hoping your contract expired with Lupozny?"

Stocky and muscular, going to flab around the middle, Skolits scuffed off a few steps in his lightweight slippers. "I knew better," he said doubtfully, plunging his hands into the seat pockets of his netherjohns. "I didn't see any harm in asking, though."

"You don't like it here?"

"Crazy about it. This is my tenth—approaching my eleventh— year. I've been here since the beginning, nearly."

"And you're tired?" I prompted him.

Skolits looked at Chaish. "Bone-tired. Deep-gut-tired." Then he smiled, a wide, glittering, disarming smile. "But two and a half months is a pretty swift sprinkle. I can stand it. It'll go by trippety-trip. And if the *Baidarka* doesn't carry me out of here, some other skater will. With some other skategrace—probably a more experienced one."

I stammered the beginnings of another question.

"I can spot novices almost immediately," Skolits interrupted. "You two don't have the attunement of a long-standing skategrace, even with all your simulator training. You're still just getting to know each other outside Honeymoon Instruction." He pointed a stubby finger at me. "Am I right?"

"This was our first interstellar crossing," I admitted.

"Another infallible way to tell," Skolits continued relentlessly, "is the eyes of the human dyadmate."

"Skolits, we'd like to ask—" I was hoping to deflect him from his path. A vain hope.

"And yours are still unclouded, just as clear and pretty as an infant's. You're not any puppy, either."

"No, I'm not." I walked away, toward the lounge's ample shower facility, its tiled walls and floors gleaming a muted and unholy maroon, then rounded on Skolits and changed the subject: "Did you like Frederick Lupozny?"

"*Like* him? Hell, no. The last person who liked Lupozny was his mother, and I wouldn't absolutely swear to that."

"Loraine Block says you've worked in the Anless system quite some time and you say since the beginning. How long, exactly?"

"Soon after Lupozny Station was built and operations began. When my latest two-and-a-half-year contract expires, though, I'll have been with the Lupozny enterprise a decade. Four contracts. No one else even *approaches* that record, Mr. Detchemendy."

"Ten years," I remarked. "Considering your opinion of Lupozny, what induced you to stick it out for so long?"

Skolits tugged sheepishly at his lower lip. "To tell you the truth, when I first came out here I was *persona non grata* with Ecumos mercantile authorities. Lupozny took me on when no one else would give me a job. I'd talked to him about a position when he was visiting his factory liaison on Greater Bethlehem, and he brought me back to Anless with him aboard the E.C.S. *Challenger*. His hiring me was contingent on my accepting a two-and-a-half-year initial contract. Once I got to work, though, I found I liked it fine—especially since a miner wasn't expected, or even permitted, to associate much with the Boss Man. That's why I kept re-upping—that and the pay."

"What first got you in trouble with Ecumos authorities?"

"Hey," Skolits said, waving his hand in annoyance. "That's prehistoric gossip. I don't even like to talk about it."

"I'd feel better if you told me."

"Sure you would." Skolits glanced nervously after Chaish, who had just stepped over the threshold of the shower room and disappeared among the gaudy maroon tiles. "Let's just say I wooleyed an Ecumos cargo master and got away with half a shipment of natural silk from Lareina II. The affair was more complicated than that, but the details don't matter. In the end, I was apprehended peddling these exotic dry goods to the go-between of a successful clothier in Bethlehem's southern capital. Justice was swift. After lockup and rehab, Corcoran Skolits—his debt supposedly paid, mind you — couldn't pick up iron filings with an electromagnet. No one wanted my services."

"Except the Greater Bethlehem representative of the Lupozny Asteroid Mining Concern, I take it."

"Yeah. That was Mr. Lupozny himself. I've never *liked* the exploitive bastard, but it's impossible not to be a little *grateful* for what he did."

"Did you kill him?"

Skolits laughed and shook his head. "Why the hell would I do that? I've got nearly ten years' money in reserve, and soon I'll be going home, back to Bethlehem. A man in my position would be an idiot to risk another lockup and rehab just because his boss had the personality of a tyrannosaurus."

I followed Chaish toward the shower room, peripherally aware that Skolits was tagging along. "Then who aboard this station had the best motive for killing Lupozny?"

"You've got me, Mr. Detchemendy. I kept my nose out of the hair-pullings and petty scandals aboard this floating tin can. Sooner or later, though, Lupozny cheated, hurt, or humiliated just about anybody he had dealings with."

Skolits enlarged upon his accusation against the dead stationmaster. He explained that when Lupozny had first opened up the Anless 32 system, after visiting it firsthand aboard the Ecumos survey ship, he had hoped to get "robber-baron rich" mining The Rocks and shipping the ore back to the refineries and mills on Greater Bethlehem. He and his two partners had formed a co-op that they believed would prosper because of the relative ease with which heavy ore can be lifted away from the surface of an asteroid and, of course, because of the sheer abundance in the Anless system of these orbiting rocks. Unfortunately, many of the asteroids proved to be "dry cows," great tumbling cinders of no real economic promise. Although Lupozny's visions of robber-baron wealth were blurred by this discovery, he capitalized on the circumstance by buying out one of his partners.

"What happened to the other partner?" I asked. Chaish was nowhere in sight, but across the shower room was another tiled threshold, another room.

"Almost a year later, just before I took my problems to Lupozny on Bethlehem, the second partner had a bad accident prospecting a real 'dairy herd' — you know, ore-rich rock — in the innermost asteroid belt. He would have died if someone hadn't been with him. As it was, he lost his right leg and completely sickened on everything connected with Anless 32. Sold out to Lupozny as cheaply as the first fellow had, even though he'd seen a flash of promise in close. Went home to Earth for regeneration therapy. That's all he got out of his association with Lupozny—just enough to foot his refooting and maybe a bit extra for his initial investment."

"You proposing him as a suspect?"

Skolits laughed again. We were walking through the shower room, and his laughter reverberated eerily from the tiles.

I halted and faced the miner. "What about Misha and Loraine Block? You think they conspired to kill Lupozny?"

"It's possible, I guess. But how the hell should I know?"

Phosphenes formed in my field of vision: **Come in here, Raymond. There's something you should see.**

"That's a utility and laundry closet," Skolits said, apparently deducing from my expression that Chaish had just sent me a message. "We clean our suits in there, rack our helmets and air-recycling equipment—not much to look at, I'm afraid."

I stepped over the closet's tile threshold, and Skolits crowded into the opening behind me. Chaish was running an iridescent finger down the flank of the spacesuit hung from a detachable bar spanning the upper rear of the room. The arms, thighs, and chest of the suit all had pockets with adhesive fasteners. Skolits's helmet sat on a shelf above the bar, blank-faced and imposing. Air-recycling equipment dangled from a hook to the left of the empty suit.

It's damp, Raymond, inside and out—as if its owner has only recently hosed it down.

I reached for the suit. "You do your own washing, Mr. Skolits?"

"Of course I do. We all do. Nobody else is going to do it for us. Have you ever seen one of these things after a miner's just come in from The Rocks? They're coated with dust, and if you don't get the stuff off, it can work its way through your suit and leave you wide open for a hematic boil-off the next time you clear an airlock. That's all the incentive I need to do my own washing."

"Where's your vacuum-suit underskin?"

"The lining garment? It stunk, Mr. Detchemendy. I'd been wearing it a long time and working hard. So I put it in the waste-conversion hopper in the lounge. That's also standard procedure."

Many miners use an airbrush to clean their suits, Chaish told me. **Of course, that's only suitable for grime on the *outside*.**

I tried to disguise the fact that Chaish had just communicated with me. "I'm sure it is," I said, responding to Skolits's last remark. "Let's go back to the lounge." I led the miner and my dyadmate through the shower room and into the rest-and-recreation area. Because Chaish was slower than Skolits, however, he kept looking back to see what was delaying her. When at length she joined us, the miner relaxed perceptibly.

"What brought you in to Lupozny Station at this precise time?" I asked Skolits, who had thrown himself onto the divan again.

"Fatigue. Simple fatigue."

"Did you have a full load of ore in your mining craft's tender?"

"No." Skolits rubbed his face with both hands. "It was more like half a load, really."

"How did Lupozny feel about miners coming in with less than a full load, especially here?"

"He disapproved heartily. But I was worn out, you understand, and it was either here or the fetch station. Here was closer."

"You seem to be all right now. Have you slept?"

"*Slept?* With everything that's happened since I came in?"

"You went with Toombs and Helmuth to see why Lupozny couldn't be roused?"

"Yeah, I did."

"What did you do—yourself, I mean—when you discovered the body?"

"I leaned over to see if he was really dead. He certainly seemed to be, blood as thick as jelly on the floor. I didn't touch the bastard, though."

"What about the others?"

"Toombs eventually nudged him over a bit, to see the wound. Synnöva hung back, and after looking at Lupozny. . . ."

"What?" I urged him.

"Well, I guess I hung back, too. That's really all there was to it. Afterwards we waited for the *Baidarka* to arrive, me in here and the others in their places."

I was out of questions, and Skolits was obviously ready for us to go. Suddenly, though, he smiled winningly and jabbed a forefinger at the vid player opposite the air-divan.

"How about turning that back on for me? I think I'm on the verge of figuring out that game."

Chaish moved glidingly to the electronic box and touched it to life. The men in duck-billed caps and striped pantaloons were still watching members of their former audience cavort and caper on their playing field. The entire scene was so removed from the insular realities of Lupozny Station that I stared at it as intently as did Skolits.

Come on, Raymond.

The bright violet strips of Chaish's respiration ribbons fluttered silently. They turned my attention away from the videoplayer, and I sheepishly followed my dyadmate out of the miners' recuperation facility.

Back in the control center we found Sinclair Toombs with the remainder of the station's other personnel, excepting only the Blocks. Hans Verschuur, Daphne Kaunas, and Synnöva sat languidly at their cubbyholes in the hub. Françoise Loizos and Krishna Rai had not yet come over from the *Baidarka*, although Verschuur acknowledged that he had sent for them and they were probably on their way. It was a glum little gathering we confronted, Chaish and I.

"What did you find out from Skolits?" asked Toombs, perched on the edge of one of the hub's metal and plastic consoles.

"I don't know," I said.

That he is the murderer, Chaish interjected.

But of course I was the only one who registered this accusation. Puzzled and surprised, I turned to my dyadmate. The chode, who do not kill their own kind, usually enter into the emotional affairs of humanity solely within the framework of the skategrace relationship, which is so special that only a minute fraction of their number ever become even vaguely familiar with the human mind. Of course, the same is true of human relationships with the chode. That we do not yet refrain from killing one another must strike them—if even a rough translation of their attitude is possible—as symptomatic of a species-wide malaise. Still, I was shocked that Chaish had singled out Skolits as the murderer on the basis of what had seemed to me an inconclusive interview. Further, her message to me pulsated with . . . well, anger, outrage, and a host of other negative emotions, all of them disproportionate to her personal stake in the death of an opportunist and bully like Frederick Lupozny.

"What makes you think that?" I asked her, undoubtedly bewildering the others in the control center. "The damp spacesuit?"

In part, yes.

"But that doesn't convict him, Chaish. There seems to be no way he could have got from the recuperation area to Lupozny's room."

A lifeboat near the main airlock gave him an exit from the station. Another in the bay just off Lupozny's quarters provided a means of reentry. There's no alarm circuit to tell when anyone enters or exits a lifeboat.

"Chaish, Mr. Toombs has already told us that none of the lifeboats attached to the station is depressurized. No one could have entered the stationmaster's room through a fully pressurized remora craft." I turned to Sinclair Toombs. "Chaish thinks Skolits killed Lupozny."

Synnöva Helmuth was the first to react. "Corcoran? He's a little queer from spending so much time among The Rocks, but he's not a murderer. His rudeness comes from not being around other people very much."

"Is Misha Block a murderer?" I asked her. "Is Loraine Block a murderer's accomplice?"

The assay officer glanced at Toombs. "No," she said, with reasonable firmness. "I've never believed that, either."

"You still haven't talked to Block himself," Toombs reminded me.

"I don't really expect his story to be any different from his wife's. Did you check out the suits in the observatory airlock?"

"I did." Toombs glanced away—up the open corridor toward both his office and the observatory. "None of them is blood-drenched inside, if that jibes with your own interpretation of events."

"I don't *have* an interpretation, Mr. Toombs. Are any of them damp?"

"Damp? Of course not."

"Skolits's was. It still is. He washed it down not too long ago."

"That's not unusual for a miner. They come in grime-coated." But his expression altered, as if a long-legged doubt about the Blocks' culpability was crawling across his conscience. "That's what the utility closet is for, cleaning dusty gear."

"Chaish says it's just as common to dislodge the grime with an airbrush as with a spray of water. Is that true?"

"Maybe. Both methods are employed. That's why the utility room is just off the shower."

"But an airbrush wouldn't be your first choice if you'd gotten blood in your suit lining and on your undergarment, too. You'd want to wash away the dried material. Some of the blood on the outside would boil away from lack of pressure, of course—but whichever portions had frozen would require more than an airbrush to dislodge, and Skolits conveniently disposed of his underskin. As per custom, of course."

Toombs took aim at the long-legged doubt making furry footprints on his peace of mind: "But Skolits couldn't have got down there, and the Blocks have a motive for conspiring to kill Lupozny!"

"And you have a motive for wanting to believe it's them who did it," Synnöva Helmuth said, her voice quavering.

Before Toombs could respond, Verschuur swiveled around to the communications console and raised his right hand for silence.

"Your friends are coming in," he told me softly. "I'm letting them into the spaceboat hangar." He nodded at Daphne Kaunas, the dark-skinned life-systems officer, and she switched on the pumps whose function was to empty the main airlock of air. A bell-like alarm sounded in the console and in the corridors of Lupozny Station, a monstrous death rattle. No one would stumble inadvertently into the main airlock while that rattle was shaking the station —a period of four or five minutes, although, because of the persistent alarm, it seemed much longer. Finally the noise ceased, to be replaced as warning by a general dimming of the station's lights and a flickering of red fluorescents in the corridors. "They're in," Verschuur said, and he again nodded at Kaunas, who activated a second set of pumps to repressurize the hangar in the main airlock. This process took another four or five minutes.

"Somebody ought to go down there to meet them," Synnöva Helmuth said.

Toombs glared at her. "Go on, then. Bring them back with you." He jumped down from the console and turned toward Chaish. "What motive did Corcoran Skolits have? Presuming of course that he could outwit the airlock alarms, the anomalies of lifeboat pressurization, and every other damn obstacle we've already pointed out to you."

Raymond, Chaish hailed me, ignoring Toombs, **come into the corridor with me for a moment.**

Without a word to the new stationmaster or anyone else, I followed my dyadmate into the corridor leading to Lupozny's quarters. Helmuth brushed past us on her way down the contiguous passage to the spaceboat hangar to greet Loizos and Rai. We watched her go.

Then Chaish put her wide-scaled back to the three human beings still occupying the control center. In the lee of her sheltering bulk Chaish opened her right hand and showed me an object that seemed to shimmer and dance like a three-dimensional phosphene. On closer inspection I saw that it was the pendant of a necklace, but so radiant and amorphous a pendant that I couldn't really tell either its color or its shape. First it was a kind of blood-black star, then an emerald crescent, then an utterly transparent disk – so many things in turn that I raised my eyes and waited for a cogent explanation. Chaish closed her satiny fingers around the object.

"What is it?" I asked, sotto voce.

The forty-ninth character, Chaish replied. **Or, rather, a chode artifact representing that character. A piece of Essencialist jewelry for those among devotees of the sect who have achieved to the highest spiritual status.**

Stymied by this "explanation," I shook my head.

I am not of the Essencialist creed, Raymond. If I were, I would not have shown this to you. The forty-ninth character is the ineffable phosphene. It is not for mere human beings to look upon. Nor should chode infidels like myself haul about a replica of this phosphene as if it were nothing but a grimy piece of currency. Simply holding it, Raymond, I defile both the character and myself. Or so our Essencialists believe.

"Where did you get it, Chaish?"

It was in one of the pockets of Corcoran Skolits's spacesuit, and it marks him indelibly as the stationmaster's murderer.

"Why? And where would Skolits lay his hands on a necklace like that?"

Chaish handed me the artifact representing the ineffable phosphene. **Conceal it, Raymond. I don't wish to carry it any longer. Conceal it on your person.**

The pendant and its gunmetal-blue chain felt alternately icelike and blistering hot. I slipped them into a tunic pocket.

"What does it stand for, the forty-ninth character?"

God. Cosmos. Essence.

"None of those things is ineffable, Chaish. You've just expressed all three of them, in a few of the forty-eight phosphenes by which you ordinarily communicate with me. I don't understand the sacred or forbidden aspect of the character."

No, Chaish agreed, **you don't.**

Confused, I looked back down the perpendicular corridor to the spaceboat hangar. Synnöva Helmuth was leading the *Baidarka's* computer officer and cargo master toward us. Neither had yet had time to unsuit. As a consequence, Rai and Loizos, both relatively graceful people, lumbered toward us in their boots. A bigger surprise was the sudden emergence of Corcoran Skolits from the recuperation facility beyond the hangar. Wearing a tunic, he hurried past Helmuth's party, careened forward, and abruptly pulled up in front of Chaish and me, his chest heaving and his nostrils dilating cavernously.

"What are you going to do now?" he demanded. "Your dyadmate's stolen something of mine!"

Tell Mr. Skolits we're going to demonstrate how and perhaps why he murdered Frederick Lupozny, Chaish declared in hardedged phosphenes.

I told him.

Ten minutes later I was fully spacesuited, except that I carried my helmet in the crook of my right arm. Françoise Loizos was at work in the hub on the main computer, rummaging its memory circuits to determine if Loraine Block had intercepted an airlock alarm. Chaish thought her own presence aboard Lupozny Station superfluous now, but I had to put her to work to achieve a thorough investigation. Krishna Rai, meanwhile, had installed himself near the lifeboat bay in Lupozny's quarters—on the explicit but secret instructions of my dyadmate, who would no longer brook any argument from me. The immediate demonstration of Skolits's guilt seemed to obsess her.

Five of us—Skolits, Toombs, Helmuth, Chaish, and I—had entered the hangar containing Skolits's crusty mining craft and the two oversized spaceboats from the *Baidarka*. The hangar was commodious, but no space was wasted. In the control center I had observed that it took only four or five minutes to evacuate this chamber of air and a similar length of time to restore its pressurization. But Chaish led us through the main airlock to an auxiliary corridor leading to the miners' recuperation facility. Above this tiny corridor, accessible by a set of narrow metal stairs, was a lifeboat bay. Chaish believed that Skolits had used the lifeboat in this housing as an escape hatch to the station's hull.

The lifeboats on Lupozny Station were remora craft—unlike the larger dinghies by which first Chaish and I, and then Françoise Loizos and our Hindi cargo master, had arrived from the *Baidarka*. And unlike, too, the mining craft that Skolits had piloted in from the outermost asteroid belt. These were cruising vessels incapable of docking with the station; they had to enter the hangar of the main airlock in order to unload and take on cargo or passengers.

A remora, however, is designed for escapes, hull-inspection

tours, short jaunts among the station's cargo canisters, and brief visits to nearby asteroids. It takes its name from those free-loading marine creatures, native to the waters of Earth, that attach themselves to whales, sharks, and sea turtles by means of a sucking disk on the tops of their heads. Each boat is a tubular creature not too different in design from Lupozny Station itself—if you mentally cut away the perpendicular pseudopod containing the station's spaceboat hangar and its access corridor.

Visualize it this way: The nose of the remora craft slips into a housing that extends from the station's hull and clasps the forward third of the lifeboat. The housing collar creates an airtight seal as soon as the remora has nosed into docking position. Inside this collar are three airtight hatches, and anyone climbing toward the lifeboat from the station must pass through each hatch in turn. None of these hatches will open unless the atmospheric pressure is the same on both sides. The final door is the hatch in the nose of the remora craft itself, positioned so that it need not line up exactly with any other hatch; it remains unblocked even should the remora enter the docking sheath catty-wampus. This hatch, like the others, will not open unless bookended by areas of equivalent air pressure.

Chaish helped me put my helmet on. **Go into the remora, Raymond. Climb out onto the hull through the aft escape hatch and proceed over the station to Lupozny's quarters. Try each of the lifeboats connecting with the bay in his room.**

"They're pressurized," I protested. "I won't be able to get in."

Skolits, Toombs, and Helmuth were standing below the metal platform giving onto the lifeboat bay. Looking down through my faceplate, I could see them discussing the likelihood of my gaining entry to the dead man's cabin. Their voices—once Chaish had sealed and locked my helmet—were virtually inaudible. I knew with certainty only that Skolits had been kibitzing our experiment from the beginning. How could we put so much credence—even a degree of credence—in the accusation of a chode, a species about whose intellectual and spiritual lives we knew almost nothing?

Chaish had still not shown the necklace she had found in the miner's spacesuit to anyone but me, and Skolits's endless stream of self-justifying chatter had finally led me, willy-nilly, to wonder if she were not indeed maliciously persecuting him for something other than Lupozny's murder. Was the simple possession of a chode artifact a crime? And was Chaish setting my own life at hazard to indict Skolits for the violation of an alien taboo?

Try to get in, Raymond. If none of the remoras at Lupozny's end of the station permits you entry, you'll still be able to come back aboard through this lifeboat. There's no real danger. My dyadmate had sensed my uneasiness; she had also discovered its cause. Her melting, mirrorlike eyes gave me back my own distorted reflection, an ugly thing, and I turned away from it to the first hatch of the lifeboat bay.

Entering the remora proved rebukingly easy. Each door opened at a crank and a tug. Passing through the last one, I found myself in a narrow fuselage designed for two passengers—three or four in a pinch—and equipped with its own small gravity generator and life-support systems, including provisions, oxygen-recycling gear, and air pumps.

Getting out of the remora onto the station's hull would be equally easy. I sealed the nose hatch, double-checked this seal, and then slid back and sidelong into the pilot's couch. Here I began to pump the air out of the remora into the storage compressors mounted aft on the fuselage. This took less than two minutes. When the interior of the lifeboat was at the same pressure as space itself, I slipped away from the instrument panel and pushed myself aft. Because the craft's gravity generator wasn't in operation now, I floated the length of the lifeboat. I braced myself beneath the escape hatch and pushed it open effortlessly. A rime of stars hung in the night overhead.

As soon as I had squeezed through the hatch onto the remora's cold, gray back, I kicked the cover shut and clambered over the docking collar to the hull of Lupozny Station. The remora would remain depressurized until someone inside the station activated its pumps from the emergency control near the stairs by which Chaish and I had climbed to the bay—or until I reentered the lifeboat and switched on its pumps from the forward instrument panel. It was imperative, however, that anyone exiting a remora through its rear-ward hatch pause long enough to close its cover—for the sake of those inside the station—and I had scrupulously done that. After-wards, I turned and made a cautious beeline toward the station's hub.

Anless 32 bathed everything in a dull red glare. Where shadows fell, however, the integument of the station was so black as to be nearly indistinguishable from the backdrop of space itself. I felt like a man walking over a precarious suspension bridge.

Off to my left rode the reassuring bulk of the E.C.S. *Baidarka*, a spidery colossus becalmed in an invisible web. Storage canisters floated dreamily along with the station as it circled its star, and I regarded these tumbling tag-alongs as companions and familiars.

My fear of Chaish's motives had begun to evaporate. It was easier—and far more reasonable—to fear the vast, indifferent night.

In my unwieldy magnetized boots – the station's gravity generators don't service the hull, of course—it took me several minutes to reach the hub and make my way to the lifeboat bays at Lupozny's end of the station. When I did arrive, I climbed gingerly over the housing collar of the first of three remora craft and tried to pry open its hatch. The thing wouldn't budge. Nor did its failure to open surprise me. I half believed that for unknowable reasons of her own Chaish was buying time: My presence on the hull was a complicated bit of misdirection whose purpose was to let her scrounge about inside for the hat with the rabbit in it. What hat? What rabbit?

I stalked noseward, mounted the housing collar, and climbed atop the second of the three lifeboats. After shuffling over the remora's hull, I bent at the waist and pulled indifferently at the hatch. Nothing, I told myself—whereupon, amazingly, the damn thing opened!

Dependent for traction on my magnetized boots, I was almost catapulted into space.

I saved myself by clinging to the hatch cover. When my boots were again safely clamped to metal, I eased them over the lip of the opening. After descending bodily into the remora, I pulled the hatch to and peered about. I expected Lupozny's killer—not Misha Block or Corcoran Skolits, but someone infinitely more brutal and bloodthirsty—to spring out of the darkness to slash my suit and leave me crumpled against a bulkhead. That didn't happen. I freed my flashlight from my belt and poled it about in a satisfyingly vain search for my imaginary nemesis. Then I went forward and activated the pumps to restore cabin pressurization.

Had Skolits, after his trip across the hull from the bay near the recuperation facility, also found an airless remora awaiting him? It didn't seem likely. What, exactly, were Chaish and I demonstrating then?

As soon as the lifeboat had attained full pressurization, I unlocked my helmet and removed it. Anxious to learn what Chaish and the others were doing, I duck-walked into the lifeboat's nose, opened the hatch, and eased myself into the docking collar. Two more such doors lay ahead. The final one admitted me to the corridor mouth off Lupozny's room. I had made it. No alarms had sounded, and the trip, if you discounted the bugaboos of my imagination, had been uneventful.

"Hello, Mr. Detchemendy. Very good to see you."

*   *   *

I jumped sideways. A pudgy brown face was staring at me from the corridor entrance. It was Krishna Rai, the *Baidarka*'s cargo master. I remembered, belatedly, that Chaish had dispatched him to the site of the murder without the others' knowledge. But why?

"What are you doing here?" I demanded.

"Letting you in," Rai informed me. "Your dyadmate instructed me so to do, using hand signs and whatnot. While you were putting on your suit."

"This proves nothing," I said, shaking my head, disappointed. "You let me in." I sat down on a bench outside the lifeboat bay but just inside the dead stationmaster's cabin. Disgustedly, I began pulling off my suit. Rai shrugged and sat down beside me.

A moment later Chaish, Toombs, Helmuth, and Skolits entered the room from the main corridor. Toombs evinced some real surprise at seeing me back inside, but Skolits quickly deduced that Rai had evacuated the remora from the interior lifeboat bay so that I could enter it, restore its pressurization, and so come aboard the station through the hatches in the docking collar.

"They're wasting your time," Skolits told Toombs animatedly. "Of course he was able to get back in. He had an accomplice." The miner gestured contemptuously at Rai, who favored Skolits with a shy, benign grin. "But the only accomplice the murderer could have had was Lupozny himself, and it isn't a damn bit likely that Lupozny would evacuate a remora just so his killer could have undetectable access to his person."

I stared at the floor. About two meters from my right boot was the yellow-green chalk loop delineating the spot where Lupozny had dropped his miniature telescope. I carried out some formless computations in my head, and these provided me with a symmetrical insight:

Lupozny had not dropped the telescope as a clue to the identity of his murderer. No, he had simply been venting, even in his death throes, the volcanic pressures of his temperament. He had tried to *throw* the telescope at his fleeing assailant, and it had landed where it had because the guilty party had been heading for the lifeboat bay.

Despite his protests to the contrary, Skolits was our man. I didn't know *why* yet, but I knew *how*, and my indignation at the miner's histrionics soured my tongue in my mouth.

Lupozny let Skolits in, Chaish told me, broadcasting phosphenes from across the room. **Approaching the station in his mining craft, Skolits used a private radio channel to request a confidential audience. The stationmaster was expecting him, Raymond.**

"Of course he was," I said aloud, toeing off first one boot and then the other. I stood and slipped out of my suit's torso sheath. A moment later everyone in the room was watching me as if I were an unfamiliar variety of snake that had just shed last winter's skin. I remembered something that Loraine Block had mentioned in passing.

"Once upon a time," I said, looking directly at Corcoran Skolits, "you were Frederick Lupozny's lover."

He met this statement unflinchingly. "So what? His affection for me died six or seven years ago, and I never had a whit for him to begin with. I did the expedient. Any number of miners out here — male and female alike — have visited this room at his invitation."

"Or command," I amended. "In any case, his preference was ordinarily isoclinic, wasn't it?"

"None of that was any of my business—"

"But you knew his preferences, didn't you? And on this occasion, requesting a confidential meeting, you let him know you wouldn't be disturbed if your interview developed into a sort of commemorative tryst, say."

Skolits lifted his eyebrows, as if to suggest that they were in the presence of a madman. But Synnöva Helmuth was scrutinizing the miner's face skeptically, and he could feel her gaze upon him. Nor was Toombs buying the man's ambiguous nonchalance outright.

"Lupozny had always liked you," I bore on. "He respected your ability, and he was comfortable with the fact that of all those ever connected with the Anless operation, you had survived the longest. That's why he was willing to renew the physical aspect of your early relationship. It pleased him that you had suggested its resumption yourself. He agreed to the secret 'audience' not because he was ashamed for others to know, but because he didn't believe this final meeting was anybody else's business. He was a sentimental ogre, this particular Lupozny."

"Damn it!" Skolits cried. "My visiting Lupozny had nothing to do with our early relationship! That was dead, completely dead!"

These words hung in the air like a net. One beat. Two beats. Three. When they finally descended, Skolits was enmeshed. He looked from Helmuth to Toombs and back again. It was the assay officer's affection and forgiveness he most seemed to crave, however, and she touched his arm sympathetically.

"Then you really were in here," she said. "Why?"

Skolits's eyes darted about among us—not in a pleading or even a self-pitying way, but like those of a captured animal comprehending the futility of further struggle. I think he was surprised to discover that no one in the room—not even Raymond Detchemendy, who had just pursued him to the cliff brink—appeared jubilant at the prospect of his fall. Lupozny, the man he had killed, had not been a popular figure.

Then I looked at Chaish, my dyadmate.

Her bodymail gleamed ferociously in the fluorescents, her eyes played upon Skolits like interrogation lamps, and her respiration ribbons fluttered audibly. She alone seemed to feel no sorrow for the miner, no inclination to forgive.

I was frightened for Skolits. He was one of my own kind, even if he was a murderer, and to see him a helpless victim of my dyadmate's terrible enmity profoundly disturbed me.

The miner shook free of Helmuth's touch and sat down in the empty chair behind Lupozny's desk. "I didn't come here to kill him," he said softly. "I came here to ask him to release me from my contract a little early and let me go back to Greater Bethlehem aboard the *Baidarka.*"

Sinclair Toombs strolled into the furry chalk outline of Lupozny's corpse, now ensconced in a cold coffin next door. "He gave you a confidential audience for that? Why the secrecy?"

"Well, it's like Mr. Detchemendy implied," Skolits confessed. "Coming in from The Rocks, I hinted to Lupozny that I wouldn't mind a friendly sort of reunion—an *intimate* sort of reunion if he'd also give me a chance to talk a little friendly business."

"But why," Toombs persisted, "did you have to meet in secret to discuss an early out from your contract?"

"We didn't, I suppose," Skolits said, staring at the clasp in which Lupozny had kept the knife that had slain him. "I just thought I'd have a better chance to convince him to let me go if I made the meeting seem . . . well, like old times." Lifting his head, he appealed to Helmuth. "You knew Lupozny, Synnöva. If you ever wanted anything from him, you had to bring out every weapon in your arsenal of persuasion to get it. It couldn't hurt, I thought, even if it was a bald-faced lie, saying I still cared for him a little." Anger had crept back into Skolits's voice, and he flipped a metal stylus off the desk with his right forefinger.

It landed at my feet. I picked it up and approached the desk with it. "And you murdered Lupozny because he wouldn't let you leave the Anless 32 boonies a couple of months ahead of schedule?

That's crazy. You said yourself that two and a half months is a pretty swift sprinkle."

Skolits looked up at me bemusedly. Then he shut his eyes, clenched his teeth, and began swinging his head from side to side in impotent anguish. His right hand punctuated this rhythm with feeble karate chops to the edge of Lupozny's desk. He was trying hard not to weep. No one spoke.

Show him the forty-ninth character, Chaish commanded me, the phosphenes drifting into my vision like incandescent grains of sleet. **Put the necklace before him, Raymond, and let him explain it.**

I glanced at Chaish. Still loitering near the room's doorway, she gave me a peremptory nod but kept her eyes fixed mercilessly on Skolits. I had forgotten the strange artifact that Chaish had found in the miner's spacesuit. I removed the necklace from my pocket, looked at the piece of stone or plastic on its chain, and then dangled the pendant before Skolits's eyes.

"Skolits," I said. "Skolits, tell us what this is."

He refused to open his eyes. "I've been waiting for that," he whispered. Aloud he said, "Dear God, even a decade didn't put me in the clear."

"Of what?" Helmuth asked, putting her hand on his back.

Skolits opened his eyes and blinked at the pendant hanging before him. "Synnöva," he said, "I didn't kill Lupozny because he wouldn't let me out of my contract early. I killed him because he threatened to keep me here as long as he himself intended to stay— four more years; six; hell, maybe another ten. That's why, seeing the knife on his desk, I grabbed it up and buried it in the bastard's chest as deep as I could plunge the bloody thing."

Skolits let his eyes slide away from the pendant and mist over with the melancholy weather of recollection. "Even with his knife in him up to the hilt, he tottered after me a few steps. I was afraid he'd catch me, shake me to pieces before he fell—do *something* inhuman and terrible. He didn't, though. I heard the telescope clatter to the floor as I struggled to open the first hatch in the lifeboat bay, and that told me he was probably done for. I came back and saw him dead and couldn't believe that I had done it. Lupozny was the first man I've ever killed, Synnöva," he concluded, glancing over his shoulder at the assay officer for commiseration.

I dropped the chode pendant and its chain onto the desk. "This," I said. "Lupozny was blackmailing you with this?"

Skolits's hand crept forward over the desk to pick up the necklace, but a shadow fell across him and he desisted. Chaish seemed almost evil in her flickering bodymail and her inscrutable self-possession. She scooped the chode necklace—with its Essencialist pendant forbidden the sight of unbelievers, of which she herself was self-confessedly one—away from the miner's grasp. Then she donned the pendant and let it glisten against the platelets of her breasts.

Tell him to explain how the forty-ninth character came into his possession, Raymond.

"You already know, don't you, Chaish?"

I believe I do. Although Frederick Lupozny may have been this man's first *human* victim, he has taken the life of an intelligent creature at least once before. Ask him what prompted him to kill one of *my* kind.

A few moments later I had Skolits unraveling, albeit jerkily, the ill-woven skein of his life before coming to Anless 32 with Lupozny. His story about bilking an Ecumos cargo master of a shipment of Lareina silk had been a cover for the real difficulties of his past. Those had begun nearly fourteen years ago on Greater Bethlehem.

In fulfillment of a boyhood dream Skolits had achieved admission to a skategrace academy on his home world, eventually obtaining a chode partner of Essencialist background and then undertaking with this enigmatic creature the initial simulator tests designed to measure the apprentice dyad's ability to navigate Black Ice. He and his partner had not done badly, although Skolits was slow to pick up on the semantic distinctions among various phosphenes, both singly and in combination. He didn't seem to have the head for it, and the patterns broadcast at him by his Essencialist dyad mate began to take on for him the quality of a severe optical affliction. He suffered headaches and nausea. Because he was slow to learn the skategrace "language," his dyad's mentor suggested that sleep-screenings, in conjunction with recorded translations, might be one means of breaking through his block. The upshot was that for a two-month period—even when he took to his bed at the end of a day of chart work and simulator tests—Skolits had no reprieve from the disorienting flurry of his partner's phosphene broadcasts. His sleep was disrupted, and his appetite failed.

"Finally," Skolits said, still perched on the forward edge of Lupozny's chair, "I lost my sight altogether. Apparently it was an attack of hysterical blindness, but to me it was real and the darkness seemed impenetrable and terrifying. The only good thing about it was that it kept out those vicious, biting phosphenes. They'd been like poisonous flying insects, stinging and flashing, and I hadn't been able to escape them even with my eyes shut. My 'blindness' kept them out, though. It also drove me crazy with fear that I'd live the rest of my life in that darkness. The thought that I might be blind forever. . . .'' His voice dovetailed to a sigh.

"What happened?" Synnöva Helmuth asked.

"A week was all it lasted. I came out of my blindness. They reintroduced me slowly to the skategrace training. Once I had cleared the hurdle of chode communication, everyone said my partner and I would be an extremely adaptable dyad. It's just that I never cleared that hurdle. I thought my partner was secretly trying to blind me—prematurely, you know, and maliciously rather than simply in the natural course of our dyadship."

"It takes about twenty years," I put in. "Sometimes longer. Maliciousness has nothing to do with it. Besides, you're permitted to retire early if you've made the requisite number of Black Ice crossings. Your fears were groundless, Skolits."

"Don't you think I know that?" he barked, standing up and staring at me challengingly. Then, as if rebuking himself, he added, "Now."

He killed his dyadmate, Chaish broadcast, plainly uncomprehending, **because he feared his dyadmate was purposely trying to blind him?** Her gaze never left the miner's face, and he recoiled from her scrutiny by turning one shoulder to her and staring at his hands.

I relayed Chaish's question.

"Yes," he said. "I killed him in his sleep, stopping his respiration ribbons, plugging the chambers with my hands. I held him to his board with the full weight of my body. My vision exploded with phosphenes as he struggled, but I didn't let go and he was dead much sooner than I had expected him to be." Skolits turned and pointed at the pendant hanging from Chaish's neck. "I found that with my dyadmate's personal belongings and took it as a keepsake. Then I fled, staying away from the main population centers of Greater Bethlehem and living off the countryside. That was when I became Corcoran Skolits, changing my real name to this one."

"But eventually you looked up Frederick Lupozny?"

"He was related to me in some distant, oblique way, and during our first interview in Lake Iguana, the southern capital, he recognized my talisman for what it was – like an idiot, I was fiddling with it as we talked. He realized that seated before him was the notorious fugitive who had murdered his chode dyadmate four years ago.

He said he'd give me a job and get me off-planet if I yielded the necklace to him and signed an initial two-and-a-half-year contract. Which I did."

"He used the necklace to ensure your loyalty," I said. "You signed three more two-and-a-half-year contracts because he threatened to expose your crime."

"No," Skolits said. "I signed those other contracts because I was content to stay out here until virtually no one on Greater Bethlehem remembered or gave a damn that the chode half of a skategrace had been murdered by his human partner many years ago. I was waiting until it was safe to go home. I was born on Greater Bethlehem, you see, and I thought I'd finally outrun my guilt and earned my passage home. I hadn't *even* seen that thing—" Skolits gestured at the pendant "—for ten years. And then Lupozny—to keep me off the *Baidarka* and to bind me to him for another interminable decade—materializes that infernal piece of chode glass and tells me I'm going nowhere until it pleases his majesty for me to go. That was when—" He stopped.

"You grabbed up the knife and killed him."

Skolits looked almost grateful that I had completed his thought for him. He sat back down in Lupozny's chair and closed his eyes. Toombs and Helmuth exchanged a melancholy glance.

"It wasn't until Mr. Toombs asked me to come with him and Synnöva to see what was wrong with Lupozny that I thought about the depressurized remora. I realized then that it might incriminate me. So while they were cluck-clucking over the body, I sidled into the lifeboat bay and activated the remora's compressor pumps. At the time, you know, I thought how lucky I was that they're such silent operators, those pumps. And I thought that finally I was home free. If I could last another couple of months, I'd be saying hello again to Greater Bethlehem. The *Baidarka* wasn't the only light-skater on The Ice."

I want no more of this, Raymond. I'm going to join Françoise in the control center. Come when you're ready.

These various phosphene patterns betrayed the depth of Chaish's agitation; they were blurred and ephemeral, so swift I hardly had time to interpret them. Then, with phantomesque grace and disdain, she glided away from the moral ambiguities and the tangled interior lives of every human being in Lupozny's room, including mine.

Synnöva Helmuth crouched in front of Skolits, her hands on his knees. "Would you have let Loraine and Misha suffer the punishment for something you did, Corcoran? I can't believe you'd let that happen."

Skolits's response was quick and cold. "Believe it," he said, not looking at the woman. "Don't be a fool, Synnöva—believe it."

I intend to remain the human half of a skategrace until the onset of blindness disqualifies me. Maybe by that time I will have obtained a partial understanding of Chaish Qu'chosh, and she of me. And in my blindness, sight. Or so I hope. They say that the blindness of a chode's superannuated human partner is not complete, that phosphene broadcasts still filter through. Good. I am hopeful that before I die my understanding of the chode and of the fallible species of which I am a member may unite in a single blinding, nonpareil phosphene. Then I will have become an Essencialist on my own terms, and my secret forty-ninth character will be forever proof against theft or misinterpretation.

In the meantime, the story I have just told has a kind of satisfying parody of a happy ending. Corcoran Skolits, you see, achieved a portion of his desire: He was able to return to Greater Bethlehem aboard the *Baidarka*, two and a half months before the expiration of his contract.

* * *

A Tapestry of Little Murders

PETER MAZARAK LEFT HIS HOUSE AT TWO-THIRTY IN
the morning. A pale, introspective young man, he drove away
brooding on two separate but troublesome concerns—the fact that
his bowel ached with a malignancy of at least two months' tenure
and the knowledge that he had just killed his wife.

Navigating the asphalt lane around the country club, Mazarak
looked out on the golf course and shaped disturbing chimeras from
its moon-dappled straightaways and doglegs. Shadows from nearby
loblolly pines played in the warp of his windshield; they resembled
slender birds trapped in the crystal prison of the glass. But that was
fancy, the confusion of his shredded sensibility. The birds were
simply shadows: moonlight divided by pine boughs along County
Club Drive at two-damn-thirty in the morning.

Aloud, Mazarak said, You have to flee the pain you create as
well as the pain inside you.

A self-mocking epigram.

Tonight—this *morning*—he fled the commission of pain that he
had not meant to inflict. The argument had resulted from his
arrival home long past a credible hour and his attempt to shift the
blame to Ruth's father. For, in menial bondage to his own father-
in-law, he huckstered farm equipment, monstrous yellow harvesting
machines. Usually these machines sat on the company lot beneath

an incandescent Georgia sun, growing as untouchably hot as electric frying pans. That afternoon, though, Daddy Coy's sales force had moved three units, and he, Mazarak told her, had stayed late in a beaverboard cubicle going over contracts and orders of delivery; hence, his tardiness.

Surely, Ruth understood. As the daughter of a man who had built his fortune peddling farm equipment (Mazarak, when he said this, envisioned Daddy Coy astride a yellow tractor, *pedaling*), she *must* understand. If his tardiness angered her, she should blame Daddy Coy or those big yellow machines—all the expensive equipment providing the young Mazaraks with such a respectable, if ordinary, livelihood. She should blame the paperwork. But Ruth knew that he hadn't worked late, as she always knew when he lied, and both pride and anxiety prevented him from speaking the truth.

Their disagreement had escalated to name-calling, the name-calling to shoving, and the shoving to slaps. Mazarak attributed the escalation to his own tension. For two months he had been redirecting his fear as feeble static, and their argument had amped it up insupportably. When he brought a fireplace tool down on Ruth's head, the release of his tension glowed within him like the coils of an electric heater, but coolly, very coolly, and he began to brood about pain.

Pain, he decided, was like matter—it could be neither created nor destroyed. This rare excursion into metaphysics left Mazarak feeling as if he had discovered a universal maxim. He had felt oddly philosophical even as he silenced Ruth's screaming gray-green eyes with the black-iron poker. In fact, the pain flaring in her eyes diminished the ache in his intestines. Standing over Ruth's body, Mazarak cursed her helplessness. He cursed her father. He cursed the pain that had prodded him out of his usual introspection into so ugly an act. And, finally, he cursed the kindly man who, only a few hours ago, had said the word *cancer* with such studied tenderness.

Now, irrationally, Mazarak fled that inescapable pain as the shadow of a crystal-thin bird fluttered in his windshield curve.

When would he reach the main highway? How long would it take to pass into the dense woods of Alabama? He had decided to flee westward, always westward, but would he ever find an exit from the maze of Radium Springs, his and his dead wife's shabbily upscale neighborhood? Would he ever see the weather-carved granite mountains toward which necessity drove him? Admonitorily, beyond two fairways and a line of loblollies, the house where Ruth lay dead gapped into view again.

Then his headlamps picked out the shape of some small living thing in the middle of the asphalt.

Pain flared in Mazarak's gut.

Whatever the creature was, under the headlamps it presented a form of surprising plasticity. Advancing from the left-hand shoulder, it moved via a series of filliping jerks until it reached the center of the road.

Mazarak ran over it. With a nearly inaudible *plip*, it exploded against the auto's heavy chassis.

Two more of the creatures appeared on the asphalt—cream-colored excrescences in the yellow light, mere distortions on the paving. Soon, though, they metamorphosed into shapeless lumps juggling one another without the aid of a magician. Mazarak also ran over these critters, which made faint but audible *plipping* noises beneath his tires—brittle explosions, like the lungs of a diver at too great a depth. Then, as far as Mazarak could see by the shimmering wash of his headlamps, the roadway accommodated endless swarms of these filliping things: amorphous lumps of migrating protoplasm. The night teemed with their pilgrimage.

Toads, Mazarak thought. The road is full of toads.

It was. In the midnight dampness, they had come out to let cool moisture seep into their hides. Now they were on the move from the lawns of his neighbors, across the asphalt, to the fetid ditch water on the edges of the golf course. Over this mad exodus fireflies winked like lanterns at sea, and Mazarak ran over toad after toad, toad after toad. Under his tires the vital amphibian plasma spilled in life-quenching gouts; it spurted away with each thumping revolution. But, grimacing at each thump, he forgot the agony plaguing him. That agony subsided. It diminished. In its place came a faint awareness permitting him to recall, with something like disinterest, Ruth's preoccupation with a toad that had lived in their backyard.

Just two evenings ago—how could Ruth no longer exist in any guise but that of memory?—the Mazaraks had walked together beside the patio wall simply to be walking together. Ruth detected a movement under her foot, gasped, and clutched at Mazarak's arm.

What's the matter? he asked.

A toad, she said. A toad pretending to be a lump of dirt.

He's not much of a pretender, kiddo, if he doesn't know how to keep still.

He knows he doesn't *have* to be a pretender.

Very analytical of the toad. How does he know?

Because he knows that *I* know him, Ruth said. He lives under the cinderblock by the water faucet and knows that nobody here plans to evict him.

Oh, good.

And he eats insects.

Too bad for the insects.

But good for the flowers, and good for us, too, Pete.

Ruth faced away, to lean against the wall. Mazarak watched the toad hop through the flowerbed and disappear under its cinderblock.

When I was a little girl, Ruth said, Daddy Coy attended a conference in eastern Colorado. He brought me home a horned toad, from the prairie.

Daddy Coy has always had a knack for giving you just what you want.

Do you know what happened to it?

It died, Mazarak said. All your fond memories about pets have tragic endings.

He had not attempted levity in a long time. Ruth turned from the wall and stuck her tongue out at him. He reciprocated. Then she threw her head back and laughed—a hard, dry laugh that altered the contours of her face.

Smart aleck, she said. Do you know *why* it died?

Mazarak lifted an eyebrow.

Well, when I first saw it, Ruth said, I thought it was suffering from a skin disorder of some kind—dishpan body, I guess. All those bumps and ridges and spines on its back, you know.

I know. A horny toad.

So I covered its body with a thick layer of hand lotion, just to smooth away the blemishes and render the poor critter attractive to his girlfriends.

Commendable.

I covered it with hand lotion every day for three days, and it died. It died in spite of my benevolent intentions.

How about that, Mazarak said. How sad.

Ruth had looked at him with enigmatic gray-green eyes, eyes that sometimes seemed to hide behind a nictitating film, and fondled his shirt collar. Then she had said:

The colored man who worked for us when I was little—did you know that he once ran over a toad with our power mower?

No. It's been a while since Daddy Coy regaled us salesmen with an amusing anecdote about the help.

Do you know what happened?

I can imagine.

The blades chewed up that toad and spat him out in hundreds of horrid pieces—gray, white, and red.

Mazarak tried to shush her, but she shook her head and clasped him fiercely about the waist.

It hurt, Pete. It *hurt* to watch that happen. The blades made one abrupt thumping sound and . . .

And the toads died under his tires. Even so, they continued to hop unperturbedly across the roadway, perishing by the dozens. With his windows down, Mazarak heard every impact, every burst, every *plipping* implosion. The toads' flattened carcasses lay strewn across the asphalt behind him, and he knew himself a latter-day avatar of the lawn man of Ruth's childhood, but to a higher and more heinous power.

He clenched the steering wheel and kept driving. When the toads' *danse macabre* at length came to an end, he found a highway that would carry him westward and pressed the gas pedal hard.

Small towns flashed into view and swept away, pasteboard tickets on the wind: Cuthbert, Eufala, Comer, Three Notch. In their dark town squares, Mazarak stared out on the empedestaled heroes of the Confederate dead. The rough-hewn piebald faces of the statues stared back. Their empty eyes haunted Mazarak, and the pain in his gut reasserted itself so severely that he cursed all heroes, living and dead alike. At last the statues vanished in the night's lacework wisteria, and the floodlit glare of a truck stop emerged from the roadside pine thickets ahead.

They can't be after me yet, Mazarak thought. It could take her folks another five or six hours to find her, maybe even more.

He pulled in. As an attendant filled his car with gas, Mazarak ate a half-melted chocolate bar. Hard brown beetles battered the floodlights around the pumps. Country music buzzed from a jukebox behind the café's screen door. Among the trucks, truckers, and haggard day laborers, Mazarak felt hugely out of place.

Just before he climbed back into his car, a trucker banged out of the café, stopped by a gas pump, and crushed three peanuts between his hard fingers. The man tossed the shells down as if they irked him and then stared over the oil-display racks straight into Mazarak's eyes. The trucker's mouth twisted, and his eyebrows deformed themselves into a hostile glower. Mazarak glanced away.

That guy looks like Daddy Coy, he thought. But a Daddy Coy

made grim and glassy-eyed by long hours in an eighteen-wheeler's cab.

When Mazarak looked up again, the trucker was mounting to his mustard-colored cab for another leg of his haul. Before he could back out of the lot, Mazarak paid for his gas, started his car, and fled. For miles, the pungent stink of a paper mill followed him, but so intense was his resurgent pain that he hardly cared.

He drove all morning and into the first light of a colorless dawn. He encountered almost no traffic, and the warm asphalt seemed to melt to the consistency of licorice, impeding motion. The world slowed, and Mazarak began having hallucinatory flashes in which he saw—of all unlikely visions—his own backyard. The farther west he traveled the more frequent became the flashes.

Christmas Day: a bright, blue, wispy afternoon, as if in Indian summer; and he and Ruth stood by the soot-blackened incinerator behind the patio wall. They had built the incinerator shortly after their marriage. A pile of loosely cemented stones, it was the only "improvement" to their property that they had ever made: an improvement that also served, with its mortared chimney and removable steel grate, as a barbecue pit. But on that Christmas Day —how many had since intervened?—they had gone out back not to grill a pair of steaks but to finish an argument. Then, no sinister animal had gnawed his bowel, no nameless organic hurt had needed concealing, and, even in his rage, he had not once considered striking his wife.

In the shadow of a tall blue conifer, Ruth had fidgeted behind his back. He was busy, though, and made no pretense of listening to her.

Pete, this doesn't make sense.

He did not reply, but obsessively dropped the contents of a large Manila envelope onto the broken coals under the incinerator grate: policies, bonds, stock certificates, sheet after sheet of ornately stenciled paper. Each sheet turned crimson along its edges, curled, and crumpled like an otherworldly flower. When Mazarak had disposed of them all, he tossed the envelope onto the coals.

I suppose you think you've redeemed your manhood, Ruth said.

Instant psychoanalysis, Mazarak said. Too damned easy.

Well, it doesn't make sense—tossing everything on the fire.

To me it does, Mazarak said. Daddy Coy can take his twenty-year harvest of insurance policies and half-ripe bonds and lug them back to his deposit box. Who does he think he is, sending us this patronizing crap?

He thinks he's my father, Pete. He thinks he's your father-in-law.

That's crap. You have a shallow grasp of the relationships at work here, babe. Daddy Coy ain't so much your father as you are his cleaving offspring, ever and always under his wing.

You're trying to make me cry. This is your egotistical notion of a noble gesture. Actually, it's insane.

Thus speaks an insane victim of her own Electra complex.

Burning those documents proves nothing, Ruth said. Except that you indulge in self-deception as an adolescent hobby.

Adolescent? Butterfly McQueen calling road tar black.

You know Daddy Coy keeps copies of everything, Ruth said. You've had it both ways this afternoon.

He turned and said, At least it's a gesture. It's better than nothing.

Then, as they watched, the incinerator's updraft carried the charred remains of her daddy's papers into the sky—through the puzzle-piece blue fringed with pine needles, up into the incandescent afternoon. When Ruth spoke again, she said only a few anguished syllables:

The ashes, Pete—they look like dying birds.

As Mazarak remembered, the brutality of the outside world shattered his reverie. Something struck his windshield—with a frightening thud. It was a bird, of course. Even though he had been dreaming of a lost time, he knew that a *bird* had hit his windshield, penetrating his farsightedness, appearing at sudden close range (as if bursting through the membrane of another continuum), and smacking against the glass. Then, bringing him fully awake, the bird ricocheted into oblivion. Mazarak sat up behind the steering wheel and endured a stinging jolt of pain.

The air above the highway had filled with wings. He had never seen so many floating scraps of plumage, like ashes billowing on the sky. All the wings belonged to mockingbirds. Mobile abstractions, the mockingbirds glided out of the tar-smeared pines on each side of the road, inscribing huge interlocking circles of descent. A paperweight snowstorm of feathers gently engulfed him, except that an occasional violent *thwok* killed for him the illusion of gentleness.

Three, four, five, six, or more mockingbirds struck his car. Oriental in their hovering beauty, they immolated themselves with all the ruthlessness of little kamikaze intelligences. Mazarak watched, unbelieving. Unbelieving, he tried to keep track. One bird undulated over the highway in chiaroscuro suspension and then rushed forward to die against the glass. Mazarak, horrified, saw that the creature had no fear, none, and that just before it struck, one of the bird's opalescent eyes reflected back at him, in blood-red microcosm, his own flawed panic. Then the *thwok*.

And still Mazarak had in his nostrils the stink of the paper mill. It had followed him all day, growing stronger rather than weaker.

How many birds died in their unreasoning attacks on his automobile? It seemed that the entire species had participated in ritual suicide. Russet smears obscured his view of the road. Mazarak turned on his wipers and discovered his mistake at once. Fluid grime swept back and forth in crimson semicircles. Soon he was looking not through the glass but at it, for a gray quill had lodged beneath one blade. It hypnotized Mazarak with a fluttery *klihk-klihk, klihk-klihk*.

His car rocked and skidded. It bounced forward like a guttered bowling ball. His tires caught the shoulder and churned through gravel. Mazarak slammed the brake pedal and, in a moment, sat quivering at a dead stop, half on the asphalt, half off. Shaking, he stared disconsolately at his cigarette-lighter knob and asked it with no sense of absurdity, *Where does all the pain go?*

That night, Mazarak found a motel and holed up in it like a lizard seeking shelter under a rock. *Holed up.* Those melodramatic Western-movie words encapsulated his predicament, for the pain in his bowel had again begun to flame, causing him to picture himself as a reptile hiding from every human eye.

But he drove all the next day without incident—*blessedly* without incident. The evening found him quartered in another nondescript roadside inn, and the following day he continued his westward trek. He spent much of his road time, though, thinking of the nightmare of his first day's travel. Killing mockingbirds struck him as the antithesis of running over toads—a crime more reprehensible, more poignant, to take part in. After all, a cold-blooded toad was so removed from humanity's rational spectrum that Mazarak could not seriously regret murdering one.

But the mockingbirds . . .

They presented a different case. In their choreographed aerial beauty, they seemed specimens of a higher life form. That they could enlist him in their destruction offended Mazarak, affording a murky clue to his own crassly motivated flight. It made his intellect touch on, if only briefly, the circumstances from which he was fleeing—and pain coursed through him.

But if he could reach the mountains, or even the shadows of the mountains, he would preserve himself; he would prevail. His pursuers might not follow him into that hard masculine country where the grain fields and the arroyo-riven prairies provided a natural sanctuary. Or they might. In point of fact, no sanctuaries existed. Some acts did not admit of escape. Some acts demanded merciless retribution, and there were always people ready to carry it out.

Mazarak began to fear roadblocks. His pursuers might capture him in the open prairie east of the mountains, before he could abandon his car and clamber into the safety of the Sangre de Cristo foothills. What would he do then? He had a few imprecise ideas about his life after eluding his pursuers and so kept driving even after stars had appeared in the tarnished pewter sky. The thought of *holing up* again, of crawling into a three-dollar-a-throw flophouse, scared him. So he kept driving, always toward the mountains, and the plains surrounded his vehicle like an ocean beneath which something persistently insidious trawls.

Then it happened again, before Mazarak could make any sort of adjustment to the onslaught. Creatures leapt through the prairie grasses—tiny creatures, the sort that you could squeeze between thumb and forefinger until their skulls crumpled in capitulation.

Kangaroo rats.

Mazarak had never seen kangaroo rats before, but he identified them as soon as they appeared on the highway in a disorganized parade of singles: fragile little animals with palsied forelegs and eyes that winked amber. Each rat tested the asphalt with a series of hops before his headlamps mesmerized them upright in the path of their own destruction.

Not again, Mazarak thought. Dear God, not again.

Then he began to count, involuntarily recording the deaths. It required focus and work. The rats made so little noise when his auto's undercarriage drove their bodies to the paving or clipped off their heads. And there were so many. How could he—how could *anyone*—keep count? But he tried, for he had a building suspicion that each rat's death put a debit in the register of his own precariously salvageable life. An even more telling IOU already weighted that register, so he *had* to keep count—merely to determine his place in purgatory.

Nine, ten, eleven, twelve, thirteen . . .

Congregations of little bodies, all tentatively leaping, crowded forward. They resembled naked little men, with undeveloped arms and flash-frozen eyes, and each death pained him, pained him deeply, even as the successive collisions drew him closer to the painless state of a crash-test dummy. Free of all rational control, his automobile rushed mindlessly forward.

Twenty? Twenty-one? Mazarak had lost track. Numbers eluded him, as the kangaroo rats did not.

A luminous mist crossed the highway, blotting out both moon and stars. The rats continued to dance onto the highway and to halt in blind petrifaction, but, because of the mist, he saw them as if through surgical gauze. Then he could *not* see them and simply hung on, riding out the intransigence of his car and listening to the rats go under, his car fishtailing and scattering wisps of fog. Finally, it carried him off the road, and even after no other awareness remained to him, the sound of shattering glass echoed.

After a long time, Mazarak awoke and struggled free of the wreckage. The sun had risen. At a distant remove, the mountains toward which he had traveled for nearly three days stood blue in the bright morning. He leaned against his crumpled car in a roadside gully and tried to orient himself—but nothing worked, nothing fell into place, the whole landscape felt *off.*

An open field bordered the highway, but it did not fit Mazarak's conception of the country through which he had journeyed yesterday. Grain grew on the prairie, stands of rippling wheat so brilliant in the sunlight that he had to squint. Each separate stalk was a miracle. Yesterday evening, the domain of the kangaroo rats had resembled a wasteland, not a spectacular granary.

Mazarak climbed out of the ditch and peered about. Briefly, he feared that his pursuers had already captured him and done something high tech to alter his perception of the world. This fear flickered out when he caught sight of a phantom that made him forget his pursuers.

Deep in the wheat field, a woman beckoned to him with the winglike sleeve of her silken dressing gown. A hood of royal blue covered her face. She beckoned again, urging him to enter the rhythmically swaying wheat.

Mazarak wanted to comply, but almost all feeling had deserted him. Even the simple act of lifting his foot proved difficult. The ground had almost no resiliency under him—no texture, no firmness. Only by visualizing the movement inside his head and then willing it could he follow the beckoning arm. In this way he approached the woman through the grain. And, as he had known she would, the woman retreated two steps for each step that he struggled to take. At last, her blue hood and white gown vanished into a farther ripple of wheat, and Mazarak halted in the long shadow of the mountains.

He shouted a name.

This name echoed away across the grain field.

Because of his shout, Mazarak almost failed to see the harvesting machine that bore down on him out of the stalks. It made no sound, and the dark figure astride the tall machine steered it toward Mazarak on his blind side. But he turned in time and looked up into the grinning countenance of the driver and the immense, silently humming blades. How high the harvester loomed—how high. This thought gave Mazarak an odd comfort, and he turned again to face the reaper head on.

All right, he said aloud.

Even when the shredding began, he would feel no pain. His malignancy had left him, and death would taste sweet. The harvester, he noted with satisfaction, was yellow, like the voluptuous sun.

* * *

O Happy Day

THE NORVEGS WERE WATCHING A DOCUMENTARY about a tribe of Sorsuni aborigines so backward that its midwives did not even amputate the tails of its newborn ratlings. The members of this archaic society made no shelters, foraged in the jungle for food, and plucked the fur from their bodies in disfiguring whorls and clumps.

"It's hard to believe there are still rats on this planet who live that way, isn't it?" said Atticus Norveg during an overlong foraging sequence.

Atticus, a large piebald rat, wore bifocals and a pair of brindle-colored slippers, which were a Muridmas gift from his wife Tamara. He had not wanted to watch the program at all, but their daughter Renata was taking a rodentology class at City College and her professor had assigned this documentary as homework. At such times, try as he might to be amiable and supportive, Atticus bitterly resented both the smallness of their apartment and their lack of a second television set.

"What's really unbelievable," said Renata, "is that the Sorsuni government is stealthily *exterminating* that tribe. They want to put a ten-thousand-acre high-rise complex right in the middle of the sacred Emmic hardwood forests."

"Which means destroying the forests along with the Emmic, of

145

course," said young Arturo, a freshman at St. Walter's Academy on Twelfth Street and Dean Boulevard.

"The Sorsuni need space," said Atticus wearily. "They're no different from us, I'm afraid."

"They're *animals!*" Renata rejoined.

"They're not such animals as the Emmic, are they?" asked Tamara Norveg, a slender dark-brown rat only lately going gray about the muzzle. She was picking out walnuts with a pointed metal tool and her own crafty fingers. A large bowl of hemispherical meats rested on the lamp stand beside her, for she had been at this task ever since finishing the dinner dishes.

"What do you mean?" asked Renata.

"Why," said Mrs. Norveg, "the Emmic don't even practice a basic form of litter control. What do you suppose *this* country would be like if every mother balked at reingesting all but two of her first-born offspring and then refused sterilization? We'd be overrun with little gutter imps, that's what, and lots of them would probably have tails, too." She peremptorily scraped a scatter of walnut shells into the trashcan next to her chair.

"Listen, Mom," said Renata indignantly. "It may surprise you to learn that reingestion isn't a *natural* maternal instinct. Besides, among the Emmic, the hardwood forests take care of litter control."

"That's right," piped Arturo. "Only one Emmic infant in seven reaches puberty, and only one in every subsequent four obtains adulthood."

Renata turned her graceful snout to Atticus, as if *he* had been disputing her arguments. "Those are pretty civilized statistics, Daddy. The Emmic *aren't* backward. They live lives of heightened simplicity, that's all, and their simplicity leaves them open to exploitation by the high-tech Sorsuni society surrounding them."

Atticus shifted his hindquarters in his chair. "If we had a territory within our borders as exploitable as the Emmic hardwood forests, we'd be doing the same damn thing. Don't kid yourself, Reni. Our leaders aren't any better than the efficating Sorsunis, and you're too old to be such a blithering naïf."

"Atticus!" barked Mrs. Norveg.

"I'm sorry, I'm sorry." He bit at a patch of semiruffled fur on his right shoulder, then smoothed it down with his tongue. "It's just that when I get home from work I'm ready to watch something a little lighter than the disgusting degradations of the Emmic. As for the continuing dastardliness of the Sorsuni, I'm all *too* aware of that. We should have bombed those bung-sniffers twenty years ago, when we could have done it without getting our own whiskers singed. The world's in a fix. It puts matter in my aching eyes, I swear it does."

"Daddy, please hush," Renata said coldly. "I'm trying to take notes."

Atticus allowed himself to be shushed. The narration had begun again, and if Renata was going to pass with honors (a doubtful possibility), he had better let her get on with her note taking. The competition for grades was bloodthirsty these days, and she had been admitted to City College only through the good offices of G. Stuart Verni, Atticus's superior at the International Grain Exchange. Verni was also a senior member of the college's board of directors.

Meanwhile, Atticus noted peripherally, young Arturo appeared to be *absorbing* the program entire. He was one of those rare intellectual prodigies who thwart the hap race for grades by effortlessly lifting themselves above it. Although Atticus loved his son, he could not forget that during his own school days he had alternately envied and despised Arturo's type. His career had been undistinguished, and he had had to fight for everything. His mind drifted back to the squalor of the Trust Avenue tenements . . .

"Look at the earth-moving equipment!" Arturo cried. "The Emmic're doomed!"

Atticus opened his eyes; he had been on the verge of dozing. Now, however, he was staring at a shard of walnut shell lying several feet to the right of the TV set, near the built-in bookcase. Tamara had inadvertently flipped the piece of shell over that way while digging out another lobe of nutmeat, but it now seemed to Atticus as portentous an object as a boulder in a doorway. Oddly mesmerized, he stared expectantly at the shell fragment.

Whereupon, from a crack between two books on the built-in's lowest shelf, a bipedal creature scurried to the shard and picked it up in its tiny hands. Atticus was too surprised either to speak or move. He watched the creature hunker down, a naked miniature of those absurd hairy primates in the City Zoo, and begin to gnaw at the sliver of meat still embedded in the broken shell. It was hungry, the contemptible little thing, but its nakedness was not complete because it had contrived to wrap a tatter of blue nest casing about its body. Atticus knew the material; it had come from his and Tamara's nest, for about two weeks ago a rectangular rent had appeared in its casing. Atticus's whiskers pricked. A wretched day at the Exchange, a family tiff over happenings half a world away, and now this . . .

"Be quiet, everyone," he said softly. "There's a hap in here with us, and I'm going to get it."

The snouts of Renata, Tamara, and Arturo turned toward him, then pointed away as they searched the room for the intruder. Electricity crackled as their whiskers quivered to the alert.

"A hap," whispered Arturo. "Is it mine?"

"In a way, I hope so," said Atticus quietly, "but maybe you'd better be praying that it isn't." He leaned forward in his chair and deftly removed one of his slippers. Then, with an angry swift ferocity astonishing even to himself, he hurled it.

Renata squeaked, and squeaked again, and then jumped from her chair and ran to the other side of the room. Mrs. Norveg nearly upset her bowl of walnuts. Arturo darted to the built-ins to determine the accuracy of his father's aim.

"You hit it!" the youngster exclaimed. "You hit it!"

The hap writhed on its knees, stunned. Arturo bent over it, uncertain how to conclude this business. His father's slipper stood upright on the cabinet's bottom shelf, and he reached for it in the apparent hope of bludgeoning the creature insensible.

"No, honey!" Tamara shouted. "Not with your daddy's slipper!"

"It's not mine!" Arturo told them, swatting at the creature and missing. (Atticus immediately understood that his son was referring not to the slipper but to the hap that Arturo kept in his loft as both a pet and a kind of living science project.) "Mine's upstairs in its cage, where it belongs!" He swatted again, ineffectually. "This one's older and thinner, and it—*umph!*—smells worse!"

Somehow the hap struggled to its feet and staggered away to the safety of the built-in. Although Arturo quickly dug out the books and bric-a-brac on the bottom shelf, the creature had fled, escaping through a crevice in the wall or a knot in the baseboard or a gap in the synthetic flooring.

"You looked like you were *trying* to miss it," Atticus accused the youngster.

"I wasn't," Arturo said, sitting back on his haunches and extending the slipper to his father. "It's just that I don't feel right pounding the brains out of *any* sort of living thing." His hackles had risen. "My hand wouldn't do what I told it to do."

"Don't take the slipper, Atticus," Mrs. Norveg said. "I'm going to pour disinfectant over it and hang it up in the kitchen. Arturo, you go wash your hands—with soap and hot water."

"Those things make me feel like I'm crawling with fleas," Renata said, coming back from across the room. "Look," she exclaimed with audible pique. "I've missed the narrator's wrap-up. Can you see me tomorrow? Professor Rattigan will ask, 'Why can't you fully summarize the current condition of Emmic society?' and I'll say, 'Because we suffered a hap attack right at the end of the program. My daddy's an important broker at the Grain Exchange,' I'll say, 'but our apartment's infested with haps.' And the smart alecks in the room will make happy whimpering noises, and some of my classmates will secretly begin calling me 'Happy Renata,' and I'll have to—"

"Shut up, Renata," Atticus said. "It couldn't be helped. You're smart enough to draw your own conclusions from what you saw. If you're not, even the narrator's *happy* wrap-up would do no good." He turned off the set and sent her to her open loft above his and Tamara's cramped sleeping space.

Arturo crouched in the bathroom scrubbing his hands, but Atticus felt crushed and diminished even by a living area empty of every intelligent presence but his own and his darling wife's. Life was a labyrinth of fatiguing complexity, and he was boxed into one of its claustrophobic side corridors, going nowhere.

Haps, of all the goddamn luck! Sniffing bungs or pulling pelage, depending on the moment's dictates, he had fought his way out of the Trust Avenue ghetto. Now, here he was at an advanced point in his stagnant career sharing condo space with two young blood-relation strangers and only God could guess how many horrid little haps. It put matter in his aching eyes.

"Atticus, you're going to have to set out some poison."

"They never—"

"Put some right there on the shelf where that one disappeared, and some more in the kitchen under the sink."

"They avoid the stuff, Tamara. They're smart that way. In fact, there's still a little heap of poison in the cardboard tray under the sink—they haven't gone near it in months, not on a dare. I thought we were rid of 'em."

"Well, we're not, and we've got to do *something*, Atticus. I've found their moist droppings on dish towels in our linen cabinets, and that one was wearing—"

"I know," Atticus replied, blinking rapidly. "I'll bait a trap with a marshmallow and stick the damn thing under the sink."

"A trap?"

"They're too cagey for poison, Tamara. A trap may be crude and old-fashioned-seeming, but a marshmallow's a fine lure. It'll work, believe me. They've got a mighty sweet tooth, haps do."

Tamara acquiesced, and Atticus trotted heavily to the kitchen to set his trap. It took him a minute or two to get the marshmallows speared on the tiny metal hook and the spring bar cocked for business, but once he had managed, he slid the trap's wooden base into position without jarring the bait loose or firing the spring. A mortal engine, primed for hap. If he caught one tonight, he would set the trap again tomorrow, and then again the night after, and so on, until he had exterminated the pesky lot or driven them into someone else's apartment.

His wife awaited him in the living room, at the foot of the steps ascending to Arturo's loft. "You've hurt his feelings, Atticus. He's crying, I think. Go up and talk to him."

"A ratling his age? Lord, Tamara, what did I say?"

"You implied that he was afraid of the hap, that he couldn't kill it because he's somehow lacking in ratty aggressiveness."

"All that? But I didn't even—"

"Go up to him, Atticus."

Atticus sighed and removed his bifocals. He breathed on their lenses and then absentmindedly burnished them on his belly fur. "All right," he said, replacing the glasses atop his snout, "all right." With Tamara looking on approvingly, he scrambled up the steep aluminum lattice to Arturo's loft. He then sat back on his haunches at the foot of his son's sleeping pallet, a nest of shredded newsprint and half-hidden adolescent trinkets. Arturo snuggled in there somewhere, sniffing audibly.

"I'm sorry," Atticus said. "It's hard to hit a moving target, and killing *any*thing—just like you said—is far from a pleasant experience."

The pile of hand-shredded excelsior did not move, but the sniffing ceased.

"Listen, Artie, I'm—well, I'm really sorry."

A moment later his son's head poked up out of the paper, his eyes glittering like fire opals. "That's okay, Dad."

"You know, I didn't stop to think you might have a hard time of it because you're taking care of a hap of your own."

"Sir?"

"Well, you know," Atticus began, struggling to express himself, "here you are seeing to the needs of the experimental hap that Mr. Ettinger gave you, and suddenly you're in a situation requiring you to stamp the guts out of another little creature exactly like it.

That poses a—call it a *psychological* dilemma. You're a very smart young fella, Artie, but you can't be expected to resolve such a dilemma in the batting of an eyelash. I'm sorry I made you think you had to."

Father and son looked at each other in silence.

Then Arturo asked, "Want to see my hap, Dad? I've got it down here with me—in its cage, of course." He ducked out of sight but instantly reemerged holding a birdcage equipped with a water tray and a bin of finely chopped peanuts.

The hap—a brown one—was standing upright with its hands around the bars and its feet spread for balance. It wore a garment of dotted-Swiss curtain material that Arturo, upon first receiving the animal from Mr. Ettinger, had conscientiously cut up and placed in the cage. Haps were practically alone among small mammals in remaining hairless from birth, and in all but tropical climates they died of exposure if not given the wherewithal to cover their bodies. In their nakedness they reminded Atticus of newborn ratlings, but he had never been able to feel any affection for them solely on the basis of that tenuous analogy.

"How's it doing?" he asked, hoping to conclude this part of their interview without an overlong report.

"Fine," said the youngster enthusiastically. "They're an amazing species—*Happicus eromicus*, that's the proper taxonomic term—with a worldwide distribution and the ability to live anywhere that we rats do."

"Do you suppose the Emmic have a hap problem?" Atticus put this question distractedly, his mind roving back to his ill-considered criticism of Renata. How to alienate your children in three easy steps . . .

"The Emmic pretty much coexist with them, I think. Sometimes, though, they eat them."

Atticus averted his gaze from the hap. "Come on, Artie. Give your old father a break."

"Sorry, Dad." Arturo placed the cage on the floor. "But the fact they're such a *successful* species fascinates me. They live in the spaces between our lives, co-opting the cracks and crevices of our shelters and picking up our crumbs and leftovers. Mr. Ettinger calls their survival mode a strategy of 'interstitial opportunism.' "

"Did he make that up himself, Mr. Ettinger?"

"Probably. He's a sesquipedalian scion of prenatal illegitimacy, with an innate proclivity for polysyllabic persiflage."

"Well, I hope he recovers." And Atticus laughed with his son, grateful that the youngster had accurately read his mood and wisely interrupted his lecture on *Happicus eromicus* with a silly joke. A high-IQ joke that Atticus would have defensively ridiculed in his own student days, but a joke for all that. Artie might yet be a winner.

"Good night, son."

"Good night, Dad."

Back in his own room, Atticus curled down into the nest and laid his muzzle across his wife's velour-soft backside. Her musky smell did not so much stimulate him tonight as offer a soothing olfactory lullaby.

"Renata's still angry with you," Tamara whispered.

"Oh God, do you want me to go up there, too?"

"That's not necessary," said Renata from her loft. "I don't have anything to say to you."

That fluffy female had ears like an ICBM warning system.

"Reni," Atticus began, staring upward myopically. "Reni, I—"

"Forget it, Daddy. Artie's always been your favorite, your little baby. I don't suppose I should expect any change in your twilight years. Don't worry, though. I'll soon be out from under your and Mom's fur. One more quarter and that's it. I'm gone."

"Renata—"

"I'm not talking to you, Daddy. I'm really not." And she refused to respond to anything else that he said. He could hear her burrowing down into her nest, burrowing down with a will and a vengeance.

Then, but for the traffic noises filtering up through the heating ducts, the apartment was silent—deathly silent. In spite of his own agitation, Tamara and Renata went quickly to sleep, and he knew that Arturo, too, had by now surrendered to dreamland. Only he of all the Norvegs had not yet succumbed, and a thousand regrets and worries laid siege to his disarmed consciousness, fluttering through his brain like great ravenous moths hungry for his memories or his self-recriminations. He lay totally at their mercy. He lay totally incapacitated by circumstance.

"No, you don't," Atticus told himself. "Hang on. Hang on."

This whispered self-encouragement steadied him somewhat. Although he still could not sleep, he held the moths of night madness at bay, imagining a world where sunlight spangled a forest floor and the weather was a caress instead of an automobile wreck. He descended toward the illusory promise of peace. If he did not quite sleep, he treaded a territory nearby.

A scurrying there in his and Tamara's room yanked him back to the moment. His whiskers tingled and his nose went up. He could *feel* his eyes adjusting to the dark, but still could not see anything. More scurrying. Haps lurked all around the perimeter of the room, Atticus convinced himself — inside the walls and ventilation system, little armies of vermin. It was Trust Avenue revisited, where he had once come upon two of the brazen critters untying a birthday ribbon from his little sister's neck.

Careful not to disturb Tamara, Atticus crept from their nest and flipped on the light. Nothing. Not a hap in view. After plunging the room into darkness again, he returned to his wife's side. Interstitial opportunism, eh? Well, they weren't yet interstitial enough to suit Atticus Norveg, not by a long shot. Until they were both soundless and invisible, he would regard their presence in his apartment as a personal affront, a challenge to the comfortable and cleanly way of life that he'd tried to forge for his family. Tomorrow he might call in a professional pest-control service. No one was going to mock his daughter with the epithet "Happy Renata," even if she did sometimes treat him abominably and likewise he her.

But the scurrying had ceased. Atticus had frightened the haps, who had apparently retreated for the night. Fine. He could resume their war in the morning. Besides, his wife's musky scent — along with the dainty systaltic motion of her flanks — had begun to lull him toward the suspension bridge of sleep. At last he crossed it. Even when one of its metal cables snapped, momentarily jolting his eyes open, he did not try to retrace his steps to the worrisome realms of wakefulness.

The first thing he heard the following morning was the television set, tuned to a network news program.

"That efficating box," he muttered. "You'd think our kids had grown up inside one of the blasted things and never discovered a way out."

"It's Renata," Tamara cautioned him. "It's for her current-events symposium at City College."

"Whatever happened to reading?"

"You're not much of a reader, Atticus. Don't bully her this morning, too. Let's all have a nice breakfast together."

So Atticus lumbered penitently to the kitchen to put on water for coffee. He nodded at Renata as he passed the living room, but either she was too involved in her newscast to return his greeting or her anger at him had not yet dissipated. Arturo, who might have had a friendly word for him, continued to nose about in his loft dressing and gathering up school materials.

In the kitchen Atticus remembered his trap. He pulled open the door beneath the sink and peered into the musty darkness there. A hap lay helplessly pinioned in the trap. The creature still lived, one of its tiny legs mangled by the spring bar. It had torn off its garment trying to free itself, and Atticus stared unhappily at a piece of blue nest casing lying in a spill of detergent granules. Alternating currents of chagrin and pity surged through him, for he had *not* expected to find the victim of his first extermination ploy still conscious, still kicking, a reproach to his methods.

"Oh no," moaned Atticus.

He picked up the base of the wooden trap so that the hap could not scratch or bite him, then lifted the entire mechanism into the light. The creature's naked body hung upside-down from the spring bar, dangling like an entrail or a miscarried fetus. When its eyes intercepted Atticus's, they shone with intelligence: minute sapphire sparks. Indeed, Atticus wondered if the hap had chosen the blue material of his and Tamara's nest casing to match the color of its own flame-bright eyes.

"They can't do that!" Renata shouted from the living room. "Who the hell do those bastards think they are!"

"What is it?" Mrs. Norveg called from even deeper in the small apartment. "What's wrong? That's not the sort of language we've taught you to—"

"Oh, the unfeeling, *stinking* animals!"

Atticus, having thought to spare the hap before anyone realized that he had captured it, shuffled about bemusedly, distracted from his half-formed intention by the anguished cries of his daughter.

"Do you know what those murdering Sorsuni have done?" Renata shouted now. "They've dropped timed-release chemical defoliants on the Emmic hardwood forests, that's what! The Sorsuni ambassador here labels the reports the beginnings of a new propaganda campaign against his country, but the network has already documented hundreds of Emmic fatalities! Come in here, Daddy! Come in here, Mom! They're showing the victims receiving treatment in one of the makeshift aid stations just over the Sorsuni border! Oh God, it's horrible!"

Atticus's flanks began to tremble. Renata had just spoken to him, but O! at what terrible prompting. The jests of history, Lord, how they did put matter in a poor rat's eyes. Well, he had better go to Renata; the Sorsuni and network news had given them a bitter pretense for reconciliation, and only a sorry father would let that pretense slip away.

The hap? Well, it was only a hap, an interstitial opportunist that had misjudged the dimensions of its happiness. Half a world away, intelligent creatures of Atticus's own species were undergoing annihilation at the behest of a barbarian regime. How could he reasonably feel any pity for this filthy little beast?

At the sink Atticus lifted the bar from the hap's leg and shook the creature into the garbage disposal. Activated, the unit's maw gurgled and pureed. A little disinfectant sloshed about the drain mouth took care of germs and odors, while a good hard spray of water from the hose atop the sink washed away any telltale signs of the hap's whirlwind dissolution. Atticus reset the trap and put it back under the sink.

Then, mind almost at ease, he trotted into the living room to comfort his outraged daughter.

*　　*　　*

Herding with the Hadrosaurs

I N '08, MY PARENTS — PIERCE AND EULOGY GREGSON of Gipsy, Missouri — received permission to cross the geologic time-slip west of St. Joseph. They left in a wood-paneled New Studebaker wagon, taking provisions for one month, a used 'Zard-Off scent-generator, and, of course, their sons, sixteen-year-old Chad (me) and five-year-old Cleigh, known to all as "Button." Our parents rejected the security of a caravan because Daddy had only contempt for "herders," detested taking orders from external authority, and was sure that when we homesteaded our new Eden beyond the temporal divide, reptile men, claim jumpers, and other scalawags would show up to murder and dispossess us. It struck him as politic to travel alone, even if the evident dangers of the Late Cretaceous led most pioneers to set forth in groups.

That was Pierce Gregson's first, biggest, and, I suppose, last mistake. I was almost a man (just two years away from the vote and only an inch shy of my adult height), and I remember everything. Sometimes, I wish I didn't. The memory of what happened to our folks only two days out from St. Jo, on the cycad-clotted prairie of the old Dakotas, pierces me yet. In fact, this account is a eulogy for our folks and a cri de coeur I've been holding back for almost thirty years.

(Sweet Seismicity, let it shake my pain.)

The first things you notice crossing over, when agents of the World Time-Slip Force pass you through the discontinuity locks, are the sharp changes in temperature and humidity. The Late Cretaceous was—in many places, at least—hot and moist. So TSF officials caution against winter, spring, or fall crossings. It's best to set out, they say, in late June, July, or August, when atmospheric conditions in northwestern Missouri are not unlike those that hold, just beyond the Nebraska drop-off, in the Upper Mesozoic.

Ignoring this advice, we left in February. Still, our New Stu wagon (a dubious cross between a Conestoga wagon and a high-tech ankylosaur) plunged us into a strength-sapping steam bath. All our first day, we sweated. Even the sight of clown-frilled triceratops browsing among the magnolia shrubs and the palmlike cycads of the flood plains did nothing to cool our bodies or lift our spirits. It was worse than going to a foreign country knowing nothing of its language or mores—it was like crawling the outback of a bizarre alien planet.

Button loved it. Daddy pretended that the heat, the air, the grotesque fauna—all of which he'd tried to get us ready for—didn't unsettle him. Like turret-gunners, Mama and I kept our eyes open. We missed no chance to gripe about the heat or our wagon's tendency to lurch, steamroll seedling evergreens, and vibrate our kidneys. Daddy, irked, kept his jaw set and his fist on the rudder knob, as if giving his whole attention to steering would allow him to overcome every obstacle, physical or otherwise.

It didn't. On Day Two, twenty or thirty miles from the eastern shore of the Great Inland Sea, we were bumping along at forty-five or fifty mph when two tyrannosaurs—with thalidomide forelegs dangling like ill-made prosthetic hooks—came shuffle-waddling straight at us out of the north.

Sitting next to Daddy, Button hooted in delight. Behind him, I leaned into my seat belt, gaping at the creatures in awe.

The tyrannosaurs were stop-motion Hollywood mockups—except that, gleaming bronze and cordovan in the ancient sunlight, they weren't. They were alive, and, as we all soon realized, they found our wagon profoundly interesting.

"Isn't that 'Zard-Off thing working?" Mama cried.

Daddy was depressing levers, jiggling toggles. "It's on, it's on!" he said. "They shouldn't be coming!"

The scent generator in our wagon was supposed to aspirate an acrid mist into the air, an odor repugnant to saurians, carnivores and plant-eaters alike.

But these curious T-kings were approaching anyway—proof, Mama and I decided, that our scent-generator, a secondhand model installed only a few hours before our departure, was a dud. And it was just like Daddy, the biggest of scrimps, to have paid bottom dollar for it, his perfectionism in matters not money-grounded now disastrously useless.

"Daddy, turn!" I shouted. "We can outrun them!"

To give him credit, Daddy had already ruddered us to the right and was squeezing F-pulses to the power block with his thumb. The plain was broad and open, but dotted with palmate shrubs, many of which looked like fluted pillars crowned by tattered green umbrella segments; we ran right over one of the larger cycads in our path before we'd gone thirty yards. Our wagon tilted on two side wheels, tried to right itself, and, failing that, crashed down on its passenger box with a drawn-out *KRRRRR-ack!*

Mama screamed, Daddy cursed, Button yowled like a vivisected cat. I was deafened, dangling in an eerie hush from my seat belt. And then Button, upside-down, peered quizzically into my face while mouthing, urgently, a battery of inaudible riddles.

Somehow, we wriggled out. So far as that goes, so did Daddy and Mama, although it would have been better for them—for all of us—if we had just played turtle.

In fact, our folks undoubtedly struggled free of the capsized wagon to *look for* Button and me. What Button and I saw, huddled behind an umbrella shrub fifty yards away, was that awkward but disjointedly agile pair of T-kings. They darted at Mama and Daddy and seized them like rag dolls in their stinking jaws, one stunned parent to each tyrannosaur.

Then the T-kings—lofty, land-going piranhas—shook our folks unconscious, dropped them to the ground, crouched on their mutilated bodies with crippled-looking fore claws, and vigorously tore into them with six-inch fangs.

At intervals, they'd lift their huge skulls and work their lizardly nostrils as if trying to catch wind of something tastier. Button and I, clutching each other, would glance away. Through it all, I cupped my hand over Button's mouth to keep him from crying out. By the time the T-kings had finished their meal and tottered off, my palm was lacerated from the helpless gnashing of Button's teeth.

And there we were, two scared human orphans in the problematic Late Cretaceous.

Every year since recrossing the time-slip I see a report that I was a

feral child, the only human being in history to have been raised by
a nonmammalian species. In legend and literature, apes, wolves,
and lions sometimes get credit for nurturing lost children, but no
one is idiot enough to believe that an alligator or a Komodo dragon
would put up with a human child any longer than it takes to catch,
chew, and ingest it. No one should.

On the other hand, although I, Chad Gregson, was too old to be
a feral child, having absorbed sixteen years of human values at the
time of our accident, my little brother Cleigh, or Button, wasn't.
And, indeed, it would probably not be wrong to say that, in quite a
compelling sense, he was raised by hadrosaurs.

I did all I could to pick up where our folks had left off, but the
extended tribe of duckbills—*corythosaurs*—with whom we eventually joined also involved themselves in Button's parenting, and I
remain grateful to them. But I jump ahead of myself. What happened in the immediate aftermath of our accident?

Button and I lay low. A herd of triceratops came snuffling
through the underbrush, grunting and browsing. Overhead, throwing weird shadows on the plains, six or seven pterosaurs—probably
vulturelike quetzalcoatli—circled our wagon's wreck on thermal
updrafts, weighing the advisability of dropping down to pick clean
the bones of Pierce and Eulogy Gregson. They stayed aloft, for the
departed T-kings may have still been fairly near, so Button and I
likewise stayed aloof.

Until evening, that is. Then we crept to the wagon—I held on
to Button to keep him from trying to view the scattered, collopy
bones of our folks—and unloaded as much gear as we could carry:
T-rations, two wooden harmonicas, some extra all-cotton clothing, a
sack of seed, etc. TSF officials allowed no synthetic items (even
'Zard-Off was an organic repellent, made from a Venezuelan herb)
to cross a time-slip, for after an early period of supply-dependency,
every pioneer was expected to "live off the land."

A wind blew down from the north. Suddenly, surprisingly, the
air was no longer hot and moist; instead, it was warm and arid. We
were on a Dead Sea margin rather than in a slash-and-burn
Amazonian clearing. Our sweat dried. Hickories, oaks, and conifers
grew among the horsetails along the meander of a river by the
Great Inland Sea. Button and I crept through the glowing pastels
of an archaic sunset, looking for fresh water (other than that slosh-
ing in our leather botas) and shelter.

Which is how, not that night but the following dawn, we
bumped into the hadrosaurs that became our new family: a

lambeosaurine tribe, each creature bearing on its ducklike head a hollow crest, like the brush on a Roman centurion's helmet.

Becoming family took a while, though, and that night, our first beyond the divide without our parents, Button snuggled into my lap in a stand of cone-bearing evergreens, whimpering in his dreams and sometimes crying out. Small furry creatures moved about in the dark, trotting or waddling as their unfamiliar bodies made them —but, bent on finding food appropriate to their size, leaving us blessedly alone. Some of these nocturnal varmints, I understood, would bring forth descendants that would evolve into hominids that would evolve into men. As creepy as they were, I was glad to have them around – they clearly knew when it was safe for mammals to forage. QED: Button and I had to be semisafe, too.

"Where are we?" Button asked when he awoke.

"When are we?" or *"Why are we here?"* would have been better questions, but I told Button that we were hiding from the giant piranha lizards that had killed Daddy and Mama. Now, though, we had to get on with our lives.

About then, we looked up and spotted a huge camouflage-striped corythosaur—green, brown, burnt yellow—standing on its hind legs, embracing a nearby fir with its almost graceful arms. With its goosey beak, it was shredding needles, grinding them into meal between the back teeth of both jaws. Behind and beyond it foraged more corythosaurs, the adults nearly thirty feet tall, the kids anywhere from my height to that of small-town lampposts. Some in the hadrosaur herd locomoted like bent-over kangaroos; others had taken the posture of the upright colossus before us.

Button began screaming. When I tried to cover his mouth, he bit me. *"They wanna eat us!"* he shrieked even louder. *"Chad— please, Chad—don't let them eat me!"*

I stuffed the hem of a cotton tunic into Button's mouth and pinned him down with an elbow the way the T-kings, yesterday, had grounded our folks' corpses with their claws. I, too, thought we were going to be eaten, even though the creature terrifying Button had to be a vegetarian. It and its cohorts stopped feeding. In chaotic unison, they jogged off through the grove on their back legs, their fat, sturdy, conical tails counterbalancing the weight of their crested skulls.

"They're gone," I told Button. "I promise you, they're gone. Here—eat this."

I snapped a box of instant rice open under his nose, poured some water into it, and heated the whole shebang with a boil pellet.

Sniffling, Button ate. So did I. Thinking, "Safety in numbers," and setting aside the fact that T-kings probably ate duckbills when they couldn't find people, I pulled Button up and made him trot along behind me after the corythosaurs.

In a way, it was a relief to be free of the twenty-second century. (And, God forgive me, it was something of a relief to be free of our parents. I *hurt* for them. I *missed* them. But the possibilities inherent in the Late Cretaceous, not to mention its dangers, pitfalls, and terrors, seemed crisper and brighter in our folks' sudden absence.)

The asteroid that hit the Indian Ocean in '04, gullywashing the Asian subcontinent, Madagascar, and much of East Africa, triggered the tidal waves that drowned so many coastal cities worldwide. It also caused the apocalyptic series of earthquakes that sundered North America along a jagged north-south axis stretching all the way from eastern Louisiana to central Manitoba.

These catastrophic seismic disturbances apparently produced the geologic divide, the Mississippi Valley Time-Slip, fracturing our continent into the ruined Here-and-Now of the eastern seaboard and the anachronistic There-and-Then of western North America. Never mind that the West beyond this discontinuity only existed in fact over sixty-five million years ago. Or that you can no longer visit modern California because California—along with twenty-one other western states and all or most of six western Canadian provinces has vanished.

It's crazy, the loss of half a modern continent and of every person living there before the asteroid impact and the earthquakes, but you can't take a step beyond the divide without employing a discontinuity lock. And when you do cross, you see fossils sprung to life, the offspring of a different geologic period. In Europe, Asia, Africa, South America, Australia, Antarctica, it's much the same —except that the time-slips in those places debouch on other geologic time divisions: the Pleistocene, the Paleocene, the Jurassic, the Silurian, etc.

We're beginning to find that many parts of the world we used to live in are, temporally speaking, vast subterranean galleries in which our ancestors, or our descendants, stride like kings and we are unwelcome strangers. I survived my time in one such roofless cavern, but even if it meant losing Button to the Late Cretaceous forever, I'd be delighted to see all our world's cataclysm-spawned discontinuities melt back into normalcy tomorrow. . . .

✻ ✻ ✻

The corythosaurs were herding. The tribe we'd just met flowed into several other tribes, all moving at a stately clip up through Saskatchewan, Alberta, and the northeastern corner of old British Columbia. Button and I stayed with them because, in our first days beyond the divide, we saw no other human pioneers and believed it would be more fun to travel with some easy-going nonhuman natives than to lay claim to the first plot of likely looking ground we stumbled across.

Besides, I didn't want to begin farming yet, and the pace set by the duckbills was by no stretch burdensome—fifteen to twenty miles a day, depending on the vegetation available and the foraging styles of the lead males.

It was several weeks before we realized that the corythosaurs, along with six or seven other species of duckbill and a few distant groups of horned dinosaurs, were migrating. We supposed—well, I supposed, Button being little more than a dumbstruck set of eyes, ears, and boyish tropisms—only that they were eating their way through the evergreens, magnolias, and cycad shrubs along routes well-worn by earlier foragers.

Where, I wondered, were our human predecessors? The time-slip locks at St. Joseph and other sites along the divide had been open two full years, ever since Tharpleton and Sykora's development of cost-effective discontinuity gates. To date, over 100,000 people had reputedly used them. So where was everyone? A few, like our parents, had met untimely deaths. Others had made the crossing elsewhere. Still others had headed straight for the Great Inland Sea—to trap pelicanlike pterosaurs, train them on leads, and send them out over the waters as captive fishers. It beat farming, said some returning pioneers, and the westerly salt breezes were always lovely. In any event, Button and I trailed our duckbills a month before happening upon another human being.

How did we become members of the corythosaur family? Well, we stayed on the lumbering creatures' trail every day and bedded down near them every night. At first, sighting us, the largest males—like four-legged, thirty-foot-tall woodwinds—would blow panicky bassoon notes through the tubes winding from their nostrils through the mazelike hollows in their mohawk crests. These musical alarms echoed back and forth among the tribe, alerting not only our family but also every other nearby clan of hadrosaurs to a possible danger. Initially, this was flattering, but, later, simply frustrating.

Button got tired of dogging the corythosaurs. They stank, he said, "like the snake house in the St. Louis Zoo." He griped about all the mushy green hadrosaur paddies along our route. He said that the insects bumbling in clouds around the duckbills—gnats, flies, a few waspish pollinators—were better at "poking our hides than theirs." He whined that we couldn't "become duckbills because we don't eat what they eat." And he was right. We were living on T-rations, tiny rodentlike mammals that I caught when they were most sluggish, and the pulpy berries of strange shrubs. We often had tight stomachs, loose bowels, borderline dehydration.

But I kept Button going by ignoring his gripes, by seeing to it that he ate, and by carrying him on my shoulders. Weirdly, it was after hoisting him onto my shoulders that the duckbills stopped running from us at first sight. By that trick, we ceased being two bipedal strangers and became a single honorary hadrosaur.

When he sat on my shoulders, Button's dilapidated St. Louis Cardinals baseball cap gave us both the crest and the bill we needed to pass as one of their youngsters. Then, in fact, the corythosaurs let us travel at the heart of their group, with all the other juveniles. There, we were relatively secure from the flesh-eaters— *T. rex*, *Daspletosaurus*, and *Albertosaurus*—that would track us through the Dakota flood plains or try to intercept us in the lush Canadian woods.

The corythosaurs did a lot of noisy bassooning. They did it to warn of predators, to let the members of other duckbill clans— *Parasaurolophus*, *Hypacrosaurus*, *Maiasaura*, etc.—know of their nearness (probably to keep them from trespassing on their foraging grounds), and to chase off rival duckbills or timid carnivores.

Button and I took part in some of these performances with our wooden harmonicas. I'd sound a few notes, echoing the call of an upright male in a register too high to make the imitation precisely accurate, and Button would blow an impromptu score of discordant notes that, totally silencing our duckbill kin, would drift across the landscape like the piping of a drunken demigod.

Anyway, by the time we had hiked almost five hundred miles, we were adopted members of the family. Or, rather, one adopted member when Button rode my shoulders, but tolerated hangers-on when he didn't. Trapping small mammals, picking berries, and digging up tubers that we could clean and eat (our T-rations ran out on the twenty-seventh day), we scurried about under the duckbills' feet, but made ourselves such fixtures in their lives that none of the creatures had any apparent wish to run us off.

Thus, we came to recognize individuals, and Button—when I

asked him to name the creatures—gave most of them the names of his favorite anserine or ducky characters: Daffy, Mother Goose, Howard, Donald, Daisy, Huey, Dewey, Louie, Scrooge McDuckbill. Adult females, because of their bulk, got monikers like Bertha, Mama Mountain, Beverly Big, Hulga, and Quaker Queen. (I helped with some of these.) We spent the better parts of three days baptizing our corythosaurs. Button had such a good time that he wanted me to help him come up with last names, too. I protested that we'd never be able to remember them all. When Button began to sulk, I told him to do the stupid naming himself.

Anyway, we wound up with three McDuckbills, some O'Mallards, a Gooseley, and a covey of Smiths: Daffy Smith, Mama Mountain Smith, Hulga Smith, etc. If, that is, I remember the baptisms correctly. On the other hand, how could I forget any aspect of the most vivid period of my life?

About a month into our trek, we ran into Duckbill Jay Chatillon and Bonehead Brett Hopkins, self-proclaimed "dinosaur men," hunters who traded "lizard beef" and "'gator skins"—welcome supplements to a marine-based economy—to the people in the fishing villages along the northern coastal arc of the Great Inland Sea.

We ran into them because they leapt from the forest through which we were hiking and filled Dewey O'Mallard, a lissome juvenile, with handmade arrows. They shot their arrows, fletched with *Hesperornis* feathers, from polished bows fashioned from centrosaur ribs and strung with rodent gut. The other duckbills yodeled in dismay, reared, thrashed their tails, and trotted off bipedally in twelve different directions at once. I'd been walking four or five animals behind Dewey, with Button on my shoulders, and when Dewey trumpeted and fell, causing general panic, I simply froze.

The dinosaur men emerged from their natural blinds to butcher Dewey. When they saw Button and me, they started. Then they began asking questions. I took Button, now crying hysterically, from my shoulders. He spat at the men and ran off into the woods. I would have chased him, but the shorter of the two men caught my arm and squeezed it threateningly.

I spent that night with the two dinosaur men. They made camp near Dewey's corpse, tying me to a cycad with a rope of hand-woven horsetail fibers. Why were they doing that? Why weren't they helping me find Button? As they field-dressed Dewey, I shouted, *"Button, come back!"* realizing, even as I yelled, that it would be stupid for him to return to the uncertain situation he had instinctively fled. I shut up.

Chatillon and Hopkins, who had politely introduced themselves, built a fire and roasted over it a white-skinned portion of their kill. They tried to get me to eat with them, but I refused, not because I wasn't hungry or despised dinosaur flesh, but because Button and I had *named* Dewey. How could I turn cannibal?

Despite their Wild West nicknames, Duckbill Jay and Bonehead Brett weren't uneducated yahoos. (To receive permission to use a discontinuity lock, you couldn't be.) But they had separated themselves from other pioneers, dressed up in spiked nodosaur-hide vests, duckbill-skin leggings, and opossum-belly moccasins, and begun a two-man trading company inspired by North America's rugged trappers of the early 1800s. Playing these parts, they had come to believe that a selfish lawlessness was their birthright.

Unable to coax me to eat, Chatillon, a slender, sandy-haired man with a splotchy beard, and Hopkins, a simian gnome with a high, domed forehead, tried to talk me into joining them. They could use another set of hands, and I'd learn to make arrows, shoot a bow, skin heterodontosaurs, butcher duckbills, and sew "fine lizardly duds"—if I let them teach me. They'd also help me find Button so that he, too, could benefit from their woodsy self-improvement program.

I talked to the hunters, without agreeing to this proposal. So they began to ignore me. Hopkins left the clearing and returned a little later with a half-grown panoplosaur to which was rigged a travois. On this sled, they piled the hide, bones, and butchered flesh of Dewey, after conscientiously treating the meat with sea salt. Then they ambled over to the cycad to which I was bound.

"Any idea where those flute-crests of yours happen to be going, Master Gregson?" Chatillon said.

"No, sir."

"Four months from now, the middle of June, they'll hit the Arctic rim, the shore of what Holocene-huggers used to call the Beaufort Sea."

"Holocene-huggers?"

"Stay-at-homes," Hopkins said. "Baseline-lubbers."

"You want to traipse eighteen hundred more miles, kid? That's what's in store for you."

"Why?" I said. "Why do they go there?"

"It's a duckbill rookery," Chatillon said. "A breeding site. Quite a ways to go to watch a bunch of lizards screw."

"Or," Hopkins said, "you could link up with some boneheads in the Yukon and tail them across the land bridge into Old Mongolia."

"Where are we now?" I asked.

"Montana," Chatillon said. "If Montana existed."

"Its relative vicinity," Hopkins said. "Given tectonic drift, beaucoups of climatic changes, and the passage of several million years."

I had no idea what to reply. The dinosaur men put out their fire, lay down under the chaotically arrayed stars, drifted off to sleep. Or so I thought. For, shortly after lying down, Chatillon and Hopkins arose again, walked over, unbound my hands, and, in the alien woods, far from any human settlement, took turns poking my backside. I repeatedly cried out, but my tormentors only laughed. When dawn came, they debated whether to kill me or leave me tied up for a passing carnivore. They decided that the second option would free them of guilt and give a human-size predator—a dromoaeosaur or a stenonychosaur—several hours of amusing exercise.

"Wish you'd change your mind," Bonehead Brett Hopkins said. He prodded the sleepy panoplosaur out of its doze.

"Yeah, Master Gregson," Duckbill Jay Chatillon said. "We could make good use of you."

Guffawing, they left. The woods moved with a hundred balmy winds. A half-hour after the dinosaur men had vanished, Button came running into the clearing to untie me.

It took us most of the day, but using the telltale spoors of shredded vegetation and sour-smelling corythosaur paddies, we tracked our family—Scrooge McDuckbill, Mama Mountain Smith, etc.—to a clearing in the Montana forest. There we tried to rejoin them. But our arrival spooked them, and it was two more days, Button on my shoulders like a tiny maharajah, before we could catch up again, reconvince the duckbills of our harmlessness, and resume our communal trek northwestward.

Long-distance dinosaurs, I reflected. We're going to walk all the way to the Arctic rim with them. Why?

Because the Gregsons had always been loners, because I had good reason not to trust any of the human beings over here, and because we had already forged a workable bond with our "flute crests." Besides, I didn't want to homestead, and there was no one around—close to hand, anyway—to tell us we couldn't attempt anything we damned well pleased.

So Button and I traveled on foot all the way to a beautiful peninsula on the Beaufort Sea, where we heard the duckbills bassoon their melancholy love songs and watched hundreds of giant lizards of several different species languidly screw. The males' upright bodies struggled athwart the females' crouching forms, while the tribes' befuddled juveniles looked on almost as gaped-beaked as Button and I. The skies were bluer than blue, the breezes were softer than mammal fur, and the orgasmic bleats of some of the lovesick duckbills were like thunder claps.

Button was dumbstruck, fascinated.

"Sex education," I told him. "Pay attention. Better this way than a few others I can think of."

The males in the mild Arctic forests blew rousing solos and showed off their crests. Those with the deepest voices and the most elaborate skull ornaments were the busiest, reproductively speaking, but there were so many dinosaurs in the rim woods, foraging and colliding, that in less than a month Button and I could see through the shredded gaps as if a defoliant had been applied. We saw boneheads—macho pachycephalosaurs half the size of our duckbills—banging their helmeted-looking skulls in forest sections already wholly stripped of undergrowth. The clangor was spooky, as were the combatants' strategic bellows.

Button and I stayed out of the way, fishing off the coast, gathering berries, trapping muskratlike creatures on the banks of muddy inlets, and keeping a lookout for the human hunters that prowled the edges of the herbivore breeding grounds. We did well staying clear of godzillas like *T. rex* and the daspletosaurs, but, more than once, we narrowly avoided being kicked to tatters by an eleven-foot-tall midnight skulker called—I've since learned—*Dromiceiomimus*. Resembling a cross between an ostrich and a chameleon, this beast could run like the anchor on a relay team. And so Button and I began weaving tree platforms and shinnying upstairs to sleep out of harm's way.

Sexed out and hungry for fresh vegetation, our corythosaur clan stayed in its breeding haunts only until late July, at which time Scrooge McDuckbill, Daffy Smith, and Donald Gooseley led the group southeastward. Button and I, more comfortable with these lummoxy herbivores than apart from them, tagged along again.

In October, catching the placental odor of the Great Inland Sea, the gravid females (including Quaker Queen, Beverly Big, Mama Mountain, Hulga, Bertha, and several demure ladies from clans that had joined us after our run-in with Chatillon and Hopkins) split off from the males and led their youngsters into a coastal region of northern Montana. We went with the females rather than with the males because the females, seeing Button and me as one more gawky kid, matter-of-factly mother-henned us on this journey. Their bodies gave us protection, while their clarinet squeaks and oboe moans offered frankly unambiguous advice.

Then, at an ancestral hatching ground, they dug out mud-banked nests that had fallen in or fashioned new nests near the old ones. Working hard, the ladies built these nests at least a body-length apart; each nest was about eight feet in diameter and four feet deep at the center of its bowl. When the nests were complete, the female duckbills squatted above the bowls and carefully deposited their eggs (as few as twelve, as many as twenty-four) in concentric rings inside the drying pits. Then they left, cropped ferns and other plant materials, waddled back, and conscientiously covered their tough-skinned eggs.

Although I tried to discourage him, warning that he could get trampled or sat upon, Button got involved. He carried dripping loads of vegetation back to the hatching grounds to help Beverly Big and Quaker Queen incubate their lizardlings. And when their eggs broke open and baby hadrosaurs poked their beaked noggins out, Button not only helped the mama duckbills feed them, but also sometimes crawled into the muck-filled nests and hunkered among the squeaking youngsters. No mother seemed to resent his presence, but what *almost* cured Button of this behavior was having Quaker Queen drop a bolus of well-chewed fruit on him. Even that accident didn't keep him from stalking the mud bridges between nests, though, watching and waiting as our dinosaur siblings rapidly grew.

Button and I stayed with our corythosaurs for more than three years (if "years" beyond a discontinuity divide have any meaning). We migrated seasonally with our duckbill family, going from south to north in the "winter" and from north to south toward the end of "summer." We saw the hadrosaurs mate in their breeding grounds, and, after the females had laid their eggs, we stayed in the muddy hatching grounds like bumbling midwives-in-training.

On each seasonal trek, we saw animals for whom we had developed great affection — Daffy, Bertha, a host of nameless youngsters — run down and murdered by the T-kings and the albertosaurs that opportunistically dogged our marches. During our third year with the duckbills, in fact, I figured out that only 64 of over 800 hatchlings made it out of the nest and less than half the survivors reached the Arctic breeding grounds with their adult relatives. Agility, stealth, and even simple puniness often saved Button and me, but the hadrosaurs weren't so lucky. Many of those that didn't fall to predators succumbed to parasites, accidents, or mysterious diseases. The forests and uplands of the Late Cretaceous could be beautiful, but life there wasn't always pretty. (Maybe our folks, escaping it so soon, had known true mercy.)

As for human pioneers from the blasted twenty-second century, A.D., Button and I had no desire to consort with them. At times, we saw smoke from their villages; and, on each of our migrations, bands of human nomads, archers in lizard-skin clothing, helped the T-kings cull the weakest members of the herds, whether duckbills, boneheads, fleet-footed hypsilophodonts, or horned dinosaurs. In large bands, though, the archers sometimes risked everything and went after a tyrannosaur. Once, from a mountainside in eastern Alberta, Button and I watched a dozen Lilliputian archers surround and kill an enraged Gulliver of a T-king. Neither of us was sorry, but it isn't always true that the killer of your greatest enemy is automatically your friend.

Chatillon and Hopkins came into our lives again the year that Button—who had long ago given up talking in favor of playing duckbill calls on his harmonica—turned eight. Along with nine or ten other raiders, they targeted the duckbills' Montana hatching grounds, shooed off as many of the mothers as possible, and killed all the mothers inclined to defend their nests. The men were egg gathering, for reasons I never fully understood   restocking the fishing villages' larders, providing a caulking substance for boats—and Button and I escaped only because the men came into the nesting grounds shouting, banging bones together, and blowing triceratops trumpets. There was no need for stealth; they *wanted* the females to flee. So Button and I hurried out of there along with the more timid hadrosaur mothers.

The next day, I crept back to the area to see what was going on. On a wooded hillside above the main nesting floor, I found an egg that had long ago petrified, hefted it as if it were an ancient cannon ball, and duck-walked with it to an overlook where the activity of the nest raiders was all too visible. Hopkins, his bald pate gleaming like a bleached pachycephalosaur skull, was urging his men to gather eggs more quickly, wrap them in ferns, and stack them gently in their sharkskin sacks.

The sight of Hopkins's head was an insupportable annoyance. I raised myself to a crouch, took aim, and catapulted my petrified egg straight at his head. The egg dropped like a stone, smashing his skull and knocking him into one of the hollowed-out nests. He died instantly. All his underlings began to shout and scan the hillside. I made no effort to elude discovery. Three or four of them scrambled up the overlook's slope, wrestled me down, secured my hands with horsetail fibers, and frog-marched me back down to the hatching site to meet Duckbill Jay Chatillon.

"I remember you," Chatillon said. "Brett and I had a chance to kill you once. I'll bet Brett's sorry we didn't do it."

It seemed likely that Chatillon would order me killed on the spot, but maybe the presence of so many other men, not all of them as indifferent to judicial process as he, kept him from it. After finishing their egg collecting, they tied my hands at the small of my back, guyed my head erect with a lizard-skin cord knotted to my bindings, and made me walk drag behind an ankylosaur travois loaded with egg sacks and another hammocking Hopkins's corpse.

At a village on the Great Inland Sea, I was locked for at least a week in a tool shed with a dirt floor. Through the holes in its roof, I could sometimes see gulls and pteradons wheeling.

I had lost my parents, I had lost Button, I had lost our family of hadrosaurs. It seemed clear that Chatillon and his egg-hunting cohorts would either hang me from a willow tree or paddle me out to sea and toss me overboard to the archaic fishes or ichthyosaurs that yet remained. I was almost resigned to dying, but I missed Button and feared that, only eight years old, he wouldn't last too long among the harried duckbills.

The last night I spent in the tool shed, I heard a harmonica playing at some distance inland and knew that Button was trying to tell me hello, or goodbye, or possibly "It's all right, brother, I'm still alive." The music ceased quickly, making me doubt I'd really heard it, then played again a little nearer, reconvincing me of Button's well-being, and stopped forever a moment or so later. Button himself made no appearance, but I was glad of that because the villagers would have captured him and sent him back through a discontinuity lock to the Here-and-Now.

That, you see, is what they did to me. The sheriff of Glasgow, the fishing settlement where I was confined, knew a disaffected family who had applied for repatriation. He shipped me with them, trussed like a slave, when they made their journey back toward the Mississippi Valley Time-Slip, just across from St. Jo, Missouri, and the unappealing year known as 2111 A.D. Actually, because of a fast-forward screw-up of some esoteric sort, we recrossed in 2114. Once back, I was tried for Hopkins's murder in Springfield, found guilty of it on the basis of affidavits from Chatillon and several upright egg raiders, and sentenced to twenty-five years in prison. I have just finished serving that sentence.

From the few accounts that sometimes slip back through, Button grew up with the corythosaurs. Over there, he's still with them, living off the land and avoiding human contact. It's rumored that, at nineteen, he managed to kill Duckbill Jay Chatillon and to catch in deadfalls some of Chatillon's idiot henchmen. (God forgive me, I hope he did.)

Because of my murder conviction, I'm ineligible to recross, but more and more people in our desolate century use the locks every year, whether a gate to the Late Cretaceous or a portal on another continent to a wholly different geologic or historical time. This tropism to presumably greener stomping grounds reminds me of the herding and migrating instincts of the dinosaurs with whom Button and I lived so many "years" ago. And with whom Button, of course, is probably living yet.

One gate, I'm told, a discontinuity lock in Siberia, debouches on an epoch in which humanity has been extinct for several million years. I'd like to use that lock and see the curious species that have either outlived us or evolved in our absence. Maybe I will. A document given me on leaving prison notes that this Siberian lock is the only one I am now eligible to use. Tomorrow, then, I intend to put in an application.

* * *

The Tigers of Hysteria Feed Only on Themselves

T RAPPER'S FARM LAY TO THE EAST OF THE FOOTHILLS shadowing the red gas pumps and the corrugated tin roof of the general store in Bay Hamlet, two miles down the road. The nearest towns were Harriston and Bladed Oak.

On the morning of his stepson's return from the war, Trapper, a thin man with a sharp nose and a balding head, stood in the gravel drive waiting for his dead wife's son to appear in a tornado of dust on the hedged-in road in front of his clapboard house. Behind him, his repair shop seethed in the summer heat. Its darkness contained a clutter of rusted barrels, deer and moose antlers, twisted automobile parts, and oil-stained girlie calendars commissioned by farm-equipment companies.

Trapper kicked at the gravel with his boot.

An hour went by.

Then the faint churning of heavy tires told the lean old man that his stepson had turned the corner by the Primitive Baptist Church, off toward the foothills. Between the road's hedges drifted the yellow cloud both concealing and ratifying the existence of a car. Soon enough, this car bounced into the drive and swayed there in the heat, like a B–52 set down on a jungle airstrip for an emergency stopover.

"Hello," a voice said. "Hello, Trapper."

172

Sonny, the old man's stepson, gave the impression that he had appeared not from the interior of the car but by parachute from the cloudless white sky. He wore civilian clothes but still looked like a soldier. His hair bristled. His lined but solid jowls were tan. Blue eyes burned out of his combatant's face, and he pulled Trapper to him with intimidating strength for a hug. He had served as a first sergeant in the army, but three days ago his retirement had gone through.

"You don't look a bit different, Trapper—maybe skinnier, is all." Sonny turned to the silver automobile. "Hey, I want you to meet Joe Luc."

An Asian youth who looked sixteen or seventeen walked around the silver car's hood with grim fury in his eyes. Slender and supple, he halted six feet away and stared at the embracing father and son.

"I'm trying to adopt him, Trapper. Hell of a job getting him into the States at all—but people over there owe me plenty, some of em colonels n generals. Anyway, until we get some stuff straightened out, I'm calling him Joe Luc."

The white sun incandesced. The smell of pesticides drifted in to them from the cotton fields behind the shop.

"He looks a tad old for adoptin," Trapper said.

Joe Luc leaned against the driver's door and thrust his fisted hands in his trouser pockets. "I am too old for adoption, Mr. Trapper." Trapper's last name was Catlaw. "I am in August only twenty-one."

Sonny led Trapper over toward the young man. "Last year, when I started trying to escape that hellhole, he told me, 'I am in August twenty-one.' He doesn't know what years are. He says the same to everybody, don't you, Joe Luc?"

Trapper Catlaw and Joe Luc stood eyeball to iris. At last the old man put out his hand and the Asian kid took it. The smell of insect-killers in the cotton burned Trapper's nostrils. Sonny and Joe Luc had to notice it, too.

"*I* know what years are," Trapper said. "Pleased to meet you."

They ate in the kitchen, at the wooden table that Sonny's mother had always kept covered with sweetbreads, fried pies, and open plates of vegetables, usually in vinegar. Trapper served his visitors pork chops left over from the previous day and iced tea made from mineral-laden farm water. (The water always made Sonny think of tin dippers and broken pumps.) Joe Luc ate and drank matter-of-factly, unoffended by the bad water or too well mannered to mention it. After the meal, Trapper scraped the chop bones into a slop pail and slid the dishes into the sink.

That evening they watched the color television set in the living room. They did not really converse, for Sonny told two different war stories three times each, waving his arms as if commanding a platoon of goldbricks. On CBS, Roger Mudd substituted for the regular news anchor, Walter Cronkite; he introduced several war stories that a host of videotaped pictures illustrated. After the news, they watched a quiz program, and Joe Luc answered some of the questions. Later they watched *Mannix*, a show about a private detective in a garish plaid coat.

After that, Trapper hitched across the hardwood floor on his game leg to change the channel. "There's a shoot-em-up-Tony I want to see." Trapper called westerns shoot-em-up-Tonys. The shoot-em-up-Tony was in black and white.

"Oh, Trapper," Sonny said, "you don't want to watch that shit."

"What do *you* want to see, knothead?"

"Not that. They're all the same. You know how it's going to come out. Hell, I'll bet you've already seen this one."

"We'll watch the shoot-em-up-Tony," Joe Luc said.

In the dim living room, lit only by the TV's monochrome eye, they watched the predictable shoot-em-up-Tony.

At the second commercial break, Sonny levered himself up off the couch and shuffled into the bedroom where he had slept as a boy. Trapper watched the door shut behind him. In that room, a featherbed awaited his stepson, and next to the bed hung the ancient pelt of a bear, moth-nibbled and stiff. Outside, a pickup clattered by. It sounded like the advance vehicle in an army convoy, growling through the night on a rutted alien highway.

That night, Trapper sat up in bed and listened to the voices drifting across the living room from Sonny's room. What time was it? Trapper got up early, but never at two or three in the A.M.

It sounded as if Sonny and Joe Luc were exchanging insults in his stepson's cramped "hunters' den," which was what Sonny had called the room as a boy. Straining to hear, Trapper cocked his head, but the darkness muffled the men's voices, which bore a distinct gookish flavor and carried only faintly. Trapper's hands began to shake. He sat bolt upright against his headboard and looked toward his open door. Even in June, he rarely sweated, but damp patches had formed under the arms of his ribbed tee shirt and a fever had enflamed his earlobes. He waited.

A bump. A half-smothered shout. An abrupt wash of light on the living room's deep-purple planking. And then—the slamming of a door.

Trapper did not sleep again that night.

In the morning, he put crispy-edged fried eggs with unbroken yolks in front of Sonny and Joe Luc. Sonny had a long, crimson-lipped cut over his left eye. No one had tended to the cut, and flakes of blood had dried in the brow. A brownish smear marked Sonny's temple; a blue swelling, his eyelid. Joe Luc, trim and exotically clean-cut in his white shirt, ate with his head down.

Buttering a piece of toast, Trapper said, "What happened to that eye?"

"Nothing happened to it," Sonny said. "What's wrong with it? Do you see anything wrong with it?"

"It's blooded up pretty good."

"Yes," Joe Luc said, looking up. "It is."

"You're both out of your heads—prolly the heat. You never could think straight in summer, Trapper."

"Know a blooded eye when I see it."

"It ain't *blooded*, old man."

Joe Luc set his fork aside and launched into a speech using words that Trapper found perplexing: "In the mountains in my country live a people who refuse to admit their pain when they suffer a hurt from themselves or others. They pretend nothing has happened. They put their faith in the hysteria of the community; out of this emotion, they believe, will come an avenger—someone who molds their pain, anger, and madness into a beast-shape. This creature rages at and destroys the source of their pain. The mountain people fear only one thing, Mr. Trapper—that the creature formed from their hysteria will turn upon them." Joe Luc wiped up his egg yolk with a crust of bread. "They fear that it will *forget* who ought to be the object of its recompense."

Joe Luc sounded just like a preacher. "If I was those people," Trapper said, "I'd go on a hunt."

Sonny pushed his chair back and knocked his plate to the floor, where it rattled but did not break. "Listen, Joe Luc," he said, "do you want me to adopt you or not? Shut up that stupid claptrap! You hear me?"

"For adoption," Joe Luc said, "I am now too old."

Sonny clenched his fists and hyperventilated. In a matter of minutes, even as the three men regarded one another in the sun-streaked kitchen, his left eye closed and glued itself shut. Sonny did not even seem to notice.

Trapper cleaned up the mess, dumped it into the sink with last night's dishes, and limped out to his shop, where a neighbor named Spurgeon Lester waited patiently for him to begin repairs on his '62 John Deere tractor.

Before noon, the sky clouded over. Thunder sounded in the east, like distant artillery.

July arrived, and even greater heat.

Almost every night, Trapper heard arguments from the hunters' den: high-pitched bickering that usually ended in the explosion of a slammed door. Trapper never got up to see what prompted or sustained these arguments. It was none of his business—except that they ought to have more sense than to rattle the brass bedposts and to slam doors at two in the morning.

Sonny came to breakfast with no more wounds (even though, unfathomably, the midnight shouting and thumping had grown steadily more violent), but his left eye had still not healed. Instead, it had turned into a swollen and gooey depression; his eyebrow had dipped down toward this vileness and interthreaded with the mucus that had replaced his once sky-blue eye. Twice Trapper had told Sonny to go to a doctor, but, in response, Sonny had shouted abuse. Now they did not talk about the eye at all.

Indeed, Trapper marveled that during daylight hours Sonny engaged in as much foolish horseplay as he had when both incandescent blue eyes had glowed in his farm-boy face. Joe Luc also behaved as he had from the start—with an Oriental formality underscoring the fact that he knew just what he wanted and needed no one but himself to obtain it. He told no more tales about the simple mountain folk and their fear-bred beast-avengers, but Trapper hardly missed such unsettling talk.

Surprisingly, Sonny and Joe Luc did not appear to suffer from the lack of sleep occasioned by their midnight arguments—but they didn't go out to work in the fields, either. They lounged about all day, drinking Coca-Colas, watching quiz programs, and playing checkers, at which Joe Luc excelled. The two got along famously during the day. Only at night did they savagely dispute.

But at two A.M. on July 31, Trapper awoke with a start. He had heard nothing—absolutely nothing—from the hunters' den across the moonlit buffer zone of the living room, not even a whisper. The house pulsed with the silence, and in the garden outside Trapper's window the earth hummed with the latent energy of a thousand buried seeds. Why weren't they at it? Didn't they know what time it was? For the rest of that night, Trapper heaved from side to side in his bed, twisting his undershirt hem between his thin fingers, searching for sleep.

In the morning, Trapper slouched into the kitchen. Only Joe Luc sat at the table, smugly buttering a piece of toast.

"Where's Sonny?"

"Still in bed, I must suppose."

They ate their fried eggs in silence.

After breakfast, Joe Luc retired to the living room and turned on the *Today* show on the big color set. Trapper could hear Frank Blair reporting the news as he exited via the porch off the kitchen, let the screen door bang shut, and limped down the steps toward the barn and the chicken houses. Passing through the barn's hay-strewn carriage area, he already knew that when he reached the chicken houses, he would happen upon the baleful aftermath of a disaster.

He did. In the chicken pens lay the tortured corpses of all his biddies, roosters, and fledglings. No signs of forced entry—no broken gates, or holes clawed beneath the chicken wire, or knocked-askew posts. Instead he found severed, eyeless heads, ineptly plucked torsos, feathers plastered against the coop's weathered boards, stuck there by a thin mortar of blood. Broken eggs everywhere: spilled yolk or bits of shell adhering in the niches free of feathers. The stink of bird flesh.

"I didn't hear none of it," Trapper said aloud.

Whoever or whatever had killed the chickens had not been hungry enough to eat them, or desperate enough for cash to tote off a few of the corpses. What did this wanton slaughter mean?

In the barn, a horse whinnied and stamped, and Trapper had the incongruous thought that a long time had passed since the United States Army had retired its cavalry horses. He limped back to the house.

In his absence, Sonny had arisen. He and Joe Luc sat in front of the television set on either side of a big leather hassock, playing checkers. He said, "Morning, Trapper," without looking up and hopped two of Joe Luc's black checkers with a red piece that Joe Luc had already had to crown. One of Sonny's fingernails had broken off all the way to the quick; the crimson plush of this wound throbbed with a hypnotizing animal vibrancy, focusing Trapper's attention. At last Sonny looked up.

"Something wrong, old man?"

"Like what?" Trapper barked. He retreated to his bedroom, closed the door, and stood there surrounded by old furniture and disheveled bed linens. After a while, he picked up a framed photo of Sonny's mother and used his handkerchief to wipe the dust off the glass over her puzzled face.

In August, the gratuitous slaughter of livestock in the Bay Hamlet area became a source of speculation among Trapper Catlaw's neighbors. In addition to his poultry, Trapper had lost an Angus bull and six heifers that he kept in the land to the north of his cotton fields. None of the meat had been eaten.

Spurgeon Lester reported that *something*—who knew what?— had disemboweled both his prize bluetick hounds, dogs valued at more than five hundred dollars apiece. He had found them in the kennel behind his house, their guts looped through the chainlink fence and scattered right up to the porch beneath his and Mrs. Lester's bedroom. Neither he nor the missus had heard a thing, not the first bugle note of their hounds' instinctive baying. As in every other such episode hereabouts, no tracks led up to or away from the site of the slaughter.

Spurgeon said, "What I want to know is, are *people* safe from this whatever we've got here, and how long will it go on?"

Trapper, a farmer and a mechanic, had no answer for Spurgeon Lester.

In the Bay Hamlet general store, you could hear gossip, rumors, unsubstantiated reports, lies, half-truths, and maybe even the truth itself. Lucas March, from this side of Cherry Creek, was out a team of matched Percherons. Seabright Johns knew an upland farmer who had lost an entire herd of white-faced cattle in the space of two nights. A woman, somebody's hysterical wife, said that the sheriff in Harriston had come upon the mutilated bodies of three black boys in a roadside ditch. That story almost answered Spurgeon's question about the status of people with this killer-thing, for if three black boys could go under, how long before this unnamable menace brought down a bona fide white landowner?

The crowd in Ferril's General passed Nehi carbonated drinks around in front of a low-slung water-filled cooler, talking nonstop.

Trapper went home to the clapboard house where Sonny and Joe Luc played their interminable games of checkers. Squinting at the board with his good eye, Sonny leveled gibes at Joe Luc, and Joe Luc smiled back with his mysterious and tolerant smile—just as if the two *liked* each other.

"Crown me, you pestiferous gook!" Sonny shouted as Trapper came into the living room from the kitchen. "Another king, god-damn it!"

Joe Luc moved a checker. "Give me the crown also, please."

"Hello, Trapper. Sit down. What's the word at Ferril's? They going to catch this thing?" Before Trapper could reply, Sonny said, "You check the mail? I'm wondering if those adoption papers aren't finally going to get here."

"Warn't no mail. Warn't no 'doption papers." Trapper did not sit down. "How can you all play checkers all day, every day, when the whole country hereabouts is under bloodthirsty nightly attack?"

"Yeah," Sonny said. "It's a honest-to-God curse, all right." He moved another red checker.

"I am always too old for such papers, anyway." Joe Luc smiled at Trapper. His dogteeth, bright with saliva, shone like tiny scimitars. He moved a black checker, tapped it for a crown, and soon thereafter won the game.

That night Trapper removed only his shoes. In his oil-grimed khaki trousers and work shirt, he climbed into bed and pulled the sheet up to his chin. A spear of light came into his room from the TV set. Sonny and Joe Luc, in chairs out of his line of sight, were watching an old movie.

Then one of them walked across the planking to turn off the set. From the sound of his footfalls, Trapper guessed Sonny. A silhouette leaned into the glow of the stuttering picture and blanked it out at the end of *The Star-Spangled Banner:* " . . . and the home of the   "

Click!

Darkness prevailed everywhere. Sonny and Joe Luc creaked across the floor to the hunters' den. Trapper scarcely breathed. His heart ticked like a watch in the breast pocket of his shirt. Crickets sang anthems in the midnight grasses.

Trapper got out of bed, limped to the door, and stood there vigilantly for a long time, his heartbeat for company. When his eyes adjusted to the living room's saturated grayness, he saw that Sonny's door gaped wide.

Sonny almost never let his door stand open. As a boy, he had been keen about shutting out the world—his brothers, sisters, parents, everyone—whenever he went to bed. Sometimes he had closed it right after supper. But now the door to the hunters' den stood not merely ajar but nakedly open. Why? Maybe Sonny *wanted* his nightly set-to with Joe Luc to wake up Trapper.

Then a lithe muscular form, a sleekness among bulkier shadows, slipped from the open door and glided through the patterns on the floor toward the front porch: an animal shape, a spooky mixture of cunning and brute strength. After it had passed, the hardwood gleamed anew, as if freshly varnished.

Trapper crossed to Sonny's room in his stocking feet. His pulse rattled in his bones like small-arms fire. Unable to check Sonny's bed, he opened the screen door to the porch and felt the cold of its poured concrete osmose through his threadbare socks. The crickets had set up a racket like a hundred thousand telegraph boards operating in unison, and the swing where he and Sonny's mother had passed most of their evenings before the arrival of television rocked slowly, its tether-chains creaking. Nothing else hinted even bleakly at life.

Trapper stumped across the porch and down the front steps. He hitched along the narrow walk between his dead wife's chrysanthemums and snapdragons to the gravel road. In the middle of it, he looked east toward the Primitive Baptist Church, but the thin moonlight allowed him a view only of the hedges flanking the road and a whitish sheen above a far stand of cottonwoods. The acrid smell of pesticides made him wonder if the buzzing of the crickets wasn't actually the drone of a crop duster, coming in crazily low over invisible telephone wires.

But he sensed nothing else at all—no hungry were-critters—and returned to the house, where he sat down in the porch swing. For over an hour he rocked. He could not have said if he were hoping to fall asleep or waiting for Sonny. Finally, he got up from the swing, limped out to the road, and looked eastward again.

Fires flickered to the northeast, as did a cancerous halo above the sharecropper's yard beyond which the Baptist church stood. The sky shone red-black. The air reeked of kerosene and something awfully like the outlawed DDT. In this nauseating nightglow, in this mysterious stench, Trapper awaited a sign.

A pickup truck jounced down the road toward him out of the lurid blaze of the Primitive Baptist Church. Its headlights bored into him like thumbscrews positioned just above his eyes. Abreast of him, the pickup halted in a spray of gravel.

Seabright Johns leaned out and said, "Spurgeon Lester's wife's been killed—torn in a hundred pieces just outside the parsonage. She'd been helping late with tomorrow's covered-dish and had started home. Spurgeon found her down the road a ways after phoning to check up on her. At first, of course, he didn't even know it was her."

Two other men occupied the truck cab, neither of them Spurgeon.

Trapper spoke up before Seabright could start spieling again: "What're them fires down there?"

"We're torching all them old empty sharecroppers' shacks," Seabright said. "The killer's more n likely holed up in one of them. We're gonna burn him out."

"What happened to the church?"

"That was an accident. Some fellas up there spilled kerosene and somebody's cigarette got loose." He sounded jubilant. "But they's plenty of fuel oil left and they're going toward Cherry Creek with it, them other fellas. Nick and Jimmy and I are going over by the Hamlet and up into the foothills. You want to come?"

"No. You can't burn up the whole countryside."

"Just the sharecropper shacks—so we can flush the bastard out —roast the son of a bitch!"

"It won't work," Trapper said.

The men in the truck cab laughed, and the pickup grumbled away, spitting rocks. Its taillights glowed like embers. When it was gone, the telegraphy of insects reasserted itself in the silhouetted foliage.

Trapper returned to the porch swing and spent the rest of the night rocking. Just before dawn, limping back to his bed, he noticed that either Sonny or Joe Luc had closed the door to the hunters' den.

On the second-to-last day in August, Trapper no longer had to imagine that the countryside lay in ruins. It did.

In a week's time, he had attended three funerals, the first one that of Spurgeon Lester's wife. The eulogies at each of these interments sounded the same predictable notes, for the preachers all extolled the virtues of the dead in voices either furred with anger or oily with self-righteousness.

Several families around Bay Hamlet had lost barns and outbuildings in the fire-setting spree in which Seabright Johns and his chums had taken part. From as far away as Bladed Oak came reports of other cases of arson—involving houses, country stores, and even an elementary school built during World War II.

Sonny and Joe Luc watched the newscasts every evening before the *Tonight Show* with Johnny Carson, but paid little heed to the reports—even though the Bay Hamlet story had begun to attract network coverage. They played checkers, asked to be crowned, and badgered Trapper to bring them Coca-Colas and cookies.

On the second-to-last day in August, Sonny got up, ate breakfast, and left in his hot silver automobile for Memphis. "I got to see what's stalling those adoption papers, Trapper. Don't expect me back till evening." He drove off beneath the white battlefield sun, a contrail of dust hanging in the air behind him.

In front of the repair shop, Joe Luc approached Trapper, who rarely encountered him outside in the heat. "Mr. Trapper," he said, "let me show you what I've done for the people of Bay Hamlet—and also for you, sir."

Joe Luc led Trapper toward the house and behind it into the vegetable garden, through rows of okra, pole beans, and carrots. They stopped only a few feet away from the old man's bedroom window.

Trapper looked at the earth beneath his window, where Joe Luc was pointing. A rectangular pit seven feet deep, and nearly as long, occupied the space between the house and the last row of dry corn. In its center, three sharpened stakes formed the upthrusting points of a cruel triangle. Trapper stared into the pit, dumbfounded.

"What's this?"

"To catch the beast-avenger that murders your friends."

"When'd you have time to dig a hole this big, knothead?"

"At night, Mr. Trapper. When I can't sleep, I come out here and work."

"I never heard it. Why'd you stick it under *my* window?"

Joe Luc chuckled. "Sir, we both know why the pit for the beast-thing must be exactly here." He continued to look amused until a sudden notion took him and he turned aside to camouflage the pit, which he did in less than fifteen minutes with cornstalks and a few sprinklings of rich country soil.

"Don't forget, Mr. Trapper, and accidentally step here."

Joe Luc went inside to watch the morning quiz programs. Trapper, numb, stared at the hidden pit as the white blister of sun rose to its zenith.

Sonny did not get back that evening, as he had said he would. Neither Trapper nor Joe Luc waited up for him.

The pit outside prevented Trapper from sleeping. Shadows shifted on the walls, rippled down the Venetian blinds, crawled over the tufted white bedspread. His leg hurt. He wanted to hear Sonny's car pull up through the gravel under the floodlights atop the repair shop. Somehow he drowsed, the warm night spicy in his nostrils.

When he awoke, the night smelled sharper, gassier. Its stink evoked animal musk rather than chrysanthemums. Someone was standing at the foot of his bed. Trapper cried out and threw the bedspread aside. He had one bare foot on the floor when a thin hand settled on his shoulder.

"Please to not be startled, Mr. Trapper."

Dressed in a white, open-collared shirt, tan slacks, and well-polished shoes, Joe Luc looked like a college boy home for the last of his summer holidays in 1948, or '52, or possibly even '58—before the unsettling events of the last decade and a half had bent the world askew.

"What do you want, Joe Luc? What the *hell* is it?"

"Hush, Mr. Trapper. The beast-thing has impaled itself on my stakes. For twenty minutes it has been rending its own bowels. Soon it will die."

"How do you know that? What makes you—"

Joe Luc shushed him, and the two men listened. Trapper could hear nothing but crickets and a queer droning inside his own head. How could this gooky greenhorn have heard anything at all?

Trapper seized Joe Luc's wrist and started to rise.

"Wait a moment, sir." Joe Luc slid over to the window by the vegetable garden but did not open the blinds. "All right. Now get dressed, and we'll go see the unraveled destiny of the beast-thing."

Trapper dressed. Did he really want to see the "unraveled destiny" of the creature that had slaughtered his chickens, felled his cattle, and so mutilated Spurgeon Lester's wife that all three morticians in Bluded Oak had called for her funeral to proceed "closed coffin." Once Trapper had tied his shoes, Joe Luc pulled him to the kitchen, although the more direct route lay out the front.

"I need a knife, Mr. Trapper—a big knife."

"Why can't you use your teeth for whatever you've got in mind?"

Joe Luc ignored this question and rummaged up one of Mrs. Catlaw's old butcher knives. Then he led Trapper through the dark rear porch and outside to the shop. There he picked up a grease-blackened rope that lay in the musty debris like some sort of filth-loving snake. After that, he found a flashlight.

Trapper waited in the flood of illumination outside. Sonny's big silver car sat in the driveway not fifteen feet away. Toads hopped about in the yellow-green glare, and a horse whinnied fretfully in the barn.

"All right, Mr. Trapper. Ready."

They stalked around the house to the garden. They peered into the pit that Joe Luc had dug. The cornstalks had all fallen into its maw, and something grotesque had in fact impaled itself on two of the stakes. The third stake curled around the creature's side like a pale exterior rib. Joe Luc shone his light on the beast, which Trapper immediately recognized as a black and royal-orange tiger. The tiger's great mouth contained moist cordage from its own intestines. And its left eye—Trapper shuddered—had none of the terrible fierceness of its right one, for a lump of pus resided in the left socket, delicately furred over.

"Good," Joe Luc said. "It's dead. Please help." He carefully let himself down into the pit. He wrapped the greasy rope around the animal several times and gave its frayed end to Trapper. Then he climbed back out, and the two men worked an hour or two—Trapper had gone numb—extricating the creature. During their labors, the sky turned a bright silver.

After a few minutes' rest on the verge of the garden, Joe Luc returned to the weretiger to skin it with the big knife. Except for a place where the beast had impaled itself and then ripped at its own flesh, the pelt was lovely—so lovely that Trapper could not watch Joe Luc peel away the vibrant golden-orange hide.

Without looking back, he limped into the house, eased into his bed, and slept all that hot summer's day—the last day of August.

A few minutes after ten of the following night, a messenger knocked at the front door of Trapper Catlaw's house. He had a registered letter for the old man. The evening was unseasonably cool, and the messenger wore a jacket with a sheepskin collar. When the messenger exhaled, Trapper imagined that he saw—or maybe actually saw—puffs of vapor in the chill of the screened-in porch.

"Sign here, sir."

Trapper signed and went back inside. Joe Luc sat in the only comfortable chair, the one that Sonny had always tried to grab. He was wrapped in the pelt of the creature that he had skinned yesterday morning. Trapper did not like him wearing it, but could not rebuke him for doing so. As always, the television set blared. A newscaster had just finished saying something upbeat about the conclusion of the latest series of peace talks in Geneva.

Tuning out the newscaster's voice, Trapper opened the bulky letter that he had signed for. He unfolded several sheets of official-looking papers with a single staple in their left-hand corners.

"These are your 'doption papers," he told Joe Luc. "It says here I'm supposed to sign them. Not Sonny—me. It don't make a lick of sense."

"No, sir."

"What should I do with them?"

"Sign them, don't sign them. It doesn't matter, Mr. Trapper. I am twenty-one on the first day of September."

The room felt like the inside of a refrigerated vault in which hunters store the dressed-out carcasses of their kills. Trapper wanted Joe Luc's tiger pelt. Stumped, he flipped through the adoption papers again. The news, weather, and sports went off, and a loud used-car salesman started bellowing at them.

"Please, Mr. Trapper."

Hunching his shoulders, Trapper eyed the boy.

"Please change the channel," Joe Luc said. "I wish to see the shoot-em-up-Tony."

* * *

Tithes of Mint and Rue

*L*ULA CARNAHAN SWEATED AT HER DESK IN THE office of Nichols's Automotive in Abnegation, Alabama, marveling again at how reliably her bulk made her invisible to men of a certain age (fifteen to sixty-five) and easygoing arrogance (eighty per cent), as if the larger she loomed in her flesh the lower she sank in their eyes.

"Hello!" cried Ronnie Guptil, searching the open bay. "Anybody to home?" A thirty-two-year-old bachelor and former classmate, he had damp barn-owl eyes and the goatee of a *Playboy*-cartoon satyr.

"Just what do I look like, Ronnie?" Lula said, waving the invoice for the brake job on his pickup. "A goose egg inside a zero?"

He pivoted, hands in armpits so that the tattoos on his biceps —a dragon and a mermaid—leapt into prominence. Then he focused, allowing Lula to emerge from a backdrop of boxed air filters and fan belts. "Geez, gal, you scared the piss out of me. No, you don't look like a goose egg. More like the goose herself."

He never should have said that. A scowl replaced the mask of tight goodwill on Lula's face.

Ten years ago, only a month after her marriage to Chance Carnahan (once the second-leading scorer and only white player on County High's basketball squad), Ronnie had copped a feel during

186

one of Chance's beer-fetching forays into the kitchen. Lula had fended Ronnie off. In those days, wearing a slimmer body, she warded off three or four of Chance's friends a week—plus, every time she ventured downtown, some redneck Casanova with Scope on his breath and hands like crayfish claws.

"Sorry," Ronnie said, sashaying over.

Today, sorry didn't cut it.

Lula rose, leaned over her desk on the palms of her dimpled hands and snarled, "A goose, eh? Fatted for the slaughter? Well, nobody eats goose on the Fourth, you peckerwood. It's barbecue and Brunswick stew or fried chicken and cabbage slaw. But you heard the words 'goose egg' and couldn't resist calling *me* a goose."

"Come on, Lula. Let me pay my bill." Ronnie reached for the invoice even as he avoided her gaze.

"You could've said I looked like a thunderhead threatening eastern Alabama. Or an ocean liner needing three or four tugboats to make it to dock. You could've said, 'If only I had one of those little American flags the Veterans of Foreign Wars hand out every Fourth, I'd stick it in your backside and claim you as a spanking-new U. S. territory.' You could've said—"

"Lula, please."

"—that if I bought just one new dress a year, I could personally guarantee every cotton grower in the South a banner year. Or that if I filled up on helium, you and a few of your buddies could hitch a basket to me and get a bird's-eye view of next year's Super-bowl."

"Nobody in high school could outthink you," Ronnie said penitently. "Nobody had more smarts."

"If I'd had the I.Q. of a chipmunk, I could've outthunk you. Most of your smarts wound up in your balls, and thinking as a pastime appealed to you about as much as manual labor. Some things never change, Ronnie."

"Come on, Lula, cut me some slack."

Lula Carnahan tore up Ronnie's invoice, flung the pieces at him, and ambled out of Nichols's Automotive impressively rolling.

Thinking to shake the dust of Abnegation off her feet, Lula bought a bus ticket to a small midwestern town she'd never seen before. (Of course, she'd only barely visited Montgomery or Birmingham.) The Greyhound left at 5 P.M. from the front of the High 'n' Dry Cleaners, where her oldest friend, Sue Rose Foyt, acted as clerk and ticket agent, and where Lula tried to explain to Sue Rose why she had decided to leave Abnegation for the Great Plains.

"The guys here all think with their gonads," Lula said.

Sue Rose said, "That's the species, honey. There ain't no other sort of man Up North, Out West, or anywhere else."

"Maybe not, but I can't stand the guys in *this* backwater."

"So why head off to another one? To godforsaken Festivity, Iowa? *Iowa*, of all places."

A cheap suitcase at her feet and ranks of plastic-covered clothes hanging behind her like the husks of the Raptured, Lula perched in her folding chair next to the counter. Squinting, her eyes resembled pinless pink pincushions. Sue Rose regarded her critically, as if recalling when everyone in town, especially Chance, had considered Lula the county's greatest beauty.

"For love," Lula said at last.

"Of what?" Sue Rose said. "Corn cobs? Grain elevators?"

Lula's eyes twinkled in their slits. "Of somebody worthy of me. Of my soulmate, maybe."

"Come on, Lula, nobody's got to travel a thousand miles to get their heart broke."

"I do." In her violet-patterned sundress, Lula shifted her weight to her opposite haunch. "I most certainly do."

"Honey, tell me why."

"Several nights running I've had a dream of this carnival in a field of corn stubble under a crooked moon. Of a sideshow tent where a man in a tuxedo tells everyone who comes in what they must do to find everlasting love."

"And what's that?"

"Sell what they have. Give to the poor. Forsake the place of their birth for the carnival midway."

"Oh." Sue Rose smirked. "Is *that* all?"

"They must devote themselves to a lost soul who walks that midway lookin' not for answers or mysteries but just for . . . a true experience."

"Some dream. Okay, Lula, have you sold what you own?"

"Mostly. Chester Philpot's agreed to find a buyer for my trailer. Plus I got a dime a title at Minna's Magic Browse for my romance novels and movie mags."

"And you've given to the poor?"

"My clothes went to Baptist Thrift and what cash I could spare to Talledega Mission. I reckon that counts."

"Sure. But you have to go to *Iowa*?" The air conditioning

thumped, throttled down, droned like a beehive. "To marry this guy in the tux?"

"Not him. He's just a ringmaster, a fella who takes us in and then introduces the *real* attraction."

"*Takes us in?*" Rose said.

"Not that way. Welcomes us, I mean."

Noisily, the bus from Montgomery arrived and idled outside like a panting behemoth, its skirts tarred with road grime, its innards as mysterious behind its tinted windows as the holy of holies in a Hebrew tabernacle.

Lula boarded the Greyhound. The driver gazed down on her with the disinterest of a biologist watching a python engorge a frog. Only a few passengers looked up, but Lula still felt like a member of another species, less a mammal than an upright amphibian. Two rows back on the left, a pair of empty seats beckoned, and Lula squeezed into the nearer. Cool air from the window vents washed over her like a blessing.

The bus pulled out and cruised up U.S. 280. Inspecting her tickets, Lula found that she must change buses three times en route to Festivity, sleeping as she traveled. For courtesy's sake, she eased over toward the window, but her left hip still encroached on the aisle seat.

In Birmingham, the bus almost filled up, but no one sat by Lulu. A soldier squatted up front until a family of three got off in Carbon Hill and he slipped into a vacated seat.

In Tupelo, a new surge of riders boarded. A tough young guy with a shaved head, angry freckles, and a swastika earring stopped next to Lula, leaned over, and said, "A hippo like you ought to buy *two* tickets, honey."

Lula lowered her book and smiled. "What makes you think I didn't, ferret-face?"

The skinhead peered around, cawed loudly, then leaned back down to whisper, "Next time you smart-mouth me, cow, I'll slice your liver out."

Lula stage-whispered back, "You'd only lose your knife," then grabbed his sweaty tee shirt and twisted it with both hands. "Make nice so everyone can hear and sit down before I hurt you *bad*."

"Sure," the man said squeakily. "No disrespect intended, ma'am." When Lula let go of his shirt, he collapsed into the seat next to hers.

"Lula Carnahan," she said. "I can't imagine you want me to call you ferret-face forever."

"Just to Memphis. I'm Walter Cheatam." The bus swung a curve that pressed him against her, and she smiled with a look that dismissed him as even a minor nuisance, much less a bona fide person.

Acid filled Cheatam's mouth, and he caught a glint from the spoon-shaped silver brooch pinned above Lula's heart. Nodding at it, he said, "Maybe you should wear one shaped like a pitchfork."

Lula said only, "My ex-husband gave me this," and fingered the brooch's curved handle.

"Husband? Somebody must've poked the poor bastard down the aisle with a shotgun."

"No way." Lula took from her purse a photo of herself as County High Homecoming Queen, sixteen years ago. "I turned my husband down twice before surrendering."

Cheatam twisted the snapshot from side to side. "This is you? Va-va-voom! What happened?"

Lula seized it and dropped it back into her purse. "Take a look. I enlarged."

"Well, that's a shame."

"The shame is, I had to."

"Had to swell up like a balloon? What crap, Miz Carnahan."

Lula tapped his knee and recounted how her teenage beauty kept provoking men to lay hands on her (not religiously) and to try to persuade her to scoot off to New Orleans or Atlanta (not always on their own funds). Worse, Chance despised jealousy as a wimp's emotion and laughed off her every report of his pals' betrayals. In self-defense she began to eat, to plump herself out with milkshakes and cheeseburgers.

At first, when Lula informed him of her pregnancy, Chance tolerated these binges. His wife had to eat for two. He even bought the silver baby spoon that, after her miscarriage, Lula had made into a brooch. She went on gorging. For a while, Chance considered this an acceptable response to the terrible hollowness she felt—but when she *kept* eating, her increasing bulk alarmed and repulsed him.

"So the bastid left you," Cheatam said.

"Yes. Eventually."

"Understandable."

Lula *squeezed* Cheatam's knee. "Maybe so. But the other guys backed off too. Fat turned them off faster than a dose of saltpeter."

"Ow!" Lula stopped squeezing. "Hope that didn't surprise you," Cheatam said. "Guys visit strip clubs for the foxes, Miz Carnahan, not the manatees."

"What surprised me was, Chance had loved me for the way I'd looked, not for my inside self. So I added some flesh to subtract the jerks pretending to be his friends."

"Deep," Cheatam said.

"If I didn't look good, Chance didn't look good. Solution: divorce."

"Maybe Chance thought your extra weight would give you like a heart attack or somepin."

"If he did, the creep's motto was 'the sooner the better.' He talked diets to me but never doctors. Then he packed up and moved—two months after my miscarriage." She rubbed the bowl of her brooch, making it shine.

In Memphis, Cheatam stood by Lula while a porter unloaded the luggage bin. Then, all solicitude, he carried her suitcase into the station's waiting area.

"Whyinhell you want to go to Iowa?" he asked.

"Haven't you ever heard of running off to join the circus?" Lula smiled, showing her dimples.

Cheatam saluted, then pivoted and vanished out the door into the city's humid predawn. Not until an hour later, while boarding her bus to St. Louis, did Lula notice that her brooch had also vanished.

From Memphis to St. Louis. From St. Louis to Des Moines. From Des Moines to tiny Festivity.

Lula arrived at 9 P.M., exhausted, her sundress stained with sweat. A skinny old man outside the drugstore doubling as bus depot told her that a couple of nights ago the carnival had set up two miles northwest of town. Festivity had no taxi or shuttle service, but if she walked out beyond the Sweet Freeze, she could hitch a ride.

Dozens of cars whooshed by—some more than once, honking scornfully—but nobody stopped. So Lula walked. Half a mile away, she saw the lights of the makeshift fair grounds and heard the shrieks of the carnivalgoers. Not until nearly ten did she reach the Carnaval Milagrosa, her legs as stunned as butcher's blocks.

Lula paid and waddled into the parade of townies on the sawdust-strewn paths. Huge canvas posters rippled before her, hyping The Flying Frenellis, The Ugly Rat Boy, The Siamese

Transistor Sisters, and Evelyn Stynchcomb (*Ten-Performers-in-One!*). Ramshackle rides banged and ratcheted. Along with screams of glee and panic, these noises stretched out over the grounds like audible taffy, gumming the very air.

Just inside the biggest sideshow tent, a carny who looked Mayan made me check my suitcase. I told him it didn't contain a bomb, but he wouldn't let me enter until I'd stowed it behind his counter and he'd given me a receipt. Then I sauntered into the tent and between its swaying panels to a stage backed with a crummy drop scene of the Eiffel Tower, with King Kong hanging off it and exposing his crotch. Somebody'd pasted a decal of Joe Camel over this area, though, and before anyone could point out how much Joe Camel's face resembled the equipment of a male primate, the show's emcee, wearing a maroon tuxedo like the ringmaster in my dream, strolled out and tipped his top hat.

"*Bienvenido*, one and all," he said. "I am Cesar Sereno, manager of the Carnaval Milagrosa. Tonight, without moving an inch, you will witness in this tent the miraculous talents—the miraculous *person*—of Evelyn Stynchcomb, Ten Performers in One." Sereno glanced toward the people still filing in. "Come in. Yes, keep coming. We haven't begun yet. Plenty of room in the pit for you groundlings." He made a sweeping gesture of invitation.

"Plenty of room if you hadn't stuck your fat lady front-row center!" shouted the beefy man next to me.

"Look who's talking," said a good-looking fella on the edge of the crowd. "A professional nose tackle."

Everyone laughed, even me, but our laughter floated up at the edges, like a sheet with a bad smell under it.

Cesar Sereno bowed to me. "The plus-sized lady down front has gravitated to our amusement as a patron. She has as much right to her space as you to yours, so please accommodate with civility to one another and let the small fry come forward so they may see without hindrance."

"Maybe the small fry don't need to see this!" cried a voice somewhere behind me.

"Maybe not all of it," Sereno admitted. "For them, Evelyn Stynchcomb will appear as *Eight* Performers in One. Later, they will exit this tent for a free frozen-banana pop or a free ride on the midway."

The nose tackle bumped my shoulder. "Move over," he said, from the side of his sturgeon-lipped mouth.

I put my foot on his instep and leaned. Then I slipped my hand into his pocket and played Captain Queeg. The balls in my palm squished rather than clicked. The man gasped. When I let go, three children—cute Iowa towheads—butted between him and me to the pit's front row.

"Without further ado," said Cesar Sereno, "the wonderful—yes, the *miraculous*—Evelyn Stynchcomb!"

Near-blackness fell. (Hints of midway activity flickered in the tent's warp and woof.) King Kong and the Eiffel Tower ascended. A second backdrop slammed down, and the lights came up to disclose an immense human figure facing it, a kind of Sumo wrestler in soft silver slippers, pearl-gray pantaloons and tunic. The new backdrop featured three cartoonish strong men. The first held aloft an automobile, the second an entire family of acrobats, and the third the Earth itself.

"Performer Number One," said Sereno's disembodied voice. "The Strongest Woman in the World."

Immediately, Stynchcomb bent forward, full-mooning us, and gripped her slippered feet just under their arches. Then, grunting, she lifted herself from the stage and continued to hoist herself upward until she hung suspended about a yard off the stage like— well, like the moon.

Everyone gasped. If Evelyn Stynchcomb could lift her own formidable bulk—a bulk greater than even mine—how could any of us at the Carnaval Milagrosa let the petty trials of our workaday lives oppress us? Meanwhile, her labored breathing told us that keeping herself aloft had a heavy price, that to accomplish this feat she paid in joules of agony. Although I ached for the pain of her energy expenditure, I felt lighter myself—as if in escaping gravity in this way she had lifted a burden from my spirit. Others seemed to experience a like freedom. We all burst spontaneously into applause. Stynchcomb let go of her right slipper, extended her leg until her foot touched down, then balanced shakily on it until she could lower her other leg and redistribute her weight. Our applause intensified.

Then she turned to face us, enormous in harem pants and tunic, her bosom a pillowy shelf, her features hidden behind an apronlike veil from her eyes down.

"Performer Number Two," said Sereno with no intervening blackout. "*La Dama Gorda*: The Fat Lady."

We gawped. What else could we do? The World's Strongest Woman had become nothing more nor less than the phenomenon

of her own person. Beside her, even I resembled a marsh wren. So
we gawped, amazed that we'd already seen what we'd seen.

In a whiskey-edged contralto Evelyn Stynchcomb spoke through
her veil: "You may ask me questions."

No one did. Stunned and self-conscious, we simply stared. "As
the Fat Lady, I have no act per se. I stand before you as model or
admonition. You may ask me questions."

"What do you eat?" said a little girl up front.

"Anything and everything. Whatever I want. Who would be so
crazy as to try to dictate my menu?"

This reply chastened even the little girl who had dared to
speak. We gazed up in browbeaten adoration, shuffling our feet and
imagining private interviews in which we formulated such insight-
ful questions that Performer Number Two told us even her most
shameful secrets.

"You disappoint me," she said. "Don't you want fair value for the
cost of your tickets?"

This time the impetuous little girl piped, "How much do you
get paid?"

"Not nearly enough. Did this crowd pay *you* to speak for it,
child? No? Then let me say that in addition to my monthly salary,
my contract guarantees that I need never pay a food bill, at any
grocery store or restaurant I visit on the road."

Nice work if you can get it, I thought.

"Someone else ask a question," Stynchcomb said. "Don't let this
kid wind up your spokesperson by default."

"Are you married?" asked a farmer to my left.

"Are you proposing?"

Everyone guffawed, relieved that someone besides the child had
spoken, grateful for the Fat Lady's table-turning reply.

When we stopped laughing, the farmer popped his suspenders
and said, "That depends, lady. I don't mind a little flesh on a
woman, but if she's got a kisser like King Kong, well, that's different.
Any chance of seeing your face?"

Immediately, Sereno said, "Performer Number Three. *La
Dama con Barba.*" Stynchcomb unveiled. "The Bearded Lady."

A curly chestnut beard clung like a chinchilla muffler to
Stynchcomb's jaw. It made her look like a lumberjack with severe
gynecomastia. For the first time—in my eyes, anyway—she
appeared freakish. Her levitation and her bulk I had seen as talent
and self-definition. The beard, though, scared me.

"Jesus," said the farmer who had wanted to see her face.

This time we had questions aplenty. Did she take male sex hormones? No. Had she always had a beard? Only since the age of thirteen. Had anyone ever mistaken her for a youthful Santa Claus? Only a drunk in Altoona. Did she sleep with the beard inside or outside the covers?

"That question sabotages the old saw that the only stupid questions are the ones you *don't* ask," said Stynchcomb.

Everyone laughed, even the asker, and I gradually began to regard her as an extraordinary woman with a beard rather than an aberration of nature. In fact, the beard lent her a dignity and an authority—even if of a masculine stamp—in addition to those attendant upon her obesity. She looked handsome too. Why would anyone fixate on me and my subversive bulk with *this* woman present? So I felt safely a part of the crowd even as I hoped for a private interview with this prodigy.

Outside, the Carnaval Milagrosa squealed and oom-pahed its way toward midnight, but, inside, time lapsed at a slower rate, as if summer had stalled and Evelyn Stynchcomb's tenure as an attraction had acquired permanence. But I must tell the rest of this story quickly:

After a blackout, doing Performer Number Four, Stynchcomb swallowed swords. She guided first one, then two, and finally three épées down her gullet, glowing like a gargantuan firefly when their tips touched the floor of her stomach. Then she whipped the foils up through her mouth, so that briefly they fenced above her head before she recaptured them—one to each hand, the third beneath her arm—and bowed with a grand smirking flourish.

As Performer Number Five, Stynchcomb devoured fire. She ate it from silver torches as I would have eaten marshmallows from the tips of straightened coat hangers. She also set her beard afire, deliberately, so that it was consumed in curls of blue flame as delicate as the beard's own chestnut curls. Her cheeks then shone as smooth and rosy as a child's.

The farmer who'd asked her to unveil cried, "*Marry me!*"

Another blackout. The crowd shuffled in darkness, and then the lights flooded up again. On the rear wall hung a scrim of Mount Fuji, with cherry blossoms in its foreground. Evelyn Stynchcomb, naked from the waist up, faced this scrim. On her back roiled an elaborate tapestry of tattoos.

"Performer Number Six," said Cesar Sereno from the wings. "The Human Cyclorama."

We gawked as Stynchcomb flexed and twisted without once

facing us, working not to become meaningful to us as a person but only to inspirit the mauve and yellow, emerald and purple, scarlet and indigo subjects inked into her back. Devotees of the storytelling tattoo, we watched in awe as gods, beasts, warriors, maidens, sorcerers, trees, temples, and machines in her illustrated flesh played out their parts in a mesmerizing pageant from which each one of us chose the sequence answering to our deepest need.

I, for instance, focused on a reenactment of that part of Plato's *Symposium* in which the god-split halves of primordial human beings seek to reunite. This drama—the origins of Love—unraveled in the small of Stynchcomb's back when a pair of upright creatures, each a cutting of the original orblike manwoman that Zeus sliced in two, found each other, embraced, and became whole again. This sequence occurred in the midst of a myriad unrelated episodes, but I had eyes only for it. When it ended triumphantly, I, too, felt an orgasmic release and burst into applause.

Everyone else in the pit, from kids to oldsters, clapped along with me. They had witnessed satisfying passion plays of their own, whether a successful dragon hunt, a flying-carpet ride over a green archipelago, or the execution of their most dreaded enemy. Evelyn Stynchcomb, as the Human Cyclorama, had delivered.

After another blackout, she reappeared, clad once again in her pearl-gray tunic, nodding in acknowledgment of yet another swell of applause.

As Performer Number Seven, Stynchcomb read our minds. She picked seven people at random and told each one his or her most troubling worry and most heartfelt wish. She mentioned the unfaithfulness of spouses or sweethearts, crop failure and debts, illnesses and misunderstandings. She prophesied true love, life-changing foreign travel, even someone's purchase of an albino dachshund puppy.

She picked me seventh. "Callula Ward Carnahan, your real first name means 'Little Beautiful One,' but you have come a thousand miles to escape the contempt of sex-obsessed men and the cancer of your own self-hatred. True?"

"I don't know," I said weakly.

"Ah, but you do. And your fondest wish—which you didn't discover until you entered this tent—is to assume my powers and change places with me."

"No," I said, horror-stricken. "No it isn't."

"Correct," Stynchcomb said. "It isn't. I won't identify your fondest wish, Lula, because I don't wish to embarrass you or anybody else—not even those among you, whom I refrained from choosing, who *deserve* embarrassment or punishment because they've borne false witness, committed adultery, stolen from a family member, abused a child, or even taken another person's life and successfully concealed the crime."

"*You* bear false witness!" a man behind me cried. "*You* do!"

A woman in khaki slacks and a white blouse pushed forward. "I've seen enough to understand that you scoff at decency, Ms. Stynchcomb. You defile your body through gluttony and immodest display. You may even consort with demons." She appealed to the crowd. "We must close down this tent—the whole Carnaval Milagrosa! The devil himself couldn't do more than this circus of sin to corrupt the people of Festivity!"

"Close 'em down!" shouted a man behind me.

"*Close 'em down! Close 'em down!*" A mob of others gladly took up the chant.

Ms. Stynchcomb lifted her hand. "Stop it!" The chanting stopped. "Everyone eighteen or under must leave the tent! To make up for your early departure, you'll get tickets for free food or rides at our exit. We encourage you to go, by the way, to *avoid* corrupting you."

When the young people had left, the woman up front said, "Removing the children doesn't remove the problem. Your act—this entire carnival—stands as an affront to our community, Ms. Stynchcomb. I had to see it myself before I could make that judgment, but now I recognize this whole enterprise as a deceit and an abomination."

Stynchcomb's eyes flashed like torches as she swung herself to the edge of the stage. "'Alas for you Pharisees! You pay tithes of mint and rue and every garden herb, but still neglect justice and the love of God!'"

This oration paralyzed the crowd. We all peered up like well-scolded kids, scarcely hearing the calliope music or the rides rumbling on the midway.

Then the woman said, "'*The love of God*'? How can a person of your ilk, a lackey of Mammon, utter such words?"

"Because the love of God surrounds us too," Stynchcomb said mildly. Then she roared, "'Alas for you Pharisees! You clean the outside of cup and plate, but inside seethe with greed and wickedness, judgment and injustice!'"

"For crying out loud," the woman said. "Even the devil can quote scripture to support his positions."

"*The Merchant of Venice*, act one, scene three," Stynchcomb said. "Dueling quotations. Shoot me another."

The woman said, "No more prattle. We'll send the sheriff out here to close you people down. We'll do it legally and make it stick."

"*Close 'em down! Close 'em down!*"

Cesar Sereno's amplified voice intoned, "Performer Number Eight. Stynchcomb the Magician, Sorceress of Grievous Spells."

Stynchcomb lifted one hand. "Begone, ye hard of heart! Begone, all doubters and despisers!"

The canvas tent panels and the backdrops on stage bellied inward, then flapped back out. The pressure in my head seemed out of phase with that in the pit, as if it had risen without warning to Ferris-wheel height. I stood alone below the stage, the only patron to have escaped banishment.

"Callula," said Stynchcomb. "My soulmate in the flesh."

"Performer Number Nine," said Cesar Sereno before I could regather my wits. "The Fabulous Geek."

Stynchcomb turned toward the voice. "I just can't do that anymore. Children don't need to witness geekery, of course, but watching it degrades adults too—not to mention the poor performer. So count me out, Cesar."

After an extended pause, Sereno said, "Okay. I don't mind rebilling you '*Nine* Performers in One.' Nine has cachet. The nine Muses. Dressed to the nines. Et cetera."

"Thank you."

"Performer Number Nine has bowed out," said Sereno. "So I present to you now Performer Number Nine, formerly Number Ten. The Discreet Epicene."

A last backdrop slammed into place. It showed a smiling Buddha-like figure, with pendulous breasts and earlobes, sitting naked amid pale-purple orchids.

"Where'd everybody else go?" I asked.

Evelyn Stynchcomb extended her hand. "Help me down." I took her hand and walked beside the stage as she crossed it to a set of stairs. She descended into the pit, still holding my hand, and faced me smelling faintly of sweat and a mild eau de cologne. "I spelled them out, kid, with no memory of any of my various performances. Some may sit in front of television sets in Festivity, some may vie for prizes at booths on our midway, but none has come to harm—not even my most zealous opponent, that dreadful woman."

"Good," I said. "But please, Ms. Stynchcomb, what's an epicene?"

"A two-in-one, friend. A hermaphrodite. As Aristophanes says in

Plato's *Symposium*, 'Once there existed a manwoman sex and a moniker to go with it, but today nothing remains but the reproachful title.' Obviously, despite his great learning and wit, Aristophanes didn't know everything. He erred in thinking the title lacked a contemporary object, either then or now."

Uneasily I said, "What do you *do* in this portion of your act?"

"At most typical performances, once the children have left, we divide my audience by sex, men to one side and women to the other, and draw a curtain straight across the pit. Then I move between the sides talking to each group so that all can hear me, but only half the crowd—the men to begin with, the women later—can see what I have to show them."

"And what do you have to show them?"

"Only the imperfect temple of my body, which God made as it is. Would *you* care to see it? You, Callula, I can give a private audience."

Lula Carnahan and Evelyn Stynchcomb left the sideshow tent, picking up Lula's suitcase on their way out, and trudged side by side through the sawdust and the concession-stand litter to an encampment of trailers and recreational vehicles behind the Barrel Spin, a ride whose dimpled metal floor dropped away so that centrifugal force pinned its riders to its wall until the floor rose into place again and the groaning cylinder ceased to whirl. Lula felt as if she had spent an entire evening in this cylinder.

As they traipsed, a baroque Ferris wheel emerged from the hazy lights on the fair side of the fairgrounds, turning under the lopsided moon. Lula could not remember having seen the big wheel on her way out from Festivity. All its cars but one held passengers, all the cars shadowy in the cloud-strained moonlight, while between its struts hung figures that from this distance looked somewhat more or less than human. Eerie music accompanied the wheel's turning, but you could scarcely hear it over the carnival's dying hubbub. Oddly, Lula understood that unless Evelyn intervened, before morning she would have to take a seat in the device's only empty car.

"Come into my den," said Evelyn Stynchcomb. "I'll show you my hanging file folders."

Lula preceded the carny into the trailer, which featured built-in bookcases, framed posters, filing cabinets, and a cozy dining booth. Stynchcomb gave Lula a cup of instant coffee with dollops of cream and sugar, then converted the booth into a bed.

On this bed, much to Lula's astonishment, she beheld in private what audiences of the Discreet Epicene beheld in public in groups segregated by sex and divided by a curtain. She also ministered to Evelyn in ways that, a few hours ago, she would not have imagined possible, much less acceptable to her as a woman of Christian upbringing. Evelyn, in turn, ministered to and accommodated Lula.

In the morning, Lula awoke alone. Alert to the silence of the cornfields and of the trailer in which she had debauched herself, she rolled over and slid open a porthole panel. The Carnaval Milagrosa had gone, even the disturbing Ferris wheel. The trampled midway remained, as did tent-stake divots, tire treads, animal dung, ticket stubs, cigarette butts, and blowing trash. Otherwise, the carnival had decamped.

Shame crept over Lula like a sunburn. What had she done? Only with Chance, her eventual husband, had she ever had sex outside wedlock.

Across the room, a slip of paper hung from a bookshelf. A note, Lula thought. She wallowed through the sweaty linen and launched herself toward the bookcase. On the shelf above the taped note lay a silver object. Lula recognized it, after a shake of the head, as the spoon brooch that Cheatam had filched from her in Memphis.

The note said, "I thought you might want this. I have run away from the carnival. Should you want to join it, I leave you my vehicle and everything in it, including my hanging file folders. Señor Sereno next plans to set up outside Blue Earth, Minnesota. Continue to pay tithes of mint and rue, but do not neglect justice and the love of God. Last night, you showed me both. Thank you."

It was signed "E. S."

Lula read the note again. Looking around, she felt sure that the RV contained miraculous secrets. She folded the bed linens, dressed in fresh clothes, pinned the spoon brooch over her heart, and moved forward to the roomy cab. How long would it take to drive to Blue Earth, Minnesota? How long to return to Abnegation, Alabama? What other destinations might beckon if she let them?

The key turned easily in the ignition. The engine rumbled in its mounts like a wind freshening over water.

* * *

Of Crystalline Labyrinths and the New Creation

There are multitudinous emanations, and sight is but one of them which is given us here in the childhood of the soul.

—R. A. Lafferty

☆   ☆   ☆

1

Ossie Safire, character,
A digger diligent and lean,
Went out one day searching for
Just one thalassapithecine.

Boomer Flats Ballads

WALKING BESIDE AN ARROYO ON A GIN-CLEAR OKLA-homa day, Ossie Safire caught sight of something: a shimmer, a shifting, *something*. Forty feet ahead of him, a shuffle of air and wind had just *unsparkled* in the gulch's clayey walls. By rockhound intuition Ossie knew that if he didn't hop down into the arroyo, whatever it was that he hadn't quite seen would disappear.

So down he hopped and strode up the arroyo talking to himself: "I'm looking for Osage pottery shards, the paleoliths of the enigmatic pre-people People, or the flipper bones and femurs of archaeo-okie thalassapithecines." (These last were seagoing ape folk of an undated inland-sea era in whom nobody *but* Ossie Safire believed.) "I am *not* looking for unsparklings of ostentatious air."

Rowdy Al LeFever had invited Ossie out to his ranch to look around. Rowdy Al, who hailed from Boomer Flats, claimed that a first-rate discovery lay in wait on his place for a dedicated rock-hound. Ossie had met him earlier that day on the porch of his lopsided, yellow, many-gabled house.

"An unusual house, sir," Ossie had said politely.

"A fella down the road once tried to build one just like it," Rowdy Al told Ossie. "He said to me, 'Mr. LeFever, there is nothing so original as a first-rate copy.' The house he built fell over nine or ten times before he got one version to stand up. 'Well, it ain't an *inimitable* house you've got here,' he said, 'but I could've never built one anything like it without seeing yours first.' Later he tore it down and built a house more like himself, but I didn't think too ill of him."

"I've come to look for rocks," Ossie had said, trying to get back on topic. "Or fossils."

"Well, nose around. Make you a find. I've heard of you, Ossie Safire, and I want you to be the first to run across this thing." Rowdy Al had retired into his yellow house, leaving Ossie to his own devices.

And so, wishing for the serendipitous, Ossie stalked the thing he hadn't quite seen and fumbled his handpick out of his rucksack. A stand of cottonwoods topped the ochre rise beyond the arroyo's far bank. Ossie was admiring their long trunks and liquid leaves as all unexpectedly it happened, *it* being a collision.

"Ow!" he said. For he had bumped into an anomaly that would soon grow even more anomalous, and had scraped his nose. He thought he saw a not-sparkle—yes, a *not-sparkle*—interpose itself between his eyes and the cottonwoods. He lifted his handpick and tapped it on the motionless wind in the gulch, upon the airy hardness that his nose had bumped. The air blocked his handpick blow and shivered Ossie Safire's wrist. This is dismaying, he thought, for if no digger at the Greater Tulsa Diggers' Consortium can credit thalassapithecines, will any of that crew believe I've found a pocket of solidified air?

But Ossie, whom dismay seldom deterred, again tapped his discovery with his handpick. He tapped up and down and laterally. He tested the dimensions of the entire anomaly, which hung from unknown heights into the arroyo like a transparent stalactite. Stooping, Ossie walked under its rounded tip. It had a radius of four or five feet and kept not-sparkling and not-glinting, all of which negative coruscations he now ignored.

(What *were* these unsparklings and not-glints? Ossie regarded the gin-clear day as one protracted flashing of the Cosmic Orderer; he thought the negative coruscations from the unseen rock winks of ordinary daylight. If this explanation sounds complicated, think how hard it was for me to devise.)

Ossie rued that he could not measure the *height* of the invisible stalactite. He threw dust on it hoping that a coating of grime might enlighten him, but the dust would not stick. It flew away on the Oklahoma breeze.

After a while, Ossie sat down on the arroyo bank with a peanut-butter-and-jelly sandwich and a flask of mineral water. He stared up at his discovery. Was this what Rowdy Al had wanted him to find? Apparently. And so it hurt that the huge, hanging rock would not be tricked into visibility. The Greater Tulsa Diggers' Consortium would expel him as a crank and a mountebank.

Eighty or ninety feet overhead, a graceful hawk collided with something and tumbled beak over pin feathers toward the arroyo. Ossie jumped to his feet, but the hawk caught itself up and, flapping with clumsy flaps, avoided a crash landing only a few feet from Ossie's picnic. Groggily, the bird flew away.

A moment later, the brightness above Ossie unsparkled. Even more unsettlingly, he felt the invisible crystal *think* something at him:

Almostal comptured of omniversilly mattessence om Aye, O resiever of m'eye enconquerumphing metamorphilology.

This isn't fair, Ossie thought. I was hunting thalassapithecines, and this annoying weirdness isn't fair—not at all, not at all.

2

An Indian, called Flashing Plains,
Found a diamond on the prairie:
Sammy, blessed with spunk and brains,
Became a lapidary.
Boomer Flats Ballads

A week later in downtown Tulsa, Ossie Safire sat with three of his pals in the Arrowhead Lounge of the Diggers' Consortium: Ignatius Clayborne, whom everybody called Clay to avoid getting knuckled; Opalith Magmani, a beautiful beast of a woman to whom Ossie had proposed four times; and the richest Indian interested in archeology whom Ossie had ever met, Sammy Flashing Plains. All three wondered why Ossie had herded them together into this cramped Naugahyde booth.

"Which idiocy must we deal with today?" asked Ignatius Clayborne. "The pre-people People or your butterflying baboons?"

"Thalassapithecines," Ossie corrected his friend, humbly.

When Sharla, the barmaid, came to their booth to take their drink orders, Sammy Flashing Plains said, "No wisecracks about firewater, you guys."

Ossie ogled Opalith and said, "I'd like a dry Magmani." He quickly emended this to "A dry martini," his mouth chock full of the dust of chagrin.

They *all* ordered martinis. "Banish the vermouth," Sammy Flashing Plains said. "There's enough wormwood in the paneling."

"Well," said Ignatius Clayborne when Sharla left to fetch their drinks.

The frog in Ossie's throat croaked. "I've hesitated to talk to you all," he began, coughing a bit, "because of the esteem in which I hold all three of you: Clay, a geologist; Opalith, a stratigrapher, dendrochronologist, and reader of varved clays, not to mention the greatest beauty to come out of Tishomingo, Oklahoma; and Sammy, a—"

"Preservationist," Sammy Flashing Plains said. "I lead palefaces like you away from our holy places to do your digging, and I thank the Great Spirit that none of you is a social anthropologist." He sported a double-breasted blue suit and a headband of Osage design. Everyone else slouched there in work clothes.

"Okay," Ossie said. "Anyhow, out of esteem, I've delayed mentioning my most recent discovery. Now, though, several well-documented recent events have made it possible to broach the subject."

Their martinis arrived.

"What thubject?" Leaning forward in unstarched khakis, Opalith was a starching creature, alert and lissome.

Ossie turned his gaze upon his crystalline gin and recalled the matter at hand. "Have any of you all been reading the *World* or the *Tribune,* or watching the television newscasts?"

Except for Sammy Flashing Plains, who eschewed the media of the technocracy, they had indeed.

"Then," Ossie continued, "you've no doubt heard of the appearance, in diverse parts of the world, of sudden geological outcroppings."

"The invisible ones?" Opalith fingered her alluring tresses.

Ossie Safire nodded.

"It's a hoax," Ignatius said. "A convocation of world political

leaders hope to take the public's mind off their manifold bum-
blings. Invisible outcroppings, indeed!"

"It isn't a hoax," Ossie said. "I've found one myself, one hundred and thirteen miles from here." He told his skeptical pals of the
unsparkling on Rowdy Al LeFever's ranch and of how he had
bumped his nose. Not one whit did he embellish, but he did refrain
from mentioning that the invisible rock had communicated telepathically with him. (Well, *almost* communicated.) By way of
epilogue he said, "Now there've been reports of similar anomalies
as far away as Jerez, Spain, and as close as Dubuque, Iowa. Nine in
all, there've been."

"I can add a tenth," said Sammy Flashing Plains, "but the report
will be the most recent and the sighting the most ancient."

"Explain yourself, you indigent aborigine," said Ignatius Clayborne.

"That's *indigenous*," Sammy Flashing Plains said. "Which, in
conjunction with *aborigine*, is redundant." He made his martini disappear. "Many years ago, when I was little more than what Clay
would call a papoose, I saw just such an unsparkling as Ossie has
described—a flicker on the sage-grown prairie. Little rib-ringed
coyote that I was, I ran home shouting, '*The plains are flashing,
O my mother! The plains are flashing, O my father!*' "

"Is this a retelling of the Chicken Little story?" Ignatius asked.

"No," Sammy said. "Incidentally, the proper name of that story
isn't 'Chicken Little,' but 'Chicken Licken,' a fact having importance because of the incantatory nature of the poem's rhymes.
These reports of invisible outcroppings may spell for us the same
sort of disaster that overtook the protagonist of the nursery fable."

"We'll all by eaten by a fox?" Opalith Magmani said.

"Of course not," said Sammy, "but it's astute of you to recall the
ending. What I suggest is that the incantatory nature of these reports
may dull us to another possibility. Expecting a political catastrophe,
we may fall prey to a totally different disaster—just as Chicken
Licken, fearing skyfall, winds up as a fox's dinner. An important
contrast does exist, however."

"Do tell," said Ignatius.

"Chicken Licken's error lay in supposing a universal catastrophe when she and her friends succumbed to a personal one. Our
error may lie in assuming the collapse of a few local governments
when the impending disaster will destroy *everything*."

"How fashionably gloomy," said Opalith.

Ossie Safire said, "What about your finding as a child, Sammy?"

"My father tried to dose me with castor oil, but my mother stopped him. She said that I'd seen only a bit of mica or tin can. I explained that I'd seen the unsparkling *above* the ground instead of *on* it, but they wouldn't listen. I went back to the prairie and found a jutting point of solidified air at waist height. I cupped my hands around it, but couldn't budge it. Finally, I draped my blood-red headcloth over it as a marker.

"When I returned the next day, my headcloth had blown into the sagebrush. I picked it out and, this time, *tied* it around the flashing crystal outcropping. But the cloth split and fell away again, for the rock inside my tiny bundle had . . . grown. I kept trying to capture it with cloth, but at last the rock point cut through the *blanket* that I had taken from my parents' bed. Then, friends, it spoke with an inside-out tongue of fire in my brain, saying *Tittle Smindian, you mayan't never trapture a manipphany of the Nu Cree Nayschun.*"

"Come again," said Opalith Magmani.

"That's what it said, inside me. I remember because *I* never thought like that, and still don't. My father spanked me for spoiling the blanket. The next day the outcropping vanished. Today I am a lapidary, a gemstone dealer, and an Indian even yet."

"An interesting story," said Ignatius. "Do you contend it has some bearing on what Ossie has told us about his own find?"

"Two plus two," said Sammy Flashing Plains.

Ossie Safire, grateful that Sammy had corroborated his account, downed his drink. He was also grateful that Sammy had recited the unseen outcropping's telepathic nonsense, for the recitation made him feel less crazy.

At least until Sammy said, "Twenty years ago, it wasn't time for what is going to happen to happen. Now, my friends, it is."

3

> *A bold quartet, they sallied out*
> *Like buccaneers or reivers*
> *To ask whose exegesis was most stout:*
> *Why, Rowdy Al LeFever's!*
>   Boomer Flats Ballads

Back out to the Oklahoma prairie they went, to the arroyo where Ossie had made his find—Ossie, Ignatius, Opalith, and Sammy Flashing Plains. Into the early-morning, blast-furnace swelter, one week later, they boomed along in Miss Magmani's jeepster. (Don't blame me if you prefer *Ms.* for the ladies. The *Miss* was Opalith's own idea, and she insisted upon it.) How that woman could wheel a vehicle. Her driving made poor Ossie wish for a headache powder or a fortifying tot of vodka.

If he hadn't known before, Rowdy Al now knew of his ownership of an invisible anomaly. He had invited four members of the Greater Tulsa Diggers' Consortium to visit his place to examine it. He would be waiting for them. And he was.

"Howdy!" Opalith hailed him, jouncing her friends up the drive to Rowdy Al's lopsided yellow house.

Out to the arroyo the rancher led them on foot. "Still here," he said as the five of them stared up at the big unflashing rock. He took off his Stetson, mopped his brow, and beheld the gin-clear Oklahoma sky. "A very quiet anomaly," he said.

"They're all over now," Sammy Flashing Plains said. "From the Kirghis Steppe to the African Sahel to Ty Ty, Georgia, U.S.A."

"Twelve sightings in all," Ossie said. "Thanks for not publicizing this one."

"Well," said Rowdy Al, "it's been behaving itself."

"Any new developments?" asked Ignatius Clayborne.

Rowdy Al pointed. "I think there's another one out in the middle of the pasture beyond those cottonwoods."

"Why do you think that?" said Opalith.

"The cattle have been crawling on their knee joints to lick the salt licks out there, and they don't usually do that. Also, it sort of winks."

"Have two outcroppings been 'seen' this close together before?" asked Ignatius.

"I don't think so," said Sammy Flashing Plains. "To avert catastrophe, we must determine the composition of these invisible rocks."

"Set up camp out here," Rowdy Al said. "Stay as long as you like." He pivoted on the arroyo bank and walked off toward his bric-a-brac-infested house. The whiteness of the day cloaked his dwindling bulk with a hieratic haze. O, did that man glow!

The others set up camp halfway between the hardness that Ossie had discovered and the one that Rowdy Al had hinted at. They soon verified that the second outcropping did indeed exist, a veritable floating mountain of invisibility, which they christened The-Anomaly-As-Big-As-The-Ritz. (Ossie's discovery, by the way, they called the Hope-It's-A-Diamond outcropping.) Its bottom hovered four feet from the ground, and it had the circumference of an oil-storage tank. Its height, no hawks having flown by, they could not even guess at.

Ignatius Clayborne set out stakes beneath the perimeter of The-Anomaly-As-Big-As-The-Ritz, strung the stakes together, and knotted orange rags to the string. He moved the offending salt blocks so that LeFever's cattle would not crawl over his pickets to get their licks in. Meanwhile, Opalith took soil samples from the area inside the flags, and Sammy circled the unseen rock trying to chip a specimen or two from its sides. Shivered wrists were all he got for his pains.

Ossie Safire hopped down into the arroyo and discovered that the Hope-It's-A-Diamond outcropping had grown. It had lengthened in parallel with the gully beneath it. If it kept growing, one day it would abut on the one where his friends labored. (The arroyo wound that way, you see.) Mazy walls of glass would divide the ranch as surely as barbed wire already did.

The moon jumped up, and they all retired to their stuffy tent. "Not a good start," Ignatius said. "What do you think The Ritz and the Hope-It's-A-Diamond are—invisible rocks, solidified air, or a flash-frozen liquid?"

"In this setting," Opalith said, "I would call those equally accurate, or inaccurate, ways of saying the same thing. The anomalies— which we cannot see, hear, or taste—occupy space, they encroach, and they grow. What does it matter if we call them rocks, air, or water?"

"Well, I'm a geologist," Ignatius said huffily.

"We can *hear* the anomalies," Ossie put in. "They ping when you tap them." He neglected to add that sometimes the rocks *thought* things at you.

"Still," said Opalith, "it's their space-occupying that frightens us. That, and their sudden popping into being, and their ability to grow."

That night, Sammy Flashing Plains rocked over his knees like a trance-taken medicine man. When Opalith dialed down the gas lanterns, the glowing gargoyles on the green tent walls faded from view. Talk mumbled off into sleep, and the night flowed down like embalming lava.

The next day, the four diggers resolved to delimit the transparent stones in space. The rag-hung cordons beneath The-Anomaly-As-Big-As-The-Ritz did this job inexactly. The flags kept them from banging into it, and the cows from crawling, but did not go far toward clarifying dimensions. Because the eroded gulch under the Hope-It's-A-Diamond made it hard to work there, the friends concentrated on The Ritz and discussed means and methods of plumbing its mysteries.

Ignatius said pontifically, "We must make this prairie-pent Gibraltar visible," and sent Opalith—who would allow no one else to drive her jeepster—to the hardware store in Boomer Flats to buy 1) an extension ladder, 2) a gallon of paint, and 3) a plastic bottle with a spray attachment.

"I got green," Opalith told Ignatius upon her return. "Your favorite."

Fortunately, he had asked for only one gallon because, once Ignatius had climbed the ladder and begun to spray, the paint—like the dust that Ossie had hurled on his first morning in the arroyo—would not adhere. Emerald droplets struck The Ritz's invisible surface and immediately slid or blew away. Ignatius, a many-freckled man, came down the ladder with a profane lack of grace.

"O Froggy," Opalith greeted him. "It looked so eerie to see you up on that ladder, balanced on nothing." And it absolutely had.

"We need a piece of canvas," Ignatius cried. "We'll wrap it, that unshpritzable Ritz. Wrapping large buildings was once a popular art form, and we can do it here, my band of brave upholsterers."

"It won't work," said Sammy Flashing Plains. "Don't you remember the story of my headcloth and the invisible rock point?" He suggested building a housing around the outcropping: a derrick-like structure or a series of scaffoldings.

Ossie noted that this strategy might prove dangerous, especially if the rock began to grow as they built.

"Then I'm going to ask Rowdy Al for some dynamite." Ignatius wrote a note to the rancher and carried it down the pasture to his big zinc mailbox.

That evening, in the gargoyle-haunted tent, Ossie's radio announced that new anomalies had made their presence known in Illinois, Texas, Nebraska, and Utah. Other parts of the world also reported more outcroppings. The four pals looked around at one another out of ash-colored faces.

Before going to bed, Ossie Safire walked outside and stood amid the cottonwoods looking toward Rowdy Al's house of many gables. All its lights were on, and jig music jogged up the rise to Ossie. Further, the silhouette of the heavyset rancher went dancing from one blazing window to another. Rowdy Al, it seemed, was rowdy in private, but you could participate at a distance in his genial rowdiness and commence to glow almost as bright as he.

Ossie crept back into his sleeping bag. To his disappointment, Opalith had again opted to sleep in work clothes.

On the third day they tried dynamite—a crate full of dynamite. On the top of the crate fluttered a tiny card whose handwritten message declared, *This is a good idea, but it won't work. R.A.L.*

It didn't work. Nor had the friends expected it to. (Still, you would have enjoyed watching Opalith and Ossie run off the cows.) However, the experiment blew up in their faces in a different way from what they had expected.

Beneath The-Anomaly-As-Big-As-The-Ritz, Ossie and Ignatius planted four separate charges. Then, after collapsing their tent, they retreated to the arroyo, where everyone took cover under Hope-It's-A-Diamond. From the dusty gulch, they detonated their charges.

Whumpf. Whuumpf. Whuuumpf. And *whuuuumpf.* O, it was like a tubercular cow wheezing out the letters of a bovine Tetragrammaton. Afterward, the four diggers scrambled like lizards from beneath their rock to behold what they could behold and saw . . . well, nothing.

Or no more than several distended balloons of dust drifting hazily through the cottonwoods; those, and the orange rags that lay all over the land. As they came through the cottonwoods on their approach to The Ritz, they did see the outsized pothole beneath the invisible rock: a shallow crater, with lumps of dirt still lumpily in it, clods of clay that the wind had not dispersed.

Said Ignatius Clayborne, "Let's search for fragments."

Down on all fours went all four of them, with a few returning, cud-chewing cows looking on imperturbably. Ossie found blades of buffalo grass, sidewinder spoors, heat-steamed cow chips, and one crazily careening dung beetle. But he found no fragments of The Ritz, nor did anybody else.

"Such a shame," said Opalith Magmani. "Such a shame."

They discovered, however, that they had altered the dimensions of The-Anomaly-As-Big-As-The-Ritz. Whole chunks around its base had disappeared, like bites out of an invisible mushroom.

"Those missing chunks," said Sammy, "have to be somewhere."

"Maybe they went back to wherever they came from," volunteered Ossie Safire. "Just like that rock point of your papoosehood."

"Uh-uh," grunted Sammy discouragingly.

"Explain yourself," said Ignatius Clayborne.

"Far from ridding ourselves of these invisible crystalline structures, if that's what they are, we may have facilitated their proliferation, growth, and ultimate imprisoning of the damnable human race."

"Boy," said Opalith, "you are one gloomy Indian."

Back in the vicinity of their dismantled tent, they listened to a National Public Radio announcer report new outcroppings in every state of the union, as well as in every country represented in the United Nations. Two streets in downtown Tulsa had filled with huge, invisible hardnesses, making them impassable; meanwhile, other cities had suffered similar inexplicable clog-ups. "We would say more," the announcer intoned, "but high-ranking government officials have asked us not to. Anyhow, it looks as if the *Rocks . . . Are . . . On . . . The . . . March.*"

Ossie Safire wandered into the cottonwoods and stood looking for a long time at Rowdy Al LeFever's house. Tonight no lights blazed in the windows, no merry figure hippity-jigged among the rooms, and the house's yellow paint looked muted and muddy. Even so, the shingles on the roof had a phosphorescent sheen, and the spirit of Rowdy Al hovered spectrally over the landscape, more in control of things than he, Ossie Safire, would ever be. Things were falling apart; no, they were growing together, and something was not quite copacetic with the world.

The-Anomaly-As-Big-As-The-Ritz unsparkled under the moon like a demonic Ferris wheel. But it did not wink at him telepathically, and Ossie emphatically wished that it would. Comfort glinted in those ominous, rocky thoughts.

4

Strew flowers all about,
Heliotropes and hyacinths.
And let that yellow house draw out
Hosannas from the labyrinths!
Boomer Flats Ballads

They awoke the next morning to find that a wall of invisible glass had grown through the cottonwood copse. They walked out of their tent and went *bang* against it. Ignatius Clayborne collided first and then Ossie. Opalith and Sammy Flashing Plains escaped this indignity. None of them, however, could escape the implications of this new intrusion. Blasted fragments of The Ritz had taken root and bloomed into bulwarks, all viewless and vitreous where they didn't belong.

"Are we trapped?" asked Ignatius.

"No," said Sammy, "but plainly it has become dangerous to remain here. Look." Today, the wind blew hard, but the leaves and limbs of only half the trees around them jiggled. The others stood as if encased in Lucite molds—which, in a way, they were, for that clear rock stuff had flowed right around the old cottonwoods, fixing them fast. "This could have happened to us," Sammy went on, "and now we'd be nothing but four human aphids in amber."

"You're one eloquent Indian," Opalith said. "Shall we pack up and go?"

"A powwow," Sammy said. "Everybody sit."

In the stand of cottonwoods, an invisible wall on one side, they sat in a ring like pipe-smoking shamans. Ossie mused that he and his pals looked like picnickers at a feast of potential panic. How did it feel to have stone lap about you like gin and congeal, with nary an olive for comfort?

"I had a dream last night," began Sammy Flashing Plains. "In it, Rowdy Al LeFever told me that our anomalies are extrusions of a catty-corner crystalline vulcanism taking place in the continuum next door. A world over there is heaving and groaning and creating so abundantly that it's splitting its own seams. These extrusions, Rowdy Al said, are extropic in nature and may not soon cease."

"What's this 'extropic' business?" asked Ossie.

"Our system is an entropic one," said Sammy. "This other continuum runs on the opposite principle, one of endless creation rather than of unrelenting dysfunction and decay. Its system makes matter out of the great spinning Nothing, whereas ours can only . . . not destroy matter, but leach away at the old creation until it collapses.

"All this, and even more fabulous stuff, Rowdy Al told me as I dreamt. And as I slept, the crystalline lava of the New Creation flowed into our camp, lapped the trees, and lovingly hardened. It flowed through the seams that we had loosened with our dynamite, through the pressure points opened by the blasts that scattered abroad the shrapnel shards of The Ritz."

"So we've abetted our own downfall," said Ignatius Clayborne.

Sammy Flashing Plains ignored him. "The most fabulous thing that Rowdy Al told me was this: 'In the New Creation, Sammy, intelligence and nature have melded into an indivisible whole. The flowing lava and the seam-bursting crystal are blessed with sentience; they possess not only the ratiocinative ability but also imagination! They can recombine human language into more compact and meaningful units of ideation—*if only we could understand those units*. Rocks won't replace humans over here, but, instead, creative mineral *intelligences.* In such a domain, Sammy, death itself dies, for death can never conquer that which lacks frail flesh and frangible bone.' And Rowdy Al urged me to rejoice."

"In other words," said Ignatius, "using dynamite was a good idea except for the fact that it didn't work."

"It didn't work as we *expected,*" said Sammy. "The downfall that Ignatius dreads holds embryonic life, and it would have occurred no matter what we did. Rowdy Al said, 'Sammy, as an Indian you see yourself as a constituent element of the world's adornment, not as a meddlesome observer with a trowel to poke at this and that. And that's good, for you're a part of the New Creation, too. You should daub on the peace paint and whoop the joy whoops, in awe and celebration.' "

"Rowdy Al's not your ordinary rancher," said Ossie Safire. "But how did he come to know so much about these invisible extrusions —when the world at large is so vastly stumped?"

"Rowdy Al," said Sammy, "has lived his whole life on the edge of an extrusion seam. When that seam, one of millions, finally flooded the earth with its faceted magma, Rowdy Al burst with power, too."

A quietness of great pregnancy sluiced around the four pow-wowing diggers, which Ignatius at length delivered of a confession: "I don't understand. And if that's true, what must we do today?"

"Walk among the walls and marvel," said Sammy. "This is the Last Day of the Old Procession."

And so the four friends walked out of the cottonwood copse, half of which stood imprisoned in otherworldly glass, and onto the undulant prairie. Unsparklings abounded in the gin-clear, blue day. The friends walked with their hands out, to feel where the Old World left off and the crystalline walls began. They walked down invisible corridors into unseen cul-de-sacs, marveling that The-Anomaly-As-Big-As-The-Ritz had mounted the sky, capturing midges, eagles, and clouds. Now it towered over woolly Oklahoma like a make-believe Matterhorn. Also, the Hope-It's-A-Diamond anomaly grew, shoving earth back from the arroyo bank as it snaked glassily along.

Aye anno feyk-meleaved usader intrurping mannakiddies' Domin-uum, but the brightful peniheritariy of the Noocleation, tinkled the Hope-It's-A-Diamond outcropping as it expanded.

Meanwhile, The Ritz telegraphed this message into their heads: *Conseal Ur-shelves in the krowslege that ayn butte-iffal et plat-O-teaudinoose whey of execristence has come to Glas.*

And as the four explored the mazes around them, similar allusive thoughts poured like funny water from the rocks.

All the world over, Ossie told himself, this was happening. All the world over, the labyrinths grew. Meanwhile, he and his companions had become separated in their wanderings.

"You should know this about the extrusions, too," yelled Sammy Flashing Plains from a different maze pocket. "Their facets, no matter the angle of the matrix containing them, lie flush with every dimension of our continuum; thus, their invisibility." Sammy's voice sounded diluted and wan.

Ossie Safire, hearing this murky thinness, realized that he and his chums would never come back together—never in this life. Sammy Flashing Plains stood over *there*, in the middle of the plain, while Ignatius Clayborne knelt over *there*, down by the arroyo bank, while Opalith Magmani—that beautiful beast of a woman—waved to them all from the cottonwood copse. What a stately woman, favored of forehead, handsome of aspect, her hand raised in a gesture of triumphant valediction, for a fresh extrusion had recently captured her. Lost, but lost to him painlessly, for on the Last Day of the Old Procession they were joined in a marriage encompassing every living creature. He didn't even need to essay a fifth proposal.

Turning, Ossie noted that the Hope-It's-A-Diamond outflow had engulfed and lifted up Ignatius Clayborne, who appeared to float in midair, a man holding himself aloft by will alone, an angel of latter-day geology.

Turning again, Ossie saw that Sammy Flashing Plains remained animate and active, although he had shed his work shirt, baring his breastplates to the sun. Now he stared into the white sky with outspread arms and took small sacramental steps that led him around in a slow, wheeling dance. He was one intent Indian, one reverent creature among many of the Old Procession.

"Farewell, Sammy Flashing Plains," cried Ossie Safire.

He struck out through the unhardened plots remaining before him, going where he had to go. Frozen cattle, suspended mesquite pods, a jackrabbit caught in midleap, and other monsters of eerie delight broke upon his vision. Invisible walls funneled him this way and that. He trod back down the ranch's whilom grazing area and found himself in front of Rowdy Al LeFever's house. His head ached with the manifold and mind-rocking thoughts with which the labyrinth had just harangued him.

The lopsided house leaned. Its foundations no longer touched the earth. White daylight congealed between the house and the ground. Slowly, the house rose, as if on a column of translucent fire. Ossie knew the column for an extrusion whose crystalline body had sufficient power to obliterate gravity.

"Ossie!" a voice shouted. "Ossie, my lad!"

Rowdy Al LeFever clasped his legs about a lopsided gable of the climbing house. He waved, and as Ossie Safire looked up, the rancher called down through the solidifying chasms. His burnished boots shot out stars of light. His face was refulgent.

"This is the New Creation, Ossie! And what you're seeing is only its magnificent leftovers, the excess and overflow of an eviternal birthing beyond our imagining!"

"But it's only rocks, Rowdy Al!"

"These rocks have life, Ossie. They're physical manifestations of the time-beyond-time in which that other creation is taking place. Look under my house, Ossie! You and Sammy heard them thinking, didn't you? In the beginning of this world, as the Book says, was the Word, and likewise at the beginning of the New Creation. The Word is what fends off death, the Word is what creates, and right here on my ranch you can see the Word at work."

The house kept climbing, alarmingly a-tilt. It appeared to pull out of the very bowels of the earth an assemblage of unlikely, frozen-in-place creatures, which rose into the sky in ranks beneath the gaudy yellow house. Trapped in crystal, these creatures had come through the distended seam between continuums *from the other side!* A sea beast, a one-horned camel, a butterfly with three vulturine heads, a furry pterodactyl, all perfect and beautiful, rose in the ascending column.

"On the other side," Rowdy Al cried, "creation does not evolve. It self-evinces spontaneously, simultaneously, and everywhere. Whatever the mind may imagine, that you find there. Look again, Ossie. The sooner you do the better Sooner you!"

The house continued to ascend on its widening column, which displayed in an up-rush of solidified time-beyond-time its hard-to-imagine wonders—not fossils merely, but the things themselves. A family of the pre-people People, a school of thalassapithecines (hairy critters with prehensile fins and eyes like tarsiers), and fish with wheels. Whatever else Ossie saw, he forgot—except for Rowdy Al LeFever waving his Stetson in farewell and singing at the top of his inexhaustible lungs a cowboy paean in praise of the universe and its glorious abundance. And then the singing modulated into the telepathic babbling of the crystals as Ossie was engulfed and fixed for all time.

For here on the edge of the Order of Unbalanced Abundance, it was the First Day of the New Creation.

* * *

Simply Indispensable

NO ONE SHOULD HAVE TO DEAL SIMULTANEOUSLY
with a spite wall, a boomeranging lover, and the coming of the
su'lakle.

No one.

Between Beirut and Damur, I own a faux-adobe towerhouse on the
Mediterranean. Its picture window takes in my shelf gardens, a
switchbacking mosaic walk, the crude but cleanly hovels below my
cliff-chiseled estate, a strip of tawny beach, dozens of jumbled
floating docks, and the green and creamy cloisonné waters of the
Med itself. Every time I behold it, this panorama storms me like a
SWAT team: it completely takes me over. If I were deprived of it, I
would . . . well, who knows?

Thing is, Bashir Shouman wished to deprive me of it. A month
back, he'd bought a wedge of cliff below the limestone wall at the
bottom of my property. He paid eight homesteader families in the
scrap-and-cardboard hovels there a total of three million Lebanese
pounds to abandon their shambly homes.

Not, mind you, because he wished to build his own magnificent
dwelling on this stony ledge, but because the purchase enabled
him to nettle me. To stab me in the heart. You see, he'd hired a
crew of fellaheen—Arab coolies—to raise a cheap ugly wall between my tower and the sea.

216

"Why?" asked Lena Faye, in response to my grousing.

"To block my view," I said. "To stand atop it and thumb his ouzo-ruddied nose at me."

Lena Faye Leatherboat had concorded in from Tulsa to share the view with me. No. I lie. Actually, she'd come to talk me into returning home from Lebanon to take up my old anchor post with Okla*Globe. And, as I soon found, to recharge an affair that had gone lapsed-cola flat months before Levant Limitless Broadcasting, Entertainment-and-News (LLBEAN to our wise-ass competitors) spirited me off to Beirut.

"No," said the leanly fey Ms. Leatherboat. "I meant, why does this Showman fella—?"

"*Shou*man, not *Show*man. For pity's sake, don't call him Showman. He'd *love* that."

"Why does he want to block your view, George?"

"Out of spite, what else? Vicious, unappeasable spite. It's a spite wall."

Tenderly, Lena Faye traced the shell of my ear with a fingertip. "What *occasioned* his spite?"

"It's a Semito-Phoenician thing. Drop a toad on one of these guys, he comes after you harder than a hockey goalie."

"What did you *do* to him?"

"Bashir Shouman hosts a products-demonstration thing called *Getting the Goods* on ShariVid opposite my own *Forum/Againstum* on Levant."

"Title's familiar, but I've never scanned it."

"My first week here, the head of the European Mercantile Authority, Tito Malcangio, was a guest. In passing, I told Malcangio that Shouman played with high-tech toys for a living. I swore *Forum/Againstum* would knock him off his mechanical camel—an expensive Iraqi amusement product I once saw him demonstrate—in less than six months. Malcangio hoo-hawed. Said Shouman besmirched the reps of all true sales and marketing pros."

"You insulted him."

"I made an observation. And a prediction. *Malcangio* insulted him."

"Then Malcangio should get the spite wall."

"He lives in Milan. Shouman's a Beiruti. Unfortunately, these days, I also qualify."

"My poor Cherokee."

On my nomaditronic bed in my library-cum-relaxall, Lena Faye and I stared at my cactus gardens and the boat lights bobbing on the horizon. Shouman's spite wall already partially blocked our view of the favela sprawling downslope. That wasn't so bad, but in another few days his coolies would have raised the wall high enough to revoke my vantage on the eastern Med.

Then I'd have no view, only a window on the stuccoed and whitewashed backside of a barrier whose sole purpose was to humiliate and vex me. It had no other use. Maybe I could post adverts on it or beam one of those premixed copulatory laser shows against it. No, nix that. The iman on Damur Ridge, if I showed such smut, would have his followers convert me into a choirless castrato. Nix everything but my mounting frustration and rage.

"Don't you have any recourse?" Lena Faye said. "I mean, of the legal sort."

"Over here, no. This isn't the fragmenting U.S. Over here, folks can do with their land just what they like—dogs, fellaheen, and furriners be damned."

"I can't believe that. Surely there's a law."

"I've asked the president of Levant Limitless—"

"LLBEAN?"

"Listen. I've asked her to pull strings. To offer *baksheesh*. To threaten. But Shouman's pit-bull intractable."

"And his wall keeps going up."

"If I lose my view, Lena, I'll—" I stuck, sighed, resumed: "With all I've got to do, with six hours of holotaping hanging over me, this view's indispensable to my mental health."

"Come back to Tulsa. You're indispensable to me, George. As I've found to my pain in your absence." When Lena Faye kissed me, I gunned the bed a dizzy one-eighty away from the window.

Facing away from the sea, gazing upon the loveliest Leatherboat ever to emerge from Enid, I felt a rush of calming metabolic chemicals.

"*Maleesh.* 'Never mind.' Nothing's indispensable. The world keeps turning."

Lena Faye had her head thrown back, her long neck agleam. She started. Something in the window had her attention. She fought to sit up. "Turn the bed back around! *Now!*"

I pivoted the bed, elevated its headrest, revved it toward the window. Shouman's unfinished spite wall had no power to deny us a view of the plasmic light show writhing like a lost aurora borealis in the midnight skies over Lebanon. This kinetic event—whatever it was—flowed lavender, lime, orange, indigo, even an eerie red. It *rained* light. This rain flashed from the tin-roofed huts, flare-illuminated the beach, painted and repainted the bobbing docks. It turned the sea into a crumpled foil mirror that caught, and muted, and softly echoed back, the multicolored cries of this inexplicable happening.

Lena Faye clutched me. Unashamedly, I clutched her too. The terrible light show continued to blaze and flicker. Then, without any incremental slackening, it ceased. The night sky over Lebanon was nothing but night sky again, an inverted bowl of moonlight and palsied stars.

"Lord, Mr. Gist, what a hello! Do you stage the same airborne gala for all your old flames?"

I hugged Lena Faye tighter.

Serious now, she said, "What *was* it, really? A new Israeli weapon? An electrical storm?"

"Lena Faye, I have no idea. I doubt it's the former. That would jeopardize the peace. An electrical storm? Who knows? Not me. I'm no meteorologist."

Before I could react, Lena Faye had pivoted the bed and dialed up Levant's round-the-clock news coverage on my vidverge wall. We watched three or four replays of the event, as taped from the roof of our studio in the Sabra Intercontinental Hotel.

Rafika Ali Sadr, the midnight anchor, noted in five or six different ways that so far no one had a convincing theory for the untoward light show, which, just moments ago, thousands of people in Beirut and environs had witnessed "live and in shivering color." Then she began airing all the conflicting "expert" feedback, and I retrieved my multiflicker in order to mute the idiotic row among the talking heads.

"Hey, Mr. Gist! I was watching that! Don't you want to find out why the sky started sizzling?"

"We'll know by morning. Why tune in the guesses of a thousand and one egotistical crackpots, whether Arab, American, or Trobriand Islander."

"But—"

"'Spontaneous ozone-layer decay.' 'Chain-reaction molecular combustion.' 'Projected hologrammatic illusion.' Do you really think any of those blind stabs on target?"

She didn't, or said she didn't to placate me. Whereupon we consummated our reunion. Thirty minutes later, Lena Faye was fast asleep, seemingly blissfully so.

Careful not to wake her, I eased out of bed and strolled to my picture window. Bashir Shouman's spite wall loomed in the darkness downslope, an architectural obscenity, the three-dimensional Muslim equivalent of a Bronx cheer. It loomed far more forcefully in my awareness than did the weird event that had interrupted Lena Faye's and my conversation. Damn Shouman. Damn him to the gaudiest hell ever imagined by a vindictive iman.

Without my view, I'd . . .

Unbidden, my vidverge wall snapped on. Faintly, it lit 1) my library, 2) Lena Faye's lovely slumbering form, and 3) my stunned nakedness before the picture window.

In virtually thoughtless self-defense, I tinted the window with a thumb touch and telegoosed the bed into another room. That left me buff upright in front of my screen as it cycled through hundreds of fi-opt channels. I tried to kill it with my multiflicker, but it refused to slide back into blank and docile wallness. In fact, I felt that it *needed* an observer; that it *wanted* that observer to be me.

I, I mean: Cherokee George Gist of the popular gabfeed, *Forum/Againstum.*

The channels on my vidverge wall stopped flipping—as abruptly, by the way, as had the spooky-ass light show. A figure emerged from the digital fi-opt signals coursing through my scrambler, a ghost of many thin and motile colors. Green predominated, the green of a diluted kiwi-fruit drink.

The head of this wraith—humanoid after the fashion of a splayed bullfrog—reminded me, with its capelike fins and the fins' hypnotic hula-ing, of a manta ray. From the hidden neck down, though, the wraith's watery greenness hinted at a narrow "chest," pipe-cleaner "arms," and static-riven "legs" that may, or may not, have ended in a pair of nebulous "feet."

The image was a cartoon, a whimsical computer-generated assemblage of migrating pixels. Whimsical and scary at once, for the creature's "eyes"—I grokked, taking hasty inventory—looked just like those of Pope Jomo I, who, along with three other religious bigwigs and a virrogate for a lottery-chosen viewer, would appear on this coming week's cablecasts of *Forum/Againstum.*

Like Pope Jomo's, the thing's eyes gleamed big, brown, and wise. They didn't belong in a manta-ray-shaped head, granted, but today's vidverging hackers can do almost anything with sendable images. Given my screen's refusal to obey my off button and the weirdness of the figure astutter on the wall, those pious eyes held and calmed me.

"*George Gist?*" My unit speakers lapped me with a "voice" like seven cellos twanging in concert.

"Guilty." I walked to my rotary chiffonier and dialed out a robe, which I cinched about myself. The robe fell only to mid thigh, but better a quarter clad than jaybird nude before the pontiff's unmistakable gaze—the peepers, so to speak, of the Holy See. I faced my image-bearing wall.

"We are the su'lakle," the creature shimmering there said in its echoey cello tones.

"'We'? You look like an 'it.' But who knows how many of you pesky cablejackers have conjured this lie?"

"'Lie'? We don't lie. But, we confess, su'lakle is a syllabic rendering of the [garbled] physical sequence by which we denominate ourselves."

"What?"

"Sorry to confuse. We are a kind of plasma-energy entity of no small venerableness."

"'We'? You keep saying 'we.' Please name the buttinsky electronic felons in cahoots with you."

"'I'—the 'I' you now see—am a concentrated distillate of the cosmic intelligence that has just come to Earth. If you prefer the singular, I will gladly use it."

"Good. On Forum/Againstum I talk to jackasses in herds. Here at home, it'd be a huge relief to entertain crackpots like you—if I really must—one at a time."

"'Crackpots'?" the thing on my wall said in its multiple-cello voice, sounding offended. "A disparaging term, correct?"

"It's late, Mr. Ukulele. What the hell do you want?"

"To appear on Forum/Againstum."

"You and ten million other humans starved for a nanosecond of celebrity."

"I am neither a . . . a ukulele nor a human being. I am the deliberately sublimated essence—the spokesentity—of an antique sentient species here self-styled the su'lakle. Don't be obtuse, Mr. Gist."

"I'd be obtuse if I bought this. A dupe conspiring in my own unprincipled scamming."

"Hardly. You see, Mr. Gist, you're—"

"Look, you've hacked your way into my relaxall in the dumb-ass guise of Manta Man, or the Stingray Kid, and I'm supposed to reward you with a stool next to the simseats of my guests this week?"

"Roger—yes. Pope Jomo, Iman Bahadori, the Dalai Lama, and evangelist Jennie Pilgrim. I'd like to palaver—rap—with them. In order to reach as many of your kind as possible."

"Roger—yes," I mocked. "Do you have any idea how long it took me to arrange this historic tetracast?"

"Mr. Gist, you—"

"Listen, vidiot, why not hack your way onto *Forum/Againstum* the same way you've raped the privacy of my home?"

"*I am no hacker, Mr. Gist. Nor a pixel-built virrogate. I observe, therefore I am.*"

"In Marx's immortal words, horsefeathers!"

"*And therefore you are too—along with your planet, solar system, galaxy, and surrounding galactic clusters.*"

"The coaxial cops will have you traced and busted by morning! And our scientists—real ones, not cranks—will know by then what caused tonight's honky-tonk glowstorm!"

"*I doubt both such outcomes.*"

"I have a warm female companion in the next room. I'm going in to her now, Mr. Ukulele. Shut my wall unit off when you're through playing around with it."

I moved to rejoin Lena Faye. The ray-headed thing on my screen began to quake more violently than ever. Its erratic motion halted me. As I watched, it *stepped* from the flat cage of the vid-verge wall into my house. There, facing me like a burglar, the su'lakle floated in three dimensions, like a person-shaped pocket of neon mist. Less than an arm's length away, it radiated neither heat nor coolth, but a dry, spreading tingle. The hairs on my knuckles stood up. My nape hairs swayed. A fine electrostatic disturbance helixed through my bowels.

"*What crackerjack systems crasher could do this—drift in air before you as an independent being?*"

"You're a hologram."

"*I am? Projected from where, by whom, and through what mechanism?*"

Like the su'lakle, I was trembling—but for different reasons. "Who knows? By Bashir Shouman. By means of a secretly deployed nanoholocaster."

"*A hologram is often a kind of telepresence, Mr. Gist. I, though, inhabit this space with you, even as the filtered-to-essentials spokes-entity of my larger Self.*"

Truth? Gobbledegook? I had no idea.

"*Touch me, Mr. Gist.*"

I hesitated, then reached out and pinched the su'lakle's eelish arm just below its, uh, "elbow." The plasmic "skin" between my thumb and forefinger had a filmy elastic moistness; it followed my tug, more like a biddable mist than a pinch of rubber, and then seeped rather than snapped back into place. I couldn't imagine a virrogate able to interface to that peculiar degree with consensus reality. Maybe the creature wasn't lying.

"*Give me a spot on* Forum/Againstum *with Pope Jomo and the other sacred worthies.*"

"But . . . but what'll I call you?"

Su'lakle, I argued, wouldn't do—not at least until Levant's subscribers understood the being's origins and nature. Even then, they'd probably regard it as just another electronic wave-function virrogate.

After all, in the recent past, randomly selected subscribers had come on *F/A* as my "Faces from the Rubble" interviewees in the identity-concealing teleguises of Socrates, Cleopatra, Torquemada, Queen Elizabeth I, Pocahontas, Sir Isaac Newton, Soujourner Truth, Teddy Roosevelt, Amelia Earhart, Mahatma Gandhi, Brigitte Bardot, Gamal Abdel Nasser, Buddy Holly, the Pink Panther, Steven Hawking, Stephen King, Jessica Rabbit, Tina Turner, and Salman Rushdie (a virrogate sent packing in midbroadcast to avert a global epidemic of Islamic riots). The su'lakle's current look, to put it frankly, had less authenticity than had J. Rabbit's.

"*Call me Joe,*" it said.

"Joe?"

"*Yes. Joe Way. A participant without a sacerdotal honorific perhaps requires* two *names.*"

Bewildered, I agreed. The su'lakle stepped back into the two-dimensional realm of my vidverge unit, then disappeared by obligingly shutting the unit off.

I summoned my nomaditronic bed back from exile and lay down beside Lena Faye. No one, I mused, should have to deal at the same time with a spite wall, an ex-fiancée, and the unannounced arrival of a star-struck plasma being.

I got up to find Lena Faye sitting in front of my vidverge at a table set with bagels, strawberry jelly, cream cheese, and a pot of Earl Grey. I joined her.

"Hey, slug-a-bed," she said. "Despite your certainty to the contrary, the world still lacks a decent explanation for last night's pyrotechnics."

"Nobody's suggested fireworks?"

"Of course. Along with dozens of other screwy guesses. But those *weren't* fireworks. The only fireworks I have any empirical knowledge of, George, took place—" nodding "—in that bumper-car bed of yours."

I spread some jam on a bagel and took a bite. I poured myself a cup of tea, which Lena Faye had brewed to a satisfying strength and temperature.

"If you won't come back to Okla*Globe," she said, "I could come here. I'd bet LLBEAN, ShariVid, or AvivTel could use another savvy PR flack, wouldn't you?"

"Say LLBEAN instead of Levant to management, they'll boot you out faster'n a CableCom inspector."

"Have talent, will travel."

"Lena Faye, I just can't think about that now. I tape the biggest shows of my career this afternoon."

"Congrats." She deformed a bagel with her canines, the jam on her mouth as red as something more dire.

"Besides, you're supposed to get me back with obscene amounts of cash, corporate flattery, and—"

"Good lovin'."

"Which you've just offered to bring *here*. Meanwhile, Okla*Globe can go jump. If this is savvy recruitment work, Lena Faye, nobody here in Beirut will recognize it."

We ate for a time in silence. Nadia Suleiman, Levant's morning anchor, efficiently ticked off all the theories so far proposed for the peculiar aerial phenomenon that'd signaled "Joe Way"'s arrival on the stage of Earthbound history. None of the theories mentioned the su'lakle, of course, or came anywhere near the bizarre truth of the matter.

It did amuse me, though, to hear Nadia report that a spokesperson for the New Millenarian Ecumenical Council convening this week in Beirut claimed that the light show marked God's joyous personal blessing on the momentous proceedings of the NMEC.

"Ha ha," I said mirthlessly.

"At least that has a certain befitting poetry to it. You just grump and cynicize."

"Because *I* know what really happened."

"Do tell."

To Lena Faye's incredulity, consternation, and mounting alarm, I did just that. She believed me. I warmed to the telling because she so obviously did believe, and tried to comfort me, and in fact eased me through the rest of the day to the taping that would secure *Forum/Againstum*'s status as the premier gabfeed on any of the global vidgrids.

*   *   *

Pope Jomo, Iman Bahadori, the Dalai Lama, and Jennie Pilgrim, spiritual leader of the World Evangelical Union (WEU), had all come to Beirut for the New Millenarian Ecumenical Council (NMEC). Other attendees included an assortment of hatted rabbis, skinny Hindu mucky-mucks, the prophet of the Baha'is, voodoo *houngans*, the head of the Eastern Orthodox Church, Wiccan hierarchs, saronged Theravada and Mahayana priests and bodhisattvas, African tribal shamans, and maybe a dozen sachems from mainline, borderline, and off-the-wall Protestant-Christian denominations.

I'd tried to round up a representative sampling of spiritual leaders for this week's episodes of *Forum/Againstum*, but the Pope and Iman Bahadori had threatened to withdraw if I made them share Levant's studio—even as holojections—with more than two other council attendees. In return for this concession, they'd offered me six hours of their precious time, all of which I hoped to tape on a single afternoon for a full week's worth of programs. No one else in the infogabshow biz had ever managed such a coup.

If not for Bashir Shouman's spite wall, my internal struggle over Lena Faye, and the anomalous shuffling of "Joe Way" into my overloaded *F/A* deck, I'd've thought myself the luckiest chap in town, if not the whole rosy world.

Levant's studio well in the Sabra Intercontinental Hotel was wrapped by a field shield. Behind the shield, as audience, sat five tiers of educated foreigners and Beiruti locals.

Envision, then, six vivid figures on the set, four of them holojections in simseats, one an eccentric emerald virrogate (who'd materialized in the well as a substantive presence an hour before the coming of the others), and me, Cherokee George Gist, in a Danish chair of shiny aluminum tubes and interwoven flaxen straps.

Iman Bahadori, Pope Jomo, and the Dalai Lama sat across from Jennie Pilgrim, me, and our flickering pseudo-virrogate, Joe Way. A dozen autocams gyro-gimbaled around us at different heights and angles, all under the control of Khalil Khalaf, *F/A*'s Maronite Catholic director.

"Good evening, ladies, gentlemen, and brighter-than-average children," I began the taping. "This evening we commence a series of shows on which I plan to browbeat our distinguished guests about their respective spiritual positions and the fading hope for harmony among religio-ethnic factions and their increasingly rigid doctrinal positions."

With courteous fervor, my handpicked audience applauded. Via satellite and fi-opt cables, millions more would thrill, later, to this same lead-in. I then introduced the Pope, the Iman, the Dalai Lama (who, even as a holofeed, didn't look much like either the dead artist Salvador or a Peruvian camel), and the large but attractive Jennie Pilgrim.

"*And I'm Joe Way,*" said the su'lakle in its many-celloed voice. "*From deepest outer space.*"

"DOS, eh?" said the Dalai Lama's holojection from his suite in the fully renovated Hotel St. Georges. "Is DOS a freshly protected cyber territory?"

"Mr. Joseph Way comes to us tonight," I said hurriedly, "as the proxy virrogate of our far-flung viewers, to represent them in a telegab of great historic importance."

"*Joe. Joe Way. Not Joseph.*"

"Johweh?" said Pope Jomo in his Kikuyu-flavored English. "I hear echoes of both my name and that of the tetragrammatic Hebrew deity."

"*Pardon me, Your Popeness,*" Joe Way said as quickly as a cello section may do, "*but, in your view, what comprises the most basic heartfelt desire of any sentient entity?*"

I tried to retake control: "If you'll wait a—"

"Salvation and eternal life in God's very presence," said Pope Jomo readily enough.

"Amen to that," said Jennie Pilgrim. The two beamed at each other. (Given their status as holos, *beamed* is something more than a metaphor.)

"Nirvana," said the Dalai Lama. "Preferably after a good leg of lamb and a glass of fine wine."

"A passionate blessed martyrdom," said Iman Bahadori, "followed by heavenly immortality."

"*Does anyone of a more secular persuasion in the studio have a differing opinion?*" asked Joe Way, the wings of his manta-ray head rippling subtly.

Beyond the field shield, several members of my audience boldly spoke up:

"*Earthly* immortality!"

"More money than King Croesus and Austin-Antilles Corporation combined!"

"Eternal youth!"

"An unending orgasm of painful cosmic sweetness!"

"Power!" cried one pale, marmoset-eyed young man. "Power, power, and *more* power!"

Lifting my hands, I stood up and shouted: "QUIET!"

My studio audience quieted.

"Better! Much better! *Forum/Againstum* isn't five minutes old, people, and you've let this green virrogate usurp both my role as host and the religio-philosophical agenda embodied, at least potentially, in the presence of these estimable spiritual leaders! Let's get back on track! Okay?"

"Actually," said Jennie Pilgrim with a melancholy sigh, "the 'most basic heartfelt desires' shouted out here testify to a real eschatological ignorance and a nasty decline in age-old Judeo-Christian values."

"I concur," said Iman Bahadori, visibly gloating.

"*Actually*," Joe Way put in, "*although wrong, these desires do have their honesty to commend them.*"

Annoyed, I turned on the su'lakle. "'Wrong'? Isn't one's basic heartfelt desire a matter of private choice? How, then, can you label any single such opinion *wrong?*"

"Mr. Way is correct," Pope Jomo said. "The basic heartfelt desires spoken out here are bankrupt illusions. None bestows true happiness because all are— "

"Happiness!" shouted a member of the studio crowd: a late response to Joe Way's question.

"There is only one route to genuine happiness," the Pope said. "Namely, the Way, the Truth, and the Life."

"*Wrong again,*" said the su'lakle. "*One's most basic heartfelt desire is the route to happiness, but that route is 'the Way, the Truth, and the Life,' or 'martyrdom for Allah,' or 'out-of-body perfection' only to those who have given up on that longing which has dwelt hidden within them since the first conscious moment of their being.*"

Khalil Khalaf gave our global audience a skillful close-up of Pope Jomo's handsome ebony face, wreathed in a smile. "As I still say, that longing, whatever it is, is an illusion. One must sacrifice it to that which has lasting, and obtainable, spiritual validity."

I couldn't help myself. Looking directly at Joe Way, I said, "But what is that longing?"

"*Indispensability.*"

Everyone—guest, studio-audience member, or tape-delayed Levant Limitless Broadcasting subscriber—gaped at Joe Way. In his guise as a pseudo-virrogate (if the oxymoronic irony of that term doesn't render it totally meaningless), Joe Way pulsed like a living mist, kaleidoscopically kinking inside the illusory integument affording him his green-glowing creaturely outline.

The Dalai Lama, a bald, brown, spexware-bearing man in his late twenties or early thirties, recovered first. "Nonsense, Mr. Way. I know many persons with the soulfulness to wish for nothing more —in worldly terms—than to live forever in that perfect instant just before sunrise. Or to make some small but lasting private contribution to our species."

"And if you want *secular* basic heartfelt desires," the Right Reverend Ms. Pilgrim said, "I've known two or three half-decent but unsaved gentlemen who longed for nothing but a lake, a johnboat, a cane pole, and lots of time to fish. For them down-home bubbas, indispensability didn't enter the picture atall."

"*These desires came upon them,*" Joe Way said, "*after the world had disillusioned or corrupted them.*"

"After reality'd set in," Jennie Pilgrim countered. "And they realized how hard this world works to thump the backsides of malingering spiritual babes."

"Amen," said Iman Bahadori, surprising both her and me.

These guests could've conducted *Forum/Againstum* without benefit of host or studio audience. Exasperated, I tried to wrench my program back from the su'lakle: "Tell me, Iman, what issues do you plan to raise at the general session of the NMEC this Friday?"

"*It nonetheless remains the case that all human beings—indeed, all conscious entities universewide—long at bottom not for power or immortality or spiritual riches, but for that attribute, alone among attributes, that confers them all; namely, indispensability, the only quality that assures the being possessing it that if aught evil befalls it, including its own extinction, the universe and all its many components, sentient or otherwise, will perish in train. Face it. All human grief stems from the hurtful knowledge that the universe has so little care for one's own existence that the end of that existence will affect neither the operation nor the integrity of the universe a sparrow's fart. Selah.*"

"How about that, Pope Jomo?" I said. "Do you—?"

"With due respect, I must point out that your flamboyant virrogate's opinion is nonsense," said the Pope.

"*Allah akbar,*" said Iman Bahadori. "The only indispensable Being is God Himself. Does Mr. Way intend to imply that we should all strive to become as God?"

"I have no problem with that ambition," said the Dalai Lama.

"Well, *I* have beaucoups with it," the Right Reverend Ms. Pilgrim retorted. "Smacking, as it does, of self-idolatrous pride."

"*Each person here wishes at heart, or once upon a time wished, that he or she were indispensable to the health of this physical reality,*" said Joe Way unequivocally.

Jennie Pilgrim said, "Gist, you've unleashed an infantile ijit on us. A mewling babe."

"*Alexander the Great died. Caesar died. So did Mohammed, Queen Elizabeth, Shakespeare, Newton, and Sadat. Even Einstein died. Ditto the Marx Brothers, Jack Benny, Buckminster Fuller, Bear Bryant, Dick Clark, Imelda Marcos, and Norodom Sihanouk. The world continued without them. Secretly, we long for such a profound in-knitting with the world that, should we grow sick, or falter, or even lapse and die, the world that these famous ones left without even rippling its basic contours would, as a direct consequence, founder in shock and fall to irreclaimable nothingness.*"

The Reverend Ms. Pilgrim wrinkled her brow at the Dalai Lama. "This is a guy thing, right?"

His Tibetan Holiness shrugged.

"*I didn't expect to encounter such denial among you,*" Joe Way said, splotchily pulsating emerald, lime, and radioactive chartreuse. "*Perhaps it's a function of the trained-up religious frames of mind pheromonically drawn to the NMEC.*"

At that, several members of my studio audience began to whistle, boo, and/or stamp their feet.

The Pope raised one long, eggplant-purple hand. "Hush."

Everyone hushed.

The hand stayed up, in calming benediction. "It seems to me that this one anonymous viewer—" the Pope gestured at Joe Way "—has stolen a disproportionate amount of our time with pathological musings of a private and, I trust, treatable nature. Now, however, I would—"

"*I know whereof I speak. Because the august telepresences here this evening refuse to acknowledge their most basic inborn longing does not mean that I have misnamed it.*"

"Look," said Jennie Pilgrim, "who are you, anyhow?"

Oh, God, I thought. Don't answer that.

"*How* do you know?" Iman Bahadori asked the su'lakle before it could ID itself.

"*Because I am in fact a being possessing the attribute for which all of you long. Indispensability. Instant by instant, I help sustain the fabric of reality.*"

Iman Bahadori raised an eyebrow. "You are God?" His lip curled in contempt. Then he began to snicker. But, thank God, he demanded neither Joe Way's immediate exile nor a sacrilege-avenging global manhunt and a beheading.

For, of course, only Lena Faye and I, of all those in the studio, understood that the su'lakle existed as the fabricated material essence of his kind rather than as the virrogate of a geographically distant human viewer.

The Dalai Lama leaned toward Joe Way. "I beg you, sir, to repeat your last assertion."

"*I am indispensable.*"

"Really?"

"*Simply indispensable. I help sustain the world. My end would speed that of this expansion-contraction phase of this particular universe at its every spatial-temporal extension.*"

"I think we'd better break for a message from Glom-Omni Foods and Printed Circuits," I said.

Khalil Khalaf, bless him, took that desperate cue and cut away to a spectacular canned pitch for hydrosnap peaches and high-torque magnelev motors.

I looked up and saw Lena Faye sitting among some Beirutis on our studio's highest tier.

She smiled. In Cherokee hand language, she signed, *Don't get rattled. You're doing fine.*

The six-hour taping floundered on. Joe Way dominated the first hour, which aired later that same evening, but had only a couple more bombshells to drop, petards he lobbed during the taping's third and sixth hours.

"*Reincarnation within this expansion-contraction phase of this particular universe does not occur,*" he informed the Dalai Lama in the third hour. "*You hope for it in vain.*"

By this time, the other guests had begun to humor him as if he were an unhinged brother or an incontinent pet cat.

"I don't hope to return to the world of *maya* as either a housefly or a bodhisattva," the Dalai Lama said. "I hope to escape the cycle of death-and-rebirth entirely."

"*You hope for that in vain as well.*"

Jennie Pilgrim shot the Pope a conspiratorial look. "Do you mean to say there's no such thing as an eternal afterlife?"

"*Depends on what you mean by eternal.*"

"Pardon?"

"*We su'lakle have gone through this six or seven times before, Reverend Ms. Pilgrim. Souls caught in each cycle's afterlife get funneled into the primordial singularity from which the* next *cosmos bursts forth. They emerge as unconscious matter. The intervals are so long, though, that most gladly, or perhaps indifferently, relinquish aware-ness out of boredom. Moreover, the crowding during the epoch of ultimate collapse is terrible. Who* wouldn't *want to pull a terminal phase-shift back into affectless nonbeing?"*

For a moment, no one—I chief among the speechless—could think of anything to say to this. Then a professor from the American University in our audience said, "The souls of sentient creatures don't migrate into a region of sempiternal superspace?"

"No way to get to it," Joe Way said shortly.

The rest of that hour, my other guests discussed the links, con-spicuous or subtle, among their belief systems. Joe Way stayed silent. In fact, I had the nagging suspicion that he had gently with-drawn his essence from the pseudo-virrogate on the stool to my right.

Toward the end of the sixth hour, despite two weeks of heavy preparation and a slew of off-camera cue cards, I'd just about run out of questions. I realized *Forum/Againstum* was in deep trouble when Iman Bahadori produced some laminated photos of his kids and I took a genuine interest.

Jennie Pilgrim, by choice a single woman, jumped to the show's rescue. She leaned around me and said, "Mr. Way, I've been mean-ing to ask, how is it, exactly, that you think you're 'simply indis-pensable' to the universe?"

The su'lakle had gone pretty pale over the past two and a half hours. His swirly-curly innards looked more like watered limeade than melting emeralds; the fins on his manta-ray head drooped like windsocks on a still desert night.

"Mr. Way!" Jennie Pilgrim insisted. *"Mr. Way!"*

At last the su'lakle appeared inhabited again. *"Forgive me. My 'mind' wandered."*

Ms. Pilgrim restated her question.

Joe Way's answer took several minutes. Anyone interested in its details need only consult—quickly—any video of my final *Forum/Againstum* broadcast. Basically (Joe Way told us), he, or his virtually immortal kind, had the ability to perform recurrent key observa-tions at the quantum level that *"support the structure of the physical universe by actualizing a sequence of key observables in such a way that the fundamental physical laws that govern the cosmos cohere."*

Pope Jomo winced. "Oh, Mr. Way, you make my head ache. Of what 'kind' are you, if not the human kind?"

"A su'lakle." And steeling myself for the inevitable hostile reaction: *"An alien energy being."*

"From DOS," said the Dalai Lama evenly. "Deepest, Outer, Space." This idea passed unchallenged, as if everyone in my studio, future-shock junkies, had already suspected as much.

A woman in a silk sari stood up. "Are you saying you can select among the many potentialities of microscopic particles? Can, in fact, direct the observer-induced 'collapse of the wave function' common to quantum mechanics?"

"Yes, I am," said Joe Way, audibly relieved.

"But no one can dictate the value—the position, or energy state, or momentum—that the specific measurement of a particle actualizes," said the woman, sitting back down. "No one."

Replied Joe Way, *"No one human. So far as I know, we su'lakle alone, at least for now, have that talent. We not only understand the structuring subatomic codes, we can twiggle them."*

(*Twiggle?*)

"How?" Lena Faye called out from her lofty perch.

"The su'lakle—I am One—intrinsically possess a quality of intensified self-reference or -observation enabling us to alter our own consciousness. We thus influence 'reality' through externally directed observations of several specific sorts."

"This must be very hard work," said the Dalai Lama.

"No lie. Often, though, we can peer through the maya of this space-time realm to the suprareality of the overcosmos."

"Again, a claim to Godhood!" said Iman Bahadori angrily.

Jennie Pilgrim said, "Mr. Gist, you've let a funny-farm hacker loose on y'all's premises."

"On the other hand, collapsing this realm into 'reality' from its various superpositions, eon after eon, eventually acquires a debilitating tediousness. Even if the actualizers—we su'lakle, along with a few other observing species across the cosmos—initially accepted that responsibility out of equal measures of self-challenge and love."

And those were Joe Way's last words during the sixth hour of our taping, an hour that wouldn't get fi-opted until this coming Saturday evening.

Khalil Khalaf signaled *Cut!* from his director's booth. I'd successfully shepherded my human guests, and the wild card of an incognito interstellar visitor, through a grueling marathon taping session.

So, of course, I began contemplating the best spot in my tower-house for another Peabody or Emmy.

Unceremoniously, Pope Jomo I, Iman Bahadori, the Dalai Lama, and Jennie Pilgrim vanished. Who could blame them? They'd given me over six solid—i.e., unbroken, substantive—hours of interview time; they deserved medals.

Only Joe Way remained on the well's floor with me, because, of course, he was a plasmic distillate of the su'lakle rather than a holojection.

As my studio audience filed out, Lena Faye picked her way down the stairstep seats to join us. We hugged each other. Khalil Khalaf eyed her from his booth. He knew for whom she worked and had no doubt why she'd come.

"Mr. Way, I have a question," Lena Faye said.

"*Please.*" (Permission to ask it.)

"Why did you bring Earth's religious leaders—all of us—the message of your local 'indispensability'?"

"*Why?*" The cello voices sounded confused.

"Yes, why? I mean, what did you, or *do* you, want us to do in response to that message?"

A damned good question. I should have asked it myself. And I *would* have, I think, if I hadn't striven so hard to make it appear that the su'lakle was "really" a virrogate of one of my randomly selected viewers.

Joe Way shifted before us. The manta-ray wings of his "head" flapped a kind of querulous veronica.

"Do you want us to do you homage?" Lena Faye asked. "You know, *worship* you?"

The gaseous emeralds swirling inside the su'lakle throbbed brighter, as if she'd blown on a green fire. "*Absolutely not,*" Joe Way said.

"What, then?"

"*In time,*" he said, "*I hope to persuade you—your species, I mean—to supplant us, the su'lakle, in the indispensability business here-abouts. Voluntarily.*"

With that, he convoluted once, slowly, and funneled upward in a keening rush that hurled him out of the studio, as if he'd popped into another continuum through the tip of that notional funnel.

Three evenings later, after the first four episodes of my *F/A* tapings had appeared, Lena Faye and I had dinner together on the sidewalk outside the Green Line Café. To stymie both gawkers and would-be autograph seekers, we sat near a trellis bearing oligs (hybrid olive-figs) and thoroughly enjoyed each other's company.

I seemed to be falling in love with Lena Faye again. Why she wanted *me*, though, I had real trouble figuring. For some months before leaving Tulsa, I'd treated her as a mere human accessory. And even since her arrival in Lebanon, our mutual sack time notwithstanding, I'd generally shown more interest in F/A's global ratings and the likelihood of more infogab awards than in shoving our relationship into something akin to permanence.

Now, though, I was beginning to perceive that Lena Faye had always seen in me the inhering specter of my better self. She had always believed in and struggled to free it, when a woman of less patience, and a less atoning vision, would have written me off as Superjerk. Now, I theorized, her fastidious observations of the microscopic virtues in me were actualizing them—collapsing them into being—in the day-to-day realm of human interactions. Maybe.

Anyway, I was thinking seriously of abandoning Beirut and of marrying Lena Faye Leatherboat.

Suddenly, a gang of youthful Shi'ites came marching toward the café jogging placards up and down; they wore stained white sandwich-board pullovers bearing upon them militant slogans in Arabic script: *Only ALLAH Is Called For. The Green Thing Is a Devil. Satan Lies in Many Colors.* One pistoning sign held a startling message in English:

> George Gist, atheist!
> We have no need
> Of his gabfeed greed
> Or Godless creed!
> Bleed him from his crown,
> Run him out of town,
> Uproot him like the weed!

"Uh oh."

Lena Faye took my hand. "Sort of catchy."

"They're looking to catch me, that's how catchy it is. I wish you wouldn't trivialize this."

"Tighten your sphincter, George. Let them go."

It was good advice. The protest, obviously provoked by the week's first *Forum/Againstum*, had a noise-making rather than a vengeance-taking agenda, even if one of its signs read like a death warrant. It seemed highly likely that Iman Reza Bahadori himself had sent these young zealots out. In any case, they marched loudly but harmlessly by.

"I'm no atheist," I said.

"No?"

"I believe—" I thought a moment. "I believe in the Great Spirit." Another thinking spell: "Or *a* great spirit."

"*The* or *a*? Which is it? Investing in lower-case stocks doesn't require much capital."

"Small investment, small risk of woe."

"Small hope of a bracing return." Lena Faye nodded after the noisy Shi'ites. "Those guys have no doubt you're *the* weed in their spiritual garden."

"Me? I'm a high-profile media spear-carrier."

"Meaning you think the demon-weed they should *really* take out after is poor old Joe Way."

"I don't think they should take out after anybody. I think they should give it a rest."

"Some people have strong opinions, Mr. Gist. Some people *commit.*"

"Some people scare the holy sand out of me."

"Not me, I hope." Then: "I believe in love."

"Great song title. It's been used, but so what?"

We left the Green Line Café and wandered along the Rue de Damas to a bistro called Hobeika's Den occupying most of the bottom floor of a bank building gutted in the anarchistic and self-cannibalizing 1980s. No signs of rubble, pock marks, or coverups today: Hobeika's Den looked spanking new, a high-tech watering hole with vidverge mirrors, game screens, a voluptuous animatronic belly dancer, and a car-park band with wired flutes, guitars, and percussion sets.

As soon as Lena Faye and I got inside, we could tell that the Tarabulus Music Militia's lead singer, a young Druze in a psyche-delically embroidered *kaffiyeh*, was singing, in a kind of bastard cockney, a hard-rock curse called, if the recurrence of one phrase means anything, "Simply Indispenserble":

"S really arfly risible,
A daftness indivisible,
To so much pride surscepterble,
E thinks e's [*bump! bump!*] 'simply indispenserble'!

"E'll avtah take some sass fum us
To be so bogon blasphemous,
Cause it's crudely indefenserble
To claim e's [*bump! bump!*] 'simply indispenserble'!"

The crowd in Hobeika's Den, or a major part of it, was *dancing* to TMM's syncopated heavy-pedal scorn. Someone had even programmed the belly dancer to punctuate the *bump! bump!*s with staccato hip swings—unless, of course, its microcircuitry simply triggered automatic kinetic feedback to whatever music it "heard."

"Cripes," I murmured.

"Don't be profane."

I lifted an eyebrow. Then I took Lena Faye's hand and led her to the cappuccino-and-cordial bar. I'd just drawn a stool out for her when a bearish man in a lapelless silver-lamé jacket and a gold-foil *kaffiyeh* grabbed the stool and shoved it toward the dance floor. Lena Faye's eyes widened. Otherwise, she showed no sign of alarm.

> "S awtuhgedder winceable,
>   At on barmy princerple,
>   Lahk e's ploom invincerble,
> E sez e's [*bump! bump!*] 'simply indispenserble'!"

"Gist, you camel-dung pig-dog dormouse! You dare to show up in public? To push your shameless mug into a place where living flesh-and-blooders can do you the infinite justice of spitting in your eye? *Phfffthhhhhht!*"

With the back of my hand, I wiped a bleb of saliva from my cheek. (Ha ha, you missed.) Then: "Lena Faye Leatherboat, allow me to introduce you to the mild-mannered Bashir Shouman. Mr. Shouman, Ms. Leatherboat."

"An honor," Shouman said, kissing Lena Faye's wrist before turning back to me. "Have a care, you pig-dog! You sully her name merely by appearing in her company! Your depravity, like your cableglom, has no discoverable limit!"

> "Allah is de Prince-uv-All,
>   But Joe Way's blubber-dense, yer-all,
>   Is skin so fiercely flenserble
> To swear e's [*bump! bump!*] 'simply indispenserble'!"

"See? See what your mendacious gabfeed has wrought? Now I know why you call it *Forum* plus *Againstum!* You stand against all decency! You lie to up-puff yourself!"

"Translation: Levant's ratings have annihilated ShariVid's in our contending time slots," I told Lena Faye.

"Say on, say on!" Shouman raged.

"Mr. Shouman doesn't like adjusting to this hurtful fact. We even plastered him *tonight*, with Joe Way sitting there about as talkative as Tar Baby."

"I could ask the Ayatollah Sadr to do string figures on my program! Or hire Kuwait's soccer team to kick around a ball in ClingFlex thongs! My ratings would also soar! But never do I pander! Never do I *manufacture* attractions!"

"I *manufactured* the Pope?"

"Not him! Not Iman Bahadori! Not the Dalai Lama! Not that veil-free Pilgrim woman! Not them, but the unscrupulous fraud of your so-called DOS 'energy being'!"

> "E sneers at pious protocols
> N kicks at commonsense, ycr-all!
> Is power's awl ostenserble,
> But, yah, e's [*bump! bump!*] 'simply indispenserble'!
> No way, Joe Way, no *waaaay!*"

"Joe Way is for real," I said.

"He's a sec-throughable holojection which some deluded people—" nodding at the Tarabulus Music Militia "—lack the commonsense to see through. They suppose your meretricious Gumby-ghost is lying, never considering that the lie springs instead from you, you pig-dog!"

"It doesn't," Lena Faye said quietly. "I know Joe Way to be exactly what he has claimed."

This assertion, from this source, gave Shouman pause. How could Lena Faye speak false? He sidestepped his doubt:

"You corrupt even the most innocent, you garbage thrower, and chaos descends!"

"Unlike your spite wall, which keeps going up."

"And will do so until it has left your towerhouse as blind as its dungball-cating occupant! You deserve to see no farther than a man in a windowless box!"

"Like Wigner's friend," I said.

But Bashir Shouman didn't hear me. He had elbowed his way outside onto the Rue de Damas. Meanwhile, it had taken nearly the last of my psychic energy to keep from trying to choke the vituperative crap out of him.

"You did good," Lena Faye told me.

The TMM combo had finally brought "Simply Indispenserble" to a crescendoing end. Now the boys were crooning, "Bright are zuh stars zud shine, / Dark izzuh sky. / I know ziss luv ufmine / Will nevuh die."

Pretty. Truly pretty. I was astonished.

At my place south of Beirut, Shouman's hired hands worked more furiously on his spite wall, as if he'd offered them bonuses to speed up its construction. Before Lena Faye's and my eyes, it was turning into something less like a wall than a prodigious monument to malice. People in shacks farther down the hill tottered upslope just to watch the ugly barrier grow in width and height.

"The bastard," I said.

"At least he's putting people to work," Lena Faye said.

"I need a bazooka. I know where to get one too. There's still a dilapidated arms depot at the old Burj Al Barajinah refugee camp, and it'd be—"

"Stop talking rot."

"Yessum."

"If you do stay here in your adobe tower, simply turn the wall's stucco backside into a laser-mural canvas. You could switch the mural out every month or week or day, depending on your attention span."

"Ha ha. I'd already thought of something like that."

Lena Faye had only four more days of her working vacation for Okla*Globe in Lebanon. On Monday morning, I'd escort her to the airport either to see her off or to accompany her back to the states. Okla*Globe's final salary package was definitely attractive, and for additional inducement there was Lena Faye herself. . . .

Meanwhile, my vidverge wall showed that, although hostile local reaction to Joe Way's *Forum/Againstum* gigs had developed slowly, it had now begun to heat up. This anger had its roots not only in various Islamic groups (the Sunnites, the Shi'ites, and the Druze), but also in the Christian community (Maronite Catholic, Greek Orthodox, Greek Catholic, etc.). Ten thousand Jews also live in Beirut nowadays, and their religious leaders were attacking me and Levant both for putting Joe Way on the show and for excluding a qualified representative of their own faith from the cablecast.

"*Two* Christians this come-lately Cherokee *goy* has on his gab-show," Rabbi Moshe Hillel Silver told Nadia Suleiman in a spot between reports of Shi'ite street protests and of a Maronite picket line outside the Sabra Hotel. "Not a single Jew. You call that balance?"

"He's right," Lena Faye said.

"I know. Tell that to Pope Jomo and Iman Bahadori."

"My, how you can crab-sidle, injun."

The protests against Joe Way and the outrageous su'lakle message of their indispensability to this region of the cosmos—and against my gabfeed for providing them a forum were now receiving at least as much cable coverage as the proceedings of the New Millenarian Ecumenical Council.

The NMEC, however, appeared to be in as much disarray as Beirut's streets, parks, and beaches. Officials from the Big Three monotheistic religions suffered excruciating trials of conscience accommodating to the session-opening prayer rituals of Wiccans, animists, goddess worshippers, voodooists, and idol devotees. And vice versa. Nor did these partisan brouhahas prevent internal bickering among all the denominations, cults, cabals, and sects within either the major or the minor spiritual alignments. A spokesperson for Pope Jomo I announced that His Holiness would depart Beirut a full two days before the closing ceremonies.

"Why?" our reporter Mitri Ahad asked this flunky.

"Unfinished business at the Vatican." The spokesperson did a rude preemptive heel-pivot.

Then my vidverge screen disclosed that a large party of Druze protesters had joined the Maronite sign-wielders on the sidewalk below Levant's studios in the Sabra. Despite their common purpose —namely, reviling me, my employer, and F/A—the two groups clashed with one another about tactics, sidewalk territory, and even the su'lakle's degree of insidiousness as an extraterrestrial Satan. Police moved in, but placard poles, with much accompanying cursing and shoving, began to jab about like pikestaffs.

"Do you think Nadia's safe up there?" Lena Faye asked.

I was about to say, "I think so," when the picture on my wall crumpled in zigzag bands and scrambled away to static. Before I could use my multiflicker to repair the picture, the static resolved itself into the manta-ray-headed phosphor-dot image of Joe Way. This image stayed two-dimensional only long enough for him to acquire focus and to step out of the vidverge as his old viridescent self. This time, though, he had to *duck* to get fully out, and when he straightened again, he resembled a hammerhead shark upright on its tail, or maybe the freak show version of the not-so-little brother of the Melancholy Green Giant.

"Joe," I said fatuously. "What's up?"

"*Ignorant members of your species don't believe I'm what I say I am, or else they assume I've somehow insulted*—blasphemed against —*their frail sectarian notions of the godhead. They think I've arrogated to myself the creative energies and the abiding omnipotence of*

*God by using your infogabshow to declare the fact of my indispens-
ability.*"

"Unfortunately," I said, "that's true."

Joe Way flickered from one side of my relaxall to the other like
a pacing would-be suicide. "*How can I ask your species to take over
the observational task of local universe-sustenance if I'm not believed? Even if I were to give you a simplified subatomic transition
kit, full instructions, and intensive techno-spiritual aid, your species'
disbelief—your intolerant wrathfulness—would probably sabotage
the takeover and with it, inevitably, much of the enveloping cosmos.*"

Lena Faye said, "Even if every human being alive believed you,
I'm not sure we'd rush to accept the responsibility you're trying to
stick us with, Joe."

"*Nonsense. It's a great honor.*"

"We probably couldn't do it," I said.

Joe kept up his spectral golemesque pacing. "*That's true. But
mostly because your kind fatuously assumes indispensability equates
with divinity.*"

"It doesn't?"

"*Of course not. The su'lakle—finite entities at least passably com-
parable to your own species—operate on a divine mandate, a ukase
from God Wholeself.*"

"What's God like?" Lena Faye said.

"*You'll never really know until you take this job.*"

"So God exists?" I said.

Joe Way stopped pacing, and with Pope Jomo's all-to-human
eyes—a su'lakle affectation of cagy ulteriority—fixed me with a
condemning/forgiving glare. Believe me, to escape it, I'd've gladly
kevorked.

"*Mr. Gist, you're descended from a man named Sequoyah, who
taught his people how to 'write.' True?*"

"Yessir."

"*This Sequoyah, alias George Gist, once said, 'We have full confidence they will receive you with all friendship.' *"

"Maybe. I never heard that before."

"*My final F/A segment airs tomorrow night, ne pas?*"

I nodded.

"*Tape a segment to append to the cablecast. Announce that to
demonstrate the earnestness of su'lakle intent, along with my capacity to do whatever I say, I will put on a 'pyrotechnic spectacle' not
long after your announcement.*"

"When exactly? And where?"

"*Midnight. Across an unmissable arc of sky over Al Biqa Valley, directly east of Beirut.*"

"But why?" Lena Faye said. "What's the point?"

"*To* make *a point. Human beings like shows. Next week, I will appear on* Forum/Againstum *again to explain simplistically how humanity may acquire indispensability.*"

"But I've already booked next Monday's guests."

"*Pshaw,*" said Joe Way. "*After Saturday night's spectacle, Levant's subscribers will clamor for my return.*"

When he was gone, back through my looking-glass vidverge unit, Lena Faye said, "*Quel* ego. Kinda like one of my beloved Superjerk's greatest hits."

We flew from Damur Ridge to the Sabra Hotel in one of Levant's helis and set down on the aviary landing pad. The disorder in the streets had come under an uneasy modicum of police control, but I was happy we didn't have to try to enter the Sabra from the ground.

In Levant's studios, I taped the add-on that Joe Way had asked for and turned around to find both Lena Faye and myself facing a uniformed officer of the United Nations Near Eastern Security Service (UNNESS), which President Balthazar Hariri regularly dismisses as UNNESSesary.

"Mr. Gist," the officer said, "I'm Colonel Patrick Rulon. I'd like to see all the tapes of *Forum/Againstum* on which the virrogate Joe Way actually speaks."

"Why?"

"Purposes of evaluation and security. Are there forms I need to fill out?"

"No, you can see them. Did you hear me tape that business about Saturday night's light show in Al Biqa?"

"I did."

Nothing else, not even a smile, just "I did." So I took Rulon to a corked booth where he could review the first and third hours of this week's cablecasts and then preview the one scheduled for tomorrow night. I gave him a multiflicker so he could fast-forward through Joe's silences or back up and replay his odd pronouncements about "the heart's most basic longing" or su'lakle indispensability.

When he emerged from the booth, in which he'd spent less than an hour, Rulon handed me the tapes. "Interesting."

"What did you think of them?"

"I just told you."

"How do they bear on Near Eastern security?"

"That stuff has *global* implications, Mr. Gist. Keep it under your hat."

"The last episode you watched cablecasts tomorrow. Then there's that Al Biqa thing."

"Yes, I know. Night." The colonel beat a tight-lipped, tight-assed retreat.

Lena Faye: "What was that all about?"

"Pissing on bushes," I said. "Territory."

The following afternoon, even before the last of the six *F/A* programs was to appear, Lena Faye and I took my Levant heli out to Al Biqa and landed on a hilltop from which we'd have a good view of Joe Way's promised midnight spectacular.

The stretch of irrigated valley to our east lay below us like a beautiful gridded quilt of lavenders, salmons, and jades. The most unusual feature in the landscape, though, wasn't the crops (leafy tobacco here, tangled grape arbors there, apricot and cherry trees on islandlike ridges), but the spaced-out wind turbines—tri-petaled pinwheels set atop spindly latticework derricks—generating power not only for the hamlets of Al Biqa but also for Sidon, Tyre, Byblos, and parts of Beirut. The blades on those turbines pleasantly hypnotized us as we picnicked on cheese and bread, polished off a couple bottles of wine, and waited for The Show.

Meanwhile, about a mile away, a convoy of military trucks crawled up a hill into a concealing stand of fruit trees. (It may have joined others already positioned there.) Also, once Joe Way's last episode of *Forum/Againstum* had concluded, groups of sightseers in buses and touring cars began to filter into the area, via the main highway from Beirut and dozens of rutted *muhafazah* roads. We saw these last arrivals by their headlamps and taillights, not by the shapes and colors of the vehicles, which, in the gathering dark, registered as amorphous creeping shadows, small smudges on the vaster, darker smudge of the valley floor.

"What time is it?" Lena Faye said.

Before I could check my digital, the sky flashed once: a great, silver-veined lilac throb.

This lilac throb, occupying more aerial territory than a hundred overlapping full moons, faded slowly away, but the sky kept glowing, as if God had turned on a monstrous scallop-shell night-light behind the star-dusted scrim of space. Someone sitting on our picnic blanket murmured, "Wow." It could have been either, or both, of us.

I don't have the heart to describe in its entirety what the su'lakle showed us over Al Biqa. Imagine the biggest and most complex Fourth of July celebration you've ever seen, heard of, or read about. Then cube it. At least.

Even that doesn't quite convey what we witnessed, though, because the bursting rockets, drifting fireballs, parachuting tear drops, and migrating color streams continuously deformed into skyborne images: fields of lion-maned flowers, roaring Niagaras, breaking tsunamis of Oriental-carpet figures, flaming baobab trees, translucent calving icebergs, oddball animals at play or at rest, faces human or disturbingly alien, spiraling keyholes to other continua. Et cetera.

"You know what's weird, George? What has my gut strings twanging really strangely?"

"What?" I was propped on my elbows, my head thrown back, my mouth stupidly agape.

"I've got a hunch they're dumbing this hurly-burly down."

I glanced over at Lena Faye.

"You know," she said, "for us. Condescending. Dumbing it down for our sakes. It could be ten times as spectacular if we had the brains, or the sensory apparatus, to take in their very best. Maybe a thousand times. You know?"

I didn't want to think about that. Usually, I hated fireworks; they boomed and hissed, scintillated and glowered, and all you could do was watch big-eyed and of course moan in orgiastic approval with the rubes around you. This thing the su'lakle had set shifting kaleidoscopically across the sky, though—it was different. I had the feeling not so much that they were patronizing us poor *Homo sapiens* as subtly trying to reorganize our brains through our eyes, to carve fresh pathways through our gray matter by preprogrammed visual stimuli, to refold our convolutions in evolutionary ways we wouldn't fully twig to until they'd left.

Joe Way's manta-ray-shaped head took shape in the fading remnants of their final image, an energy-storm parody of *The Creation* from Michelangelo's Cistine Chapel work. That was what *I* saw. Lena Faye read into it the spare and moving cover illo on Art Spiegelman's *Maus*. (Who knows what everybody else on hand beheld or thought they did?) She and I agreed, though, that emerging from this last image was Joe Way. The head, with its weirdly compassionate eyes, floated over Al Biqa, appearing to sustain its hover by means of its fins' endless rippling. This head occupied as much sky as the first lavender throb had done.

"*In order to acquire indispensability,*" Joe Way began in a thundering overture, "*you must—*"

From the ridge a mile away, the UNNESS vehicles parked amid the fruit trees began firing a concentrated barrage of scathing laser energy at the su'lakle. Vehicles hidden in other parts of the valley joined this attack. The rays—dozens upon dozens of them—launched upward in furious, vindictive assault. Bombs detonated in Joe Way's cheeks and boccal region. The energy comprising and tethering together the features of the entity's startled face began to dissipate. One of its rippling wings detached and floated off toward Tripoli, pulling into tatters as it drifted. The other, hit several times in a row, vented an emerald glow of gigantic phosphenes and evaporated. Shortly thereafter, Joe Way closed his Pope Jomo eyes, and the midnight sky—the *old* midnight sky—reasserted itself, sealing Lena Faye and me, Al Biqa, Lebanon, and maybe even the world itself into the benumbing boxes of our work-a-day lives.

I scrambled up and shook my fist at the UNNESS encampment a mile away. "You idiots! You blooming xenophobic idiots! You may've just ruined everything!"

"They couldn't hurt the su'lakle, could they?" Lena Faye said. "Beings who sustain the cosmos."

"Look!" I told her. "Just look! Where is he? Where are they? What's happened?"

The valley filled with the honking of all the touring cars and buses whose drivers and passengers had come out to witness the midnight show. Honking, cursing, keening. An obstreperous mix-and-match symphony of outrage and disappointment.

My God, I thought, the whole planet sounds sick, grievously wounded. Sick unto death.

I guess it takes a while for a system as far-reaching and complex as the universe to unravel. Despite the chaos, anger, and traffic tie-ups in Al Biqa after UNNESS's ostensible preemptive strike on the su'lakle, most sightseers managed to get safely back to their homes. Lena Faye and I, of course, simply lifted off from that hilltop and whirly-birded homeward.

On our way, seeing the flairs and bonfires illuminating a multi-vehicle collision, we took the time to land, investigate, and help two badly injured people—a woman in her fifties and an unrelated child of five or six—aboard our Levant heli for transport to a medical facility. Indeed, I flew them to the Danny Thomas Memorial Hospital in Beirut, refueled on its roof pad, and undertook three more such missions—Lena insisted on coming along on all of them

—before returning to my towerhouse on Damur Ridge. We arrived home just before dawn. There, we turned on my vidverge unit for reports of the aftermath of the fatuous UNNESS assault on the su'lakle.

Instead, we got Joe Way in his viridescent manta-ray-headed guise. This time, though, he refused to step away from the screen into the authentic three-dimensionality of my relaxall. He peered out at us like an alien prophet.

"Joe!" Lena Faye cried. "I thought they'd destroyed you! Your species, I mean!"

"*Fat chance,*" he replied. "*They disrupted the surface of a hologrammatic display projected from the interstices of this spatial-temporal continuum. Nothing more. That ill-advised action, however, has determined me—us, if you like—to abandon the task of observation to you without delay or instruction. I return to offer my apologies, for I know you two human beings, at least, as entities somewhat better than even you yourselves suppose and so not necessarily deserving of this kind of abrupt rejection. As for your species as a whole . . .*"

"You're leaving?" I said. "You're simply going to pull out? What will happen to us? Joe, we don't know diddly about universe-sustenance!"

"We haven't succeeded all that spectacularly in holding our own planet together," Lena Faye added.

"*Shit will happen,*" Joe Way said. "*Some of it will result from active manipulation of macrocosmic, as opposed to quantum, forces, and much of it will mystify and frighten you. This manipulation will be punitive. But the worst may stem from the psychic impact of our withdrawal on adjacent observer species, many of whom will follow our lead in abandoning the sustenance game. That's all I care to impart. Goodbye.*"

"Wait!" Lena Faye and I both called out.

But Joe Way faded away, and my vidverge unit commenced to operate exactly like a vidverge unit.

Since then, despite repeated U.N. pronouncements about the legitimacy—yea, the *urgency*—of its laser disruption of the unpredictable alien energy beings who'd appeared on *Forum/Againstum* as "Joe Way," the cable-watching public has reacted with either withering scorn or outright indifference. Maybe the latter response is the more common. After all, most folks assume the entire Joe Way phenomenon just another example of TV hype, from the distillate's "scripted" remarks on my show to UNNESS's self-authorized and, yes, highly colorful "ambush" in the valley.

Firm believers in Joe Way, however, want an investigation into the incident. They also demand the literal head of the chief administrator of UNNESS and a concentrated international effort to retrieve and reassemble the insulted alien(s). They have no faith in the U.N.'s promises that the untoward events of the last few hours—occurrences that seem to require the suspension of immemorial "natural laws"—will cease as soon as the jet stream gets back to normal, or martens reinfest the cedars of Qurnat as-Sawda', or the planets of our solar system realign.

"Right," I say. "Or Siddhartha Gautama reappears wearing an NBA warm-up jacket, some Bombay Gear tennis shoes, and a pair of virching goggles."

We sit in my relaxall either monitoring the vidverge unit or looking downslope at Bashir Shouman's spite wall, which his busy-busy fellaheen workers completed yesterday while Lena Faye and I were picnicking in Al Biqa. It effectively blocks our view of the beach, the docks, the sea. Shouman's hired hands left themselves some stuccoing to do on its uphill face, but why should I care whether something so evil in intent and true to its function looks finished? My consolation, now that Lena Faye and I appear to be trapped here, resides in the certain knowledge that the wall will prove useful to Shouman for only a short while longer.

Sadly, with no one to make the key quantum observations that undergird the structure of the universe, the universe will cease to cohere. The center won't hold; things will fall apart. The problem appears as grave to us as was the ruination of the ozone layer to our grandparents.

Okay, *graver*.

"About five minutes ago," Lena Faye says, "I realized that reality truly is breaking down."

"How?"

"Your bathroom scales. They weighed me seventeen pounds lighter than yesterday. Impossible, of course. On the other hand, George, I *feel* lighter—you know, semiafloat even when my feet're touching the floor."

"I know." I *do*: Sometimes, walking, I curl my toes to get better purchase, to keep from drifting away.

The vidverge unit gives us a window on the anomalous events now occurring in the outside world. (The available vidgrids keep changing, though. Levant holds steady, but CNN, ShariVid, ABC Overseas, and Okla*Globe have fi-opted out, leaving behind either static, noisy Milton Berle kinescopes, or geometric test patterns framing the profiles of Amerindians like Pontiac, Tecumseh, and Geronimo.) The first anomaly that Nadia Suleiman reported today was the disappearance at the end of its runway of any flight attempting to leave Beirut International. The big jets would lift off, squeeze into a shimmering slit in the air, and vanish like a magician's pigeons. At least three jets got airborne—and vaporized or interdimensionally transported—before airport bigwigs noted that such wholesale fishiness was bad for passenger morale, ordered an investigation, and closed the facility down.

Other strange things have occurred. Without any warning, the bank building housing the Green Line Café reverted to its rubble-filled condition of over thirty years ago. No one was hurt but the drum-set operator of the Tarabulus Music Militia, who had stretched out under a table after last night's final session. A Syrian soldier vacationing on the Ramlet el Baida beach spontaneously grew a tail (apparently, a spider monkey's) and began collecting money in a stolen fez. The Ferris wheel on this same beach started releasing its cars at the top of its arc, until not a single gondola remained, and people citywide could see the released cars drifting upward and southward like giant bubbles. The streetlamps on the Avenue Charles Helou grew palm bark, heavy green fronds, and coconuts that looked exactly like bowling balls. The horses running in the eighth race at the revitalized Hippodrome crossed the finish line in a neck-and-neck tie without even a nose's difference among them. Elsewhere, the Canadian army invaded Alaska, the Eiffel Tower lifted off with a hundred-some tourists aboard, the Taj Mahal turned into a tangy-smelling construct of melting tangerine Jell-O, and at least a million two-foot-long lobsters with WIN WITH TIM buttons taped to their carapaces swarmed ashore on the southernmost tip of the Malaysian peninsula. An oil firm struck a *crème-de-menthe* deposit in Tierra del Fuego. Denver, Colorado, collapsed into an immense sump of some kind, and all over the world statues of sundry eminent persons began coming to life, no matter how long their commemorated subjects had been dead.

At long last, here on Damur Ridge, night has fallen. For a while, I doubted that it would. I figured snow might fall, or pfennigs from heaven, or the self-pared toenails of feathered protodinosaurs. Lena Faye and I look out the picture window of my towerhouse. Kon Ichikawa's 1958 film *Enjo* flickers on the backside of Shouman's spite wall, subtitleless. I have no idea how it's being projected there, from where, or why. The acting has an earnest panache.

Above the pain and melodrama of *Enjo*, the sky is visible.

Shouman's spite wall has not risen high enough to blot it from our view. I think of TMM in the Green Line Café doing "And I Love Her" after pounding out "Simply Indispenserble." And I pull Lena Faye to me as snugly as I can. She rests her head on my shoulder. Friendly stars blaze in their familiar places, but the full moon shines down—pale, knobby, and large—like a face on Mount Rushmore.

"It's bad, isn't it?" Lena Faye means the cosmos, or this goosy portion of it, without the su'lakle.

"Yeah. I'm afraid so."

"I can't fly home, but if you'd like to be alone, I can get myself a room in a hotel – the Sabra, maybe."

I look Lena Faye straight in the eyes, replay the TMM cover beginning "Bright are zuh stars zud shine," and shake my head.

"Uh uh," I tell her. "Tonight, Ms. Leatherboat, I couldn't possibly do without you."

Once again, we look outward and up. The spite of our kind rebounds on us immediately, for overhead, without any fuss, the stars—all of them—have begun to go out.

* * *

Last Night Out

SOME WILL NOT UNDERSTAND THAT ON THE EVENING before our suicide attack M. and I visited the strip club not as a last vulgar gift to the animal in us but as a way to bolster our scorn for the reputedly innocent people we planned to kill. This strategy worked every time that we paid our cover and ducked inside. The smells of spilled whiskey, warm beer, and frank male rut never fail to replenish my outrage; they also firm my fluctuating sense of righteousness, may God forgive me.

On this slow Monday night, few other patrons vied for the bartender's attention. What do you fellas want? he said.

A blonde young woman in hand-tooled crimson cowboy boots and a glittery red thong strolled the high counter behind the bar, dipping or shoulder twisting in time to the recorded techno-rock. In the dark mirror behind her, her reflection mimicked her dance, and M.'s pupils dilated to encompass both images even as he squinted against the offense they embodied.

Come on, fellas, the bartender said. Order up.

My friend would like a Manhattan, I said.

And you?

Bring me a Bloody Mary.

You got it, the bartender said. But I have to say, your pal there don't much look the Manhattan type.

M. smiled but only with his mouth. I'm *not* the Manhattan type, he said. But this is a—a special occasion.

I placed both hands on the bar and leaned toward M., who eyed the strolling girl with a hard-to-read hunger. Even after more than a year together, he could startle me with odd enthusiasms (for bluegrass music or salt-water taffy) and untimely cruelties (as when he told a ticket taker at a movie that she must lose some weight or expect lifelong spinsterhood). Please say no more, I whispered.

A *very* special occasion, M. said more loudly.

Tattoos of blue barbed wire circled the bartender's upper arms. A hot-white pearl shone in one of his earlobes. No kidding? he said. You get promoted?

Tomorrow I get promoted, M. said.

But you're partying in advance.

M. clasped my neck and yanked me up next to him, the heat from his nostrils warming my jaw. Tomorrow, he said, we both get promotions.

Not that I aint glad to have yall here tonight, the bartender said, but most folks wait until *after* to tie one on.

I broke away from M.'s grip. The woman in boots assumed a vulgar hoochie-coochie crouch. She winked at me and rolled her shoulders.

Circumstances do *not* permit us to wait, M. told the bartender. *Carpe diem*, as you folks sometimes say, Bubba.

The bartender's ruddy face darkened. *What?*

Seize the moment, seize the day, seize the nation, said M., returning the muscular American's glare.

Please, I said, our drinks.

Through the smoke haze and the syncopated air, the bartender studied me as if I had dropped from the moon. You bet—one Bloody Mary and one Manhattan. He looked at M. You want a marshmallow in that?

Of course not, M. said. A pearl, perhaps.

The bartender stared at M., then swung his concave red face toward me. Longer I talk to your arrogant friend, he said, the more doubts I develop about what he's got in his wallet. You follow me, little man?

M. produced his wallet and riffled a bundle of crisp bills under the bartender's nose. Does this sedate your suspicions? My friend and I have jobs. Good jobs. High-paying jobs. We fly airplanes.

Pfaugh, the bartender said. But he fetched our drinks, slammed them down, and swaggered away.

Unbelievers all around us, alone in our pocket of obedience, M. and I drank and watched the show.

Good women are obedient, M. declared. Give them money, and they'll do almost anything you ask.

I thought, Good women guard their unseen parts because God has guarded them—but these hid their feet in boots and showed what the obedient conceal. M. stuffed bills into my hand and nodded at the woman on the runway.

Go on, he said. Buy yourself a harlot tonight. Before noon tomorrow, virgins will surround you.

Soon, my money deep in her boot, the blonde slid along my thighs at a table in the club's center. A chair away, M. had his own dancer, and the techno-music gave both women a strong beat by which to shimmy and beguile. May God forgive me, I am but a man, and I roused. M. had no such difficulty. He threw his head back and laughed in pleasure and contempt, his responses bound to each other like twin infants with a single angry heart.

Perhaps I sneered, for the blonde, still straddling my knees, tilted her head along with her shoulders. You don't really like me, do you?

Her words took me aback. I gave you money, I said.

Yes, to do what I'm doing.

Why do you do it? Does money have such value?

Apparently. She barked a laugh, then looked at me coyly. You can call me Marie. When I made no answer, she said, Or you can let me move on to a man who'll appreciate me.

A man who appreciates you, I said, would never let you set foot here. A man who appreciates you would beat you before he let you—

Let me what?

Disgrace both yourself and your family.

Ah, an uptight God-squad member. Is this another Save the Strippers campaign? Did your church take up an offering so you and your stuck-up friend could go fishing for our frail female souls?

I did not reply to these impertinences.

Let me tell you why I do this. God gave me this body and set me down in this place. When I had no idea what calling to follow, He appeared in a dream and told me that if I applied for work here, the manager would hire me, and in two years I'd have enough money to start college in nursing or chiropractic. You know what, fella? I just about do.

God told you to strip for school money? I said.

As sure as I sit here. I've had visions off and on since I turned eleven.

You've deluded yourself.

No more than you and ugly Mister Moses have. She nodded at M. Coming in here to win my poor lost girlfriends and me for Jesus.

You badly mistake our purpose.

You badly mistake mine.

Both the bartender and the club bouncer had occupied themselves elsewhere, and I shoved this Marie person off my lap and begged M. to end his heart-steeling frolic and to hasten from that pit of iniquity. He waved me off, but I persisted, and at length he got rid of his naked succubus by giving her more money and a copy of The Recital. Thus bolstered, we departed. Soon we would bind the hands of women more modestly dressed than these, but no less deluded.

In the ruins of the fallen towers, an ash-covered fireman found a copy of a charred document in a script unintelligible to him. He passed it along to a law-enforcement agent and trudged back to the unending search for bodies.

* * *

The Procedure

FROM THE BLUEJOINT PRAIRIE ON WHICH THE SPACE port lay, the city of Ganhk resembles an assemblage of glassware on climbing red-slate shelves.

I stumbled from the *Desideratum* with my fellow steerage passengers, many of us Corderists, and saw the planet's most famous city glittering across the plain like an exotic bottle collection. (Locals call the planet Doen, but everyone else uses the name of its Ommundi discoverer, Sagence.)

Shielding my eyes, I steadied myself on the tarmac and ogled Ganhk's sparkling glass battlements—immense pastel replicas of test tubes and retorts. A magnetrain would take us to this city. There, in a chapterhouse of the Galenic League, a surgeon would destroy the tumor that made and sustained me Corderist.

A female voice said, "What do you think, Drei?"

The strangeness of this new place—its light, gravity, and smell—had unsettled me, but how could I fail to admire the artful sanity of its design?

"Lovely," I said. "Nothing lovelier under heaven."

"A lovely place to have one's hope of heaven cut away," my friend said.

"If that can really occur, maybe we'll find heaven here on Doen itself."

253

The smile on Zarafise Koh's face hinted that our long glide through iduum space had multiplied rather than allayed her misgivings.

"Pray," I advised her.

"Why? Haven't the lucidists shown that prayer doesn't work, except maybe as an anxiety inhibitor?"

"Then use it in that way," I said.

"I've never found it more than fitfully helpful," Zarafise said. "Besides, nothing so irrational could ever work here on Sagence."

She had a right to her bitterness. On the other hand, no one had forced her to come. The majority lucidists—of Doen, Trope, Tezcatl, or any of the other Ommundi worlds—would never perform the procedure on an unwilling patient. The idea of a coerced surgery appalled them. However, any sufferer of a cultural or a maverick superstition who *wanted* the procedure could have it, free of charge. Ommundi footed the entire bill, offering transport (in steerage) to Doen, preliminary psychotherapy, and the procedure itself. Doen's physicians had pioneered this technique and then restricted it—as a spur to the planetary economy and a boost to their prestige throughout the Commonweal—to medical facilities in Ganhk. Lucidists who objected to this restriction on a procedure designed to eradicate superstition, to let in the light of reason, earned the monolithic cold shoulder of the planet's most powerful nation.

In any case, Zarafise Koh had come voluntarily to Doen, which she called Sagence. Hundreds of other religionists, including Corderists like me, had accompanied her. Among our number you could also find animanists, witnessers, eldeists, nirvanim, mahdiacs, and vacuum baptists. All of us had a shot at the procedure as the best way to assimilate fully to the dominant lucidism of the Ommundi Commonweal. Like me, Koh had her doubts that Ganhk's surgeons would truly rescue us from either our faiths or our marginalization.

Children popped up on the tarmac, almost as if they had ridden hidden elevators to its surface. They wore scarves of incandescent blue, green, yellow, and red. They tripped about us, barefoot or slippered, charming almost every one of us from iduumship steerage. The children had come as escorts. To the amplified strains of *Wind Is to Sky as Voice Is to Mind*, they took our hands and skipped with us across the tarmac toward the white pylons of the magnetrain cradle.

"Such spry, loving children," said Zarafise as the children tugged us along.

"They don't appear brainwashed." I smiled as I said this.

Zarafise frowned, then grinned in acquiescence as the children danced us up into the magnetrain cars.

Don't ask me either where our escorts vanished once we had boarded that ivory train or how the city of Ganhk absorbed such a flood of believers once we'd poured onto the tiled reception platform among those daunting bottle towers. You would think that the efficient processing of so many patients would require long lines, reception gates, a storm of broadcast directions and announcements, but none of these methods prevailed.

There on the platform, a petite girl separated me from Zarafise Koh and the others and led me into a tunnel through which citizens strolled like people on holiday. In every tributary, the tunnel had a beveled skylight and well-spaced festoonings of plants and banners. At length, it funneled us into a chapterhouse of the Galenic League.

"You have Dr Garer," the elvin young woman said. "Through there." She nodded at a porcelain-edged doorway.

"But you didn't ask my name," I said. "How do you know I'm intended as Dr Garer's patient?"

"Whoever I chose was hers. If another had chosen you, you would have gone elsewhere."

"Everyone on the *Desideratum* has an individual doctor?" No prior briefing—and we'd had dozens had mentioned this fact. Mentioning it would have eased many anxieties.

"Ganhk has thousands of doctors," the girl said. "And here on Doen we love every citizen of the Ommundi Commonweal."

Spoken, I thought, like an amiable little robot. But she smiled, and the light in her eyes sparked from within, not from the foyer's pale lavender wallglow.

Dr Garer pushed aside her amanuensis screen and struggled up from behind a fortress of disc filers, research aids, and one brand-new-looking *book*. She seized my hands, her gray head lowered but her gray eyes searching my face. For what? A sign of my fanaticism?

"I'm Dr Pinalat Garer, a counselor-surgeon originally from Iiol." She smiled. "Iiol is a small village west of here."

Standing a hand taller than I, she hunched her shoulders to minimize the difference. Her work jacket featured cloudpanels and a few disconcerting blue blinkthreads. In fact, it dazzled me—just as, in worshipful settings, the icons of Corderism have always done.

"And your name?" said Dr Garer.

"Drei Roh Sfel."

"Well, Citizen Sfel—"

"Please use my friendname," I said. "Drei."

"All right," said Dr Garer uncomfortably. She levered her amanuensis screen around to summon the Drei Roh Sfel file. It took her seven clicks to get mine (I have fortuitous namesakes on more than five Ommundi worlds), but my date of birth and the thumbnail bio authenticated the file for us.

"Do the procedure on me," I said. "Cut away my susceptibility to the God delusion."

"Easy," said Dr Garer, pointing me to a chair. "No surgery without therapy. No therapy without empathy. No empathy without acquaintance."

"No acquaintance without intimidation," I said.

Dr Garer looked surprised. "You were forced to enroll as an excision candidate?"

I shook my head. "Oh no. No single person compelled me. No one threatened violence, or any other penalty, if I decided to remain a . . . a dupe. I came freely."

"But you remain of two minds about it?"

"Of course. Lucidist views have such widespread force that one always feels the pressure to, well, to *shed* that pressure."

"Societal pressure?"

"What else?"

"Everyone feels that, Drei. You can shed some of it simply by saying no to superstitious cant."

"I have to feel that no before I can voice it."

"Certainly," she said.

"Meanwhile, throughout most of the Ommundi Commonweal, it's a stigmatizing thing to believe as I do."

"Which makes you a good surgery candidate. I can remove the growth responsible for your delusion, thus freeing you from any societal stigma as well."

"Ah," I said. "The rehabilitated believer."

Dr Garer heard my sarcasm and rubbed her cloudpanels, which crackled with holofabric lightnings.

Either my long trip or Ganhk's strangeness, if not both together, suddenly undid me. I covered my mouth and fought to suppress a sob. This sob sounded, even to me, like the wheeze of a steer toppling in a slaughterhouse.

"Go ahead," Dr Garer said. "No shame. Let it cycle."

Given permission, I wept.

"You've agreed to what you must regard as a soulectomy," said Dr Garer. "Of course you grieve. You view the procedure less as a cure than as an assisted suicide."

I had hoped for, but not really anticipated, this degree of under-standing. I looked up.

Dr Garer said, "We honor such responses, but remember that you come to them in error, through the insidious agency of the growth that I want to remove."

"Lambs to the slaughter," I said. "Passive sheep."

Dr Garer said, "This pathological self-abuse stems directly from the tenets of your belief system, which has its own origin in a delusional soul structure."

Bemused, I shook my head.

"Would a passive lamb have had the courage to contract for the removal of such a structure?" Dr Garer said. "And to come such a distance to bring it about?"

"A stronger believer would never have admitted the need," I said. "A stronger believer—"

"—would never have come," Dr Garer said.

"Exactly. I've surrendered to spiritual genocide. So of course I scold, I second-guess myself."

"Go on."

I said, "I see the surgery that you want to do, and that I still *think* I want done, as aborting the god-seed that makes me *me*. I envy your intellectual and emotional freedom, but I also envy the militant faithful, whom I've betrayed by choosing to come here."

I stopped. Was this same conversation occurring in five hundred other chapterhouses? Was Citizen Koh undergoing a like shake-down elsewhere? If so, damn the Doenr lucidists for their ages-old strategy of Divide and Conquer.

I put my hands in my armpits. None of my fellow, or even my enemy, religionists could see or hear me, but God, I still believed, could. I appealed to the First One through the holy go-between of the Ladlamb, El Cordero.

"Praying?" said Dr Garer.

"Trying to," I said. "Not allowed?"

Pinalat Garer chuckled brightly. "If it harms no one else, do what you feel inclined to do. After our procedure, the urge will no longer afflict you, except as a rare vestigial tic."

"Does that mean you sometimes pray?"

"A silly blurt or two during crises." Dr Garer shook her iron-gray head in happy self-reproach. "Even lucidists still have tailbones, Drei. That doesn't make us monkeys. Not permanently, anyway."

I smiled, but, as I did, I prayed, knowing at once both peace and shame.

I slept that night in a room of the chapterhouse to which Dr Garer belonged: a room clean and spare, with a reedlike mat on one wall, a handheld summoner, and a port through which I could view the city without yielding privacy. Ganhk did not consist solely of glassy buildings and vivid slate tiers, but also of ragleafed trees, lofty stairwalks, and a river cutting through it in a series of locks and waterfalls. Engineering rather than naked geography had made Ganhk beautiful.

Zarafise Koh and my other steeragemates had similar digs in other chapterhouses of the Galenic League, private rooms to which preprogrammed child guides had delivered them. Dr Garer had advised that I spend the evening sorting my thoughts, preparing for further talk, and resting. Sleep would help me vanquish my iduum funk and my tendency to second-guess myself.

"Avoid loud music, crude teledramas, oversavory food, and recursive self-debate," she had said. "Most of which you've processed already or you'd have never come."

I longed to see Zarafise or any other Corderist. In fact, I would have happily spoken with even a turncoat mahdiac or Eastern vehiclist. I didn't believe what they believed, but I knew what the prospect of having the physical source of their faith removed felt like. Like agreeing to one's own lobotomy. Like watching a loved one jump into an annihilating flow of ice or magma. Like death and grief at the same time.

But for additional counseling sessions, my procedure could have happened on an outpatient basis. Often, on Doen, it does, for Doen has a low incidence of religious fervor. When it does occur, it occurs amidst born rationalists (lucidists, as they style themselves here) who have already laid the groundwork for the patients' acceptance of the procedure and their subsequent reintegration into Sagency society.

As far as my own wounded faith would allow, then, I trusted Dr Garer, awaiting the procedure with an odd mix of surrender and foreboding. I also prayed for El Cordero to come dwell in me throughout the lightscalpeling designed to evict Him from my person: *Help me stay the course in slaying You.*

But prayer, although I kept recommending it to others, had

never counted among my own spiritual gifts. Even as a creature of faith, I fell victim to thoughts of the city outside the chapterhouse, imagining its amusements and temptations—from the aesthetic to the carnal, from the noble to the base. The summoner on my bedtable had keys for food, research aid, and the referencing of millions of sites, activities, and services planetwide. It also allowed me to set the coordinates for the screen on which the unit showed these items. I enlarged or shrank the screen, shifted it in amoeboid swoops from wall to ceiling, and dimmed or brightened it, wholly on whim, perching at the end of my bed to watch the wall or lying supine to see the strange shenanigans on the ceiling.

The screen showed me that Ganhk had crooneries (singing bistros); stairway museums; falconing tournaments; concert walks; neurotheaters; disembodiment booths; pornoporia; cafés specializing in offworld cuisines; wet-, hard-, and software shops; greenhouses; costume boutiques; lock kayaking; and roving street shrinks, among hundreds of other lures, kicks, and helps, including even a daily fishing meet on the Kivit.

I wanted to go out with a friend. I didn't want to sit like a prisoner in this resort for alien invalids trying to pray—meditate—myself to an acceptance of my soulectomy. But I was a lutemaker from a hamlet in an emerging backwater nation on the far edge of the civilized iduum and lacked the balls to try a midnight escape.

My final sessions with Dr Garer began early the following morning in a revolving aerie atop the chapterhouse. The view gave me God feelings, not so much of power as of awe. Dr Garer pointed out various places and eventually diverted my attention to the red-slate ramparts west of us.

"My own village, Iiol, lies beyond those mountains," she told me. "We call them the Bloodbones."

"You hail from a mere hamlet, just as I do, and yet you came to adulthood with no spiritual training?"

"The notion that matters of the spirit belong only to those formally indoctrinated in a ritualized faith is as false as the idea that a religionist lacks intellect," Dr Garer said with a trace of heat. More calmly, she added, "I don't feel estranged from creation because I deny a quasipersonal creator. Neither will you, Drei, after the procedure."

I said, "How exactly *do* you regard God?"

"As a concept, not a personality. A metaphor, not a lord to whom self-abasement is due. If I sometimes think of God in a backward or oldfangled way, I attribute it to the stress of a bad specific moment or the firing of synapses in my reptilian hindbrain. And I go on functioning as a human grown-up in synch with the rhythms of Doen as one living world amid a vast galaxy of sentient worlds."

"Whereas I don't?"

"I don't know, Drei. Most religionists—although not all—get stuck in a narrow sacral system based on an analogy with the parent-child dynamic of our own biology, itself a product of evolutionary forces. Think how arbitrary that is. And how limiting."

I gazed out at the minarets and retorts of the city. A lutemaker could follow this argument and even credit it to a degree, but it denied the possibility that God may have shaped the so-called parent-child dynamic on the narrow sacral system defining the God-human relationship. However, the mere thought of explaining this to Dr Garer fatigued me.

"Tell me about the procedure," I said. "My procedure."

Dr Garer used a video screen and an electronic pointer to show me the odd structure (the word *growth* exaggerates the size and the changeability of such a minuscule tumor) triggering and feeding my faith. It was more like a nit-sized speck than a nodule, more like a piece of gristle than a cyst. It grew on the interior of my left lung, very near the heart. From it radiated—if only on the 3–D raychart—a targetlike aura of yellow and flame. The rings about the bud of my faith were many times larger than the tiny bull's-eye at their center.

"Air and blood," I said, fastening on the tumor's proximity to both lungs and heart.

"You're remarking on its location," Dr Garer said. "That's fine. Except that after Dr Uten Venlet developed his original theographic techniques, he discovered that the structure popped up in different places in different patients, from the cerebral cortex to the genitals. Last year, I found one behind the knee of a sullen Kozlukti nun."

"If she'd had her leg amputated," I said as a tease, "would she still've needed your procedure?"

"Oddly, yes. The structure has latent subsidiaries that may crop up almost anywhere."

"Then how can your procedure truly rid anyone of faith?"

"By its thoroughness. Also, we never perform it without intense before and after counseling."

"Like this?"

"Like this," she said.

Looking down, I saw naked children thrashing in a lock of the

Kivit River, in a nook of the banking complex, under a tree with boughs like huge beige culverts and leaves like tattered green scrolls. Nearby, adults cast lines into the water and extracted on bronze lures river creatures more like featherless birds than trout.

"So when do I have it?" I said.

"Day after tomorrow, if you keep making progress. Do you still want it?"

"I think so. One favor, though."

"What's that?"

"An evening out with a fellow Corderist. You've separated us, I think, to insure our biddability as converts."

"I'm sorry, Drei. That just isn't so."

"Then let me see her this evening."

"Who?"

"Zarafise Koh." Another evening under chapterhouse arrest, I added, would drive me crazy.

"I'm glad to agree," Dr Garer said. "And maybe tomorrow you and Citizen Koh will visit my homeplace in Iiol."

My eyes betrayed my suspicion.

"To prove we don't keep you confined to some evil end," she said. "To show how one devoid from birth of God possession can live, and live richly."

That evening, Zarafise and I strolled through Ganhk. We rented lines, sonic spinners, and a small Kivit pool under a moonlamp. Here we angled for a type of Doenr river life called goldfinch. This name, the rental man said, was a pun, albeit one opaque to us. The water, though, had an ebony depth allowing blurred vision to the bottom: fins, wings, flukes, streamers, eyespots, scales, maybe even slippery vestigial feet. Zarafise had an earache and a blister inside her lip. The earache stemmed from her body's failure to adjust to local gravity and barometric pressure, the blister from worry.

"What is it?" I said.

"I'm refusing the procedure," she said. "You should too."

"Why?" (Here we went again.)

"If this structure exists in us, there's a reason. Cutting it out is an evil intervention."

"Name the reason for the appendix. Or the tailbone. Or my own useless extra nipple." To shock her out of her inflexible piety, I pulled up my tunic and drew an invisible circle around a wen on my so-called milkline. Zarafise slapped my hand down.

"Stop that!"

"People here swim naked," I said. "I doubt a blemish on my skinny flank will offend them."

Zarafise cast her line and quickly pulled in a goldfinch, which glittered as if with hammered coins. I helped land, unhook, and release it, putting her three catches up on me.

"What will you do?" I said.

Zarafise, once she had made up her mind, rarely recanted a decision. "Begin working off the cost of my error. I have a job in the chapterhouse."

"A job a machine could do better," I said. "It'll take you years to pay off your debt."

"As I work, I'll testify. This was the Ladlamb's plan for me from the beginning."

"Sagence tolerates but doesn't encourage the God-stricken," I said. "You'll have a hard time here."

"I've known harder times in harder places."

We left the banks of the Kivit for another stroll, this time to gawk numbly at the city's architecture, a mélange of functionalism and fantasy, serviceable rectangular structures wedged amongst the tall sinuous bottles so conspicuous from the spaceport. The light of seven moons twinkled from or leaked through the city's pastel bridgeways, domes, and spires. Many pedestrians wore polarized eyeglasses.

"No churches," said Zarafise Koh. "No cathedrals."

"Did you really expect any?"

"Not even their gutted shells. At least on a world with a bona fide history, Drei, you get their petrified remains."

"Other structures stand in for them."

"Like what?"

"Hospitals," I said. "Art galleries. Chanceries."

"The sick die hopeless, the pictures lack substance, the ceremonies ring hollow."

"That's the bias of a zealot," I said. "Ganhk strikes me as joyous, alive."

"You don't need the procedure," Zarafise said. "Dr Garer has already performed it on you."

Not so. But our counseling sessions and my recent exposure to Ganhk's charms had prompted me to defend the place.

"I've had enough," Zarafise Koh said.

I took her back to the chapterhouse in which she'd spurned her role as patient for the roles of an indentured servant and a secret agent for the Ladlamb. Then I returned to the Kivit (rejecting prayer much as Zarafise had rejected the procedure) and had a strip of broiled goldfinch with a mug of Sagency mead. I had thought to debauch myself in one or two of Ganhk's pleasure spots, but that raw urge had flown and I hiked back to my chapterhouse well before midnight.

The next day Pinalat Garer and I traveled by magnetrain to Iiol. She wore sandals, a voluted blue wrapsuit, and a wide snood in which her iron-hued hair swung gently. Sitting beside her as our train hummed through a cut in the Bloodbones, I felt like a truant schoolboy.

It rained as we hurtled along. Somewhere toward the front of our car, a young man crooned: *"This magnetrain Calls the magnet rain, And all who deign To drink it again Have surcease of pain On their travels amain!"*

I liked this man's tenor and longed to accompany him on a lute of my own making. His song had three more stanzas, none very original or cogent, but his voice transfigured them. I heard the sacred in that voice. Dr Garer tapped her knee, but probably heard only his lilting tenor, the swift schussing of the train, a billion ricocheting raindrops.

In Iiol, we walked in this downpour through an orchard of toadstool-shaped treehouses to Pinalat Garer's girlhood home, where her father and mother still lived: Girmisur and Dulatod Garer, old Sagency with frank eyes and straight backs, dressed for our arrival in silken capes and culottes.

They greeted us, gave us bread, soup, and ale, and withdrew up a helical wooden staircase to a loft in the cap of their house. Thick forest grew about, but among the trees were other such houses. Iiol itself tumbled down the hillside below, an array of shingled shops and kiosks.

"This is my room," Dr Garer said, pointing me to a chair.

By her room, she meant not merely a dormitory but a living space redolent of her personality. It boasted paintings, toys, paperweights, a dulcimet, books, slate sculptures, holograms, rainstaves: items that had helped formulate or that currently amused her adult self. These things—not so much things as precious totems—shut out the outside world without turning the room itself into a prison cell.

"Cozy," I said. "A kind of shrine to you."

"Far from it," Dr Garer said. "Shrines mummify and honor, but this place gives me a kick in the seat."

"Your parents don't use it while you're in the city?"

"Yes, they do, but they try to keep it neat for me."

"They idolize you."

"Again, far from it. They respect me for who I am and what I've done. I'm their posterity, as my work is mine."

"Dying holds neither terror nor hope for you."

"The *act* of dying holds terror for me, especially if it occurs away from help. But *being* dead? That's nothing."

"What hope in utter nonexistence?"

"Perfect peace," said Dr Garer. "Why would anybody want the turmoil of hell or the boredom of your Corderist heaven?"

I stayed mute. In fact, I could not envision an afterlife, although God, as drover and deliverer, still seemed to me not only an option but also a prerequisite. I didn't want my First One to stand in that capacity, though, especially if my conviction on that point convicted me of foolishness or delusion among my freethinking peers. Zarafise Koh did not feel that way, of course, but she would spend the remainder of her life a captive of her Corderism and a servant of the Sagency.

"Take a walk or a nap," Dr Garer said. "Do as you like."

A soft rain still fell, so I stayed indoors flirting with a nap. Pinalat Garer moved about quietly. At length she took up her dulcimet, to play the song of the man on the magnetrain. Music filled the study, drenching me in warm impalpable light.

Lightning blasted the toadstool house nearest the Garers' or, rather, the antenna atop it. A crack of thunder concussed the air and the trees, rattling the house's windows. The air glowed. The hair on my arms did a brief writhing dance. Iiol was not Ganhk, nor Ganhk Iiol, and suddenly the lucidism of the city felt fragile and remote.

From the Garers' loft, a cry: "*O storm storm storm!*"

"Shhhhhh," someone hissed. "Shhhhh."

Pinalat Garer and I stepped from her room to look up the staircase. Girmisur Garer came pounding down it. He had shed his cape and hiked up his emerald-green culottes. His dugs swung on his chest like heavy ivory balloons. Blue veins and red streaks marbled his flesh, which jounced as he landed on his big ugly feet at the bottom.

Dr Garer rushed over and took her father by the shoulders: "Chaba, it's only a thunderstorm. Steady yourself."

"I know," he said. However, he didn't seem to care. The whites of his eyes had the size and the plushness of meringues.

"Go back upstairs, Chaba. Put on your cape."

Thunder spoke again, grumbling above Iiol like an air force of giant saurians. The woods quaked, as did Iiol and the sunset side of the Bloodbones.

Cried Girmisur: "*O storm storm storm!*" He stripped off his culottes and darted outside in only a loincloth.

"Girmisur!" called Dulatod. "*Girmisur!*"

"Stay here, Mezi," Dr Garer said. "We'll get him."

Girmisur preceded us into an evergreen thicket, heedless of strewn cones and needles. He broke off two branches thick with gum and held us at bay, flapping them menacingly.

"Chaba, lay the branches down. Come back inside."

He ignored Dr Garer and trotted up the hillside between toad-stool houses and trees onto an apron of scree that rose on a long slope to the peak. Trotting, he brandished his fronds and struggled to stay upright. Amazingly, three other geezers from Iiol, one baby-naked but skeletal, had reached the scree and started up it carrying branches. Eventually, Girmisur and they reached a ridge-line of crimson slate and stood on it four abreast, staring down at us with awe-stricken eyes.

"Who are they?" I said. "What're they doing?"

"A raindance," Dr Garer said. "They're educated rustics like my chaba. They understand their folly, God forgive them."

Naked or nearly naked, Girmisur and his friends looked like elderly chimps in the throes of an elemental madness. Each thun-dercrack provoked them. Girmisur or another rushed partway down the slope, toppled, cut himself, and struggled back up to the ridge-line, where the other old men flailed away at him with their branches. The rain and the din drove them, sustaining a frenzy that seemed both to embarrass and to offend Dr Garer.

"Shouldn't we go after him?" I said.

"No." Pinalat Garer gripped my wrist. "To go up there is to buy into that nonsense."

"I feel helpless watching." Which I did. One of the men had bloody gashes on his forehead and knee.

"You could pray," Dr Garer said.

I looked at her, not knowing if she meant this as a rebuke or as permission. So I prayed silently that Girmisur Garer and his friends be spared harm from the storm's fury and their own unseemly fits.

Instead of calming down, the old men began to hoot, jumping about and swinging their fronds even more violently. Dr Garer grimaced and hugged herself. I stood beside her, miserable in my strangerhood and futility.

The acquaintances or families of some of the other old men

joined us under the screeline. Dr Garer nodded at them, and they at us. Then everyone waited in the rain and lightning for the revelers to abandon their frenzy and rejoin us. At length, they did, but Girmisur last of all. Dr Garer and I climbed through the gravel to meet him and escorted him to the house. Dulatod greeted us with towels and hot fragrant drinks.

"Put him to bed," Pinalat Garer told her mother.

"It doesn't happen that often anymore," Dulatod said. "Not in ages, and we've had other storms."

"I enjoyed it!" Girmisur said. "It was exhilarating! It was—!" He smiled, a faraway cast to his eyes.

I wondered if my prayer had helped bring him down without injury. Probably not. After all, the other waiting Iiolr had taken their crazy chabas or grandchabas home without benefit of prayer, and one old man had hurt himself quite badly. Girmisur went to bed—in a room behind the kitchen—and that was the last I saw of him during my stay in Iiol. Dulatod returned to Dr Garer's study and apologized for Girmisur's antic fit and my soaking when I tried to help him.

"I didn't mind," I said truthfully.

Mother and daughter looked at each other, and Dulatod said, "Forgive him, Pinalat. He can't help himself."

"Why can't he?" Dr Garer rubbed her hair with a towel. "All my tests clearly show he lacks an enthusiast node. He's never had one."

"It's chemical," Dulatod said. "Chemical, chimerical, and chimpanic." She grinned. Her grin expanded into a smile. Her smile progressed to laughter.

"If he once saw himself, he'd desist forever," Dr Garer said, also laughing.

"Forever," said Dulatod.

"He looks like an enraged baby."

The women forgot me, making tender fun of the only male in their household. When they heard Girmisur snort in his sleep, they rolled their eyes and broke up again. Just then, I meant as much to them as a doorstop. That was fine. I relished my facelessness and the women's evident affection for an old fool.

Back in Ganhk, I underwent the procedure. The lightscalpel found, cut out, and scorched the tumor that had given vigor if not life itself to my Corderism. The structure afterward lay in a basin, an obscene bit of charred pink.

The procedure relieved me of my enthusiast tendencies, at least for a time. I went to work in Ganhk handcrafting lutes, dulcimets, and guitars from materials altogether new to me, instruments that sold well and cropped up in the hands of young men and women on Kivit's riverwalks.

I saw Zarafise Koh several times, but always at a distance, running errands for her chapterhouse and twisting her fingers about as if threading beads, even though she never had anything in them.

When it stormed, I liked to go up into a glass building and walk through a skybridge. The Kivit boiled, and the courtyards clattered. At such times, I imagined Chaba Girmisur cavorting like a lunatic ape in the scree above Iiol.

A checkup twelve days after the procedure indicated that a fresh structure had begun to grow under my left arm. I asked for a meeting with another physician. Dr Garer suggested a colleague. When his test results duplicated hers, I returned to Dr Garer. She did the procedure again at a cost that my work barely enabled me to meet. This time I stayed tumor-free nine days.

"Take it out again," I told Dr Garer.

"And the cost?"

"I'll sell my tools and equipment."

"There's no guarantee it won't come back, Drei."

"Remove it anyway."

She did, and a fresh structure appeared five days later in my groin, like a piece of gravel. At great cost, surgery again excised it, but three days later Dr Garer found another tumor at the base of my thumb. A colleague, Dr Kets, offered me the surgery again, this time as an outright gift.

"No," I told him. "Enough."

Although I ache to live on Doen as a lucidist, I am clearly one of those in whom the structure repeatedly grows back. At night in bed this knowledge bewilders me, but during earthquake and storm it goads me irresistibly to my feet.

Tomorrow, I go hunting Zarafise Koh in earnest. I want to put something like hope—maybe even an evergreen branch—in her hands.

Simultaneously, to my chagrin, I want to invite Pinalat Garer to a picnic on the nearby bluejoint prairie. Despite my affliction, she could say yes.

* * *

Help Me, Rondo

OPEN ON:

A patio with a life-sized ceramic statue of a lop-eared puppy atop a stone pedestal, which WE CIRCLE slowly. CRASHING SURF SOUNDS from the beach below the patio.

A WOMAN'S VOICE

"What charms us in a puppy—its big head, its outsized feet—unsettles us in a grownup *person*. When disfigurement accompanies this unexpected bigness, we stare or look away depending on our upbringing, our allotment of gall, our degree of fascination with the grotesque. Even when we look away, we may *want* to look back, to obsess on the disfigurement that we have escaped (if only outwardly), and to take comfort from our own, well, normality."

Two brutal-looking hands seize the puppy statue and fling it away. SOUNDS OF BREAKING PLASTER briefly override the SURF, which grows LOUDER as the hands withdraw, and as we TRACK over the empty pedestal toward an uninhabited beach and the surging ocean beyond.

DISSOLVE TO:

EXT. SMALL BEACHSIDE HOUSE—DAY

The words GULF HARBORS, FLORIDA // SUMMER, 1950 appear

superimposed on the house and a middle-aged WOMAN in a print dress who stands on her walk watering her zinnia and Mexican sunflowers. After six or seven beats, the legend fades, and a change of light causes the woman to start. A shadow falls across her, that of a YOUNG MAN. Continuing SURF NOISES do not prevent us from hearing her speak in the same voice we just heard.

MABEL

"You almost gave me a heart attack. Yes, people call me Mrs. Hatton, Mabel Rouse Hatton. My husband Rondo passed away a little over three years ago. No, not here—on the *other* west coast, California's, not Florida's. I came back to Tampa for the funeral and lived there again for a year before buying this little place.

"What? Do I think you *resemble* Rondo? What a question. Almost no one looks the way Rondo did, kiddo.

"*Really?* I can't think of another soul who's sought me out claiming to be his son, and you almost certainly have no right to that honor. Okay, given your agitation, I'll take you just as seriously as you like. Ah. Your jaw, your hooded brow, the subtle broadening of your nose, your lips, even the incipient gapping of your teeth—yes, they do in fact put me in mind of Rondo, but a much younger and fresher Rondo, with a touch of acne, and the lilt of hope and ambition still in him. If you honestly don't know your biological parents, I can see how you might assume yourself—in your orphanhood Rondo's bastard offspring, but I don't like, or buy for a minute, what such an assumption says about him.

"Sorry. I'm not laughing at *you*, only at your fancy that Rondo could have cheated on me with some chippie and taken no responsibility for their woods colt. He didn't *do* that sort of crap, kiddo.

"Okay, what *do* they call you? Frederick Coby? Frederick *Price* Coby. Nice name. Rondo's Daddy Stewart's middle name was Price—a coincidence, no doubt. You can find scores of Prices in any good-sized city's telephone book. Hattons don't crop up that often, but you don't call yourself Freddie Hatton, do you? Sorry, I mean *Frederick.*

"Well, whatever you call yourself, you should savvy your disease well enough to know that acromegalics don't inherit pituitary adenomas. No, those tumors arise spontaneously for reasons members of the hallowed medical profession just haven't fathomed yet. A sneaky mutation occurs in *one* cell of that puny gland, the cell divides and redivides, and a tumor forms; the tumor induces a veritable *flow* of growth hormone, and if it catches you after puberty—

as it did with you, I take it—you don't turn into a modern Goliath, but instead into a kind of, well, twentieth-century throwback to the face and physique of the reviled Neanderthal.

"Has anyone *diagnosed* your acromegaly?

"Oh. You've diagnosed yourself, from Rondo's films. Well, of course. Everyone should go to the movies to find out what's ailing them. I learned from *Gone with the Wind* that I suffer from intermittent narcolepsy. *Miracle on 34th Street* revealed a case of stomach flu—severe nausea. And, you're right, critics of the three films of Rondo's directed by Jean Yarbrough had even worse discoveries about their health. You must still go to a doctor, though, Frederick.

"What do *I* think? From my eleven-plus years' experience as the wife of an acromegalic? Well, you could narrowly pass as a candidate. Tell me your age. Eighteen? Interesting. Born in '32, between Rondo's divorce from Immell James and his marriage to me. That year gives you an argument, I guess, but still defies everything I know about Rondo's state of mind *and* behavior during that unhappy time.

"Well, I've just about drowned these flowers. Since you've hitchhiked all the way here from the Bay, come on inside. You deserve at least a lemonade. Or, once indoors, a bottle of beer or a gin-rickey pick-me-up. Inside, you won't look like quite such a befuddled urchin, and even my nosiest blue-nosed neighbors can't see through stucco."

INT. MABEL HATTON'S HOUSE—LIVING ROOM—DAY

MABEL

"Come in, come in. Let your eyes adjust, then flop down on that beach settee and put your feet up while I fetch you . . . okay, a lemonade. Maybe you really are just eighteen. If you were older, you'd've wound up fighting the Nips or the Jerries and might not've made it to my door at all. What? You'd've flunked the physical, anyway? Only if you suppose the docs at our induction centers better diagnosticians than the high-cost quacks in private practice, which, unfortunately, supposes the preposterous.

"I recognize acromegaly because I married it and then lived with it for nearly twelve years. Besides, Rondo and I saw *The Monster Maker* not long before Rondo died, a dreadful Producers Releasing Corporation flick about a researcher who injects one of his enemies with a serum that *causes* the disease. Rondo and I felt sure the goons responsible for that one had him in mind when they dreamt it up, really insulting crap that hurt Rondo's feelings. *My* feelings, too, for that matter.

"Anyway, most doctors have never *seen* a case of acromegaly, and yours, Frederick, is so fresh and basic that even a Johns Hopkins grad could be forgiven for taking you as simply someone naturally heavy-featured, a young longshoreman type. You have a well-muscled, an *athletic* build, and don't much resemble the hideous brute you seem to think you do.

"Here. Lemonade. Do you like it a little tart? Rondo used to. Let me turn up the window unit. Sweat's beaded across your lip like a mustache of pearls, and the smell of it—no, don't wince, I *like* it, it brings back memories of bygone intimacies and of Rondo's intolerance of temperatures higher than sixty-five—well, that smell soothes me. Maybe someone ignorant or hyperfastidious would think you careless of your personal hygiene, but not I, Frederick, not I. Do you have a headache, too? Would you like a Goody's powder to dissolve in your lemonade? All right, suit yourself.

"I won't crowd you, I'll sit over here in this upholstered monstrosity Rondo used to love. I had it shipped back to Tampa from our little place in Palmdale—Beverly Hills, sort of—not long after his interment in February of '46. Actually, it's good to see a man relaxing in my house again. Don't shake your head, you absolutely qualify as a man. And, say, making a home for Rondo in a town with shameless libertines like Errol Flynn, Howard Hughes, and some other rats I won't even mention was tough. On the other hand, fighting the Lotus Land ethos put legs under me, Frederick, it filled my every minute in that parched and rootless desert with meaning.

"You smile, as if a man as ugly as Rondo had no choice *but* to stay faithful. Don't kid yourself. Some of the floozies who gravitated to Hollywood would have banged Cheetah, from *Tarzan of the Apes*, if they figured it'd get them a part, and some of them probably did. Anyway, swarms of frails tried to make love to Rondo, especially during the stretch he had from '43 on, starting with *The Ox-Bow Incident* and running through *House of Horrors*, where he got top billing over, well, actors you probably never heard of. But Rondo never nibbled. He stayed true. He hurried home to me and our little house on Maple Drive, always appreciating that I saw past his looks to the core of American goodness around which he'd shaped his whole off-screen personality. His *real* self.

"Rondo would've blushed, or even scolded me, to hear me say

bang, much less *fuck* or any other Anglo-Saxon term for carnal relations, and I can see I've either stung or disappointed you, too, haven't I? Well, that's okay. I *admire* your ability to blush. I like an innocently boyish man. Still, you *do* savvy that Rondo Hatton couldn't possibly have sired you—either on me, because we hadn't married yet, or a forward old flame from Hillsborough High, or some harlot starlet with bedroom eyes and rocking-chair runners for heels. Don't you?

"I'll shut up for a while, we'll listen to the air conditioner and readjust ourselves to the mystery of each other's presence. So sip, sip, sip your lemonade, Frederick Coby."

FLASHBACK (1922)—RONDO'S BEDROOM (TAMPA)—NIGHT

A few years after returning from service in France under a former classmate, Captain Sumter L. Lowry, Rondo dreams that a cloud of sulfur-bearing gas seeps into his bedroom through the cracks around his door.

Panic-stricken but paralyzed, he rests on his cold floor while a figure in a gas mask approaches with a blinding glass bulb on the end of either a gun barrel or a peculiar futuristic dowsing rod. In the bulb's hot glare, the gas dissipates, but the figure does not retreat, and Rondo's extremities—his hands in particular—inflate like rubber gloves attached to invisible canisters of hydrogen. Each hand grows monstrously huge and clawlike. Rondo's face shrinks into a small agonized appendage of his enormous hands.

Rondo SCREAMS into this nightmare, "Help me!"—with neither sound nor prospect nor result. His impotent gigantic hands fascinate him. Even in this wretched state, he cannot look away from them.

INTERIOR—MABEL HATTON'S HOUSE—LIVING ROOM—DAY

MABEL

"What happened to Rondo may not happen to you, Frederick. All my researches show that acromegaly sometimes goes into remission. It spontaneously limits itself. You can't go back to the way you looked before your pituitary tumor provoked the first telltale somatic changes, but the disfigurement stops. It doesn't worsen. In your case, if the process halted within the next year or so, you could anticipate an altogether normal life. *I* find you attractive. I'd bet this house that other females—gals at least as strapping as and a lot younger than I—find you pretty dishy, too.

"Now *that* blush hasn't got a thing to do with the heat, it says I've either hit the mark or missed it by—not much. Those dewy eyes of yours have wooed and won over their share of pneumatic demoiselles, haven't they? I'll bet you look pretty swell in boxing trunks, too, like Garfield in *Body and Soul* or that new young Lancaster fella in *The Killers*. Ha! You just get redder, Frederick, as crimson-plush as a knife slice across the thumb. I like that, too.

"Actually, in his younger days, Rondo cut a swashbuckling figure himself. He set a breeze blowing around a lot of pretty skirts. He sowed his wild oats, his devil-may-care tares, his libidinous rapeseed. I'm talking figuratively, of course, but until Rondo fixed on my figure alone, he had an eye for figures and a figure for the distaff eye. Sadly, the movies stressed the brutishness of his acromegaly, the way he'd devolved into a lumpy human ogre, but as a kid your age, Frederick, he ran track, pole-vaulted, and excelled on either side of the line of scrimmage as a footballer. But for his disease, he might have impressed Henry King, the director who discovered him out at Rocky Point, as a second Douglas Fairbanks rather than as a shudder-provoking character actor. And girls saw him, then, as more Gable than Karloff, more Lew Ayres than Lugosi. He could buckle a swash, Rondo could.

"Another lemonade? No? Well, let me show you his photo with an elite high-school fraternity called 'Ye Royal G. G.' Unbutton your collar while I fetch it from my keepsake room, my 'Mausoleum of Remembrance' as one of Rondo's irreverent cousins insists on calling it. I had the photo matted and framed after the funeral. No, don't get up. I'll bring it to you. Wholly my pleasure.

"Move over a bit. I'll hold it for you so you don't smudge the glass with your fingerprints. Look. That's Rondo, front and center on the bottom row, broodingly Valentinoesque if you want my cheerfully biased opinion. Ten princely specimens of white Southern manhood, circa 1912, in their tuxedos and emperor-penguin shirtfronts.

"All right, take it. You do hold it with intuitive respect. Maybe you see yourself peering back out from Rondo's deep-set, forebodingly hooded eyes. For years, Frederick, I badgered him to tell me what the 'G. G.' in 'Ye Royal G. G.' stood for. For years he either changed the subject or hit me with absurdities like 'Goober Gluttons,' or 'Gallant Galoots,' or 'Good-looking Gorillas.' The subject embarrassed him. After the failure of his first marriage—or Miss Immell's failure to forgive the coarsening of his features even as she embraced the coarsening of her own values—well, after their divorce, Rondo couldn't even *think* about that club without cringing. The ethos of the guys—carnal opportunism—disgusted him. The more brutish he started to look, the quieter and more self-critical he grew, as if God had afflicted him with acromegaly as an ironic way of scourging his vanity *and* of ennobling him.

"Yes, he did, Frederick—he told me during the filming of *Moon Over Burma*, six years into our marriage. 'Ye Royal G. G.' stood for 'Ye Royal Gonorrhea Guards.' Isn't that terrible? Laugh if you like. All right, laugh because it sounds no less an absurdity than Goober Gluttons. And it doesn't, does it? But this time he had truly confessed the club's dirtiest and most fundamental secret. He swore that the remorse he felt as the high mucky-muck of these smug adolescent playboys had served, over time, to redeem and cleanse him.

"He said, '*I stand shame-faced before myself, Mabel.*' His exact words. He never had a line that good in any movie, and he never said any line that he *did* have with such heartbreaking conviction. You smile? Well, you smile because you've seen *The Spider Woman Strikes Back, House of Horrors, The Pearl of Death*, and *Jungle Captive*, and you know Rondo couldn't say 'Bless you' without making it sound scripted, much less 'Stop screamin'.' Even *I* knew Rondo couldn't act. Never, under any circumstances, would he have made a matinee idol in the talkies, but off-camera he lived as soulfully as anyone. Film could never capture his *low-key* intensity.

"He always believed the mustard gas he'd inhaled in the trenches outside Paris triggered the adenoma that caused his disfigurement. He saw it as divine punishment for his riotous youth. More than one Beverly Hills doctor told him no medical evidence linked his pituitary tumor to chemical exposure. The Krauts gassed thousands of doughboys, but not every doughboy came home with the clock of acromegaly ticking inside him. And you, Frederick, you were *never* gassed, were you?

"But Rondo didn't believe in accidents, he thought God had finessed him into the trenches as the first step in a redemptive process that included marrying Immell, two-timing her, growing uglier, suffering her rejection, and meeting Henry King when he came to Florida to film *Hell Harbor* in '29. Rungs on a ladder. Links in a chain. He felt God sculpting his flesh toward a highly fraught transformation, but during the breakdown of his marriage he started to think the process simply punishment for him and a shadowy warning to others. Only when he met me, and I loved him in spite of his looks, did he begin to reckon that the process had a wholly different object.

"Namely, reconciliation. Here, Frederick, give me back the photo. See this card attached to the back. The skull and crossbones on it was the official insignia of Ye Royal G. G., a nod to Tampa's history as a haven for buccaneers, a nod to its annual Gasparilla Festival. Three months before Rondo died we made plans to come home in February to see the mock pirate invasion of the old port city. Little did I know that Rondo would join that assault in a one-man ship exactly the size of a coffin."

FLASHBACK (1945)—A HOLLYWOOD ROAD—NIGHT

Once beyond bit parts in his films of the late 1930s/early 1940s—an ugly face in *The Hunchback of Notre Dame*, a leper in *The Moon and Sixpence*, a moll-abusing freebooter in the Bob Hope comedy *The Princess and the Pirate*—RONDO HATTON began playing villainous lunks at the dispatch of smarter guys who befriend or patronize him for their own purposes. In *House of Horrors*, his screen credit, superimposed on his misshapen face emerging from the dark, reads

Introducing
RONDO HATTON
as THE CREEPER

Introducing. As if he has sprung full blown from Boris Karloff's forehead, or the smoky bowels of an Eastern European golem factory. As if he hasn't already essayed the part of the Hoxton Creeper in a deft Sherlock Holmes adventure, with Basil Rathbone, called *The Pearl of Death*. As if he never existed to the world at large until reeled into shambling visibility by the camera work of Maury Gertsman.

Coming home from a prerelease showing of *House of Horrors* at director Jean Yarbrough's place, Rondo and Mabel joke about this credit and his belated birth as a movie star—if only of cheap Universal programmers that in less than a year the studio will jettison as antithetical to its strategy of luring the affluent postwar public away from bowling and their newfangled television sets.

"I liked how your lip imperceptibly twitches in that moody opening shot," says Mabel in their late-model Packard.

"Yeah," says Rondo.

Mabel says, "You can talk like a grown-up now. No stupid screenwriter's limiting you to grunts and snarls."

Lightning crackles above the pepper trees in the Santa Monica foothills. Rondo glances sidelong at Mabel, a look of happy menace on his face, his upper lip raised at the corner, as he mutters:

"That lip twitch was my opinion of the word *Introducing.*"

"When you acted that scene, you couldn't even see the word, Rondo. The credits all came in postproduction."

"I read the screenplay and had a hunch. Unlike most of the ugly creeps I play, I *can* read."

"You always die in Universal's programmers," Mabel says. "Can't they dig up a screenwriter with brains enough to imagine some other ending?"

Rondo smiles. "I should get the girl. *Get* as in *win,* not as in *choke to death.*"

"You already have a girl, remember? I just think the silly sameness of the plots would stick in your craw."

"Why?" says Rondo. "They play like my own life, where I do the bidding of others, like when the Army sent me to France to shoot Huns or when you talked me into coming out here and looking up Mr. King again. And, eventually, I *will* die."

"You haven't died yet."

"Just a matter of time, sweetheart. Did you see me in that walking-shadow bit? That wasn't just me walking along in those shots. That was acromegaly on the march."

"You've outlived Roosevelt," Mabel reminds him.

"He had twelve years on me, and poliomyelitis. Scuttlebutt has it that he was also messing around."

"Which you don't do."

"No, ma'am. And which I wouldn't even if I could."

They drive. Then Mabel says, "I've figured out why they call it *House of Horrors,* Rondo."

A roll of his eyeball, a flicker of his brow. Liquid rivets PING off the Packard's cream-colored body metal. "It's not because Martin Kosleck's crazy sculptor gives the Creeper asylum in his studio," Mabel says. "It's because that stuck-up art critic pegs him dead to rights as a no-talent."

"So?" says Rondo.

"So the horrors in Kosleck's house aren't you, big boy, but the godawful papier-mâché statuary in his studio." Mabel folds her arms over her bosom as if she has just decoded an abstruse cosmic mystery.

Rondo LAUGHS. The rain CLATTERS down.

INT. MABEL HATTON'S HOUSE—THE KEEPSAKE ROOM—DAY

MABEL

"Frederick, come in here. I know you want to see what I've got in here. I don't invite just anyone for a look-see, but you've gone out of your way not only to see Rondo's last five films but to find me here in Gulf Harbors. But I *won't* hand-deliver an engraved invitation. Either join me now or kindly remove yourself from the premises.

"Ah, the Spider Woman has enticed you into her web. Let me look at you looking. The spectacle of someone else's awe never fails to excite me. I brought all these lobby posters, stills, and tabloid clippings from L.A. when I returned to Florida for good. But not until last February, on the third anniversary of Rondo's death, did I fix up this room as you now behold it.

"Some acquaintances and purported friends have accused me of living in the past, of turning my den into an idolatrous shrine. Do you know what I told those impertinent folks? I told them either 'Fuck you' or 'Go away,' always suiting the squelch to the character of my tormentor. Ha!

"I don't see it as *living* in the past to commemorate one's personal history. The past made us who we've become, after all, and it ought to partake of a little more glamour than a pile of broken seashells, don't you think? 'Remember the Alamo.' 'Remember the *Maine.*' Should we forget that FDR pulled us through the Depression or that Hitler tried his damnedest to exterminate the Jews?

"Maybe I've gone a *little* haywire here—your eyes say as much —but that dramatic photo of Rondo in a black fedora and black leather gloves recalls a filmmaking era at Universal that will never come again. I bought those gloves in a darling shop in North Hollywood. One afternoon in the Brown Derby, Rondo and I argued over whether we should send a copy of that shot to one of his impressionable nieces.

"There—Rondo and Basil Rathbone. There—Rondo as a wrangler. There—Rondo as Moloch the Brute. And there—Rondo lit from below to accentuate the alleged gruesomeness of his facial features.

"But I don't consider this room a shrine because I neither live nor worship in here. Besides, some of the keepsakes—look at those shelves—commemorate *my* accomplishments. This little Santa effigy in the satin-hemmed coat? I used to make dozens of them every fall to put in L.A. department stores on consignment. And that generously cupped brassiere hanging on the wall, as if some female miler burst chest-first through the plasterboard? (Ah, the famous Frederick Coby blush again.) I patented its design in the '30s and have drawn residuals on it in dwindling sums ever since. Without my contributions to the Hatton household, honey, Rondo wouldn't have lasted a season in Celluloid City. And those felt dummies of the Creeper? My doing again, as I'm quite proud to say.

"A memory room, sure. But a tomb or a shrine? Uh-uh. If it has any religious overtones at all, they spring from Rondo's hardheaded refusal to believe in accidents and his silly conviction that the God of the Universe *wanted* him to star in penny-pinching Universal horror flicks. The lug believed that. And even if he wasn't very good, he enjoyed the work—lousy scripts, the occasional insensitive cast member, cheap publicity campaigns, tyrannical seven-year contracts, and all—because he believed that.

"Take this copy of Rondo's Bible and let it fall open where it will. The Book of Isaiah, right? Okay. Start reading at the thumb smudge.

"'For he shall grow up before him as a tender plant—' No, don't stop. I'll recite it with you. I know it by heart, just as Rondo did: '—and as a root out of dry ground: he hath no form nor comeliness, and when we shall see him, there is no beauty that we should desire him.'

"Good. Keep going.

"'He is despised and rejected of men: a man of sorrows and acquainted with grief: and we hid as it were our faces from him; he was despised, and we esteemed him not. Surely, he hath borne our griefs and carried our sorrows: yet we did esteem him stricken, smitten of God, and afflicted.'

"More, Frederick. Don't listen to me reciting it with you. Just keep reading.

"'But he was wounded for our transgressions, he was bruised for our iniquities: the chastisement of our peace was upon him; and with his stripes we are healed.' Okay. Now drop down to the chapter's last verse and read: 'Therefore will I divide him a portion with the great, and he shall divide the spoil with the strong; because he hath poured out his soul unto death; and he was numbered with the transgressors, and bare the sin of many, and made intercession for the transgressors.' Good. Let those final words echo in you a moment, then close the book."

FLASHBACK (1938)—A HOLLYWOOD PRODUCTION LOT—DAY

As the first "ugly man" contestant in *The Hunchback of Notre*

Dame, Rondo, wearing no makeup to speak of, loses to CHARLES LAUGHTON, who plays the cathedral's bellringer, Quasimodo, with the help of disfiguring latex strips and a prosthetic hump. After the filming of these bits, Rondo goes looking for Laughton, not really hoping to talk with him but simply to fulfill Mabel's fannish request to "dig up some dirt" on the pudgy British-born star.

There, amid a swarm of PROP MEN and EXTRAS, stands the bandy-legged gnome, with director WILLIAM DIETERLE. Rondo's nerve almost crumples, but the reporter's instinct that served him so well at the *Tampa Tribune* asserts itself and he saunters up, his hands in his back pockets, his chest thrust out like a locomotive's cowcatcher.

"Yes?" says Dieterle evenly.

Rondo addresses both men: "If we'd had a contest based on the looks God gave us, I'd've won hands down."

Dieterle smiles wanly, but Laughton, who would stand at least Rondo's height if not stooped under his artificial hump, looks up with popeyed interest.

"Even without this painful rigging," he says, "I'd give you a run for your money, Mr. — "

"Hatton. Rondo Hatton."

"Have you ever seen me in a movie in which my countenance appeared more or less *au naturel*, Mr. Hatton?"

"Sure. *Mutiny on the Bounty. The Old Dark House.*"

"Then you already know that I have a face like the behind of an elephant."

Rondo and Laughton twinkle at each other, an exchange that Dieterle does not remark, and Rondo tactfully withdraws. A few minutes later, Laughton also leaves the set, probably to begin the arduous process of having his naked face restored to him by makeup artists George and Gordon Bau.

INT. THE HATTONS' BEDROOM—THAT NIGHT

Lying in bed next to Mabel, Rondo says, "I'll bet he's telling his wife that today he met the ugliest living human being he's ever seen."

Mabel says, "Elsa Lanchester? The bride of Frankenstein?"

They LAUGH for ten minutes.

An hour later, unable to sleep, Rondo sits on the edge of their bed in his satin pajama trousers flipping an Indian-head penny that he found on the set that morning. Mabel, whom he never meant to keep awake, lies beside him waiting for him to complete this arcane ritual and to rejoin her under the covers.

Heads. Tails. Heads. Heads. Heads. Tails.

On the seventh flip, Rondo drops the penny, and it SCREES across the floor and vanishes under a Biedermeier chest of drawers. "Crap," says Rondo. Then, more LOUDLY, "Crap!" He GRUNTS and rises, the box springs TWANG, and Mabel says, "For Pete's sake, Rondo, let it go, it's only a goddamn penny."

"I hadn't finished with it. *It* hadn't finished with *me.*"

He flings his damp pillow across the room, knocking a picture askew. Sweat waterfalls down his flanks. His temples throb. He picks up the chest of drawers by one end, toppling a regiment of bric-a-brac, and then haphazardly scoots it forward.

He hears a SNAP, like an anklebone breaking, and drops to his knees to feel about for the penny. Mabel says he might have better luck if he turned on the light, but he tunes her out—just as, more and more often, he tunes out the dismaying news from Europe on their cathedral Philco. With hands as nerveless as rubber gloves, Rondo gropes about. Either the penny has disappeared into another dimension or it continually takes effective evasive action.

Rondo sits back on his heels and HOWLS.

Mabel's hands knead the taut muscles in his shoulders. "Mr. King promised you'd find work," she says. "It'll come. You don't have to decide our future on a coin toss. Talk to me, baby."

Rondo HOWLS.

"Come on, baby. Come back to bed."

"My lucky coin!" Rondo SHOUTS, sounding rage-filled and piteously ridiculous even to himself. He cannot help it. The probability of finding work in the picture mills of Hollywood does not concern him. He has no doubts on that score. In fact, he chose to flip the coin in part *because* he had no fear of going unemployed.

"Talk to me, Rondo." Mabel massages his neck, leans into his clammy back with maternal solicitude. "Talk to me, baby."

He can't. He HOWLS.

INT. MABEL HATTON'S HOUSE—THE KEEPSAKE ROOM—DAY

MABEL

"Do you see how every photo—not counting the head shots, I mean—underscores the strength and brutality of his hands? Well, of course. The Creeper was supposed to *strangle* all his victims. Creepily enough, upon occasion Rondo couldn't even open a jar of pickles. I had to do it for him. The thickening of his tissues, as the acromegaly cruelly progressed, trapped his nerves, particularly in his hands, rendering them as weak as a baby's. I'd pinch the web between his thumb and index finger, and he wouldn't really feel it, not even if I brought my nails together.

"Not that I did that very often, just now and again, as a test. Sometimes—rarely—he registered the pinch and looked annoyed. Believe me, Frederick, I took heart from his annoyance. Maybe his faith had triggered a previously hidden immune mechanism and set him on a miraculous path to recovery. But could even a miracle counteract the fact of his overgrown bones and cartilage? Can a toad become a tadpole again, or a crippled boxer an unblemished altar boy?

"There—Rondo with Tyrone Power. There—Rondo with Henry Fonda. There—Rondo with Gale Sondergaard. There—Rondo with Charles Laughton and Cedric Hardwicke. A life in Lotus Land had its compensations, but we never hobnobbed with any of these people.

"Everybody—directors, actors, writers, probably even grips—segregated themselves according to the money they made. Top-flight stars didn't party with B-picture types, writers who made three hundred a week cold-shouldered the stiffs who made a century and a half, bigwigs from Warner Brothers wouldn't think of knocking back a few with the chiefs from RKO. We didn't party much at all, but when we did, we usually wound up with either Universal-serials people or folks from the poverty-row studios along Gower Street.

"At one cocktail party, a hack from Omnivore Pix or some such staggered up to Rondo and me and pitched a movie idea to Rondo as if Rondo actually had some clout. The guy'd written a screenplay for a film that would require live actors and actresses to assume the roles of Disney *cartoon characters*—Donald O'Connor as Mickey Mouse, Deanna Durbin as Minnie, Groucho Marx as Donald Duck, Fred MacMurray as Pluto. (Live actors as cartoons, I don't think I've ever heard a lamer idea.) Anyway, the hack thought Rondo would make a picture-perfect Goofy. He wanted to go out to his car for the screenplay so Rondo could show it to Mr. Dieterle or Mr. King and start the project rolling. As politely as he could, Rondo told the guy that Mr. Disney might not take the unauthorized use of his creations too kindly.

"'Why?' the nutzo said. 'None of his people will have to draw 'em. So if Walt gets nasty, we just offer him a cut, right?'

"Well, maybe my story doesn't have anything *obvious* to do with the weakness in Rondo's hands, but I doubt that anybody anywhere

else in the world would have approached my husband with a prop-
osition based on his alleged resemblance to Goofy. On the other
hand, lots of stars and stagehands treated Rondo well, accepting
and encouraging him. Given all the depressing stuff I've told you
about acromegaly and Rondo's dark nights of the soul, I thought
you might appreciate something . . . *airier.* I don't want you to lose
heart. I don't—

"What? You want to hear how he died? *Really?* If I were in your
huaraches, Frederick, I might *never* want to hear it. What if I told
you that on the set one day an actor pulled out a Colt pistol—not
a prop—and shot Rondo point-blank in the heart. You look
shocked. Of course, in all but a couple of his last films, exactly that
sort of death carried Rondo off and the film itself into its closing
credits. But okay, I'll tell you quickly because Rondo's real death
happened almost as fast as a trigger squeeze, and maybe that news'll
give you solace.

"Late in '45, a sailor from Tampa, a guy Rondo'd met working
for the *Tribune,* turned up in the Navy hospital in Los Angeles with
pneumonia. Tom began coming over as often as he could convince
his doctors that a home-broiled steak and a bull session with
another Tampan would speed his cure. Well, he convinced them a
lot so we saw him a lot, and since I liked Tom, too, if he couldn't
make it over, his *absence* haunted our house.

"Around Christmas, Rondo had a peculiar cardiac incident
while toting a plant from our house to a neighbor's. Tom left the
neighbor's—we'd gone there ahead of Rondo—to look for him and
found him on the sidewalk, a terra cotta pot shattered at his feet and
an impenetrable fog in his eyes. But Rondo got better and never did
stop talking about returning to Tampa in February for the Gasparilla Festival. The incident scared *me,* though, because acromegaly
ups the risk of heart disease, and the doctors had no reliable treatment for either the symptoms or the excessive flow of hormones
that produce the symptoms. They still don't.

"On the second of February of '46, while I pan-fried some
venison, Rondo fell in the shower. Tom had come to visit again, and
he burst into the bathroom to help. Rondo perched hangdog and
naked on the edge of the tub looking as white as bleached rice. I
telephoned the fire department for an ambulance. Just when the
driver and a medic ran through our door, Rondo died. With Tom's
help, those guys got him covered and laid out on our bed, and what
happened after that, Frederick, I couldn't tell you if you held a
blowtorch to my feet. He didn't hurt long, though, which suggests a

measure of divine justice because his disease had tormented him, mentally *and* physically, for twenty years or more, God rest his soul.

"Do you wish I *hadn't* told you?

"Rondo can't help you, Freddy, unless you take courage from his. And doctors can't help you unless they develop a foolproof way to regulate the flow of growth hormone from your pituitary.

"I can almost guarantee you that Rondo wasn't your daddy, though. His acromegaly often shut him down as a lover. Even if he'd had Casanova's staff and stamina, he never wanted any kids, for fear—a foolish one, I'm told—they'd inherit his affliction. So don't look to Rondo or to yesterday's medicine for your salvation, baby, 'cause it just won't come from either place. It just won't.

"Give me your hand. Maybe Mabel can help you. I *know* how you feel. Grief feels terribly like fear, and I've come through mine to a certain calm. So why don't you stay for dinner? I'll boil some shrimp, and while we eat, you can tell me your story."

EXT. A PACIFIC ISLAND—INFINITE DAY

Hangdog and naked, he steps into a coracle that carries him westward to the sky island, Rapanui. On its shore, he beaches this boat and stalks inland, up the grassy slopes to the great stone heads standing like sentinels above the sea. Recognizing himself in every tall face, he offers a prayer of gratitude—gratitude that the sculptors of these artifacts did not afflict them with either feet or hands.

BRIGHTEN TO INCANDESCENCE

* * *

A Lingering Incandescence: Notes About the Stories

ACK IN 2001, A REVIEWER UPBRAIDED ANDY DUN-
CAN for disclosing too much in the endnotes to his award-win-
ning inaugural collection, *Beluthahatchie and Other Stories*. This
reviewer felt—no doubt sincerely—that Duncan's remarks dis-
charged the stories of some of their mystery and radiance.

I disagreed. Good stories do not cease to stir us simply because
the author elects to write about their origins, the fuel in their
engines, or their influence, if any, on the world at large. Granted,
neither gossip nor analysis nor self-praise will redeem a bad or an
indifferent story, but they may sometimes create a sense of privileged familiarity that heightens rather than diminishes our esteem,
breeding gratitude rather than contempt.

I *like* personal notes in story collections, whether Harlan Ellison's signature rants, or Thomas Pynchon's wry self-putdowns, or
the stew of manifestos, aw-shuckses, and reminiscences flavoring
the back pages of the annual *Best American Short Stories* volumes.
Such notes tickle, bemuse, or annoy, depending on how the
author's hat and eye are cocked. If nothing else, they prove that
flawed, self-doubting writers can sometimes shrug so craftily inside
their skins that wings of silken beauty break through the rents. (At
other times, of course, an unplaceable odor may escape, but we
might like a good anecdote about that as well.)

284

So if you share my passion for story notes, read on. If you don't, how did you get this far? Here, however, let me warn you that I placed these notes at the end of my book on the assumption that you would read them *after* reading the stories. If you read them *before* the stories, in one or two cases you may spoil, or at least compromise, a surprise embedded in the narrative. But suit yourself.

Initially, publisher Gary Turner and I envisioned *Brighten to Incandescence* as a *Best of* compendium, not as a gathering of uncollected stories. It evolved into the latter once editor Marty Halpern began reviewing the available stories and decided that a book of uncollected tales would make the more attractive commercial package. (Besides, Gary had already noted that hostile critics could decoct, from our provisional subtitle *The Best of Michael Bishop*, the daisy-cutter acronym BOMB.) And I was pleased to find that I had written enough stories to fill a seventh collection without reprinting a title from the previous six short-fiction volumes or, forgive me, immolating Quality on the altar of All-Inclusiveness.

Marty helped me separate sheep from goats, sorghum from sawdust. Several stories that I still like—"In Rubble, Pleading," "Spiritual Dysfunction and Counterangelic Longings," "Three Dreams in the Wake of a Death," and "Cyril Berganske"—did not get in because either Marty or I adjudged them less successful than stories that made the cut. On another day, though, we might have chosen differently.

Of the seventeen stories in *Brighten to Incandescence*, "A Tapestry of Little Murders" leapt the earliest from my brain and my gray IBM Selectric (which I junked regretfully in 1986 for a word processor). Even in 1970, I had long wanted to write a psychological horror story with the kind of intricate and haunting pattern evident in the late British writer A. E. Coppard's "Arabesque: The Mouse." Coppard first drew my attention in a thick blue trade paperback from Simon & Schuster called *Reading I've Liked* edited by Clifton Fadiman. In Tulsa, Oklahoma, in the early 1960s, I bought this 908-page doorstop in its thirteenth printing for $2.25. Fadiman included two other pieces by Coppard, "Felix Tincler" and "Dusky Ruth," but, as fine as they are, neither stunned me as did "Arabesque: The Mouse." Here are its first two sentences:

> *In the main street amongst tall establishments of mart and worship was a high narrow house pressed between a coffee factory and a bootmaker's. It had four flights of long dim echoing stairs,*

and at the top, in a room that was full of the smell of dried
apples and mice, a man in the middle age of life sat reading
Russian novels until he thought he was mad.

How could anyone, mad or sane, not read on?

"A Tapestry of Little Murders" does not rival "Arabesque: The Mouse" in either style or concision, but I still like it for its presumption, and I've revised it a little, as I have three or four other stories, for its appearance here. When I submitted "Tapestry" to Edward Ferman at *Fantasy & Science Fiction* in 1970, I did so without using quotation marks to indicate dialogue. Ed added them to keep from irking or confusing anyone, but I have never thought dialogue without quotation marks, if skillfully done, irksome or perplexing, and so I have restored their . . . absence. Besides "Tapestry," I shaped and sold seven stories while a commissioned instructor of English at the Air Force Academy Preparatory School near Colorado Springs, Colorado.

However, I wrote "The Tigers of Hysteria Feed Only on Themselves," my tenth sale, in 1973 in a drafty clapboard rental house in Athens, Georgia. I recall little about the writing other than that it came quickly and that I could not avoid structuring it as a parable about our self-destructive involvement in Vietnam. It appeared in *F&SF* in early 1974, well over a year before the North Vietnamese army captured Saigon, but I claim no rare insight or prescience. The war had seemed endless, if not altogether lost, as far back as the Tet Offensive of 1968. My father, nicknamed "Sonny," and my step-grandfather, Cody Philyaw, provided the templates for Sonny and Trapper Catlaw, whose monikers still evoke the men for me. (Both died over a decade ago.) My setting, an isolated farm in Arkansas, also derives from family history.

"Of Crystalline Labyrinths and the New Creation" owes everything but its original maddening length to that cunning fantasist and oversized leprechaun, R. A. Lafferty. When Virginia Kidd, then my agent, sent it to Robert Silverberg, a Lafferty admirer and the editor of the top-flight hardcover anthology series *New Dimensions*, Silverberg winced and called it a "stunt." Roy Torgeson, a Lafferty admirer and the editor of the second-tier paperback anthology series *Chrysalis*, proved more receptive, or more gullible. He bought the story at almost twice its new wordage, ran it in the final spot in *Chrysalis 7*, and declared me in his introduction the author of the "only genuine *lafferty* ever written by anyone other than 'The Man' himself" and as "a genius . . . of sorts." (Punch *of sorts.*) In 1979, out of respect for a writer now shamefully neglected, I had written my so-called *lafferty* in logorrheic high spirits, but what it really needed was a ruthless blue-penciling. Twenty-two years later, I've given it one.

Not long after I wrote the foregoing paragraph, Ray Lafferty died —on Monday, March 18, 2002, in Broken Arrow, Oklahoma. Although he allegedly stopped writing twenty years ago, Lafferty left to posterity some of the funniest stories and most lyrical oddball novels in the history of our field. In his hilarious novella *Space Chantey* (1968), he created a classic science-fictional pastiche of Homer's *Odyssey* long before the Coen brothers transposed that story to the Depression Era South, as they do in their hit film *O Brother, Where Art Thou?* First published as half of an Ace Double, *Space Chantey* is now sadly out of print and exasperatingly hard to find. My copy disappeared from my shelves years ago. His major collections—*Nine Hundred Grandmothers* (1970), *Strange Doings* (1972), *Does Anyone Else Have Something Further to Add?* (1974), and *Lafferty in Orbit* (1991)—feature dozens of his most inventive and flamboyant tales, but try to find any of them nowadays without recourse to the Internet. (Thank God for Lafferty's fans, who have done yeomen work to keep his memory alive.)

I have Lafferty's signature on two or three of my copies of his work, but I recall meeting him only once, at a convention in either Memphis or New Orleans. He had fallen asleep on a sofa in the hotel lobby, and his head had slumped forward, pressing his chins into his chest. As Jeri and I walked through the lobby, I paused to look at him and resisted with all my will an incongruous impulse to kiss his naked pate. Today, I wonder why I didn't simply do it.

SF and fantasy writers seem to collaborate more often than do mystery, romance, or western writers. Think Kuttner and Moore, Pohl and Kornbluth, Niven and Pournelle, Ellison and Everyone. This volume contains two collaborations, "Murder on Lupozny Station" with Gerald W. Page and " 'We're All in This Alone' " with Paul Di Filippo (with whom, as "Philip Lawson," I have also written two mystery novels, *Would It Kill You to Smile?* and *Muskrat Courage*), but other partners have included Craig Strete ("Three Dream Woman"), Ian Watson (*Under Heaven's Bridge*), my cousin-in-law Lee Ellis ("The Last Child into the Mountain"), and, again, Jerry Page ("Scrimptalon's Test"). In this field, far from an extraordinary showing.

Some collaborations, especially on novels, begin deliberately.

The writers converge, brainstorm, and knock out the necessary words. Other collaborations, often on short stories, arise when a writer gets stuck and calls on another for help. If I remember correctly, both the sf novella "Murder on Lupozny Station" and the serial-killer fantasy " 'We're All in This Alone' " evolved from a cry-for-help impasse. Jerry Page, author of many fine solo stories, including "The Happy Man," and editor for several years of *The Year's Best Horror Stories*, approached me in 1979 with a locked-room space-station mystery that he had not yet finagled into a finished-feeling shape. I read Jerry's story, hit upon the idea of adding an enigmatic alien pilot, and ran from there. We both liked the results, as did Ed Ferman at *F&SF*, for many years a low-key but stalwart patron of my work.

" 'We're All in This Alone' "—forgive me this violation of chronology—grew from an abortive effort of mine. In the spring of 2001, *I* cried for help. I mailed a manuscript titled "Squawk" to Paul Di Filippo in the hope that he could rescue it from the desk drawer in which it had moldered for five-odd years. Paul advised an operatic overhaul, featuring more crime-oriented melodrama and less of Lingenfelter's moody intellectualizing. His suggestions triggered a fresh burst of enthusiasm and some frenzied reactive plotting. I press-ganged the work of the late, still controversial British artist Francis Bacon into our story and spent three or four hours on-line viewing photographs of Bacon's unsettling paintings. Several of the "squawks" in this version appeared without byline in a daily feature in the *Atlanta Journal-Constitution* called "The Vent." None, so far as we know, precipitated a murder.

"O Happy Day," also the title of a very different story by Geoff Ryman, appeared in the fall of 1981 in a short-lived magazine edited by Eric Vinicoff, *Rigel Science Fiction*. Ellen Datlow, fiction editor at *Omni* and a reliable friend of my work, had passed on it for exploiting a one-note "gimmick," the transposition of humans and rats. So why include it here? First, I have an irrational fondness for it. Second, the switch in perspectives freaks out many readers. Third, the story owes many of its effects and intermittently even its tone to my favorite book, *Gulliver's Travels*. Fourth, without a whisker of evidence, I like to think that "O Happy Day" mystically inspired James Patrick Kelly's classic story "Rat." (It didn't.) And, fifth, I have an irrational fondness for it.

Nearly every science-fiction writer who came of age in the late 1950s or the 1960s had to write a rock 'n' roll story. Some excelled at these. Think Gregory Benford ("Doing Lennon"), George R. R.

Martin (*The Armageddon Rag*), Lewis Shiner (*Glimpses*), Howard Waldrop ("Flying Saucer Rock & Roll"), Pat Cadigan ("Rock On"), Michael Swanwick ("The Feast of Saint Janis"), and legions of others. Me, I first heard the Beatles melodiously caterwauling "I Saw Her Standing There" in Payne Hall, a dilapidated dormitory on the University of Georgia campus, in December 1963. Life changed. The Brits invaded. If you weren't the Beach Boys, the Supremes, or James Brown, you had better hail from the British Isles or you couldn't get no airplay, much less no satisfaction.

Oddly, I didn't write the first of my own rock 'n' roll sf stories until 1983, two-plus years after John Lennon fell to a murderer's bullet outside the Dakota apartment building in New York City. Ed Ferman featured "With a Little Help from Her Friends" as lead novelette in the February 1984 issue of *F&SF*, with a striking quasi-psychedelic cover by Ron Walotsky. I revised it late in 2000 for an eight-story packet of electronic offerings from Fictionwise.com, and, in 2001, Carl-Eddy Skovgaard translated this new version into Danish along with two other stories, "Saving Face" and "The Bob Dylan Tambourine Software & Satori Support Services Consortium, Ltd." George Harrison's death of brain cancer in October 2001 shatters it as prediction, of course, but I never saw it as prophecy, preferring to view it as a parallel-timeline tribute and eulogy. Besides, its real protagonist is Eleanor Riggins-Galvez.

I wrote "Thirteen Lies About Hummingbirds" in 1990 or '91 for Charles L. Grant's anthology *Final Shadows*. The first two *Shadows* volumes had contained my stories "Mory" and "Seasons of Belief," respectively, and I did not want to miss out on an appearance in this valedictory collection. The title comes—obviously, I suppose—from the famous Wallace Stevens poem "Thirteen Ways of Looking at a Blackbird." As in "A Tapestry of Little Murders," I tried to weave a series of anxiety-inducing events into a strange but evocative pattern. Today I believe that "Thirteen Lies" *almost* works, and I fret about its falling just shy of elegance.

Sometimes I enjoy writing a story on the basis of a specific editorial assignment, rather like a newspaper reporter. Some fiction writers shun or deride this practice, on the grounds that it stifles the muse or produces hackwork for hire. Occasionally, it does both, and the resultant stories reflect well on neither their flailing authors nor their out-of-options editors. In my case, if I like an editorial assignment, I often write stories that gratify my aesthetic sense and also my dread-tinged longing to confront and master a challenge.

On four occasions, the first in the mid-'80s, Byron Preiss

approached me with assignments that I could not refuse. For a lovely fact-and-fiction volume titled *The Universe*, I took his dare to write a science-fiction story about quasars, although I had only a layperson's inkling of what quasars must look like, consist of, or do. My fervor and my research, however, resulted in "For Thus Do I Remember Carthage," a tale bringing together quasars, Augustine of Hippo, and an alternate Roman North Africa. Then, for a companion anthology called *The Microverse*, I fashioned a meditative story about littleness, "The Ommatidium Miniatures." After "Miniatures," for *The Ultimate Frankenstein*, I stitched together a grotesque brute of a story called "The Creature on the Couch," which, however, led me to write my own favorite among my category novels, a homage to Mary Shelley and baseball called *Brittle Innings*.

And "Herding with the Hadrosaurs"? This time, with Robert Silverberg as co-editor of *The Ultimate Dinosaur*, Preiss challenged me to write a story using the latest paleoecological discoveries about "dinosaur migrations." I applied myself to the literature and then adopted the venerable, if hokey, sf convention of the time-slip to dispatch a family of "pioneers" into the Late Cretaceous to do battle, sort of, with big extinct beasties. Frankly, I rank this story third among my efforts for Preiss. Again, a reasonable person might ask, why include it here? Because many readers extol it, finding it a fast-paced hoot. Both "For Thus Do I Remember Carthage" and "The Ommatidium Miniatures" tend to the cerebral, but "Herding" unrolls as an exotic, danger-beset, first-person journey.

"Simply Indispensable" arose from my perception that not a few people—myself shamefully included?—find the idea of self-extinction less menacing than they do the notion that the universe will proceed just fine without them. They desire immortality less than they do a taste of cosmic indispensability. These thoughts triggered the hypothesis of alien energy beings—Joe Way and the su'lakle— whose "recurrent key observations at the quantum level" sustain the entire cosmos. Michael Morrison, whom I met at the International Conference on the Fantastic in the Arts in Florida in 1994, gave me good-humored advice and the straight skinny about quantum physics, even bestowing upon me a textbook that he had written. Thus, I dedicated the story to him; here, I absolve him of any scientific errors that it may commit. (Incidentally, the name *su'lakle* derives from that of an indispensable sf-and-fantasy writer, and my decision to use a Levantine setting predates our attack-inspired preoccupation with matters Islamic and apocalyptic.)

Although hardly an opinion of apocalyptic dimensions, I find Chihuahuas both silly and obnoxious. I like dogs in general, but this breed inspires only my irritation, a bigotry requiring painful atonement, either now or posthumously. Once, in the late 1960s, when our friends Mike and Claudia Brown accompanied us to a party in Colorado Springs, the host answered our knock and three Chihuahuas stampeded toward us yapping like tiny demons. "Here come the rats," Mike observed, memorably. A few years later, here in Pine Mountain, Jeri and I often visited an elderly neighbor who lived in one room in a large Victorian house, her only companion a trembling, bug-eyed Chihuahua that bared its teeth at us while prancing about on her tufted bedspread. Maybe I should have admired Paco's courage, but I always wound up contemplating how he might sound if I imprisoned him in a coalscuttle.

In 1994 (I believe), Gardner Dozois invited me to contribute to an anthology of original ghostly love stories. I figured that his brief would elicit stories more tragic, frightening, or elegiac in tone than otherwise and resolved to go against the grain by submitting a comedy. And so I wrote "Chihuahua Flats," which generally gets a positive reaction when I read it aloud, even from auditors who later confide that they own a Chihuahua or two and that my story *nails* their prickly possessiveness. As a result, I like Chihuahuas a bit better than I used to and have even considered acquiring one for a pet—if a mutant parvovirus wipes out every other breed, not excluding chows, pit bulls, and neurotic cocker spaniels. (Dare I admit that our neighbors on King Avenue, the Phillips family, own a Dachshund-Chihuahua mix that I sometimes feed table scraps and stoop in the darkness to pet?)

"The Procedure" developed quite differently. Somewhere I read a review of a short story (whose author and title I forget) about a medical intervention, or a genetic manipulation, that "frees" our species from the tyranny of the religious impulse. I have always suspected that this impulse constitutes a portion of whatever gives substance to our humanity (a debatable point, I know), and so I wondered what might happen if an organic cure for the organic religious impulse proved reversible. This idea gave birth to "The Procedure," just as my desire to write a colorful off-world science-fiction story midwived it. Scott Edelman, editor of *Science Fiction Age*, a profitable magazine whose publisher yanked the plug because it did not make as much money as its sibling wrestling periodicals, bought "The Procedure" and ran it in his July 1996 issue.

Earlier that year, Jacob Weisman at Tachyon Publications in

San Francisco had asked me to read Mary Shelley's five known fantasy and/or sf stories and to write an introduction to a small collection showcasing these works, *The Mortal Immortal*. I agreed —*if* I could write my introduction in story form rather than as an orthodox critical essay, and Jacob okayed this approach. Everything else that one needs to know about "The Unexpected Visit of a Reanimated Englishwoman" occurs in the story itself, except that I read it at the International Conference on the Fantastic in the Arts in March and that David Hartwell printed it in a special number of *The New York Review of Science Fiction* (August 1996) before the small, handsome volume from Tachyon appeared.

(Oh, yes, one more thing: When James Patrick Kelly and his wife Pam, avid gardeners both, came to Georgia in late February 2002 for Slipstream 3, a literary conference at LaGrange College, I took them to nearby Callaway Gardens for a look around. On this trip, I learned that the tree I called a "Japanese tulip tree" early in my story is actually a *saucer magnolia*. Until the Kellys' visit, I had indulged this taxonomic error for twenty-eight years. Anyway, *no* Japanese tulip tree appears in this collection, and I wonder how many other misconceptions plague my private stores of "knowledge.")

The year 1996 was also my first as writer-in-residence at LaGrange College, a Methodist-affiliated liberal-arts institution twenty miles north of Pine Mountain. On the recommendation of friend and colleague John Kessel, author of *Good News from Outer Space* and *Corrupting Dr. Nice*, among other titles, I used *Writing Fiction: A Guide to Narrative Craft* by Janet Burroway as my creative-writing text. Late in the course, I asked my students to do an assignment from Burroway requiring them to write a story in which one of their most cherished beliefs proves untrue. As I had done on every other assignment, I wrote my own such story, "Sequel on Skorpiós." I like this brief story a lot, but honesty requires me to confess that it both accepts and sidesteps Burroway's challenge. It appeared in the British magazine *Interzone* in August 1998 and then a year later in the United States in *Dark Regions & Horror Magazine*.

"Tithes of Mint and Rue" evolved from another editorial challenge. This time Edward E. Kramer invited me to write a story based on a character in the sculpture of a mysterious Ferris wheel by artist Lisa Snellings. I watched a video of Lisa's remarkable kinetic sculpture, chose the fat lady as my character, and, once I began writing, sent her by bus from Abnegation, Alabama, to

Festivity, Iowa, to meet a redemptive strangeness. The anthology in which "Tithes of Mint and Rue" appeared (along with stories by Neil Gaiman, Gene Wolfe, Edward Bryant, John Shirley, Nina Kiriki Hoffman, and a host of other idiosyncratic talents) Ed and Lisa called *Strange Attraction*.

The book garnered healthy reviews, and Lisa sent each contributor a distinctive harlequin statuette for making the project work. For reasons that I don't fully understand and have no plans to inquire into, I received *two* such sculptures, which now adorn the mantels of my facing upstairs offices. One harlequin balances on a blue globe and exults over a hand of cards; the other demurely holds aloft a ball-shaped candle.

Over a decade ago, in a letter or at an ArmadilloCon in Austin, Texas, Howard Waldrop told me that if I ever wrote a story about Rondo Hatton, the disease-deformed horror actor of the 1930s and '40s, I could use his title "Help Me, Rondo." "I might never get around to writing my own Hatton story," Howard said. Researching Hatton demanded ingenuity, but The Internet Movie Database (www.imdb.com) provided photographs, brief biographies, and film lists, and I ordered and pored over a video of Hatton in a potboiler called *The Creeper*. Bob Ross, a movie reviewer for the *Tampa Tribune*, my friend Andy Duncan, and others offered usable tidbits about Hatton, but when I ordered a back issue of the horror-film fanzine *Midnight Marquee* with a detailed article by director Fred Olen Ray (another contributor to *Strange Attraction*), I struck the mother lode.

Ray's essay, along with a photo-crammed history of Universal Studios, provided the grist for my take on Hatton. An invitation from William Schafer and Bill Sheehan to contribute to an original Subterranean Press anthology proffering the photomontage illustrations of J. K. Potter as inspiration gave me the impetus to start writing. With the topic of my story already in mind, I cheated and looked through a sheaf of Potter's photo illustrations until I hit upon one that suited my preconceived agenda. The form of this novelette, let me stress, is a deliberate hybrid—part short story and part screenplay, a movie for the mind. I submitted it in the spring of 2000, and it appeared in *J. K. Potter's Embrace the Mutation* in 2002.

Of this story, South African reviewer and critic Nick Gevers wrote, "Michael Bishop has a well-practiced knack for rendering quintessential American voices, an admirable sort of Southern ventriloquism; in 'Help Me, Rondo,' he looks somewhat obliquely

at the Hollywood career of the acromegalic Rondo Hatton, employing the hectoring, incisive tones of Hatton's wife as his biographical
scalpel. In so doing, he also quietly, wrenchingly, tells a horror story
of monstrous orphanhood."

I wrote "Last Night Out," the newest story in *Brighten to Incandescence*, a week after the September 11, 2001, attacks on the
World Trade Center and the Pentagon. A former resident of Pine
Mountain, Marjorie Salamone, the daughter of Hubert and Lillian
Champion, died in the airplane-bombing of the Pentagon, only a
week or so after moving into an office in a remodeled, presumably
hardened section of the building. Since that date, our town has
dedicated a plaque to Mrs. Salamone at the site of a memorial to
five or six generations of community veterans. Reading or watching
news stories about how two of the hijackers visited a strip club only
days before turning an airliner into a flying bomb created in me, as
it did in most people of goodwill, a horror-tinged disgust. Also, the
seeming contradiction between the alleged religious impulse
behind the atrocities and the terrorists' premature secular celebration of this mayhem made me obsess about their mindsets.

After reading the last paragraph, a friend pointed out that al
Qaeda's own terror handbook recommends that its agents shave
their beards, shun Islamic garb in favor of Western clothes, and
mingle with the heathen locals—all to deflect suspicion. This
purpose, he added, seems sufficient to explain the hijackers' visit to
a Florida nudie bar. Perhaps. But why, given the alleged God-
driven nobility of their purpose, a strip club? Why not a baseball
game, a Bach concert, a fund-raising chicken-Q, or a rodeo? Most
of us can surmise their motives—a sense of entitlement, the
repressed cry of male libido, a contempt for female "weakness" (as
embodied by the compassion of women, as well as by their
threatening sexuality), and a feeling of superiority to their dissolute
Western counterparts. Despair didn't seem to enter into the motives
of the four hijacking crews—at least not so much as a pathological
sense of mission. In any case, "Last Night Out" tries to make fictive
sense of what struck me as total madness in quest of absolute evil. I
confess, though, that it remains the document of an outraged partisan. When religion and patriotism couple, their mutant offspring
prod us to spiritual wastelands that some may seek to reproduce
in the world itself.

Here, let me note that my son Jamie created the striking wrap-
around cover for this Golden Gryphon Press volume. Nepotism
may have helped him get the assignment—I asked Gary Turner

and Marty Halpern to give him a chance—but talent enabled him to fulfill it. And Jamie's quirky take on my title and on the individual stories allowed him to weave—digitally—the lovely web of images gracing this book. Behold the forked lightning incandescing above Mary Shelley and Atticus Norveg on the back cover and limning the doleful profile of horror star Rondo Hatton on the front. Behold the saucy Chihuahua head on the spine—Jamie's revenge for untold paternal indignities inflicted on him over three decades. Still, I hope that other examples of Jamie's computer artwork will illustrate my fiction tomorrow and tomorrow and tomorrow.

And so you have read the stories behind the stories, and also the cover. Although I don't much credit the sorts of afterlife that most religions promise, I do wish to believe that before we FADE TO BLACK, we BRIGHTEN TO INCANDESCENCE, either here or later, and that the heat and light of our passage persist in forms beyond our ken. It's not only "pretty to think so," it's healthy, and even the bleakest of these stories defy the ice of nihilism by taking spark from an inward fire. May they both disturb and warm you.

Michael Bishop
Pine Mountain, Georgia
May 2002

Three thousand copies of this book have been printed by the Maple-Vail Book Manufacturing Group, Binghamton, NY, for Golden Gryphon Press, Urbana, IL. The typeset is Electra, printed on 55# Sebago. Typesetting by The Composing Room, Inc., Kimberly, WI.